Nazareth Hill

By Ramsey Campbell from Tom Doherty Associates, Inc.

Ancient Images
Cold Print
The Count of Eleven
Dark Companions
The Doll Who Ate His Mother
The Face That Must Die
Fine Frights (editor)
The Hungry Moon
Incarnate
The Influence
The Long Lost
Midnight Sun
The Nameless
Nazareth Hill
Obsession
The One Safe Place
The Parasite
Waking Nightmares

NAZARETH HILL

Ramsey Campbell

A Tom Doherty Associates Book

New York

Carm

This is a work of fiction. All the characters and events portrayed in this novel are either fictitious or are used fictitiously.

NAZARETH HILL

Copyright © 1997 by Ramsey Campbell

This book is printed on acid-free paper.

A Forge Book
Published by Tom Doherty Associates, Inc.
175 Fifth Avenue
New York, NY 10010

Forge® is a registered trademark of Tom Doherty Associates, Inc.

Design by Susan Hood

Library of Congress Cataloging-in-Publication Data

Campbell, Ramsey.
    Nazareth Hill / Ramsey Campbell.—1st ed.
      p. cm.
    "A Tom Doherty Associates book."
    ISBN 0-312-86344-6
    I. Title
    PR6053.A4855N38   1997
    823'.914—dc21   96-6567
                                           CIP

First Edition: June 1997

Printed in the United States of America

0 9 8 7 6 5 4 3 2 1

For John and Ann—
eminently lunchable!

ACKNOWLEDGMENTS

As always, Jenny was there throughout the writing, and Tam and Matt helped by just existing. Pete and Dana Atkins also knew, in Cape Cod, exactly what a writer needs while at work. I've always thought that specifying where a book was written has no use other than to make the reader envious, but in case I'm wrong, let me admit that in the process of being penned this novel travelled back and forth from Wallasey to Albufeira, Rome, Cape Cod, and straight on to Danvers, and having returned home yet again, went to Manchester and to Swansea. Still, the only place a story is ever really located is inside the author's head.

CONTENTS

ROOMS NOBODY SEES

Years later Amy would remember the day she saw inside the spider house. She knew as soon as the family came out of the church that they wouldn't be going for a drive. Half an hour ago she'd seen the rusted moor over the yellowish cottages of Partington, but now the late October sky had fallen on it, or rather a fog had. Above the marketplace surrounded by dark grey roofs pinched steep, and beneath the hem of the fog attached to the sky, the hulk of a building riddled with black windows squatted in its park. Her parents were lingering in the church porch while the priest remarked on how tall she was growing, which only made her feel smaller, unless it was the sight of the building too big for the town that did. Then the priest said "Watch out for witches" and took his bright scrubbed face into the church, which released a faint scent of incense to mix with the moist autumnal smell.

"Funny thing for a priest to say," Amy's father remarked.

"He means the day, Oswald," said her mother.

"I know it, but just the same, a priest. So long as he doesn't think too much that's of yore is a joke."

"Don't be digging up your antique words, you sound more ancient than me."

"She isn't ancient, is she, Amy?"

"Only like you."

"That's you put in your place," Amy's mother told him, and pulled at her polo-neck to cover more of the little ruff of flesh under her chin before zipping up her padded jacket a last inch. "Well, are we bound for home?"

Amy's father unzipped the top of his an inch to compensate, letting his broad throat slump. "Looks like the day for a spooky stroll."

"Careful you don't give her nightmares. I'd be happy to stay by the fire."

"We haven't heard from my younger lady yet. What's your idea of a Sunday well spent, Amy?"

All the business with jackets was making Amy's arms feel restricted by hers, and eager to swing. "I don't mind a walk."

"That's right, you keep us fit," her father said, and raised his bushy eyebrows at his wife as he lowered his mouth at both ends and in the middle. "We're too fond of hopping in one car or the other at the least excuse."

"Some of us don't have the option if we want to go to work."

"So long as the books can do without you when the elements are like this." He closed the gate of the small steep churchyard after the family. "How's this for pleasing everyone, Heather? We'll sit by the fire with my roast and my pumpkin pie when we're back from a healthy trot over the top."

"A little trot."

"Over the hill and back again," he said, which might have sounded like a nursery rhyme to Amy if she hadn't known which hill. She was eight years old, halfway to nine, and more reassuringly, with her parents. She grabbed their hands through two bunches of padding as the family turned along the main road.

They couldn't walk abreast for long. At the first sharp bend the forty-foot-high wall, which held back the earth beneath a terrace of cottages, leaned out so assertively that the Priestleys were crowded off the token pavement. An iron cross as big as Amy and as mossy as the gritstone bricks secured the wall, but she always expected to see the invisible belt buckled by the cross give way, spilling a chunk of Partington across the tarmac. Instead she heard the faint rumble, made monotonous by distance, of the motorway. Below the bend were the first shops—Hair Today, Twist the Chemist's, the post office which was also a wine shop, could be deduced from the breath of the red-faced postmaster. For the moment the house in the park was out of sight, but most of the side streets to the west of the main road meandered towards it as though, Amy imagined, it had taken hold of them. Hers didn't, and as she and her parents turned the corner of the Scales & Bible, beyond whose frosted windows she heard the bony click of dominoes, she found she was glad that home was on the other side of the main road.

All the same, she liked the streets near the marketplace—their bulging bricks yellow as sand, the lintels of darker stone that gave each window a permanent frown as if the cottages were intent on remembering something they never quite could, the sights of small compact rooms beyond those windows that weren't veiled with white net, which Amy realised was meant to look demure but which put her in mind of underwear. On Moor View, which presumably had one from its upstairs rooms, a hand appeared beyond a window white with soap and rubbed an oval of glass clear to display a woman's preoccupied face. Along Gorse Cottages, the first cross street, two little girls in witches' masks and pointed hats were waving premature sparklers pale with daylight, wands whose magic they were trying to invoke. At the junction of Moor View with Market Lane, where the outer corners of the houses were rounded rather than square, a man on a ladder was handing up slates to a man on a roof. Beyond the lane of houses squashed together twice as tall as they were broad the shops crowded along Market Approach, Cards & Bards and The Cosy Cafe and Furry Friends, the pet shop, and Hiking & Biking and Knitty Knatty Knora and Hat A Head and The Cakery and The Chopping Block, as the butcher's son had renamed the shop as if to prove himself as witty as his neighbours. Passing his shop brought the Priestleys into the market square, and now there was very little between Amy and the spider house.

The market stalls had been cleared away as usual late on Saturday afternoon, amid an hour's worth of clangs and clanks that had resounded through the town, and the square was deserted, watched only by a black cat in the window of one of the farm produce shops which boxed in the square. A few scraps of sodden litter moved feebly in a breeze which felt to Amy as though something large and very cold had expelled a breath. The car park beside the marketplace was the quickest way home, but her parents' fattened hands were leading her into Little Hope Way, past The Sweet Tooth and All Your News. In a moment she could see only the building beyond the rusted-open gates of the park on the hill.

Its double doors alone were as broad as most of the houses of

Partington. Three narrow windows were set in a great deal of wall
to either side of the doors, and two more sets of six gaped above, the
smallest beneath the roof. Where the front of the building wasn't
black with slime, it was scaly with moss. Four chimney stacks so big
they looked misshapen occupied the skeletal roof, through one of the
many holes in which Amy thought she glimpsed movement, as if the
house was only pretending to be dead. She was at the end of the brief
street by now, and being led across Nazareth Row. "All right, Amy?"
her mother said.

The ruin was pretending to retreat, but held its ground and rose
above them, and as it did so it grew. Amy tried to grasp her parents'
hands more firmly, because they felt as though she had hold of little
more than padding. "Yes," she said, and tried to believe herself.

"If anything ever is wrong you'll be sure to tell us, won't you?
Don't ever let things stick inside your noddle and get to the point
where you can't talk about them."

"She said there was nothing, love. Leave her be before she gets
like—leave her if she wants leaving."

"Really there's nothing," Amy said in an attempt to head off
whatever subject had made her mother's fingers stir uneasily. "I just
wish we didn't have to go by the spider house."

Her father stared down at her without breaking his stride. "Why
are you calling it that? You know it's got a name."

"No need to shout at her, Oswald."

"I wasn't, was I, Amy? We wouldn't call that shouting. But you
know the name, that's what we're seeking to establish."

"Yes, dad."

"There's my lady. Sing it out, then."

Amy would have preferred not to say it aloud while the house
was growing so fast, revealing that it was as deep as it was broad.
Now she was through the pitted wrought-iron gates in the variously
askew railings, and the gravel path was making so much noise underfoot that she considered using it as an excuse not to speak. Her
father's gaze wasn't about to relent, however, and so she murmured
"Nazarill."

"Turn up the volume a notch or two. You'll be getting no marks
if you answer your teachers like that in school."

"She isn't—" Amy's mother started to protest, but Amy interrupted louder. "Nazarill."

"And why is it called that?"

"Because this used to be Nazareth Hill, you said."

"That's it. Nazareth Hill. Nazarill. That's been its name ever since I can remember, so why do you insist on calling it the other silly thing?"

Amy didn't know. Perhaps its ominous stillness reminded her of a spider crouching in its web; perhaps because, since she'd glimpsed her father's fear of spiders despite his efforts to conceal it from her, it somehow stood for fears of her own that she would rather not define. She hadn't the words to express that idea. "I'm sorry," she tried saying, and thought she had placated him enough that he wouldn't mind her steering him and her mother off the path, placing the solitary oak tree between the family and the ruin.

Acorns crunched beneath her feet, and the undergrowth wet with fog insinuated a chill through her soles as she passed into the shelter of the gnarled ancient branches. The cracked trunk as wide as the whole family cut off her view of Nazarill—and then her father grabbed her waist with both hands. "Let go a moment," he told her mother, and swung Amy onto his shoulders. "I'll show you there's nothing to be frightened of."

Amy found herself sailing up towards a twisted branch thicker than his arm. The remains of a rope swing dangled from it, and as the rope, which looked and felt drowned, brushed her face she thought the branch was about to thump her head. Her father ducked before she did, and only a few drops of water tapped her on the scalp while he bore her out from beneath the oak, encompassing her hands in his. As his footfalls on the soaked grass turned shrill with the grinding of gravel, the house reared up against the overgrown summit of the hill beneath the rubbed-out sky and came for her.

She thought her father meant to fit his hand around the dripping greenish brass knob and open the massive mouldering doors. Until this moment she hadn't known how much she didn't want to see them opened. But he veered towards the nearest hole where a window had once been, and jogged her with his shoulders to tell her this was just a game. The movement sent a drop of icy water from her scalp to crawl down the nape of her neck. "Now then, look here," he said in a half-joking tone that the ruin threw back flattened and chilled. "Tell us what you see."

The long secretive windows were too high for her parents to see

in, Amy realised. Only she could, and before she had a chance to resist, she did. She saw a smaller room than she was expecting. Its
floorboards were littered with greyish plaster that had fallen from
the walls and ceiling, where it had been replaced by various colours
and textures of fungus. The room was so dim that she could barely
distinguish the far wall, from which an unhinged door leaned into
an oblong of blackness. Nothing was about to loom out of that blackness, Amy told herself—not if she spoke up soon enough. "It's just
a room," she said with all the voice she could find.

"That's all. Just a room in an old mansion nobody cares for." He
was addressing her mother as well, who'd begun to chafe her upper
arms as if that could have some effect through the padded jacket.
Though he'd said that was all, he hitched Amy up and tramped to
the adjacent window. "Same in here, I'll hazard."

It was—too much so for her liking. Even if she ignored the oozing greenish fur of the walls and the bony fragments scattered across
the bare floorboards, the doorway of this room was open too. It was
black as a strip of film on which something was preparing to appear.
She shivered, not only because the trickle of water had found her
spine. "Can't see anything bad," she told her parents and the room.

"Any spiders visible?"

"No, dad. I said."

"Then that must mean there aren't any, mustn't it? There's no
earthly reason for making any kind of a fuss."

"I suppose."

She ought to have agreed with more enthusiasm, even if his idea
made no sense. Dissatisfied with her response, he strode to the next
window. "I can't imagine you'll see anything in here either. Let us
know when you've had enough."

"I think she has already, Oswald. You've made your point, I think."

As he turned towards her mother Amy disengaged one hand, in-
tending to use her collar to catch another drop of water before it ran
down her back. She was facing away from the window when she
heard a faint movement behind her: a muffled shifting of metal—
the kind of noise abandoned cans might make if a stray animal was
among them. She twisted not just her head but her whole upper body
around to see into the room while she dabbed at her neck. Then the
drop of water escaped down her spine as she was overwhelmed by
a shudder so violent that it wrenched her other hand out of her fa-

ther's grasp—that she overbalanced into the room.

It was smaller than the others, a cramped cell whose bare walls streamed with moisture, and it smelled as though its contents had been kept locked away for many years. Perhaps whatever was imprisoned had died there, because she could see it crouched in the farthest corner, its withered limbs clenched like a dead spider's legs around its ragged scrawny torso, its blackened twigs of fingers digging into its cheekbones as though it had torn all the flesh off them. Nevertheless those fingers moved to greet her fall. They unstuck themselves from either side of the yawning grimace revealed by the shrivelled flesh, and reached blindly for her.

Her legs slid off her father's shoulders. She might have grabbed the edges of the hole that had once been a window, she could have closed her ankles around his neck, but her thoughts were too slow. Hands seized her waist and dragged her off her perch. She kicked wildly and felt her left foot strike her father's back, and then she was standing on the chill wet grass, where her mother had set her down. "Keep your feet to yourself if you don't mind," her father protested. "That hurt."

"Don't blame her, Oswald. You nearly let her fall. She's had enough now. Are you fit, Amy? You're fit, aren't you, sweet?"

Amy felt as if she was swaying although, as far as she could judge, she was standing quite still. Her mother crouched to peer into her eyes. "You didn't see anything nasty, did you?"

Amy's knees started to knock—she thought she heard them drumming like a substitute for speech. "Are you cold?" her father suggested, and audibly wanting this to be the case: "Is she coming down with a cold, do you think?"

Perhaps that was all; perhaps the glimpse of the cell and its occupant was the beginning of a fever, the kind that gave you nightmares even when you were sure you were awake. Amy drew a breath that tasted of fog and sent a shiver through her while she tried to brace herself to ask someone to lift her up so that she could see she'd been mistaken. Then her mother said "Let's get you home in the warm."

At once that seemed a decidedly preferable alternative, but the scrutiny wasn't over. "That's all that's wrong, isn't it?" her mother said. "That and nearly toppling in."

Amy was prepared to swear to it if doing so took her away from the ruin, except that she was suddenly afraid her denials might be overheard—might bring an object which had ceased to be a face into view over the windowsill, to prove it was real. "I think so, mummy" was as much as she dared say.

"Of course it is. Just look at you." She stroked Amy's hair back and pushed it under the padded hood before steering her towards the gates. The gravel bit dully into Amy's feet through her shoes, slowing her down. It seemed to be delaying her father too, and when she was past the oak she risked a glance over her shoulder. She might have thought the ruin was creeping up behind him, the fog having sneaked down to encourage it, to give the impression that within the grounds only the building and the bedraggled tree were solid. All the windows were dark as holes beneath a rock. "Hold my hand too, daddy," she pleaded.

"Here I come," he said, but hardly did. "So long as you weren't shivering because of me. Neither of us would harm you for the world, I hope you know."

"Of course I do," Amy said, stretching her free hand out to him as far as her arm would reach. He plodded towards it and at last was close enough to take it loosely in his padded grasp, to which she clung in order to hurry him along with her mother through the gates standing in patches of rust on the gravel. Then the pavement of Nazareth Row was soothing her feet, not threatening to trip her up like the approach to Nazarill. She urged her parents along Little Hope Way to the marketplace where, as they turned towards the car park, she allowed herself another backward glance disguised as a smile at her father.

The ruin was dissolving into the mist, the edge of which drifted like a series of visible breaths in and out of the lockjawed gates— the advancing breaths of Nazarill. She tried not to rush her parents across the square in case they noticed her panic, but the shops with metal pulled down over their faces looked as though they were hiding from the sight she was struggling to believe she hadn't really seen inside Nazarill. The car park, its desertion emphasised by the hundreds of rectangular white outlines on the glistening tarmac, was no more reassuring. At least the main road was beyond the dormant barrier, the shops and inseparable houses winding homeward and, better still, intervening between her and Nazarill. The fog was waiting at the first bend, panting silently, but that needn't matter—except that her father halted short of the bend and slapped his forehead as though to crush an insect. "I should look in on the Prices. I was saying to you, Heather, with all that hi-fi equipment I saw being delivered they need their insurance topping up."

"You're never going to plague them on a Sunday, Oswald."

"They won't thank me if they're robbed overnight or the house catches fire while they're not covered, will they? You can never be too safe. I wouldn't call that plaguing anyone."

"I only meant they might appreciate their day of rest," said Amy's mother with a wink. "Who knows how they may be occupying themselves."

"Let me make a note at any rate, so they don't slip my mind again."

"Catch us up," Amy's mother said, already trotting downhill.

Amy looked back to see her father unzip the pocket that contained his electronic notebook and pull off a glove with his teeth so as to type as the fog edged closer behind him. It was moving only because she was, she managed to appreciate, and he was beginning to pace down the hill, if very grudgingly, as her mother ushered her into Pond Lane.

Amy had never known it to lead to a pond, only past two ranks of cottages to six pairs of the newest houses in Partington, but now the fields below it were a lake of fog. Her mother unlatched the gate of the first new house and preceded Amy up the jigsaw path through the small but elaborately planted garden, all its darkened leaves sagging with dew. She turned her keys in the door and shied her gloves into the base of the coat-stand as a preamble to typing the code that quelled the alarm. "Close the door, sweet, before the cold follows us in."

Though Amy closed the door as slowly as she could, there was no sign of her father. She'd shut him out from the warmth of the waffles of radiators, the line of her paintings climbing above the plumply carpeted stairs, one for each year of Amy's life. Her mother was tugging Amy's gloves off to throw in the coat-stand, unzipping Amy's jacket and peeling it off with a vigour that yanked Amy's sweater out of the top of her corduroys, but Amy felt as if she was somewhere else until she heard a scrabbling behind her, at the front door. It was her father's key, of course. "I hope that's you for the day," her mother said to him.

"I wanted to see how our treasure was. How are you now, Amy?"

Amy saw the closing door sweep a trace of fog out of the hall. "I'm all right now we're home."

"We'll see how you're doing tomorrow, shall we?" he said, and having already begun to address her mother "I may ring the Prices to see what they'd like me to do."

"I was thinking of an early dinner so the invalid can go to bed."

"Dinner in an hour, then. Best place on earth, the land of Nod."

"Have a nap now if you want, Amy."

"Just let the mat have another go at your shoes first."

Amy wiped a crumb of mud on the upside-down welcome as her father watched before delivering herself a nod of approval and heading for the kitchen. "Hot chocolate, sweet?" her mother said.

"Yes please."

As the kitchen stuttered alight her mother said "I'll bring it up to you" with a firmness which seemed to give Amy no chance to stay downstairs. She had to believe the house was bright enough to keep out anything that lived in the dark, and besides, mustn't the clanking she'd heard inside Nazarill mean that the thing in the corner had been chained up? Perhaps it had been a dog that had strayed into the building, broken chain and all. Whatever it had been, surely if she never told anyone—didn't even think about the glimpse—it would leave her alone. She switched on the light above the stairs and shivered only once as she trudged up to her room, where she lit up the overhead light and the gnome with a bulb in him on the bedside table as well.

Her dolls lined up at the foot of the bed or dangling their ropy legs from her bookshelves looked as glad of the light as she was. She hauled the curtains shut with their cord before levering one shoe off with the other and the other with her foot, then stuffed her feet into the rabbit-faced slippers she'd been given last Christmas. She straightened up Greedyguts, whose egg-shaped body had slumped over its stomach on the top shelf, and took down *A Child's Cornucopia,* her best book.

She had often been read to sleep with rhymes or fairy tales from it when she was younger, but it was special mostly because her mother had bound it for her at the bindery in Sheffield. Each of the leather covers was etched with a golden peacock's feather that was also a pen—the first time Amy had seen her transformed book she'd thought it had grown wings. Now it seemed heavier than usual; perhaps the fever she wanted to believe she'd caught had weakened her. She folded her arms around the book and sank onto the bed, where she opened the cover with a satisfying creak of the ribbed spine. At that moment she heard her mother's muffled voice below her in the kitchen, as though the sound was rising from the book. "So what were you thinking of, Oswald?"

"When was that, dear?"

"You know good and well. At that wretched old house."

"Yes, they should have pulled it down years ago. It's an eyesore and a temptation to the young."

"Amy didn't want to go near it, so what were you trying to prove?"

"I don't know if prove is the word. I just thought it was time—"

"Don't put on that tone, I'm not one of your customers. Time for what?"

"I'm sure neither of us wants her growing up frightened of her own shadow."

"She isn't and you know it. All her age play at being scared of that place, it's like a fairy tale to them. Do you know what I think, Oswald? I think it was you it affected, not her."

"Now whatever makes you say a silly—"

"You started at her when she mentioned spiders. It was yourself you were concerned about, not her."

"I'd like to fancy at least it was both."

"Fair dos, I'll give you that, but what was the point of carrying on at her?"

"I simply wish she wouldn't go on about arachnids. You won't tell me they don't bother her when she keeps bringing them up."

"That's because you do, for heaven's sake, and if you don't we know when you're keeping the subject to yourself. I wish you had today. If she'd seen anything in there it would have been because of you."

"I was trying to help her not grow up like me."

"There must be better ways of helping. And we'd rather she grew up like you than—"

"I wasn't thinking that, love. It wasn't in my mind at all. We both have plenty to offer her. We just have to watch what we pass on to her."

"I pray it's that simple," Amy's mother said almost inaudibly, and then the house was silent. Amy thought its warmth meant that her parents were comforting each other—about what, she would rather not know. Perhaps her father's nagging had indeed caused her to see worse inside Nazarill than was there. She began to leaf through *A Child's Cornucopia* while she waited for her mother to bring her hot chocolate.

She couldn't help wondering which fairy tale her mother thought Nazarill was like. Here was the house that helped lure Hansel and Gretel to the old cannibal witch, here was Red Riding Hood going inside a cottage and eventually inside a wolf until the woodcutter chopped her and her grandmother out again. Both tales seemed to have lost some of their appeal, and Amy didn't altogether like the flapping of the pages in the midst of so much silence. Then two pages near the middle of the volume parted, showing her a poem she hadn't encountered before, *Mad Hepzibah*. Maybe until now the pages had been stuck together.

> *"Come dance with me, young and old, out from the tree.*
> *There are songs to be sung, there are marvels to see.*
> *Come dance with me, young and old, under the moon.*
> *You'll have wings on your shoulders and dew for your shoon."*
>
> *"Dance away to the moon, Mother Hepzibah, flee.*
> *In the morning they'll come to play prickles with thee."*
>
> *"Let them come to my hovel, whoever they are.*
> *I've games that I'll play with them," says Hepzibah.*
>
> *"They've come, Mother Hepzibah, come with the dawn.*
> *Your cat she is drowned, your friends they are flown."*
>
> *"Good day, Master Matthew, for that's who you are.*
> *Will you trip the old dance with me?" says Hepzibah.*
>
> *"Bring her with us, stout fellows, bring her to the oak.*
> *She'll dance us a jig 'til her neck it is broke."*
>
> *" 'Tis no dance with no partner, and it's Matthew I name.*
> *In a twelvemonth from now you shall see me the same.*

I'll come for to find you, wherever you are.
And we'll dance in the air," says old Mad Hepzibah . . .

Amy had reached the foot of the left-hand page when she heard
her father calling her. She let the book close on her forefinger. At
some point she must have dozed, because her Save the Children mug
was standing next to the illuminated gnome. A wrinkled skin had
formed on the surface of the chocolate in the mug, which she didn't
even recall being brought to her. She gulped the barely lukewarm
drink as her father raised his voice. "Amy? Dinner."

"Coming. I just wanted to find out . . ." She laid the book face
down on the pages she was reading and switched out her lights.

Her father was walking from the kitchen to the dining-room to
collect the dish of lamb he'd placed in the hatch, her mother was
pouring soft drinks. Both parents confined themselves to smiles at
her until her father had performed his Sunday ritual of carving the
joint and spooning out the vegetables, at which point he said "How's
the invalid?"

"I'm fine, I think." Amy had the impression of saying so on his
behalf. "Maybe I was just cold. I wasn't really scared. I'm not scared
now."

"That's the main thing," he said, and raised the greyer of his eyebrows at her mother. "We're in agreement, aren't we?"

"If Amy says it I'm sure it's so, because she's the only one who
knows."

Amy wasn't certain what she knew; she felt as if she couldn't
quite focus the conversation or herself. She set about chewing the
first mouthful of lamb, which she was unusually and uncomfortably
aware was flesh. It wasn't going down, only growing larger. Her efforts must have shown on her face, because eventually her father said
"Has my roast run out of charm?"

"I just don't think I'm very hungry, dad."

"I suppose it can be resurrected, but it won't be the same. Can you
be tempted to some ice cream?"

If that was intended to make Amy betray that she was hungrier
than she'd admitted, it didn't work; she shook her head. "Would you
like to go to bed properly?" her mother offered.

"Yes please."

"Off you scurry, then," her father said. "You can leave the

washing-up to us this once. We'll be up when we're done to see how you are."

Amy wished she knew. Some of the mouthful of lamb had lodged beneath her tongue, and she dashed to the bathroom to rid herself of it before attacking her teeth with a brushful of toothpaste. She washed her face and untangled her hair, which the fog had rendered wild. In her room she pulled on her pyjamas and wriggled under the portly winter quilt, on which she turned over *A Child's Cornucopia* to finish reading the verse. But the pages at which the book lay open were full of a poem about an old washerwoman who scrubbed clothes so hard she wore a hole through to the far side of the world.

Amy turned to the previous page, then to the one that followed. Both contained stories which, like the washerwoman poem, she already knew. She was ranging back and forth through the book in search of *Mad Hepzibah,* rubbing every right-hand corner between finger and thumb in case the verse was trapped between two pages stuck together, when her mother intervened. "I shouldn't start waking your mind up if it's sleep you want, Amy. Your father's just finishing the dishes and then he'll look in."

Amy thought that might be time enough to find *Mad Hepzibah,* but her mother lifted the book out of her hands and replaced it on the shelf. "You're like me," she murmured. "My mother always said they wouldn't be able to screw the lid down on me until I'd found out the end of the book I was reading."

She sat on the bed and took Amy's chin in one cool gentle hand while she stroked her forehead with the other. "That won't be for a very very *very* long time. I only meant you and I love books. Shall I tell you one of the stories my mother used to tell me at bedtime?"

"Yes please, mummy."

"Let me think of one." She carried on stroking as if Amy's forehead was a lamp from which she would conjure a tale, but then she said "Don't mind if you have to make allowances for your father now and then. He's got the harder job, having to deal with people instead of just books."

"I know what he's like. He's my dad."

"True enough, we all know one another inside out. Let's always stay this close." She took Amy's hands in hers and embraced her with her deep blue gaze, and let her wide pink lips relax into the smile that felt to Amy like being kissed to sleep. "Once upon a time there was a princess called Amy, going on nine years old. . . ."

Amy listened to the tale of the princess and the enchanted castle, where every room contained a prince who wasn't quite good enough for her. One prince turned out to be bald when his hair came off with his crown, another left a tooth in the piece of her cake she gave him to sample, a third got so worked up by telling her how beautiful she was that his glass eye popped out. . . . Amy laughed at each of them, although each laugh had farther to travel to the surface of her drowsiness. She wanted to stay awake until her father came to see her, and perhaps she would have a chance to search through *A Child's Cornucopia* before she drifted off to sleep.

She must have nodded off, because she missed the end of the story. Her mother was silenced, and had let go of Amy's hands—indeed, was no longer in the room. Here came Amy's father, his silhouette flickering with a light she had never seen in the house, and all at once, though she didn't know why, Amy wanted to cry for her mother and dodge out of the room. But her mouth gaped like a wound, and she couldn't move. The light flared up, and she saw where she was. It wasn't the bed in which she had fallen asleep, nor did she recognise the room.

Four hats hung in a line on the wall to her left, three black bead necklaces adorned a dressing-table mirror beside them. That was all she had time to take in before the flames behind her father in the doorway leapt up so fiercely that their reflection in the mirror illuminated his face. His eyes looked brighter and more dangerous than the flames, his grimace bared his teeth and their gums too, but his voice was calm as ice. "Your mother's dead, and you're mad," he said, "and you're staying here in Nazarill."

She didn't know if the cry which responded was hers, it was so distant and muffled and so unlike any noise she would have wanted her mouth to produce. A light invaded her eyes, and as she blinked wildly to regain her sight she saw her familiar bedroom, her father stumbling through the doorway as he wrapped his dressing-gown around himself, her mother following him. "Quiet now, quiet," he urged in the voice she knew. "We're here. Were you dreaming?"

"Yes," Amy pleaded. "I didn't like it. It was nasty. It was horrible." Her tongue was functioning again, and she was home, with her par-

ents holding her hands with the hands she'd always known. Soon they
and the room would feel solid enough to persuade her she had only
been dreaming, but for the moment she was clinging harder to a
thought than to her parents. Whatever she did, she would never
again in her life go anywhere near Nazarill.

1

NEW FOR OLD

Hedz Not Fedz was the smallest of the shops at the upper end of Market Approach, but its window displayed more items than its neighbours, Pawnucopia and Charity Worldwide, put together. A notice in the bottom right-hand corner of the window, THESE PIPES ARE FOR ORNAMENTAL USE ONLY, did little to obscure the view. Someone or a wind had knocked over the four-legged sign that alerted users of the market to the existence of the shop. Amy unfolded the sign—HEDZ NOT FEDZ: EVERYTHING LEGAL—to the length of its chain and planted it on the pavement, then she hitched her Mexican canvas bag over her shoulder and let herself into the shop.

Wind chimes announced her arrival, but Martie barely glanced up from thumbing a price tag onto the contents of a box on the counter. "What kind of pipe is that?" Amy said over the strains of a tape of "Walk Right In."

"Electric. Press here and you don't even need to suck."

"Competitive."

"Just in time for Christmas," Martie said, and jabbed one stubby thumb at the tag. "Maybe we'll see where the money's hiding. As long as you're up on those classy long legs, why don't you make me a space in the window."

Amy dropped her bag with a thud of books on the bare floorboards, which she always thought looked earthy from the years when the shop had been a greengrocer's. She had to move bead necklaces and ammonite pendants and incense holders and hologram badges and crystals nesting in padded boxes before she was happy with the spot she chose, between an African carving and a book of Eastern philosophy, for the new pipe. She went outside to see how it caught the eye, and returned as she heard a shutter rattle down a shop-front in the marketplace. "I'd buy it," she said.

"You might get some funny looks at home."

"I get those anyway," said Amy, fingering the stud in her left nostril.

"You'd be disappointed if you didn't, wouldn't you? I remember feeling that when I was sorting out who I was." Martie glanced past her and frowned. "There's a look I can do without, though."

Amy turned and saw only the top of a head, its scalp cropped even closer than Martie's, ducked low as if to butt the window. Then the security guard from the marketplace straightened up from scrutinising the electric pipe and marched into the shop, donning his cap and tugging its peak towards his small suspicious eyes. The notes of the wind chimes were almost drowned by a spitting hiss of the phone that was clipped to his belt. "Can we give you any kind of a hand?" Martie asked him.

"Better keep them well away from me." He devoted a few moments to clattering the compact disc boxes in their racks until those at the front of each row had toppled forward, then he pointed his bony mottled face, which was so hairless it looked plucked, at Martie's broad calm pouchy one. "I won't ask where they've been in front of this young lady," the guard said.

"You'd rather wait until we're alone, you mean."

"I'd find out then if you're a feller or what, right enough." The guard bared his top teeth with a sticky sound, then produced a concerned frown that wagged the peak of his cap as he said to Amy "Don't tell me there's anything for you here."

Whether his concern was genuine or not, she hated it. "There's my friend Martie."

"Where?" said the guard before using the sole of one foot to indicate Martie. "Oh, that. Short for Martin, is it?"

"Martha," Amy said, furious with herself for having been provoked into responding, "and you know it, Shaun Pickles."

"How would anybody know that without getting closer than decent folk should? I wouldn't let you work your Saturdays in here if you were mine."

"You don't get an offer like that every day, Amy."

"I couldn't stand it," Amy said, which wasn't enough. "Maybe you should stop your sister Denise working in the tobacconist's if you're so worried," she told the guard.

"She's sixteen and that's legal."

"So am I," said Amy, adding "nearly" in her head.

"You're the only thing in here that should be, then."

"Which means you aren't," Amy said, and felt as if she was back in the Partington Primary schoolyard, scoring argumentative points too petty to be proud of. "Aren't you supposed to be seeing that everything's locked up for the night?"

"I'll be doing my rounds, never fret. That's why I came, to say if you want to go home through the precinct you'd better finish with her. If you want to walk through now I'll lock up after you."

"Forget it, thanks. I don't want to take you away from your prowl."

"If you don't walk up with me soon you'll have to go all the way—"

"Do you know how boring you are?" Even this seemed insufficient to put him off, and she was wondering how terse she had to be when the chimes sounded again. "Hi, Rob," she said, so enthusiastically that her boyfriend hoisted his brows and eyelids and sharp chin to mime a pretence of surprise. "Rescue me."

"From—oh." Rob tugged at his earring and gave the guard a single blink of the eyelashes Amy envied. "I remember when we met," he said.

"Guilty folk do."

"My first week at school, it was," Rob told Martie, who'd emitted a derisive snort. "He got me in a corner and wanted to know what sort of a name Robin was. 'Some kind of a bird, are you?' and for a bit of variety 'Bird's name, is it?' and poke poke poke in the ribs. And when I told him of course it was, even that didn't cheer him up."

The phone on Shaun's belt hissed, and he slapped it like a gunfighter. "So," he said tightly, "here I am."

"Here we both still are. Pathetic really, isn't it?"

"So what are you going to do about it?"

"Maybe tell our friend what we used to call you at school."

"It'd be like the rest of the rubbish you talk." Shaun exposed the underside of his upper lip before stalking to the door. "Some of us have work to do instead of playing silly bloody games," he declared, and did his best to slam the door behind him, but its lazy metal arm defeated him.

"Obsolete," Rob and Amy chorused, an insult they'd made up between them, and then Rob said "What did he want anyway, Aim?"

"To lead me to market."

"Best place for," Martie said, and thought of an improved word, "hams like him."

"The sooner he's for the chop the better."

"Has to do something to bring home the—I won't say it," said Rob.

"I'm glad that's over," Amy said, and to Rob with the roughness she knew he didn't mind "And what did *you* want?"

"Wondered what we were doing on Sunday."

"Don't mind. Maybe go to Sheffield or Manchester now all the shops are open, if we're up early enough for the bus. Anywhere that isn't here. I don't mean here here, Martie."

"I know. Only the man from the jar had one thing right, you better hadn't hang around unless you want to be locked out."

"They shouldn't be able to lock so much up. They never did when I was little." Amy grabbed her canvas bag, and when doing so failed to displace her anger, punched Rob's chest. "Was that for anything in particular?" he said mildly.

"For being a man," said Amy, knowing her anger was futile, which made it worse. She opened the door and shoved him out with a hand beneath the warm silky hair that spilled over the back of his neck. "See you on Saturday," she told Martie, and followed Rob.

Most of the shops that enclosed the marketplace were shuttered: branches of a travel agency and a wine merchant and a pasta chain, which made Amy imagine bonds composed of spaghetti, and two clothes stores and a family video library and a bookshop that sold more greetings cards than books and a store full of televisions and cameras and hi-fi piles, all gleaming black. . . . Four years ago the leases of the properties around the square had been bought by Housall, a Sheffield firm, and now only shops you saw in every English town could afford the rent. Housall still permitted the market to continue, though most local people bought their provisions from the giant supermarket that had opened in the mall off the motorway. Pickles and an older guard were striding about the tiled square, checking that shops were locked, and both jangled their keys at the couple crossing their territory. Rob and Amy ignored them except to hold hands more firmly, and strolled between the fifteen-foot-tall gates into Little Hope Way, towards the sky over the moor.

The afterglow had turned the western sky the lucid green of a ray of light from a prism. Against the glow, the jagged ridge and its filaments of heather were outlined with a clarity they never had in daylight—the clarity of the single star displayed by the blackness advancing from the east. Amy began to imagine the distances that darkness brought to the sky, but her attention sank to the hulking lump of dusk on the hill across Nazareth Row. "I used to call that the spider house when I was little."

"Arachnological. What was behind that?"

"Why did I, you mean? Someone else asked me that once, I think. I used to because . . ." A window to the left of the front doors lit up, driving the memory, which she wasn't trying very hard to recover, back into the dark. "I forget."

"Sometimes you have to."

"Sagacious," Amy said, and kissed his thin cheek to let him know she wasn't satirising him that much. "Are you coming in or what?"

"I've got a wodge of history to write up. I'll call you later."

"Byeh," Amy said with feeling, "history. Boring dates of boring people doing boring things. Don't put yourself to sleep." Having relinquished Rob's hand, she gave him a push. Partings always made her feel awkward, inclined to linger, increasingly unable to think how to leave. "I don't expect I'll be going anywhere," she said, and walked up the gravel drive that divided the wide lawn in front of Nazarill.

Though Housall had gutted the interior before rebuilding it, they'd left the facade almost unchanged. Cars were parked on an extensive rectangle of gravel to the left of the building—the photographer's Land Rover, the homeopath's Morris Minor, the Celica belonging to one of the librarians, the journalist's second-hand Porsche. As Amy came abreast of the sprawling stooped oak tree, the building the colour of bone greeted her with a silent explosion of security lights. She stepped off the drive onto the white stone threshold of the plate-glass doors and checked the mailbox beside the twin columns of nine bellpushes, to find an envelope brown as wet sand, addressed to her father. She held one end of it between her teeth while she used her key, and saw herself grimacing above a huge protruding tongue as the door swung inwards. She'd hardly set foot in the building when the doors met behind her with a sound like the echo of a distant tolling bell.

Whenever she arrived she thought she was meant to feel as though she'd entered a country house or an expensive hotel. The floor of the broad corridor was fattened by a carpet of an even darker brown than the panels of the walls, the lower halves of which were paled by a glow from behind the skirting-boards. Three mahogany doors were set into either wall, but four of the doors led to empty apartments a year after Nazarill had been renovated and advertised as the most desirable residence in town. About twenty paces took her to the stairs, which were spread from wall to panelled wall with carpet as thick as the heel of her hand.

She couldn't hear herself climb. The only sounds were a trickle of central heating through a concealed pipe and a faint clawing, presumably an attempt at escape by the cat that belonged to the magistrate who lived on the middle floor. Amy kept slapping the banister, though the brass tube felt clammy, to summon forth a low grudging hollow note for company. On the top floor she jangled her keys all the way along the corridor, where two dim blurred versions of herself slithered over the panels. One appeared to be gnawing a bone and to have placed the number 13 on its head as she gripped an edge of the envelope with her teeth while she unlocked the mortice her father had had fitted, and then the Yale lock.

The inner doors were all shut tight, which meant that the farther end of the panelled hall was dark. Smells so slight she recognised them only from familiarity greeted her: leather bindings, incense lingering in her bedroom, the larger of the two long thin rooms to the left of the hall. She elbowed the switch just inside the entrance and buttocked the door shut as the hall lit up, revealing its framed illustrations from a Victorian children's book which, as a baby, she'd pulled to bits and which even her mother had been unable to restore. She seemed to remember disliking the oversized heads and excessively wide eyes of all the subjects of the pictures, but now she would have disliked objecting to them when it had been her mother's idea to frame them. All the same, having transferred the envelope to the hand that had held the keys, Amy stuck out her tongue at the old woman being tossed over the moon in a basket as she let herself into her room.

By now she'd made it feel reasonably like home. The overhead light in its multicoloured globe found her in the mirror of the dressing-table opposite the door. As she ducked to see that her complexion was no worse than the last time she'd looked, she appeared momentarily to assume both the necklaces decorating the arch of the mirror. She hung her embroidered peaked cap next to its two friends on the wall, between her Clouds Like Dreams poster, the four pallid androgynous faces of the band keeping watch by the door, and the bookcase, where books and compact discs and tapes crowded together beneath the neat top shelf full of books her mother had bound for her. She dropped her tapestry coat near the wardrobe and her school uniform on top of the coat, and once she'd changed into a T-shirt and skirt and tights black enough to suit her, remembered to take her father's letter into the main room.

Unlike her bedroom but like the one facing hers, it had a window. Through the double-glazed sashes Amy saw the whole of Partington, the streets trailing downhill like dimmer tendrils of the marketplace to capture the luminous snake of the main road, whose head and tail were chopped off by the darkness of the moors. Several stars had pierced the eastern sky, but the night above the marketplace was always blank. As Amy dropped the envelope on the glass top of the polished oval dining-table, she saw the older guard locking the scrolled iron gates beneath the extinguished early Christmas lights. She tugged the velvet curtains shut and slipped a tape of a Vile Jelly concert into the player in the hi-fi stack. The sound level indicator splashed her hands with red as she straightened up and headed for the kitchen to brew herself a cup of herbal tea.

As she switched on the fluorescent light, the topmost branches of the oak stirred beyond the kitchen window, against the dark hump of the summit of the hill, the first step to the greater darkness of the moor. The tree continued to fumble at the air while she hung a tea-bag in her mug and awakened the red eye of the electric kettle. The light from the kitchen must have startled a bird off its perch. Vile Jelly sang "We're just a spark in the darkness of time" as she retrieved her bag from where she'd dropped it in the hall. By the time the electric mandolin solo was over she'd spread out her schoolbooks on the dining-table. The kettle summoned her with a hiss of steam and a

click of its switch, and in the silence between songs she heard a restless movement near the door of the main room: a stealthy shifting
of metal, and a murmur suggestive of a breath—the expansion of the
radiator. It was blotted out as Eve Exman broke into "Stay with me
till we see each other" while Amy poured water into her mug. She
fished out the hanged limp bag at last and consigned it to the plastic bin, and waited for the branches outside the window to finish
swaying, then slapped the light off before they finished. "Fix your
head," she told herself, and tramped away to confront her school
homework.

*Shakespeare's art is one of inconsistency and contrast. Discuss with
reference to "Macbeth."* Amy remembered enraging the English master by insisting on wanting to know how Lady Macbeth could have
breast-fed if she'd had no children, which he had eventually declared
was the oldest and most boring and irrelevant question about the
play. She gazed about the room, if not for inspiration then to distract
herself from the lingering unresolved question, at the mock-leather
suite with arms like sculptures of Swiss rolls, the actual leather lending distinction to some of the books that her mother had bound, the
television squatting over the videorecorder next to a pair of shelves
overflowing with her music tapes recorded from television.... Then
she leaned over to grab from the arm of the sofa the handset that
controlled all the audio and video equipment, and would have turned
the music low if the track hadn't commenced its sixty-second fade,
which allowed her to be certain that she was hearing a knock at the
door.

She pushed her bandy-legged chair away from the table and ran
down the hall to peer through the spyhole. A figure in an ankle-
length black dress embroidered with silver was already dwindling
into the globular section of corridor, and Amy recognised the way
its hair was drawn back straight into a ribbon only to multiply its curls
and shades of blonde halfway down the slim back. She tweaked the
latch and heaved the door open. "I'm here, Beth."

Beth Griffin turned from not quite aiming her key at her lock
on the far side of the corridor. "Don't let me interrupt if you've
friends in."

"There's just me."

Beth rubbed her high forehead and let the hand trail down her
long nose to brush her mouth, which was so small it might have been

her shyness made flesh. "I thought I heard you talking to someone as you came out."

"Not me. Maybe you heard my tape."

"Maybe." The bass riff which heralded the next track had thundered out, but Beth sounded less than entirely convinced. "So," she said, discarding the subject with a vigorous shake of her head. "I know at your age listening to music that loud needn't mean you haven't got a headache, but have you been having fewer?"

"None since last week."

"And when's your—" Beth peered along the corridor towards the sound of a door opening, although it wasn't on the top floor. "Your time," she said.

"Should be after the weekend."

"And you have the headaches mostly in the daytime, you were saying."

"Some of them are called teachers."

"Just like the olden days when I went to school," said Beth, having blinked at the Priestleys' hall as if in search of the closing door. "Carry on with the nat mur. Take a tablet whenever you feel the need, and if that doesn't help, you know where I am."

"I'll turn it down if you want to come in."

"I won't now. I will be later, won't I? I'm presuming the meeting is still on."

"Should be."

"It'll be worth it, won't it?" the homeopath said, and when Amy let her unenthusiastic response stand "We'll all be meeting finally, all of us there are."

"I may go out."

"You'll be missed. Well, I'd better . . ." Beth swung her keys in a gesture that suggested her door had become a magnet, and followed the hand with the rest of herself. "I hope I'll see you later," she said before abandoning Amy to the secretive light of the corridor.

Away from her office Beth was sometimes painfully unsure of other people, and surely that explained her uneasiness throughout the conversation, Amy thought as she shut herself in. All the same, as soon as the control was within reach she turned the music up. "This is the way your world ends," Eve Exman and the rest of Vile Jelly yelled, "so don't make any plans . . ." Amy couldn't think for the volume, but maybe once it cleared out her head she would be able to work. The guitars howled like missiles and sirens, and just as they became unbearable they were cut off. That was the band's joke, because after five seconds they would rise again, fiercer than ever. But the lull enabled her to hear a key turning in the lock, and she found herself welcoming company as she hurried to wait in the hall.

2

BESIDES THOSE INVITED

"I've called a meeting of my fellow Nazarillians for this evening," Oswald said, "but before I leave you I'd like to be certain we understand each other."

Betty Raistrick leaned over the tray, whose scalloped oval framed a turn-of-the-century seaside photograph, and pulled the knitted cosy down on the teapot as though she was adjusting a baby's bonnet. "You aren't saying my hubby didn't know his job."

"As if I would, Mrs. Raistrick. I'd rather say he was devoting so much time to his clients that he forgot to be concerned for himself."

"That means for me as well, and it was going on for years."

"I'd say that shows how long he must have been hiding the strain." Oswald gazed into the widow's wrinkled face, on which age appeared to have redistributed some of the white hair, and tried to penetrate its stoicism. "Maybe if I'd looked in more often I might have noticed something."

"I don't see how when I never did."

"He must have been determined not to worry you. What I'm driving at, you shouldn't have to be responsible for anything he kept from you."

"Shouldn't I feel responsible for not seeing how he was going?"

"Feel, well, none of us can help what we feel. But be, I don't think so in your case. Responsibility, now," Oswald said with sudden inspiration, "I'd lay that at the door of whoever burgled this house."

"Your firm aren't going to care who, are they? Only what they have to pay."

"That rather is the nature of the business, I'll admit."

"And how much that'll be is up to this man they're sending from Manchester to see what Stan didn't insure."

"I should have asked Stan or you to let me look everything over. That's what I intend to do in future if my clients will allow me." Bracing himself with a breath which he hoped wasn't noticeable, Oswald said "I keep thinking of a case like yours."

"God preserve whoever it was."

"Amen," said Oswald, and not much less awkwardly "What the survivor did when she knew the adjuster was coming, I only mention this, she took all the jewellery that hadn't been stolen, you see the similarity to your situation, and some other, other items, and left them with a friend, so that when our chap, not ours, I should say, made the valuation she, seemed to have, been—" His breath ran out with a croak, and his nostrils itched with the breath he used to say "Fully insured."

The silence struck him as exposing the words for an unreasonable length of time before Betty Raistrick said "What was her name?"

"You'll pardon me if I can't give that out."

"But you're telling me she got what she asked for."

"That was my point, exactly. She wasn't actually a client of mine. You'll appreciate I heard about her off the record." The fibs Oswald had expected the widow to welcome were multiplying beyond control or sense as she gazed rather sadly at him. "I just thought I'd let you know that similar, that other people . . ." he said, not far short of a plea.

"Well, you did. Thank you for putting yourself out on my behalf." The widow dug her ivory-handled stick into the carpet and levered herself to her feet with the nimble stiffness of a figure in a pop-up book. "Safe home," she said, using the stick to dislodge the pink snake of a draught excluder so as to let Oswald out of the house, and he was trying to think of a suitable wish in response to her words when the front door withdrew its tongue of light. "I tried," he muttered, and unlocked the Austin to fling his briefcase in before following it almost as roughly with himself.

The dashboard lit up and showed him the time, which it would have been impolite to check while he was in the house: already ten past six. He swung the car across the narrow lane, sent it backwards until a twig of the hedge squeaked against the rear window, threw it into first gear and drove uphill. He was doing his best, he tried to convince himself as he braked at the main road before driving into Moor View opposite. Close to half of that street was safe because of him. Fire and theft, he thought as he passed cottage after small neat cottage, and the Crowthers at number five had a plan that in due course would pay for their eleven-year-olds at university, Lester Keene two doors up knew his policy was keeping pace with his stamp collection, the Whitelaws on the corner of Gorse Cottages were insured against any harm their Dobermans might do. "Never be too safe," Oswald murmured as he turned onto Nazareth Row, from which several huddles of cottages faced the park. A few seconds later the Austin coasted left onto the gravel.

With its imposing facade and long elegant windows, Nazarill was as near as the town came to a mansion. Only the four disused chimneys rearing against the charred sky gave the place a slightly eccentric air. Oswald lined the car up close to the much-travelled Porsche and paused a moment to admire the stature of the building, then strode around to the front, ducking as a security light attracted a large fly or a moth. As the fierce lamp reduced the insect to ash, Oswald fished his keys out of his overcoat and let himself in.

The glass doors excluded the sounds of the town—dogs barking not quite in unison, a woman's quick clipped footsteps on a pavement, the yipping of a car alarm—and the warmth of Nazarill embraced him. Together with the silence and the discreet light of the panelled corridor, it felt like balm. It soothed him all the way to the top, where only the jingle of keys approaching his door broke the quiet. When he opened the door he found Amy waiting in the hall.

He gave her the smile which pinched his lips together. She was still Amy, however much he sometimes thought she was trying to appear not to be, her shoulder-length hair tinged green and pink, a stud gleaming in her left nostril, three rings adorning that ear, two jostling above the lobe of the other. He caught himself hoping that no more of her was pierced beneath the black T-shirt and mournful miniskirt and funereal tights. As though the burden of metal inhibited the movements of her pale thin oval face, she only raised her eyebrows and brightened her eyes momentarily to acknowledge him. "Had a good day?" he said.

At least, he began to; but the hi-fi had no patience with his standard phrase. What sounded like the effects of tortures he would rather not imagine commenced shrieking from the speakers, and he dodged into the hall and pulled the door shut. "Amy, could you turn that down for heaven's sake."

"Pardon?" he saw her pronounce.

"Down," he said, shoving his keys into his pocket and slapping the air with that hand. She only gazed at him, but the uproar started to diminish. "There, it's obeying you," she said, audibly now.

"I'm not quite senile yet, Amy. We both know it's just the end of a song, if song's the word. Please lower it before somebody complains."

"Who?"

"Do it, please, unless you want me to turn it off."

The electronic agony subsided, and the next track immediately began. It was almost a ballad. "If this isn't heaven I'll stay for a while . . ." "I thought you liked this one," Amy said.

"It's a relief." At times Oswald found the melody and even some of the words running through his head, but the nearest he could venture to admitting that now was "I do quite."

"I'll turn it down when it gets louder."

"Don't need to be told again." He felt defeated, not least by having said that, which was no doubt as unnecessary as he saw she thought it was. He hung his coat in the bedroom wardrobe and was heading for the kitchen when she informed him "An envelope came for you."

"Only an envelope?" When she didn't think that worth a smile he tried to vary her gaze by saying "Do I have to guess where it is?"

A shrug of her head and one shoulder directed him to the envelope in the midst of the scant space on the table that wasn't claimed by her homework. He scarcely needed to rip back the flap to recognise the kind of letter he'd been sent: a personal message for MR. OSWALD PRIESTLEY and his family. Have you ever wondered how you and your family would cope with a serious illness, MR. PRIESTLEY? If you had to wait for treatment, MR. PRIESTLEY, how long would your family be able to survive financially? . . . "Private medical care," he said. "I don't think we need that, do we?"

This time Amy shrugged both shoulders, and he dropped the wad of crumpled paper in the kitchen bin. "Will you be long at your homework?" he said. "We ought to start putting the food out quite soon."

"You can now."

"Don't clear away if you haven't—" But she was already gathering her books with a vehemence he might have taken personally. In a very few seconds she was across the hall, and he heard a thud on the floor of her room. The ballad ended, and just as a voice screamed "Time to go to *hell*" Amy marched back to grab the control and kill the tape. "I didn't say you had to switch it right off," said Oswald.

"Well, I did."

"Have you eaten?"

"Lunch."

"Feel free to have a nibble as we carry through."

"I'm not hungry."

"You still need to eat, Amy." He heard himself urging food on her as he'd never had to years ago, when her waist had been as slim as it was now. "I've provided for you and any other vegetarians," he said.

"I'll have something later."

"Don't make it too late. And I hope you don't mean in your room."

"Why not?"

"I'm sure everyone would like to meet you for a kick off. As well as which, we could do with a few less plates vanishing into your room."

"I thought we were having paper plates."

"We are tonight, but I'm talking about generally. I've been hunting for at least one knife and fork, and I can't imagine what you do with all the spoons."

Amy gazed at him until he began to feel as petty and absurd as it was clear he sounded to her. "Well, I'm seeing to the spread," he declared.

Some of the topmost branches of the oak were fingering the light from the kitchen. As he opened the tall refrigerator, Amy's reflection appeared at their tips, which seemed to cast her up to hover in the air while she approached along the hall. "These are all meatless," he said, handing her a tray in the hope she would be tempted. When he followed with a trayful of sausage rolls, however, he found her gazing at the vol-au-vents and murmuring to herself. "What's that, Amy?" he said.

"Flights in the wind."

"Really? If you say so." Even when he realised she was translating the name of the snack, his unease didn't quite dissipate. He sent himself back to the kitchen, to be trailed by Amy at half his speed. Between them they set the table, although since she was being more than usually averse to the proximity of meat, most of her effort was devoted to laying out plastic utensils and paper plates. She was creating an artistic arrangement of them when Oswald finished his last sortie. "You were going to bring forth some of the hoard from your room," he reminded her.

"I'm going to."

"You've already proclaimed your intention. For a change, how about—"

The apartment door buzzed with a sound too urgent to have time to be musical, and Amy darted towards it. "I'll answer that," Oswald said, "while you—" and raising his voice as he pursued her into the hall, "Amy, I said I'll—"

He gave up and assumed a welcoming expression, because she had opened the door. Beyond it was a man almost as wide as it, the neatness of his pinstripe suit and discreetly silver tie rather contradicted by the way his shirt was barely able to contain his overhanging stomach. Until he mopped his round face with a handkerchief which he then returned to his breast pocket, his forehead looked as moist as his slicked-back raven hair. "Am I early?" he rumbled as though his throat needed clearing. "I lost your chitty with the time on it. Just say the word and I'll plod back down."

"Don't think of it. I did say sevenish," said Oswald, although he'd been precise. "I'm Oswald. This is my daughter Amy. Am I right in thinking you're the photographer, Mr. . . ."

"Dominic Metcalf. If you ever want a memory preserving, I'm your man. And you're . . ."

"I sell insurance." Oswald had anticipated how Metcalf's face would grow guardedly polite. "Don't worry, not to you, not now. That isn't why I asked everyone in."

"It'll be good to rub shoulders." The photographer's gaze strayed over the framed illustrations along the hall and came to rest in the kitchen. "Do I recall some reference to food?"

"I hope there'll be enough. You won't have eaten, then."

"Advisable to leave a corner of the old tum free, I thought."

"Make a start by all means."

If Oswald hadn't quite suited his tone to his words, that failed to trouble the photographer, who surged through the doorway as if he had only now been invited and gave Oswald's hand a belated pudgy shake before veering into the main room, where he sprawled in the nearest armchair despite its eloquent creak and visibly restrained himself from swinging his legs over an arm of the chair. "I'll be up and about once I get my breath," he panted. "Shame they didn't put in a lift instead of all those stairs."

"Stairs don't get stuck," said Amy, having closed the door and followed the men into the main room.

"Stairs and a lift as well then, young architect. Is that what you aim to be when you grow up?"

"I think we're in at least two minds about how we'll end up when we're even older, isn't that the situation, Amy?"

That earned Oswald such a glare for being patronising that Dominic Metcalf regressed the subject. "Do we have any sense of what this place used to be?"

"The council offices were here when I was Amy's age, before we all started to be administered from Sheffield."

"Sheffield's not a dirty word, is it? I've a studio there."

"I've clients, and this young lady goes to school there, don't you, Amy? I should think at least half the town goes off there every weekday, or to Manchester."

"What was it first?" Amy said.

"Here? Why . . ." said Oswald, and found he meant both words as a question.

"More offices, I shouldn't wonder," the photographer said. "Offices breed offices, you know."

"It's too old."

She made that sound as though it was the fault of someone present, and Oswald was about to take control of the conversation when the door uttered its buzz. "Why don't you see what Mr. Metcalf—" he commenced, not rapidly enough, because she was already out of the room.

"Dominic by now, I hope. Or Dom if that sticks in your teeth."

"Dominic's no bother. Excuse me a moment," Oswald said, and leaned into the hall. Amy was admitting their next-door neighbours, the male half of whom gave her a grin which he maintained while striding up to Oswald. "Leonard Stoddard," he announced to the photographer, "and here's Lin when she's finished inspecting."

His face appeared to have been intended for a slightly larger head and to have been put on not quite straight, an asymmetry which his grin exaggerated. His tall but stooping wife had minutely curled short hair not unlike a poodle's, except that it was even redder than her husband's, and bright quick eyes which were busy examining the illustrations in the hall. "Are these from a book?" she asked.

"That's right," Amy said, not necessarily in answer, "you're librarians. Wasn't there a book about here?"

"About what was that, dear?"

"This place. Nazarill."

"Now that I couldn't tell you. My stamping-ground is discs and tapes. Stamping-ground," she repeated so as to nudge a dutiful laugh out of her partner. "Does the idea of a book set off any bell with you, Leonard?"

"Not a tinkle. I could consult the screen for you if you remind me, Amy, isn't it?"

"Nice to see a book being put to so much use." His wife turned from the big-eyed children trooping after the Pied Piper and said to Amy "So how do you spell yourself? The usual way?"

"You can spell when you want to, can't you?" Oswald said, and sent Amy an apologetic look, too late.

"I just meant our Pamela's taken to putting an H on her end. She's imaginative that way. Nice to see, we think."

"She's twelve," Leonard said to Amy. "She was wanting to meet you, but she's shy when there'll be people."

"You could zoom next door and see her if you like."

"And if you hit it off there might be some extra pocket money for you when we need, we mustn't say a baby, but a sitter."

"Go now if you've time, before it's lights out," Lin suggested, and blinked at a knock on the door. "That's never the hermit come out of her cell."

"I know who it is," said Amy, and answered it without bothering to use the spyhole. "Hi, Beth."

The homeopath twisted round as Amy sidled past her. "Are you really not staying?"

"I'm coming back. There's just my dad and—oh, here's some more people."

Oswald hurried to welcome Beth Griffin and whoever else was approaching. "In you come," said Lin to the homeopath, "nobody bites." "Don't be too—" Oswald called after Amy, but the door of the neighbouring apartment was already closing, and now his guests overtook it: Ursula Braine, a florist redolent of her trade; Ralph Shrift, who examined the framed illustrations, cocking his head and levelling an upturned palm at each of them, as though considering them for the gallery he ran in Manchester; Paul Kenilworth, a violinist who murmured "I hope nobody is troubled by my practising" and betrayed some pique when several of the guests had to have that explained. While Oswald produced drinks for the party to serve themselves from the sideboard, more people arrived to be let in by Beth as if doing so was a form of therapy. Peter Sheen entered toying with an expensive personalised ballpoint, as much an emblem of himself as of his journalism; Teresa Blake raised her wide flat face and surveyed the gathering much as she might have scrutinised them from her magistrate's bench; Max Greenberg seemed barely able to see them with his watch repairer's vision, despite thick lenses which appeared to float his eyes out of his face. Beth retreated to her apartment to fetch chairs, and the first of the doors she'd left ajar invited in the owners of Classic Carpets, Dave and Donna Goudge, who had carpeted the whole of Nazarill and whose His and Hers names were greeted by Lin Stoddard with an approving squeal. Alistair Doughty, a printer whose hands looked flushed from being scrubbed, turned up just in time to help Beth transport four straight chairs, which they lined up beside the door of the Priestleys' main room. A pause ensued while those who weren't pouring themselves drinks looked at the chairs, and then Leonard Stoddard said "Shall we call the meeting to order? We're all here, aren't we?"

The florist raised a fist towards her mouth to emphasise a prefatory cough. "I think there's still . . ."

"We don't need to wait unless everyone wants to," said Oswald. "I didn't mean this to be anything formal. I just thought it would be useful for us all to meet and talk."

"About anything special?" Dave Goudge said, seating himself at one end of the sofa and pulling his shirtsleeves over his wrists while his wife performed much the same actions at the other.

"Security occurred to me. I haven't lured you here for a presentation," Oswald assured the party, several of whom had begun to look wary or tricked. "I think a building is never as secure as it can be until the people in it have discussed how."

"You'll have some notions, I imagine," said Ralph Shrift, swinging one of Beth's chairs away from the wall so as to sit astride it and rest his elbows on the back.

"Leonard." Lin patted the arm of her chair to summon her husband away from Amy's videocassettes, which he was tidying under the pretence of examining the handwritten titles. "There was something we wanted to bring up, wasn't there?"

"There was."

"The tree outside," Lin said to the magistrate. "We were wondering what the position was."

"More or less upright, I should say," Teresa Blake responded, which by now was also a description of herself.

"The legal position," Leonard said, with one syllable doing extra duty as a laugh. "We thought you'd know whether it can be cut down."

"Pardon me, but who'd want to?" said Beth. "It's part of the character."

"I've known some of those I could do without," Peter Sheen remarked, extending and retracting the tip of his ballpoint with the hand that wasn't delivering frequent sips of Muscadet to his mouth.

Max Greenberg's eyes swam to find him in the twin bowls of the lenses. "You're speaking of people, are you, or places?"

"I've come across plenty of bad examples of both."

"Each makes the other."

"Which brings us back to the tree, I believe," Leonard said.

"Bad's a bad word, maybe," said his wife, and gave him back the subject with a reproachful blink.

"Fair enough then, dangerous. We think it's seen better days and ought to be dealt with before it keels over. If it does it'll come straight for this side of the house."

"It scratches at the window as it is whenever there's much of a breeze," said Lin. "Last night it kept our Pamelah awake."

"I don't see how she could hear it through the double glazing," Paul Kenilworth said with a kind of perverse satisfaction, "if nobody can hear me sawing away on the fiddle."

"Perhaps it's just young girls, how they get, you understand," Leonard said to the party at large. "I wasn't meaning there were any in the tree, but now I think about it, that's another danger."

"We don't want children trying to climb it and breaking their necks," Lin clarified.

"Nor adults either. It's up to them if they want to break their necks, but my point is that tree could be an invitation to a burglar."

"Handwritten in gold and tied up in a bow."

Lin's image brought the Stoddards to a halt, and Alistair Doughty looked up from inspecting his fingernails, presumably for traces of ink. "I know what you mean," he said, though not to Lin. "Just the other night I had someone peering in my window."

Donna Goudge sat forward, unsheathing yet another inch of her black-nyloned thighs. "Aren't you on the same floor as us?"

"That I am. Middle," he explained for the benefit of anyone who mightn't know. "There I was, nodding off in front of the evening's tripe on the box, and this, I'll call them a bee in front of the ladies, this bee sticks their face right up against the glass."

"Not a window-cleaner?" Dave Goudge said.

"Not at getting on for midnight, and not with a face like that either. I'd cross the street if I saw it in daylight, and let me tell you I've been on the lookout for it ever since."

"Male or female?" Teresa Blake enquired, lowering herself onto a straight chair as carefully as she was balancing her brimful wine-cup.

"God knows, and maybe not even its mother. Swinging about, it was. You'd have thought it lived up there. Sticking its tongue out at me, and then it was off before I could get to the window."

"We can certainly look into deterring trespassers," the magistrate said, having rendered the wine in her cup more manageable. "I don't mind talking to our friends at Housall, since my sitting on the bench seemed to impress them. Shall I tell them they might want to put some gates up?"

"Anything that keeps us private," Dave Goudge said with another tug at his cuffs.

The general murmur suggested that his listeners thought agreement was too obvious to need putting into words, except for Beth. "Won't there be a right of way by now?" she said.

"There ought not to be," Teresa said as though addressing a contentious lawyer, then softened her tone. "The land hasn't been public since it was railed off and this place built."

"As what, do you know?" Oswald said.

"I don't need to."

"That's settled, then," Ralph Shrift declared, placing his cup on the seat between his legs and clamping the sides of his face with his hands to direct it at Oswald. "You were going to tell us your plans for us."

"I thought we could take a few minutes to discuss organising ourselves," Oswald said, a proposition which the door seemed to greet with a derisive buzz. "I'll just . . ." he said, and tramped out, expecting to find Amy without her keys. But the newcomer was a man with a round startled face, his eyes almost as pale as his shock of blond hair. "Sorry for the lateness. It was my father," he said, and delivered a handshake whose firmness might have been intended to counteract the indirectness of his words.

"I've seen you," Oswald said, feeling apologetic himself. "You're making something of the grounds. I hadn't realised you were one of us."

"Down on the ground," his new guest said, which it took Oswald more than a moment to interpret as referring to the floor on which the other lived. "You won't know the place when I've done with it. George Roscommon, by the way. No garden too large or too small."

Oswald thought that a somewhat extravagant claim, but kept his feelings to himself as he closed the door and followed the gardener in time to hear him own up to his name. "Oh, hello," George Roscommon then said.

"Oh, hello," said Ursula Braine, echoing his casualness so exactly that it was clear how well they knew each other. There was an embarrassed silence until Dominic Metcalf told the gardener "You're my fellow denizen of the unpopular floor."

"That was something I thought was worth discussion," Oswald said. "Four apartments on these gentlemen's floor and one on the first. I'm sure we all want to see them occupied, but I wonder if we might like to vet prospective tenants."

"I'm all for keeping out undesirables," said Teresa Blake. "That's another word I can have with Housall, a vetting committee. I take it that will include any adults who aren't able to be here."

"It would have to," George Roscommon admitted, and as though further to confirm that, the phone rang in the hall.

"We've been thinking up safety measures," Oswald said as a cue to someone to develop the theme while he took the call. As soon as he lifted the receiver from its white slab on the wall a cracked voice demanded "Is George there? *George.*"

"He's just arrived. This is . . ."

"I'm his father," the voice complained, which at least made its gender clear. "Who else were you expecting?"

"I can't say I was expecting anyone."

"Can't or won't, Mr. . . . ?"

"Priestley. Would you like a word with your son?"

"I'll have that when he comes down. Just tell him I'd appreciate it if he wouldn't dally on the way."

"Well, I really think that's up to—" When Oswald found himself talking to an electronic drone he hooked the receiver into the slab. He hadn't succeeded in wording a message for the gardener by the time he felt compelled to go back into the room. "My father," George Roscommon said at once. "Sorry. I know."

"You wouldn't like him to join us."

"Hardly possible with all the stairs."

Metcalf panted in agreement, and Oswald felt bound to ask "Is he by himself?"

"That's how he was left. More than likely he won't say he was when I get back."

Only the florist looked as though she wanted to respond to that, and when she didn't speak, Oswald did. "You could tell him the security is in hand if that would help. Now that we'll all be able to recognise one another I'd like to propose some kind of watch scheme, nothing formal, just keeping an eye on who's in the building and what they're up to if that should seem called for."

"No quarrels with that," Dave Goudge said at once.

"None at all," Donna said.

"I think that about exhausts my ideas, but not my catering. Would anyone care to fall on some more of this food?"

The Goudges and Paul Kenilworth took this as an excuse to leave, pleading previous dinners, and Oswald might have lost faith in his cuisine if Ralph Shrift hadn't backed off his chair and refilled his plate, declaring "Better tuck than I serve at my private views." He inspired Dominic Metcalf both to return to the spread and to propose taking a photograph of all the occupants of Nazarill once it was fully peopled. "Shouldn't you snap us before the tree goes, if it's going?" Beth said, which both the printer and the watchmaker attempted to explain to George Roscommon before the florist claimed the subject as a pretext to speak to him. By now Peter Sheen was replenishing his plate enthusiastically as any journalist at a junket, and even the magistrate was nibbling a snack to go with her drinks, too late to hinder their effects. "I must be going soon," she said more than once, and eventually "Before the prisoner gets too restless."

"Who's that?" Max Greenberg demanded.

"My companion. If she thinks she's been left by herself too long she's liable to start clawing the walls."

Even once her listeners gathered she was referring to her cat, her words caused an odd awkwardness which she relieved by draining her cup and making her determinedly stable way along the hall. Some or all of that was the cue for the party to break up. The Stoddards were the last to leave. Oswald watched them along the corridor, and had finished throwing plates and cups into the kitchen bin before he heard the key in the lock. "Did you make a new friend?" he said.

"Maybe."

"What was she like?"

"All right."

Amy's replies would become resentful and even less informative if he pursued the subject, and he opened his hands towards her to signify he was resigned to having nothing to hold onto. As he headed for the main room she said "Do you want any help?"

"Please." He remembered what he'd asked her several times, and reached into her room to switch the light on. "First, if you could finally—"

The room lurched out of its dimness, and he saw a spider as big as his hand flexing its legs on the bed, its web stretching from the pillow to the floor and laden with shrivelled insects. "You filthy—" he gasped, then saw there wasn't a cobweb, only a patterned black silk scarf. But there was a spider, clinging to the light-bulb for an instant before it withered into a wisp of smoke which Oswald had the appalled impression he could smell. The room appeared to shrink and darken, and then, as he stumbled backwards, it regained its habitual size. "I can't get anything while you're in the way," Amy said, and saw his face. "What's wrong?"

"Nothing. Just a, a bit of a dizzy spell. One sip too many. Nothing to do with you." Oswald retreated hastily into the main room, although the sight of food made him feel rather sick. "Just make sure in future you keep your room clean," he said in a voice so fierce he hardly recognised himself.

3

DOWN FROM THE HEIGHT

"Well, it's back to the books for me," Max Greenberg said.

George watched Ursula murmur a parting remark to Ralph Shrift at the far end of the frustratingly dim corridor. The art dealer threw back his head as if to catch the laugh he then let fly as he admitted himself to his apartment, which brightened the corridor only to renew if not intensify the dimness. "Ah," George said, and feeling that was impolitely unenthusiastic "Oh yes?"

"A good few hours before this will be hitting the pillow." The watchmaker raised his bottled eyes to emphasise how he was pointing a manicured finger at his scalp, but George was seeing Ursula begin to descend the stairs, her loose dark green dress hinting at the swaying of her hips, the glossy black pennant of her hair at rest now, walled off from the wind across the moors. "So long as you don't strain your," George responded, and in a breakneck attempt to head off the imminent word, "though I'm sure it's worth doing, the reading is, of course."

"It comes with the calling."

"I see." By now they were at the stairs, but Ursula was no more than a whisper of footsteps beyond the bend in the staircase and a lingering trace of perfume, which made George feel tethered by the conversation. "In the sense of quite seeing that it would," he said, and when descending in silence proved unbearable "With me, now, I'm afraid it's rather fallen by the wayside."

Max Greenberg waited until the bend to turn on George a look of magnified surprise not far short of a rebuke. "Don't you think you could be storing up trouble for yourself?"

"Perhaps as I get older I'll find my way back to the, how shall we put it, the way." It struck George that if he'd been less intent on Ursula he wouldn't have allowed the chat to round on him. "Do you study every night?" he said, and stepped down far enough to see her in the process of opening her handbag outside her door halfway along the corridor. "My grandfather did, a chapter without fail before he went to bed, except of course, well, not of course, but with him it was the Bible rather than the, the one you have. Not that I'm suggesting there's any difference," he went on, his words stumbling helplessly downhill, "obviously neither's better than the other, assuming you want my opinion."

All this had brought him to the middle floor, where he became aware that the watchmaker was gazing at him with some bemusement. "We aren't still talking about my books," Max Greenberg said or asked.

"Well, I thought I . . . if I'm not . . ."

"The books I'll be preparing for my accountant."

"Ah. Yes. I should have . . ." George managed to swallow any further comment, though that meant he had no obvious excuse to linger on this floor, and more reason than ever to feel embarrassed. He watched Greenberg unlock his door as Ursula reached in her bag for her keys, and then Max said "What time have you?"

It wasn't clear from his tone whether this was a farewell or a sales pitch. "Twenty past ten," George said, having peered at the dim grey face of his digital watch.

Ursula used raising a tiny round dial to her face as a pretext for leaving her keys in her handbag. "Almost nineteen minutes past."

Max exposed his wrist with a good deal of ceremony, displaying the various hands and dials of his Rolex. "Nineteen minutes and thirteen seconds," he said in the accent of a gentle warning, and with a nod that acknowledged his listeners as the couple they were trying to appear not to be, trotted into his hall.

Ursula dredged her keys out of her bag and having pushed her door open, gazed at George. "Here he is," he said. "No mistaking him. Can't tell the difference between accounts and the Talmud."

She propped the door open with the bag and walked almost soundlessly towards him. "George . . ."

"Can't even come up with the name when he needs it, or much else either."

She halted two paces short of him, unlike her perfume. "Are you coming in for a quick mug?"

Some perverse enjoyment was to be had from pitying himself at a distance, and he found it hard to relinquish. "What are you offering?"

"Whatever you'd like to put in your mouth. You can have a nip if you're good."

"That might just do it. Better not, though, in case downstairs he starts getting how he gets. We don't want him pestering the Priestleys."

Ursula seemed unaware of stretching her right hand out to him, flexing its fingers so slightly they couldn't be convicted of beckoning. He knew how soft and firm her hand would be, and her arm, and her breasts with their nipples tilted up to greet him. . . . She was glancing back at her ajar door. "Say you aren't feeling abandoned," he said. "By me, I mean."

"Just making sure nothing goes in my flat I don't want in there."

"What would?"

"Nothing really, I suppose. I just thought I saw something little running up the stairs tonight when I came home. Maybe it was Miss Blake's moggy. I don't mind having that come to visit." She peered about the corridor before turning her attention fully to him. "What were you saying again?"

"Only that the old man's in a mood to start ringing around if he thinks he's been left too long."

"I'll just have to water my plants and take Inspector Wexford to bed with me, then." She relented at once, finding one of George's hands to squeeze and relinquishing it before their contact would have become irresistible. "Don't listen to me, you've enough on your shoulders, not that you have to put up with it all by yourself. Isn't it time you introduced us?"

"Maybe soon."

Ursula tossed her head, netting the dimness with her hair. "I'd better let you go. Unless . . ."

Her pause seemed to take hold of his groin. "Unless, yes?" he said with some urgency.

"I only thought you might dash down if you felt like it and see if he's asleep so you could wander back up."

"Except he might wake."

"It was just a silly woman's idea."

"Less of the silly," George said, feeling her withdrawing from him although she was standing still. "If he is asleep I suppose I could leave him a note."

"Saying what?"

"I'll think of it," he said to counteract her sudden skepticism. "That I'm not at the Priestleys' and they don't know where I am, for a start."

"Will you call me if you're staying down?"

"That I will." It occurred to George that he was sounding decisive about taking the least decisive course. "Let me find out what's happening," he said, and hurried downstairs, tugging his keys free of his trousers pocket. He inched the key into the left-hand door at the foot of the stairs, and edged the door open, holding his breath.

Smells of leather and boot polish met him. Though the polish smelled fresh, that needn't mean his father was still awake. He switched on the hall light and eased the door shut, and had taken one muted step when the old man started to grumble in the main room. "Who's that? Is that you?"

"Who else is it going to be?" Louder and with less of a sigh George called "It's George, father."

"See you don't leave that lamp on. That's money you're spending, and one day you'll know."

"How could I forget," George muttered, and slapped the switch. Darkness like the heavy smells made visible sprang from the panelled walls as he trudged towards the solitary light and his father's wheezing. "I thought you'd gone to bed."

"That's what you thought all right." His father gripped the arms of the reclining chair with his arthritic hands and heaved his upper body erect, dragging his legs after it. Above the severe stripes of his pyjamas and dressing-gown his pouchy face looked loosened by inactivity, the grey lumps of eyebrows drooping over eyes whose brown had faded like an old photograph, the cheeks increasingly unable to support themselves and the lower eyelids, the nostrils of the long flat nose no longer bothering to withhold their hairs, the bottom lip exposing its underside in a constant expression of petulance. "You thought I'd be dead to the world because I didn't know the score, did you?" he said, the last few words expiring in a wheeze. "I know how to keep myself alert and don't you tell anyone otherwise. Here, put these away since you're up."

He'd been polishing yet another pair of his boots, these for walking rather than climbing, their soles as thick as his hand at the ball of his thumb. George balanced the cloth and the tin of polish on top of them and bore them into his father's bedroom. As he elbowed the light-switch, the stack of gear opposite the foot of the rumpled untucked bed—boots, rucksacks, ropes, pitons, hammers—emitted a muffled clank, no doubt because his weight on the floor had disturbed the heap, though for a moment he imagined some small animal lurking in it, which dismayed him. He dumped the boots on top of another pair and knuckling the light off, strode back into the main room. "Father, I really do think you should consider finding someone who'd appreciate—"

"Don't be starting. You can sell what you like once you've planted me, but as long as you can bear to put up with me, every stick of it stays."

"I thought you didn't like waste."

"None of it would be wasted if you used it instead of prancing about in other people's gardens. Get yourself fit while you've some legs," the old man said, dealing his own a slap which made him snarl with pain.

"Father, please be careful of yourself. Gardening keeps you fit, believe me."

"Pulling up daisies is your idea of exercise, is it? Look at you. You're as feeble as you ever were," the old man said, although rather than looking at George he was lolling his head back. "Forever trailing after me and your poor mother and whingeing whenever we wanted to climb."

"If that's the mood you're in I'm going to bed."

The old man brought his gaze down from his memories, and George saw his eyes were wet. "Maybe before you shut me up in mine you'll have the decency to tell me what went on upstairs."

"I was about to," George said, blinking moistness back. "We had some good times though, us and mother, didn't we? We had some laughs."

"A few. Aye, there's always the past." His father rubbed his eyes to focus on him. "She was proud enough of you, I'll leave you that. Used to say you made something of the land when we only trod on it."

"We can make something of the present too, can't we? I thought you were pleased we landed here."

"I'll like it better once I know how many rooms we've got."

"Five, the same as everybody," George said wondering if his father had convinced himself they'd been given an inferior apartment. "This one, two bedrooms, kitchen, and the one nobody can live without."

"There's more than five in here. There's some that are smaller."

"There aren't, truthfully, I swear. Just the airing cupboard by the kitchen, and everybody will have one of those."

"I'd watch out, swearing round here. You never know who might be listening."

He was rambling, George thought uneasily; it was his age. Then the old man said "Go on, get it over with. Call whoever it is."

"I don't know what you mean, father."

"Don't give me up for doolally just yet. That's the fourth time you've looked at the phone since you came in."

George couldn't recall having done so that often, and felt as though part of himself that hadn't grown up had conspired with his father to betray him. "I'll take it through," he said, picking up the cordless telephone from beside his father's chair. "Shall I make us both a drink?"

"Not this late, not with my bladder," said his father with a look which declared that he knew the offer was an excuse to get George out of the room.

George ran the cold tap in the kitchen and filled a glass so as not to seem entirely dishonest, and gazed out at the gleaming husks of parked cars as Ursula's phone began to trill. One pulse would signify that she had been waiting eagerly for him, two that she was resigned to not seeing him, three that she wanted him to realise she was disappointed in him, four that she'd had enough of him. . . . "Hello?" she said breathlessly, cutting off the fifth trill.

"Hello."

"You're busy."

"I think I'd better be."

"I'm with you."

"I wish you were."

"Another time, perhaps."

"Perhaps." Belatedly afraid that she would think or choose to think he was referring to more than her meeting his father, George stammered "Soon, I hope, for you and me."

"I expect so. No," Ursula said, and having denied him the breath he was about to take, added like a mother promising a child a treat "I'll go so far as to say you can count on it. You look after your dad tonight and I'll look after you another."

"That improves everything." George would have been happy to prolong their companionable silence if his father hadn't uttered a peremptory wheeze. "Well, I'd better . . ."

"Go and be dutiful."

"And you be beautiful," he said, surprising himself.

"I'll try. Sleep tight."

"Don't let anything bite," George said, and felt he'd spoiled the mood. As his father wheezed more vigorously he broke the connection and took the phone back to its niche among the climbing manuals and souvenir chunks of rock shelved in the main room. "No need to try," he murmured, having realised he should have told Ursula that.

"First sign of madness," his father cautioned, and stared harder at him. "Which reminds me. Who was the crazy woman who kept cackling like a witch?"

"Nobody I know."

"Then you must be going about with your eyes shut and your ears plugged. Cackling away all the time I was on the blower to your friend upstairs."

"There was nobody like that. It must have been a crossed line."

"I thought she was laughing at me." To George's relief, he seemed mollified, at least on that subject. "So what did I miss up there?" he said, clawing at the lapels of his dressing-gown to cover his cobwebby chest.

"Mostly talk about security around the place."

"What's up with it?"

"Nothing, father. No reason to get worked up. That old tree may be cut down in case it endangers the building. I won't be mourning it. It's too dark underneath, for one thing."

"Too dark for what?"

"For anything to grow, it seems like. And there was talk of some kind of security watch, not that I imagine there'll be much to watch for. This place is built like a fortress. Nobody with any sense would try to break in."

"How am I supposed to know who's meant to be in?"

"Shall we have everyone round for a drink? It can be an early Christmas party before I drive you round to see your friends. And once the weather's better I'll take you some of the places where you used to walk and climb."

"You're a good lad sometimes." The old man dug his fingers into the arms of the chair and attempted to propel himself out of it, then subsided with a deflated wheeze. "Give us a hand up, will you? All this waiting round has tired me out."

"You needn't have waited. I'd have told you all about it in the morning."

The old man gave him a look that summed up a whole paragraph of rebukes. "Just help me out of this."

George stooped over the chair and slid his hands through his father's clammy armpits to hoist him to his feet. "Tickles," his father snarled, writhing so violently that George almost couldn't hold him, and emitted a series of protests which seemed entirely random as George, having managed to sneak an arm around him, helped him out of the chair. "Not so fast" and "You're squeezing the breath out of me" and "Mind, you'll have me—" and "Can't you see I'm—" was some of what he said before they succeeded in reaching the hall. When George attempted to steer him towards his bedroom he said "I want the—" George held that door open, and shut it as his father wavered to the toilet, slapping the tiled wall at each step. Then there was silence which an eventual flushing betrayed as having concealed a shy hushed urination, and his father emerged to blink about him, unsure which way to turn. George led him by the elbow into the master bedroom, but as soon as his father had lowered himself in a series of arrested motions like still photographs onto the edge of the bed he protested "I can manage now."

George was closing the door when a car glared out of the dark where the moor met the sky, then prowled away into the night. Though the old man pretended the view which his son had insisted he take meant little or nothing to him, George had caught him enjoying it when he thought he wasn't being observed. George eased the door shut to leave him alone with it, and was making for the bathroom when his father said in a voice that might have been intended only for himself "There was someone else in here before."

Since nothing followed except at least a minute's creaking of the bed, George advanced to the bathroom. He washed his face and scratched his scalp with a comb through the flat blond turf of his hair, he brushed his teeth and awakened their nerves with a handful of water, he directed his stream at the bowl above the pool in deference to his father, and then he turned off the bathroom light and tiptoed along the faintly glimmering hall to his bedroom.

It was practically bare. He liked that, and the starkness of the few items of furniture—the wardrobe and chest of drawers as white as the rectangle of the bed, its pillow squashed by the tucked-in sheets; the dressing-table in whose mirror he checked that his outline hadn't sagged during the day. He inserted himself in the bed, trying to leave the sheets undisturbed, a game he'd played since early childhood. His hand found the cord above the pillow and let the room reveal its nature: total darkness.

He liked the dark. It made the room feel smaller, close as the sides of his bed, as if the walls had moved to contain him in a cell that was as remote from the rest of the world as he wanted his sleep to be. Keeping his hands beneath the sheets so as not to be tempted to reach beyond the edges of the bed felt like making a pact with the room. He closed his eyes, inviting the darkness to render his mind blank. He was descending into sleep, past memories which floated upwards and were gone for the night, when it occurred to him, too gently and vaguely to jar his mind awake, that in some way the Priestley household more than resembled his own.

4

THE BREATH OF A SPIDER

"You do understand, don't you?"

"It's your decision, Mrs. Raistrick. So long as you're comfortable with it, it's not for me to understand."

"I don't want you to feel I've let you down, Mr. Priestley, when you've been so kind."

"I've no reason to feel let down that I know of. I thought you might have some."

"I won't have you thinking that." The widow sat forward so vigorously that her chair thumped its hind legs on the worn carpet of her sitting-room. "You mustn't blame yourself because my husband wasn't as thorough as you. I hope you won't blame me for not doing what you said those other people did who weren't your clients."

"I only wanted to make you aware of all the options."

"You did, and I'm grateful, but I wouldn't have wanted my hubby thinking I had to lie because of him."

"Of course if you believe that's involved . . ."

"Don't you, Mr. Priestley?"

Oswald had meant to sound agreeable without committing himself, but her eyes were asking more of him. "We can hope," he said as positively as he could.

"And we can pray, can't we? That never harmed anyone."

"I'm sure that's so," said Oswald, and had to clear his throat. "Well, I just dropped by to see that things were as all right as they could be."

"Oh, they are. I've still got the house and what's left in it, including all the memories. And with the money your firm is paying me I'm having an alarm put in, that's one thing I'm sure of."

"Not the only one, I hope."

"You're right. We can be sure of ours who've gone before, can't we?"

"I won't argue with that," Oswald said, reflecting that she mightn't be so certain of her late husband if he himself hadn't lied to her on niggardly Raistrick's behalf. He pushed himself out of his chair and felt a floorboard of the small room shift uneasily. "Well, I suppose I'd better . . ."

The widow raised her hands as though lifting a large flat piece of dough, a gesture which ushered Oswald to the front door. As he opened it she gave him a sudden brief fierce hug and stepped back, fixing his eyes with hers. "You and yours look after each other," she said. "And if you don't mind me saying this, since you've been such a friend . . ."

Though he had no idea what he was inviting, Oswald felt bound to say "Please."

"I wish you were as secure in yourself as you deserve to be." She took hold of the latch and began to swing the door back and forth. "I'll pray for you. I know you'd do the same for me," she said, and to stop herself presuming further, shut the door.

Three paces took Oswald to the wooden gate, which felt metallic with frost. The night sky was cloudless, pinned up with stars, and every streetlamp and lit window was so sharply defined that their outlines appeared to have been cut out of the dark. Nevertheless he had to persuade himself to take a deep breath. It didn't taste even faintly of fog, and so he released it as a long gasp of relief and marched himself uphill.

Foggy nights were still bad. Any sight of the lamps at the edge of Partington starting to blur was enough to revive the most dreadful night of his life. He would feel the inside of his head growing raw, scraped hollow by the memory, which had room only for itself. Four years had digested some of it: the hours he'd spent wondering how far out of Sheffield Heather had managed to drive before the avalanche of fog had spilled down the Pennines; the number of times he'd had to reassure Amy as the radio broadcast another fog warning; the way the silence of the telephone had become a presence which he hadn't dared acknowledge, even to himself—but the fading of these impressions had isolated worse. When Amy's anxiousness had sent her to the bathroom he'd sneaked out of the house, willing Heather's car to appear, and as a wind had dashed cold fog in his face, it had brought him the sounds from the motorway, the siren of an ambulance and then another and another, so tiny and distant he'd tried to believe they weren't there at all.

He'd listened for as long as Amy was upstairs, but then he'd had to go back inside, telling himself that an accident had blocked Heather's way home. If he'd let himself think otherwise he would have had to act, and that would have frightened Amy for no good reason, he'd convinced himself. He'd watched television with her, watched some comedy show which had made the half an hour before the next news bulletin begin to seem endless, until Heather's friend Jill from two doors up Pond Lane had come to ask her advice—about what, he never knew. Since she hadn't heard the sounds from the motorway, he'd felt able to ask her to sit with Amy while, as he'd said, he went to see if Heather had broken down. He'd had to drive the four tortuous miles of unfenced road with excruciating slowness, but in retrospect it seemed to have taken him no time at all to come in sight of the motorway, or at least of the fog on it, pulsing a lurid blue around a gathering of puffed-up lights. Those had shrunk into clarity as he'd driven as far as the police van which had blocked the slip road; they'd glared into his brain as he'd seen the six cars mashed together among the ambulances—seen that the red Ford Anglia in the midst of the destruction was, despite the lockjawed grimace of its front and the jagged gape of its windscreen, unmistakably Heather's. The pileup had smashed it around the wrong way, so that it was facing him, but all he'd managed to distinguish within the dark interior had been a glittering, a regular dripping of light on a great many fragments of glass. Beyond the wreck two men had been carrying a white cocoon on a stretcher to the nearest ambulance, and he'd lurched out of his car too fast to switch off the engine or slam the door or for the police to stop him. The fog had hacked at his throat, the icy tarmac had bruised his feet, and he'd continued to run—because there had been nothing else he could do—when he'd seen that the contents of the cocoon were entirely hidden, even the head.

"It wasn't Amy's fault," he declared, loudly enough to wrench

himself back to the present, where a cat emitted a terse yowl somewhere ahead. He was on Moor View, the unseparated cottages of
which flattened his footsteps and cast them back at him. He'd allowed the memories to come too close; he felt as though ice had penetrated his innards and was tightening around the core of him. If he
hadn't needed to ensure that Amy wouldn't be infected by his fears
he might at least have been with Heather in her final moments, but
how could he give such an idea any room in his thoughts? Amy was
still his and Heather's little girl, and Heather would have been the
last to blame her. The fault was entirely his, and perhaps Amy needed
him to say so. Perhaps, he thought, she was old enough for him to
tell her the whole of the truth.

All the same, as Nazarill spread into view at the top of the road,
he found he was glad that she was staying overnight at a classmate's
in Sheffield—that he was returning to a flat empty of deafening
music. Whenever he asked her to turn it down he felt reduced to a
parody of himself, and by no means only then: whenever he had to
remind her yet again to clear away her school homework, or the
plates from the snacks she ate between meals and consequently at
them, or the cassette boxes she scattered throughout the apartment,
even in the bathroom. . . . Those were also times when he missed
Heather, when he was most aware of his incompleteness.

As he reached the top of Moor View he heard a man's voice
yelling "Stay in there till you're told." A door slammed inside the end
house on the right, and one of its bedroom windows turned black as
Oswald passed through the gateway. The streetlamps of Nazareth
Row stood on the pavement opposite, their cobra heads warning the
cottages off, and as though in further deference to the great house,
their orange glow fell short of it. The tinge grew ashen less than
halfway along the gravel drive, on either side of which the blurred
shadows of the railings, exhausted by having been stretched so far,
petered out on the orange-stained turf. Between the edge of the
glow from the road and the outermost point at which an approach
would trigger the security lights was a band of dimness some fifty
yards wide. Oswald's toecap lifted a fragment of gravel, which clattered ahead of him and was extinguished like an ember. At that moment, up beneath the oak tree that was fingering its own darkness
on the grass, something moved and then was motionless.

Oswald halted amid a brief shrill clash of gravel. The movement he'd glimpsed had been too large for a bird, and it had seemed too stealthy to be up to any good. Was that an intruder's head which he could just distinguish among the stooped branches, or a furry swelling on the trunk? He craned himself towards it, digging his nails into his thighs to maintain his balance; then he stepped off the drive, which delivered itself of a faint stony squeal, and tiptoed across the grass.

The cage of branches seemed to flex itself towards him. He stepped beneath one which had rooted its tip in the ground as though the oak was trying to drag itself into the earth, and a smell closed around him: old wood, decaying vegetation, and an odour far less pleasant, suggesting that some animal had voided itself under the tree. He wished he had first gone close enough to the building to trip the lights. He was trying both to locate what he'd glimpsed and to avoid treading in the source of the stench when he realised where, and hence what, the movement had been. Of course, it was the length of rope attached to a high branch; only that morning he'd seen Amy and the girl from the next apartment taking turns to swing, though the Stoddards wanted their daughter to keep away from the tree. He spied the vertical line of the rope cutting through the tangled silhouettes of branches, and took hold of it to throw it over a branch too high for the girls to reach. Just as he realised that the rope weighed more than it should, the object at the end of it swung into his face.

It was as big as his head. Its furry body squirmed against his lips and filled his nostrils with the worst of the smells beneath the oak. Unless he dodged out of its reach its legs and then its jaws would fasten on his face, but his hands were glued to the sticky rope down which the spider had run to wait for prey. The darkness under the tree seemed to collapse towards him, filling his skull and immobilising him. Then, at about the level of his forehead, he heard the most appalling sound he could imagine ever hearing: a moist eager bubbling hiss—the breath of a spider.

So that was where its mouth was, very close to his eyes. His teeth began to chatter. Their shivering raced through him, his hand dragging helplessly at the rope, his legs performing an agonised dance as though to anticipate how they would writhe while the spider fed. He was willing himself desperately to be somewhere else, even if his body had to stay where it was, when the security lights blazed across the lawn.

The tree trunk stood between most of the glare and the thing at his face. For a moment he thought all that the light had achieved was to blind him, and then he realised that the shock had loosened his hold on the rope. He flung it away and staggered backwards, and saw Teresa Blake standing outside the glass doors, rubbing her arms through the sleeves of a slate-grey suit before shielding her eyes to peer about the grounds. "Pouncer," she was calling. "Good Pouncer. Here, puss." The rope swung out of the hulking shadow of the trunk, and Oswald saw that its burden was a black cat with a noose around its neck.

Before he knew why, he put the trunk between himself and the magistrate. Absurd though it might be, he blamed himself for not having recognised immediately that it was her pet on the end of the rope. As it began to swing into the light again, he steadied the rope and closed his hands around the animal so as to lift it, in the hope that would slacken the noose. His thumbs met across the plump furry chest, and his touch convulsed the animal. Its eyes bulged, its mouth gaped to release another strangled hiss, and as its body folded up over its stomach, it dug all its claws into Oswald's wrists.

"Devil," he cried in a whisper as sharp as a scream. His wrists felt as if white-hot handcuffs had been locked around them. He hurled the cat as high as his arms would stretch, but the claws hooked themselves deeper. The pain tugged his arms down, too hard, too far. The rope jerked taut, hauling at its branch, and Oswald thought he heard and felt the wood snap. Then the claws snatched themselves out of his flesh, and as his grasp slackened, the cat was plucked from his hands. The branch sprang back into position and flourished the animal at him, wagging its pop-eyed silently snarling head on the broken neck.

Oswald gripped his wrists as though he could squeeze the pain out of them, and heard Teresa Blake raise her voice. "Pouncer, come in now. I know you're out here, you sly little thing." A clash of gravel indicated she had stepped onto the drive. He thought she was making for the tree until he saw her tramping around the far side of the house in the direction of the car park. He backed along the shadow of the tree, and glanced nervously towards Nazareth Row in case anyone was watching. Nobody appeared to be, and what right had they to spy on Nazarill? When he was close enough to the gateway to have just arrived, unnoticed by the magistrate, he responded to her increasingly terse shouts. "Miss Blake? Is anything the matter?"

She turned so quickly that the action carried her several unsteady steps towards him. "My pal," she called, lowering her voice as she came. "Something startled her this morning. She ran out as I was leaving and I couldn't get her back before I had to go."

Her progress was jabbing her darkest shadow at Oswald, but he wasn't about to betray that he felt accused. He made himself glance at the tree, and react with a mime of restrained dismay, and hold up a hand to arrest her, and managed not to wince as the cuff of his over-coat dragged itself over his wrist. "Stay there, Miss Blake. I'm afraid—"

"Are you all right, Mr. Priestley? Can I help?"

"I'm fine, thank you for asking. Nothing wrong with me." Oswald let his hand drop and shook the cuff down. "Only I'm afraid I can see—if you can do your best to be prepared—"

"Try and calm yourself."

Oswald could imagine her saying that to the guilty in front of her bench while regarding them much as she was gazing at him. "The same to you," he muttered, and having discovered that his hands were clasped, pulled the right one free to indicate the rope. "I'm sorry, but that's her, isn't it? Or him."

The magistrate ducked to peer under the branches. Her eyes widened, her face shook, and then it composed itself into an expression which she must surely reserve for the worst offenders. "Who did this?"

"I think—"

"Yes, continue. Go on. Speak up."

"I'd say by the look of things it may have done it to itself."

Her face swung towards him, and so did the cat's. "You think it was a poor harmless little cat's fault, do you?" she said.

"Obviously not fault, no. I was meaning an accident. The girls were swinging on it earlier, mine and the one from next door, the rope, you understand. They must have tied it like that, one of them, and your, it must have, I don't know precisely, fallen out of the tree and unfortunately ..."

None of the eyes which appeared to be accusing him blinked. "I'm sure neither of them meant any harm," he said desperately. "Mine's a vegetarian."

The dead gaze was worse than the living, and both gathered on him for considerably longer than seemed reasonable before the magistrate uttered words to go with hers. "Are you helping me, or do you just mean to watch?"

"What would you like me to do?"

"I'll hold her while you take the rope off her," Teresa Blake said as if that should have been obvious.

"I'll try." Remembering the force with which he'd hauled the noose tight, Oswald wasn't optimistic. As Teresa raised the corpse with her hands cupped under its spine, he had an impression of her preparing to take down a criminal from the gallows. He edged between the rope and the tree trunk, nearly tripping over more than one root, and the magistrate said "Where are you going?"

"To do as you asked." If he didn't keep to the shadow of the oak she might notice the marks on his wrists. He dug his nails into the snarl of rope with all the force he could bring to bear, and the bones of the snapped neck ground together against his fingers. Pain flared in his wrists, his nails started to peel away from the flesh; the cat's head sagged against his hands as though it was trying to nuzzle him. It felt like a spider again. He wrenched at the rope in a frenzy, and it untwisted itself so suddenly there might have been no knot at all.

He loitered, his smarting wrists hidden behind him, while the magistrate cradled the head to stare into the face. He was thinking of stealing away when a glass door threw an extra portion of light into his eyes, and George Roscommon emerged onto the wide step to raise one hand in the shape of half a megaphone to his mouth. "Who's there? I can see you behind there."

Oswald nearly shot up a hand to wave as he stepped out of the shadow. "It's me and Miss Blake. Her, it's met with an accident."

"I'm not quite getting . . ." The gardener advanced several tentative paces, and his habitually startled look diminished into genuineness. "Oh Lord," he said, and lowering one shoulder to peer over it through the railings: "Did somebody . . ."

"Mr. Priestley believes she got caught in the rope."

"It shouldn't have been allowed to stay," George said, dealing a low branch a thump with the side of his hand which made several branches creak and grope around him, and bent his head like a mourner towards the cat. "Will you . . . may I take it . . ."

"Speak up if you've anything to say."

"Only that if you wanted her buried, I could."

Oswald took this as his cue to leave. "If you'll excuse me . . ."

"Yes. Yes, of course. Thank you." It wasn't clear which of the men Teresa was addressing. Oswald sidled between two rooted branches, just as she said "Are your hands always scratched like that?"

He felt as though the cage of wood and shadows had closed over him. As he struggled not to respond until he knew whether a lie or an abject apology would escape his mouth, George Roscommon said "Not this badly usually. I'm dealing with a place that's been left to itself for too long."

"Weren't you a bit scratched at the get-together?" Oswald improvised in case that helped, and fled across the glaring lawn to Nazarill.

As the doors gonged together he felt as though they had shut out the incident. He managed to fish forth his keys without scraping his wrist on his pocket, but removing his overcoat to hang it in the wardrobe brought the tweed into contact with the scratched flesh. He imagined how Heather would have looked after him, taking his wrists in her cool hands and wanting to know what he'd done. He held his wrists under the hot tap in the bathroom until the searing grew unbearable, then splashed disinfectant over the red weals and bared his gritted teeth at his tearful face in the mirror. "At least you aren't hanged," he growled, and went in search of ways to occupy himself.

In the kitchen he transferred the contents of the washing machine to the dryer. While the drum embarked upon its churning he took from the refrigerator half of a steak and kidney pie and set it in the microwave, and then he found himself drawn to the window of the main room. Teresa Blake was standing on the lawn in front of Nazarill, where the gardener had dug a border as yet unseeded. The cat, arranged to look no worse than asleep, lay in her shadow on the grass. When another shadow joined hers, of a man brandishing the silhouette of an outsize hammer which it took Oswald a moment to identify as a spade, he retreated to the kitchen.

Eyes followed him, but they were only paper. He didn't need to hide his stinging wrists. He wouldn't have been able to do so from Heather, but she wasn't there to see him; even the smell of the books she'd bound was fading. All at once he felt as though he had wished her away for fear of being observed. What could he ever do that would make him afraid of her seeing it? The microwave chirped like a simplified bird, and he sprang the metal door open and removed the plate to the kitchen table. He'd sat on the bench with just a fork when he made himself fetch a knife. Heather had never liked his eating with a fork alone; it set Amy a bad example, she'd said. He'd guided Amy worse than that, he thought as a whiff of the wrong kind of incense reached his nostrils. They'd hardly been to church since Heather's funeral.

He fed himself a mouthful, then sprinkled more salt than he supposed was good for him on the pie before he took another, and still had the impression that the taste was avoiding him. He strode chewing into the next room and searched in the rack beside the hi-fi for something of Heather's. Here was a tape of some of her favourite music, including songs with which her mother had sung her to sleep. He slipped the tape into the player and brought the velvet curtains together on the view of the shadow of a spade, its head swelling each time it flung the ghosts of clods of earth across the grass.

The speakers broke into song as he returned to the bench, and at once he wished he had played another tape of Heather's. "If you were the only girl in the world. . . ." Suppose Heather's mother were indeed the only person in a place he dared not begin to visualise, what would her state be now? Growing old had loosened her already feeble grasp on her sanity: suppose she was condemned to an eternity of madness? His thoughts had already gone too far, but there was no arresting their momentum. Suppose the fear which Heather had admitted to him—that despite all the control she exerted over herself, in time she would become like her mother—had been realised at her own death?

It couldn't be. He mustn't give the notion any kind of life. Even if he couldn't snuff out the image of her mother walled up in a place the size of her mind and crawling with all the nightmares in it, he mustn't imagine that of Heather. Was controlling his imagination the best he could do? Did he care less about her than Betty Raistrick did for her late husband—so little that he wouldn't pray for her because he wasn't sure it worked? "Please God," he mumbled, and swallowed a tasteless lump of pie so as to speak louder. "Please. . . ."

He had little sense to whom or to what he was praying. He'd

ceased to believe in much since Heather's death. The tape was singing about the Garden of Eden, "just made for two," and he felt as though he'd cast himself out by giving up the vague beliefs he'd retained from his childhood—please God, cast out only himself. He switched off the tape before any more words could catch at him, and emptied the contents of his plate into the kitchen bin. He couldn't pray while he was eating, and a little fasting wouldn't do him any ____ ____ ____ ____ er ceased its rumbling he unplugged it and headed

He hadn't felt to pray since he was Amy's age, and he found that doing so now would ____ ____ ____ e him feel hypocritical. He sat on the edge of the single bed and gazed at the small shelf of Heather's favourite books, which she'd bound for the love of them, before he turned to the photograph on the dressing-table of Heather and himself with six-year-old Amy on his shoulders, the adults stretching out their hands towards the sandcastle she'd made. He held that image in his mind as he clasped his hands tight, ignoring the pain in his wrists, and shut his eyes. "Please," he murmured. "Please don't let her be suffering. It isn't fair."

That wasn't praying, it was wishing, and it sounded worse than childish—superstitious. He knew how to pray, he just had to remember, though trying felt like his fumbling attempts to unknot the rope which had proved only to be twisted. His failures at the tasks seemed to be entangled in his mind, as though one had caused the other. Which were the first words everyone who was taught to pray learned? He found them in a corner of the dark cramped place his mind was threatening to become, and he clenched his hands together. "Our Father—"

What came next? Though his parents had always disagreed, until now he had never thought it mattered; yet surely if you said "Our Father Who" that assumed you were addressing a person, whereas "Which" implied some less imaginable and reassuring presence. His need at the moment seemed to leave Oswald no choice. "Our Father Who—"

A smell of Amy's incense troubled his nostrils, and at the same time he heard a scratching at the window. It couldn't be a branch; none of those came close. His eyes fluttered open and stared at the curtains, whose heavy material concealed every inch of the glass. When his trapped gaze began to make them appear to shift, he pushed himself reluctantly off the bed and trudged towards the curtains until he had no option but to grasp handfuls of them. Their softness sent an unexpected shudder through him, and he wrenched them apart to the length of the rail.

A black fly as shiny as coal was bumbling against the pane. The glow between the gates of the market lent its body an orange outline. It was inside the double glazing, otherwise he wouldn't be able to hear the small muffled thuds of its body against the glass. As if Oswald's realisation was a weight he'd loaded onto it, the fly immediately plummeted to the bottom of the sash.

Its attempts to escape might have caused the noise which had alerted him, but equally that might have been the sound of legs scraping the glass—the legs of the spider that was waiting for its prey to falter. It wasn't as huge as the one he'd thought was on the rope; perhaps its legs could stretch no wider than his grimace of loathing and panic was dragging his lips. Its elongated slim-waisted body was exactly the dark brown Amy's hair would naturally be. As it reared up to seize the fly, which it clawed down with its front legs and thrust into its glistening jaws, Oswald saw it raise itself to greet him.

5

THE RUMOUR OF A BOOK

The day of the photograph was the first and last time Amy met all the living occupants of Nazarill, though for a while it seemed she might never leave the building. Her father made her wait until he'd finished looking dissatisfied with himself in the bathroom mirror, and didn't even ask for her opinion of his appearance. She was finally in the corridor and about to ring Beth's bell when Leonard Stoddard poked his head out of his apartment. "You wouldn't like to see if you can hurry Pammy up, would you? Maybe she'll listen to you, being a girl."

Amy had no idea how he meant that, and told him so with her eyebrows. "I'll see you down there, dad."

"Here's Amy," Leonard Stoddard called along the panelled corridor. "Don't keep her waiting or she won't be your friend."

His wife Lin and a mixture of scents emerged from the bathroom. Her hooded track-suit was much like his, except mauve rather than dark green. "She won't sit, your father means," she amended with a frown at him which tugged her red curls lower on her forehead, and having stooped past Amy to the outer corridor, raised her voice. "If you're really set on wearing that, Pammy, just be sure you bring a coat to put over it while we're waiting to be snapped."

The door truncated the start of a conversation in which Amy heard her own name, and then the youngest Stoddard called it. Amy strolled along the hall to the equivalent of her bedroom. From her previous visits she knew there were almost no books or magazines in the main room and altogether too much lace, but there was even more of the latter in the girl's room: bordering the counter-pane, worn by the three dolls lined up at the foot of the bed and the one reclining against the pillow, extending the hem of the curtains white as an underskirt—curtains that were only pretending they had a window. The twelve-year-old was letting down her long auburn hair to brush, having apparently decided it needed the blue ribbon which went with the bridesmaid's dress. She waved at Amy over her shoulder, a gesture that sent her hamster scurrying into the depths of its elaborate cage in a corner of the room. "It's all right, Parsley," Amy murmured.

"He knows you. He'll come back up in a bit," the younger girl said as though the animal's flight had been Amy's fault. "Will you look after him at Easter?"

"I may be on a school trip too, Pammy. Aren't you Pamelah any more?"

"It got boring."

"I know what you mean."

The girl lifted her hair with the ribbon and peered at Amy in the mirror. "Thought you weren't going to Spain."

"Someone in my class had to cancel, and I want to go now. My tongue's hanging out for a bit of time away."

"You'll be old enough to move somewhere of your own soon."

"Next summer."

"Where?"

"I mean I'll be old enough. I don't know yet if I want to get a job so I can move out of this old place or wait till I go to university." Being taken to be more in control of her life than she was made her feel even less so. "I'll decide after Spain," she said.

"Would your dad see to Parsley for me?"

"I expect so. I don't think he minds furry things. I'll ask him when I tell him about the trip."

"Haven't you asked him?"

"He was in bed when I got home last night. I went with Rob to hear Perfection Kills in Manchester," Amy said, and as the younger girl jumped up, having tied the bow in her hair: "Don't forget your coat." She didn't like telling people what to do, Rob excepted, but it worked. Pam, as Amy was determined to think of her, draped a hooded coat over her shoulders before hurrying out of the apartment, leaving Amy to secure the door.

They weren't alone in being late. As they reached the ground floor, where the daylight at the far end always seemed brighter for not having been able to penetrate the upstairs corridors, Mr. Roscommon was pushing his father in a wheelchair towards the entrance. Both men wore dark suits, white shirts, and ties; the old man was tugging the knot of his tie up as though to support his faded drooping face. "Thank you, ma'am," he wheezed at each of the girls when they held the glass doors open, and Amy felt like a nurse letting a patient out of a hospital.

The air was prickly with the imminence of snow. Beyond the two gateways the marketplace was full of Christmas. Fairy lights deadened by daylight festooned the shop-fronts, and every one of the dozens of stalls which had sprung up for market day appeared to have something to celebrate. Some of the shoppers had abandoned fingering the goods to watch the activity in front of Nazarill, where Teresa Blake was helping organise the composition of the photograph while Dominic Metcalf finished setting up his three-legged camera beside the oak. "There you are, girls," he said, mopping his forehead. "If you could go and stand with your—"

"Stand with your parents, there's two dears."

For an instant, until she hardened herself to give the thought no chance to touch her, Amy heard the magistrate telling her she had two parents. Teresa Blake's gaze had already moved on. "And where will you have Mr., both the Mr. . . . ."

"Would you and your father like to go in the middle, Mr. Roscommon? Between Miss Braine and Mrs. Goudge."

"Don't ask where I want to go," the old man grumbled, but discovered some gallantry within himself as he was wheeled into place. "Harold Roscommon," he told the women. "I don't mind being set between two such lovely jewels."

"Watch out or you'll be sharing me," Donna Goudge said to Dave.

"It wouldn't be the first time."

This provoked several sounds behind hands from the rest of the party, who otherwise concealed their awkwardness by making room for the newcomers. As Amy's father took hold of her shoulders to move her into the gap between himself and Ralph Shrift, Teresa

Blake said "Are you keeping your gloves on for the photo, Ursula? You'll show the rest of us girls up."

"It's either that or have my scabby hands spoil the picture," the florist said.

Amy's father put his hands behind his back as the magistrate paced along the line-up. She'd suggested this photograph for printing in a Housall brochure to advertise the empty apartments of Nazarill. Amy shrugged her shoulders to rid herself of a shiver at the chill in the air, and the photographer called "If you're ready, Miss Blake . . ."

"No panic," said Max Greenberg, covering up his watch. "She's seeing we're presentable. It must come with the calling, that kind of an eye. I wouldn't want to look less than my best for her."

"We need to be quick," Dominic Metcalf protested, "if we don't want the shadow."

A trough of darkness was widening on the border between Nazarill and its tenants as the sun sank towards the moor. Amy thought she saw her shadow and the others lengthening in front of her, and had a momentary impression that they were straining to creep away from Nazarill. "I think everyone's as correct as they're likely to be," Teresa Blake said, but had scarcely taken her place next to Amy's father before she stalked towards the photographer. "Go away," she shouted. "Go along. Just go."

She was addressing three girls of about Pam's age, who had advanced to the end of Little Hope Way and were posing in imitation of the subjects of the photograph, giggling and pointing as though everyone who'd emerged from Nazarill was mad, redoubling their efforts now that the magistrate had encouraged them. "Ignore it, Pammy," said Lin Stoddard as they spotted the bridesmaid's dress.

"It's the market that attracts them," Peter Sheen declared with all the conviction of one of his newspaper columns.

"The quality of the goods is to blame," Paul Kenilworth said.

"Spoken like a guardian of culture," Ralph Shrift told the violinist, and Amy thought he was being ironic until he added "We might wonder how much that's undesirable can be laid at the door of the shop that's jeering at the law."

"Which shop are you saying ought to be shown it isn't wanted?" Max Greenberg enquired.

"Heads and whatever the rest of the name is that's trying to be clever. The place that promotes putting things in one's head."

Amy felt betrayed. "Don't you think some of your artists may have?"

"If any have they'd better keep it to themselves. Art should be a way of controlling the imagination, not indulging it. I'm very much opposed to anything that threatens the mind."

"Maybe living here does, living in a dead place like this."

"It's not so bad as small towns go," said Beth.

Harold Roscommon gripped the wheels of his chair. "I'd not have rushed if I'd known there'd be so much sitting around. Tell him when you're ready and he can bring me out again."

"Stay there, Mr. Roscommon," Dominic Metcalf pleaded, drying his forehead anew. "We're ready now."

"Not till whoever's stopped in there comes out you're not."

"We aren't waiting for anyone. We're all here."

"We're not," Harold Roscommon said, hitching himself around to jab his knuckly forefinger at a window. "I just saw someone poke their head up in there."

"You couldn't have, Mr. Roscommon. Especially not there."

"And why not, pray?"

"That's the apartment next to mine. Nobody's living there. I expect you saw a bird, the reflection, I mean. If everyone's set . . ."

"I thought you said we were," the old man complained, and with even more venom "A bird."

"What did you think it looked like, father?"

"Worse than me."

"Smile," the photographer called. "Let's see some teeth."

There was a belated flurry of activity as, having set the camera's fuse, he ran to join the other subjects; Pam gave her father her coat to hold, and he almost knocked Alistair Doughty backwards in his haste to conceal it behind him. The three spectators at the railings yelled with laughter as Dominic Metcalf arrived panting at the right-hand end of the assembly, and he gave them a rueful smile in time for it to be caught by the camera. "We're done. Preserved for posterity," he said.

"Should you take another to be sure?" Peter Sheen said, clicking his ballpoint for emphasis.

"I can if you like," the photographer said, though his panting sounded more enthusiastic than he did. He tramped to the camera, sending the three girls towards the marketplace, where they scattered as uniformed Shaun Pickles approached them. Metcalf rejoined his fellow tenants and held a smile just long enough for the camera to record it, then rubbed his chest while he gave in to a bout of puffing. "That's done it," he eventually said.

"And very well done too," Alistair Doughty told him. "How about some words to go with it? A picture's only half of one without a caption, and I don't say that just because I'm a printer."

" 'There's a refuge for you in Nazarill,' " Ralph Shrift suggested as he cloaked himself with his overcoat and made for the doors, letting the Roscommons precede him with a squeak of wheels. The Stoddard family followed, having raised their hoods against the wind, and as Amy saw the hooded figures enter the building she shivered without knowing why. Rather than take refuge inside, she veered to the window the old man had identified. Resting her hands on the stone sill, which was as cold as she imagined the bottom of a well must be, she hoisted herself up.

Reflected branches crept ahead of her and reached into the largest room. They had to be the reason why she felt that something beyond the window had stopped moving as she'd focused on the interior. The room looked more than newly decorated, it looked unentered, but could this be why she had the impression that its appearance was not its true nature? Before she had a chance to decide, her father grasped her by the elbows and lifted her down, and steered her firmly towards the doors. "Don't start that, Amy, please."

She freed herself and folded her arms fiercely, squeezing her breasts. "Start what?"

"Nothing if you say it's nothing. The poor old chap was confused, that's all."

She wasn't going to argue when her eyes were growing heavy with the threat of angry tears. She rubbed them hard as she ran into the building and up to her floor, where Peter Sheen's and Ralph Shrift's doors were closing opposite each other, while beyond them Leonard Stoddard was ushering his family into their apartment. "Leonard?" Amy called.

"Miss."

"Did you have a chance to look up what I asked you about?"

"Whoops." Apparently that meant no, since he continued "Remind me. I've had to be the complete librarian these last few weeks, not just setting up word processors for library users who want to try and write, exhibiting their work for the public to read."

"You said you'd see if you could find the story about Nazarill."

"I shouldn't think there's much of one."

"I'm sure I saw it in the library once, in the fiction part."

"Is it quite an old one?" Lin Stoddard asked over her husband's shoulder. "When did you see it, do you think?"

"When I was little, and I remember it was a bit dusty, or I might have had a look in it."

"We wouldn't have it now, I can tell you without checking."

"Wouldn't you keep it when it's about somewhere local?"

"Not a novel, no. Maybe not even a history if it's just about a building this far out. It's all to do with balancing the books," Lin said. "If we didn't sell the old stuff we wouldn't be able to afford the things I'm sure you like, videos and music tapes and discs."

"I thought libraries were meant to be for books," said Amy, and knew she had partly because her mother would have.

Amy's father moved her out of his way and jangled his keys. "Amy," he warned her.

"Do you think it's fair of libraries," said Leonard, "to just be for people who can read?"

Amy gave up, not least because the phone had become audible as her father opened the door. She waited while he ran to grab the receiver, into which he gasped their name. "It's 'Can I speak to Amy?' " he found more breath to announce.

"Don't you know who it is?"

"Whoever's red and comes bobbing along."

She'd liked his singing that to her when she was little, but now he'd robbed the words of their appeal. She didn't look at him as he passed her the receiver. "Hi, Rob."

"Have you finished posing?"

"Do I ever?"

"Does anyone? What are you doing now besides that?"

"I'll meet you in the market if you want. I'm going down to ask about a book."

"I'll see you at the stall then, shall I?"

"You won't see me in one," Amy said, and hooked the receiver into its niche.

Her father had closed the fish-eyed door and was leaning against it. "Before you fly the coop, Amy, I must say I sometimes think you might behave a shade better."

"Like when?"

"Flouncing into the house as you just did, for instance."

"Because of how you were going on at me in front of everyone."

"Nobody would have noticed if you'd restrained yourself from making such a fuss."

"What do you expect when you were talking to me as if I was her age next door?"

"You aren't so much older. Do remember I'm the adult and you're the child. Forgive me, but I still have to be in charge."

"You won't be for much longer."

"Calm yourself, Amy. Don't just babble. You've more control over yourself than that, or you used to have."

"Soon I'll have all I want."

"Perhaps you'd care to enlighten me on what that's meant to mean."

"It means next summer I'll be able to move out and live anywhere I want and you won't be able to stop me once I get to be sixteen."

"I very much hope you won't," her father said, and held out his hands, revealing the scratches he'd told her he'd suffered while trying to rescue the magistrate's cat. "I hope we'll stay together as I know your mother would have wished."

Amy blinked hard and swallowed the taste of tears, and felt as though all the eyes on the walls were scrutinising her. "You aren't expecting me to live the rest of my life with you, are you?"

"Let's not presume to see too far into the future. I'm simply asking you to put these mad, these foolish ideas out of your head. Concentrate on getting to university so you can make something of yourself."

"I'm something now. I'm more than that, I'm someone, and you make me feel I'm not."

"I really think that's a shade unfair. You've a good deal more freedom than I had at your age. My father used to say more always wants more, and I'm starting to see what he meant."

"More of what?" Amy demanded, and her need to feel released found words. "It can't be more if you already said I could, can it?"

"I'd require to know what you're talking about."

"You said I could have gone to Spain if there'd been a place."

"That's so, but to speak the truth—"

"There is. Someone's had to drop out."

"Well, never mind. We'll go somewhere next summer to make it up to you, the father and his daughter who'll be so grown up he won't recognise her. If you've set your heart on going abroad I may even consider that if you do a few more of the things I ask."

"Dad, I've said I'll go on the school trip."

"What possessed you to undertake such a thing?"

"You did."

"I'm sure the very most I said was to come home and tell me if there was a place."

"Well, there is, and I have. I had to say I wanted it so they'd keep it till I told you. I have to confirm on Monday. Please, dad."

"I may as well give you the answer now. I'm afraid it has to be no."

Amy felt as if the hall had narrowed. "Why?"

"The way you say that is sufficient reason."

"I can't help sounding how I feel."

"I pray you'll try. Your mother would have wanted it, I fancy."

"Stop saying that," Amy cried, and controlled herself before he made her sound even more childish. "She'd have kept her promise if she'd said I could go, and she'd have wanted you to."

"Very cunning, Amy. Try applying your cleverness to some worthwhile purpose before it becomes warped."

It was as though whichever way Amy turned to escape her trapped emotions he was already there waiting. "You haven't said why I can't go."

"I don't want you straying so far without me at your age. As you keep reminding me, you wouldn't even be sixteen."

"I'd be with the school."

"With the teachers whose idea it was to take children to Spain, which I fear doesn't say much for their judgment. I made it my business to learn about the country after you brought it up. I hadn't realised they tolerated drugs there. I thought the Spaniards were supposed to be God-fearing folk."

"Some religions use drugs. Some books even say Christ—"

"No more talk like that, thank you. Don't be so wrongheaded. I'm glad the libraries are cutting down on books if they're that kind. And I hope the drugs situation wasn't any part of why you were so anxious to visit Spain. You're far too close to that sort of wickedness as it is. Concerning which—"

"I can't talk any more now." That was imminently true; her lips were beginning to stiffen with her struggle not to release her feelings. "I'm meeting Rob."

"If he cares for you he'll wait, won't he? I'm not asking you to talk but to listen. You heard what Mr. Shrift said about the shop you frequent. Your mind is precious, Amy. It's your soul, and I can't imagine anything more evil than interfering with it."

"Then don't. I want to go now. I'm late."

Her father raised his eyes heavenwards, revealing tears on their lower lids, but she was more aware that he hadn't shifted from his post in front of the door. "May I enquire what is so much more important than talking to your father?"

"You heard. You were listening. You always do."

"Why are you so obsessed with a book all of a sudden?"

"I want to see what it says about here."

"Not much, I'll warrant, if it's nothing but a story. If you're going to devote so much effort to a book it's a shame it isn't schoolwork. Why should we care what our home used to be? It's what is made of it that counts."

Having been sapped of words, Amy stared at him. Her eyes had begun to smart before he said "How long do you propose to be?"

"Don't know."

"Where are you planning to go after the market?"

"Don't know."

"Will you be home for dinner?"

"Don't know. Shouldn't think so."

He gazed sadly at her, and she met his gaze with the smouldering lumps of frustration her eyes felt like. Abruptly he shook his head and glanced aside. "Lord help us, child, you've an evil eye sometimes," he muttered. "Don't be out all night or anything approaching it. I'm certain that your room needs cleaning."

The moment he stepped forward, Amy dodged past him and snatched the door open. The sight outside was no relief: it was more of the same—it even had small round dead solitary eyes to watch her. She slammed the door and ran down the corridor, which might have been absorbing what light there was rather than exuding it from its hidden source. On the stairs she felt as though the dimness and the way the carpet hushed her footfalls were dragging at her with their very lack of substance, leaving her nothing to fight. The confrontation with her father was reason enough for her to storm away, and the empty gates beyond the glass doors had never looked so much like freedom.

She stepped off the threshold with a clash of gravel. The air was as refreshing as an iced drink after the stagnant heat of the corridors. She was enjoying the touch of a wintry breeze and the whisper of the oak tree when she heard a clang from the marketplace. She must have been detained in Nazarill for longer than she'd realised; they were dismantling the market stalls.

As she sprinted out of the shadow of Nazarill the gravel threw diluted sunlight in her face, causing her to blink as if she'd just emerged from a windowless cell. She dashed between the gateposts and across Nazareth Row, and was in Little Hope Way before all her vision returned to her. In the midst of the clangorous dismantlement at the end of the stub of the street, many of the stall-holders were continuing to advertise their wares: Christmas cards, decorations, wrapping paper, cheap imported toys, a one-word shout for each species of goods. All Amy's attention was for the stall close to Hedz Not Fedz, which sold Hardly Owned books and was the nearest Partington had to a bookshop. The trestle table was half bare, and the bald though bearded owner was loading a carton of hardcovers into the rear of his van. But Rob was at the stall, and told him "Here's someone who wants you."

The bookseller gave Rob's earring and long eyelashes a doubtful glance before turning to confront Amy with much the same expression. "What are you after, girlie? I've packed up the romances."

"I packed them up years ago."

He swung a box of horror paperbacks, all their spines black, into the vehicle. "Wuh," he said in token of his effort. "If it's best sellers you want you'll have to climb in the back."

"Not those either. I'm looking for something old."

"Will I do, even if I'm not as pretty as your friend the pirate?"

"I don't think my dad would approve."

"I reckon he has to be broadminded." The bookseller grinned at himself and returned to his job. "How old?"

"I thought you might know. It's a book called *Nazarill.*"

"Woogh." At first it seemed he was reacting to the name, but this carton must have been heavier than its predecessor. "That's about the place up there on the hill."

"I knew it had to be. Is that all you know about it?"

"The place? Started out as a monastery from what I've heard tell."

"I didn't know that," Amy said, although for an instant she felt as if she had, and more if she could only grasp it. "How about after that?"

"How nasty do you like your history?" The bookseller hefted a carton in which Bibles and books on the occult were squashed together. "What's your interest, can I ask?"

"I live there."

This time he uttered no sound as he loaded the van, and was slower in straightening up. "You'll have heard it was a hospital."

"Not that I remember."

"After they pulled down the monastery, that would have been. They weren't so enlightened in them days. What they called a hospital would put you off your food, how they treated people."

"Not so different from some of the hospitals now," said Rob.

"Doesn't say much, does he?" The bookseller heaved the last carton to himself and dumped it in the van. "Wugh," he said, and rubbed his beaded pate, then closed his hand around his beard. "This book you're after, it won't be about any of that. Poor man's Dickens is my impression, about when your place was offices."

"Do you know where I could find it anyway?"

"I'll keep an eye out if you want. Wherever I am I go rummaging for books." He seemed engaged by her seriousness. "It shouldn't cost you much if I can get it," he said.

"About how much?"

"Less than a chain for your wrist."

"I can live with that. I'll keep coming back then, shall I?"

"Any time you want to light up my life," the bookseller said, and folding up the table, slid it into the van. "I'm here every week bar Christmas. What do they call you?"

"Amy Priestley."

"More by name than nature, is it? Not much wrong with that." He emitted a final expansive grunt as he slammed the rear doors of the van. "I'll put it by for you if I snaffle it," he said.

As the scraped vehicle piebald with imperfectly matched paint chugged away through the car park Amy said "I wish you hadn't interrupted when you did."

"If I hadn't when I did I wouldn't have when I didn't, would I?" Rob said, and to give her no chance to sort that out "I didn't know you went for older men."

"Apart from you, you mean."

"Brat."

"Cradle-snatcher." Amy watched the van's exhaust fade, then turned on him. "I mean it, Rob. I wish you'd just let him talk. I think he was going to tell me some more about Nazarill."

"What would it change if he had?"

"I don't know, do I? I'd like to find out the kind of place I'm living in, that's all."

"Don't look at me."

"Maybe you'd know if you ever came in."

"I get the feeling your dad wouldn't like me invading his haven."

"He'll have to if we want him to. He's having to get used to me."

"Traumatic," Rob commented, and looked away as the framework of a clothes stall collapsed with a sound like the shutting of a huge gate. Did he think she was demanding too much of a commitment of him? She took his cold hand and folded his long fingers around hers to make him feel wanted without needing to talk, just as Martie stepped out of Hedz Not Fedz and ventured along Market Approach. "Amy?" she called.

Her broad pouchy face was less placid than usual, perhaps because the chimes of her door had brought Shaun Pickles out of a half-demolished aisle of the market. Amy ignored him and pulled Rob with her into Market Approach. "What's happening, Martie?" she said.

"That's what I wanted to ask you." Martie widened her eyes before narrowing them as though to adjust the spaces between the lines of her frown. "Did you know your father meant to . . ."

Amy clenched her hands, and made them relax when Rob winced at her grip. "What's he done?"

"Try not to be angry with me. I can't very well go against him, you not being sixteen yet." Martie shook her head so hard that Amy imagined she saw her cropped hair move. "He says you aren't to come in my shop any more," Martie said.

6

IN THE DARK ROOM

"Anything more for you, Mr. Metcalf? Anything at all."

"Thanks a heap, Nico, thanks from a heap. I couldn't, really. You've outdone yourself." Dominic dealt the mound of his stomach a tender pat, and then his gaze strayed to the dish that was being placed before the nearest diner. "Dear me, that does look tempting."

"A portion of Garides Skordates for Mr. Metcalf, Melina, and some more bread for the sauce."

Dominic reached to empty the bottle of Othello into his glass, only to have the owner of the restaurant do so. "Some more red, Mr. Metcalf? Everything on the house."

"I shouldn't, you know. Well, maybe just one. Food without wine is like food without company, only half the pleasure."

Nico pushed his chair back and stood up. "It's always a pleasure to feed anyone who enjoys it so much."

"I didn't mean a whole bottle," Dominic murmured after him. He'd made his token protest, even if it went unheard. By the time Nico's wife brought the plateful of king prawns in garlic and wine sauce and a basket of bread, Dominic had drained his glass and refilled it from the second bottle of Othello. Several further dishes which looked irresistible had arrived at nearby tables, and he seemed to need only to glance at these to impel one of his hosts to bring him a sample: a kebab, a stuffed pepper, a barbecued lamb chop, pork with coriander. . . . All this helped him see off the bottle, and then there was syrupy baclava for dessert, and coffee brewed on a bed of hot sand, and Metaxa. When he'd finished inhaling the sharp aroma of grapes he found his lips with the snifter of brandy. "To your hospitality," he declared for at least the second time that night.

Melina and Nico picked up their glasses of ouzo that were standing on the bar. "Without you we aren't here," Melina said.

Dominic supposed that was as true as her grammar was quaint. When very eventually he left, having shaken hands twice with Nico and exchanged hugs with Melina, he had to make way for a party enticed in by the work he'd done on his hosts' behalf. Much of the window was occupied by his photographs, of three tables laden with the entire menu—even he hadn't been able to eat it all—and of the staff of the bank that held the restaurant's accounts celebrating someone's promotion: clerks dancing on the longest table and displaying as much thigh as they would on a beach, an assistant manager jigging so vigorously he had to hold onto his spectacles with the hand that wasn't around his partner's shoulder, the manager's eyes gleaming as she smashed yet another plate. Since the photographs had been exhibited the restaurant's takings had doubled, and Dominic was happy to accept some credit for it, despite suspecting that he'd simply corrected a misconception that a place called Nico's had to be Italian. Tonight it was so popular that both sides of the road on the outskirts of Sheffield were full of parked cars nosing one another's rumps, and it took Dominic some minutes to manoeuvre his Land Rover out of the trap that had been built around it. He had to get home, he kept telling himself as frustration extended the unpleasant pounding of his heart to his sweaty hands, to develop the photographs he'd taken in front of Nazarill. If he didn't tonight he wouldn't have time before Christmas, what with the seasonal increase in his work.

The Land Rover's front bumper inched itself clear of a smugly immobile Jaguar at last, and Dominic trod hard on the accelerator, then slowed the car as the sight of windows flickering with rainbow trees reminded him he was on a residential street. He sped up once the houses grew fewer and larger, and soon there were only trees beside the road, their branches decorated with dead bulbs left behind by a fog. Now and then a bulb fell to shatter in the headlights on the tarmac, and Dominic had drifted into watching for the next to fall when several revellers staggered out of an unexpected pub. Singing "God rest ye Jerry mentalmen," they reeled straight in front of the car, and

only a swerve which almost put the vehicle in the ditch of the unfenced road saved them. Dominic had to stop and press his forehead
against the windscreen, his sweat fogging the glass, before he trusted
himself to drive on. "Crazy. Shouldn't be let out," he mumbled, and
tuned the radio until he found a programme of carols to soothe him.
At last he drove towards the motorway, braking at every curve of
the deserted road.

Apart from the occasional midnight lorry, he had the motorway
to himself. Once he reached a stretch he knew went on for miles, he
allowed his speed to build up. He was shaking his head at the spectacle of a white sedan approaching fast behind him—he was ex-
ceeding the limit himself, but the other driver's speed was insane—
when its roof began to flash like a multicoloured Christmas light, and
he saw it was a police car. As he braked too hard it raced past him
and down a slip road. The siren howled away into the dark, and a
radio choir announced a silent night, which struck Dominic as an especially bad joke, since he was anything but calm and bright. He had
to force himself to increase speed so as not to appear as suspect as
he felt all the way to the Partington exit.

Five minutes off the motorway an orange glow became visible beyond the rocky slopes, as though there was a fire above the town.
When the Land Rover reached the top of a long curve of road he
saw the chains of light that were the streets trailing down from
Nazarill. The light drew him like a fire, even if he couldn't feel it. As
he turned uphill at the Scales & Bible it made all the ground-floor
windows of his building appear dimly lit to greet him. He couldn't
quite persuade himself that wasn't the case until he came to Nazareth
Row and saw that the whole of the ground floor, and indeed the rest
of Nazarill, was unlit.

Some animal, no doubt a cat, dodged away from the limit of his
headlights as they swung between the gateposts. The radio began to
sing "It came upon a midnight clear," but had pronounced only those
words when the tuning strayed awry, substituting a shrill mutter for
the rest of the carol. Whatever the voices were chanting was in a language foreign to him, and he switched off the radio as the gateposts
crept together in his mirror. The animal became part of the dark beneath the tree as Nazarill lit up its facade, and Dominic drove
through the glare to the parking area.

The slam of the car door sounded flattened, boxed in. The harsh light drained the facade of colour and coated the windows, turning them blank and dead. His gravelly tread in the midst of so much stillness made him feel conspicuous, as though he was being watched through the opaque panes. "Hardly," he mumbled, and tried singing "It came upon a midnight clear," but could remember no more words. He pulled out his keys with a jangle keener than the clash of gravel and let himself into Nazarill.

The external glare stopped short of the corridor. As the glass doors tolled behind him, the glow of the interior set about becoming visible. The close stagnant warmth revived his sweating, and he unbuttoned his coat as he twisted the key in his lock. The door fell away from him, pulling him into its hall, and he slapped the lightswitch. "What are you lot up to in the dark?" he said.

None of those addressed answered him. Being taken unawares was their constant state. Here was a bridegroom stumbling over his wife's train as he lunged in pursuit of his windblown top hat, and next to them a mother poised to strangle her five-year-old who wouldn't sit still for the camera. Opposite these framed photographs were a flautist whose musicality was summed up by the grimace of the pianist behind her, and a hotelier who'd insisted on rearranging himself and his Great Danes so often that one of the dogs was cocking its leg against his seventeenth-century chair. Usually talking to these and their kind in the various rooms relaxed Dominic in proportion to the trouble the sitters had given him, but tonight it didn't quite work, perhaps because even once he'd tugged the chains of the tubular lights above the frames, the hall seemed unduly dark. "Too much to drink, that's what it is. Anybody going to tell me off? Thought not," he said, and stumbled to the bathroom.

A young woman who'd fidgeted so much during her coming-of-age portrait session that she had almost come out of her strapless dress was waiting for him. "I should avert your eyes if I were you," Dominic advised her, "not that there's much to see." He took out the little he had and emptied the great deal for which it was the solitary egress, then sent himself to the kitchen for the blackest coffee he could make. While the percolator accumulated its bubbling he peered over a swelling and dwindling patch of his breath on the window at the tree, from which he had to persuade himself broken branches were dangling, not ropes. When the percolator uttered a peremptory click he half drained a mug of coffee before refilling it

to take to the darkroom. He'd known he was for Nazarill the moment he'd seen he would have a windowless room.

The amber glow of the safe light seemed not so much to illuminate the room as to stick like honey to its contents: the single eye of
the enlarger poring over the baseboard, the plastic tray lining up
opaque jars of chemicals beside the tray that isolated the develop-
ing tank. He stood the mug in the space between the tanks on the
bench and leaned into the hall to switch off the light. "Don't get up
to anything while I can't see," he murmured at the photographs,
only to find that the joke hovered in the dimness of the room, so that
he had to remind himself the appeal of living alone was that there
was nobody to let unwanted light in. "Here comes the dark," he said
loudly, and punched the switch and closed the door hard, rustling the
long envelopes which protected negatives. "On with the job," he
said.

His voice sounded unnaturally close to him, as though it had very
little space to move. He gulped a mouthful of the orange medicine
into which the safe light had transformed the coffee—it even tasted
of the trace of chemicals in the air—and went to the smaller of the
benches to fetch the negatives of the Nazarill session. He'd slipped
them out of the envelope and into the negative carrier, and was
holding them under the enlarger lamp to examine them for dust, before he realised he was holding a school photograph.

Nobody could have moved the negatives. He'd selected the wrong
envelope, that was all. Sheathing the strip, he inserted Nazarill in the
carrier and held it at an angle beneath the enlarger lamp. The line
of tiny black-faced figures stretched along the front of the building,
their eyes and their hair albino white. Behind them the windows and
glass doors were black as granite slabs embedded in the bony facade.
One window wasn't quite so black; it contained a paler mark. It was
his bedroom window.

He might have thought the mark was the reflection of someone's
head, except none of the other windows showed anything similar.
Perhaps it was simply, though annoyingly, a flaw in the negative. He
wouldn't know until he made a print how bad it was going to look.
"Let's be seeing you," he murmured, and switched off the enlarger
lamp while he set up the easel on the baseboard and arranged a sheet
of printing paper in it. Having minutely adjusted the lens, he switched
on the lamp.

Often he would expose the first print in sections to judge how much time it required, but he gave this one the full twenty-five seconds before extinguishing the lamp and preparing the trays—developer in one, stop bath in its neighbour. "Now we'll see who you were," he said, feeding himself a gulp of coffee to stave off a chill that had invaded the apartment. He raised the frame of the easel and picked up the exposed sheet by a corner of its border to float it in the developer.

He always enjoyed these seconds of seeing the picture at last, yet as he stooped over the tray he felt as though the thick dimness was weighing on him, helping the drowned image to draw his head down. He held onto the corner of the print with the tongs and agitated the sheet gently in the fluid, and had never been so conscious of performing a ritual. The lined-up faces paled against the front of Nazarill, and wisps of cloud sprang up like unkempt hair above the roof. For a moment the window at which he was peering appeared to swallow the presence it was framing, and then the pane crystallised around the shape. "Dear God, look at that," he blurted, and crouched forward in case a closer scrutiny might refute the evidence of his eyes.

There was a face in his bedroom, not the reflection of the back of anybody's head. It was nobody he'd ever seen or would have wished to see. Though the head was bald, he couldn't tell if it was male or female, or its age. It had been wrenched into a grimace that could hardly be called an expression, the jaw gaping wider than any mouth should go. The neck was as thin as a child's wrist, and the head was thrown back on it. Dominic gripped the edge of the bench with his free hand so hard the fingers trembled, and just as the print started to disappear, having lain too long in the developer, he saw from the position of the head and neck that their owner was being dragged back into his bedroom. He groped wildly for the stop bath tongs to transfer the print into that tray before the image could darken further. At that moment he heard the door open behind him.

He was twisting his head and upper body around when the whole of his spine seemed to lock. The door had opened about a foot, and all the darkness of his flat appeared to have massed beyond it, but that wasn't why he felt unable to move; he was hearing the words he'd last spoken. He'd meant "Look at that" only for himself, just a turn of phrase which shock had driven out of his mouth. He hadn't meant it as an invitation, and surely it could have brought no response.

He didn't realise he was holding his breath until his chest began to throb. If he didn't move, he thought he might collapse, but he was terrified that moving could draw some attention to him. Then the darkness beyond the room, or something in it, inched the door open further, and he saw in the gap a dim round object hovering some inches above the floor.

The plastic tongs fell out of his hands and clattered on the bench. His fingernails dug into the wood, and the jabs of pain released him. He straightened up so violently that at first he was afraid he had damaged his spine, and then he saw how helpless he was. The nearest light-switch was beside the darkness, not even separated from it by the door.

He sucked in a breath which seemed to fill his head with fumes and took hold of the enlarger. Snatching out the negative carrier, he wrenched at the lamp housing until its top clanged against the column of the stand. He scrabbled at the switch for the lamp and seized the column with both hands to tilt the heavy enlarger and direct the beam across the room.

At once he thought it wouldn't work. By the time it reached the doorway, the light was so diffused that its glow was scarcely visible. Yet it did work, altogether too well. As though the latent contents of the darkness had been enabled to develop, the round object wavered upward, and he saw its face—the face from the photograph. Its jaw gaped as the body scuttled on all fours into the room.

It halted just inside and raised itself on arms like dead branches, twisted and scrawny and peeling, as though to locate him. It cocked its yawning almost noseless head and turned it back and forth, and he thought that whatever was left in the puckered eye-sockets was unable to see. The spectacle would have paralysed him, except that the prospect of waiting to be found was even worse. The crawling figure wasn't really there, he managed to think; it was like a photograph the building had somehow taken, an image that the fabric of the place was projecting. The thought allowed him to lower the enlarger onto the bench, although his pulse made his fingers feel swollen and unstable. The base met the wood with a faint thud, barely audible through the pounding of his heart but loud enough to send a surge of panic through him. He launched himself at the hall, flinging out an arm which felt as though it was wrapped in thick rubber to grab the door and throw it wide.

The gaping head turned away from him, and the heel of his hand thumped the edge of the door. He'd grasped the wood and realised how it could help him vault into the hall, from which he would dash into the corridor and out of Nazarill before he let himself remember how unfit he was, when something caught his feet. The feel of it suggested he'd trodden in a mass of cobwebs, but a glance showed him the hands that had closed on his ankles. As he kicked out frantically and tried to find breath for a scream, the figure swarmed up the front of him, growing more substantial as it came, though it still felt even thinner than it looked. The dead face rose level with his, a tattered stump of tongue jerking deep within the hole of a jaw, and the shrivelled eyes found him.

7

THE ABSENT GUEST

At twenty-five to midnight on Christmas Eve, Oswald put his coat on and left the Roscommons' get-together to determine why Amy hadn't come back. The building was as silent as the night was meant to be, and he didn't meet her on the stairs or in the top corridor. He pressed the bellpush on their door and fitted his eye to the spyhole, but could see nothing through it. He fished out his keys and unlocked the door. As it swung away from his push, a song hit him in the face.

"I'm as old as anyone I know," a man was singing at the top of his ravaged voice, if singing was the word, and in the midst of the up-roar which seemed to be doing its best to drown him out, Amy was using the phone in the hall. Oswald shut himself in to give himself a chance to speak—shout, rather. "What in hell's name do you think you're doing?"

"I've got to go, Rob. See you tomorrow." She repeated most of this in fragments before hooking up the receiver and fixing Oswald with a wide-eyed gaze. "What does it look like?"

"Turn off that evil row for heaven's sake. Tonight of all nights peo-ple don't want to hear that kind of heathen racket."

"Which people? Everyone's downstairs."

"I'm surprised it isn't giving them a headache there, and you as well. You're supposed to suffer from headaches, aren't you? Isn't that why your friend across the corridor gives you pills a proper doctor wouldn't countenance?"

"Could you hear my music before you came in?"

"I'm hearing it now. Watch out you don't want to be heard some-time and find out nobody can," he said, lowering his voice and sharp-ening it so that it was just audible through the squirming squeals of instruments that had once been guitars. "You still haven't done as I asked."

Amy had met his warning with an incredulous stare, which she took with her on the way to stopping the tape. "Back in your box, Useful Bacteria. Old people don't like you."

"Thank you, Amy," Oswald said, attempting not to sound sarcas-tic. "Do try acting a bit less of the mad thing while you're off school."

She stalked out of the main room and pushed up the baggy sleeves of her sweater, which was the black of most of her clothes, as a pre-amble to folding her arms. "Mad like how?"

"Oh, Amy, don't pick at everything I say. You'd think you were the adult and I was the child," said Oswald, and felt her gaze draw-ing words out of him. "Deafening yourself whenever you're meant to be concentrating on your homework, that can't be good for your mind, can it? And just explain to me if you can what you thought you were doing when I came up. Couldn't you be bothered to turn it down while you were talking, or did you put it on to do his ears more mischief than they've already been done?"

"I think you're the one who sounds mad."

"Come along," Oswald said with all the authority he could sum-mon, "or we'll be late for mass."

Without her decision being in any way predictable she marched into her bedroom and emerged shrugging on her long black coat, which emitted a whiff of incense. "Don't forget you're to clear out that room during the holidays," he said.

God only knew what her room was like. He hadn't ventured to look in it since he couldn't quite remember when. If a spider had managed to invade his window, what might her untidiness have bred? At least the spider had died between the panes; he made himself look at its clenched withered form every morning and night. "Shake a leg, Amy. Or if you're feeling energetic, shake both," he said, as much to move her stare as her.

He'd locked their apartment and had succeeded in hastening her down to the ground floor when Harold Roscommon leaned out of his doorway and beckoned him with the hand that wasn't gripping the frame. "Any sign?"

George turned from murmuring to Ursula. "Father, Mr. Priestley didn't—"

"Don't be so sure you can say what he did. What about it, Mr. Priestley? Did you hunt down the lost one?"

"She's behind me."

"Better watch out, then. Don't they still say that at the panto when the witch or the demon comes on? It's behind you. I didn't mean you, lass. I was asking your pa if he found the feller who made us all line up like inmates."

"Mr. Metcalf," Oswald realised at last. "I can't say I saw him, not that I was looking."

"I thought you were meant to be in charge of the place and the rest of us."

"No, father, you remember, I told you. The idea was for us all to keep our eyes open."

"All except for me, since I'm never taken any notice of."

"I'm sure Mr. Metcalf just forgot he was invited," Ursula said.

"I didn't see him to remind him," George admitted.

Several of the guests appeared behind him. "I'd have thought he was the last of us to pass up the chance of a spread," Alistair Doughty said, inspecting his fingernails while he waited to sidle by.

"Must have had a better offer," said Paul Kenilworth, and waved his long fingers at the Roscommons as though he was practising to take up the piano. "No discredit to your evening. He does rather seem to live to stuff himself."

"I'd lay a bet he'll stuff himself into an early grave," Ralph Shrift declared.

"He hasn't yet. He's in there watching."

"I don't think so, father. I don't think you could have seen—"

"I see a damn sight more than I'm given credit for. I saw his eye just now at that prison peephole over there. If it wasn't him, you tell me what it was."

George hunched his shoulders and let them drop, and Oswald crossed to Metcalf's door. Having rung the bell, he peered through the bulging lens. An eye stared back at him—his own, backed by darkness. When the bell brought no response he moved away. "It must have been a reflection of one of us, Mr. Roscommon."

Harold Roscommon uttered a disgusted grunt and limped into the hall, where Max Greenberg flashed his Rolex at him, saying "Nearly Christmas."

It would be in less than fourteen minutes, Oswald saw from his own watch. He'd dawdled as though Nazarill needed him to oversee it—as though he'd elected himself to the role the old man had suggested. "We'll have to run, Amy, or we'll be late."

The air beyond the glass doors doused him like a cold bath, pure and invigorating. "Feel that," he said to her, but she was striding away from Nazarill so fast that the toes of her long black boots flung gravel across the lawn to clatter against the oak. As he ran after her into Nazareth Row he couldn't help wishing that just for once the market gates had been left unlocked. Surely the closing of the short cut to the church was a small price to pay for security, and besides, his was by no means the only family hurrying downhill. Amy betrayed no interest in all the windows planted with trees, so that he needn't regret having assumed she was too old for a tree this year—could admit to himself he would have felt it was more heathen than the celebration ought to be.

Ten minutes' jog in Amy's wake brought him to the upper edge of Partington, where the gate of the small steep churchyard squeaked to welcome each newcomer and many of the headstones sparkling with frost appeared to have stooped to greet them. "Good girl," he gasped, not that she seemed to take this for praise, as they hurried through the stone porch into the aisle. They'd just found space in the right-hand rear pew when the congregation rose to its feet, and Oswald felt as though it had waited for him.

The organ blared, the song-sheets rustled, the voices rose with the incense. "O come all ye faithful . . ." Oswald felt uplifted, by his sense of a community at worship and by the presence of so many of his clients in the church. He'd helped make them safe, and now they were helping him in return—helping him worship here so that he would be able to pray at home. It occurred to him that the thick unyielding walls of the church were by no means unlike those of Nazarill, and perhaps Harold Roscommon was right to believe it was somehow Oswald's duty to keep that building peaceful. When he rose to join in the final carol he felt renewed, transformed by the season.

"All Christian men rejoice, with heart and soul and voice. . . ." At first he couldn't grasp what was intruding between him and these sentiments—why the words were going wrong in his head—and then he heard that Amy was singing not "Christian men" but "Christie Annes." When he nudged her, harder than he'd thought he would, she retreated along the pew, leaving him to raise his voice to drown any other changes she might make. The carol was over before he managed to regain a sense of being part of it, and as the priest vanished into the sacristy Oswald took hold of her arm, to rebuke her for refashioning the words. He hadn't spoken when she pulled herself free, muttering "I'm going to the grave."

She meant Heather's. It had been years since they'd visited it together. "I'll come with you," Oswald called after her, only to be halted in the porch by a diminutive couple who were waiting for him. "Merry Christmas, Mr. Priestley," said Jack Pickles, peering up at him from behind tortoiseshell spectacles which might have been chosen to tone in with his freckled scalp and the last of his reddish hair.

"A joyous Christmas to you both."

"And many more with children in them," said Hattie, who seemed determined to live up to that name whenever she left the house: tonight she was crowned with a pink creation that resembled a giant sugar whorl at least as much as headgear. "Where's our Shaun?" she demanded, having already found him, and urged him by one elbow towards Oswald. "Here he is, up there. You remember Mr. Priestley who saw to our insurance. Wish him the compliments."

Her son's mottled face was in the process of rearranging its colours. "Ha," he mumbled immediately before "Happy Christmas."

"Leave the boy now, Hattie. He's not usually such a drooping snowdrop, Mr. Priestley. You should see him do his job. Isn't the light of your life with you?"

"She was ahead of me. Sorry if she didn't speak. You know how they can get at her age, or perhaps you don't. That's her over there in the black."

"God bless her," said Hattie, rubbing out a tear with a fingertip. "It's the book and its cover and no mistake."

Oswald was wondering why he wasn't as touched as she was by the sight of Amy, her lips moving as she confronted the granite column of the gravel plot on the far side of the churchyard, when Jack Pickles said "You've been seeing quite a bit of her lately, haven't you, son?"

"When she worked by the market," Shaun admitted.

"You won't have seen her working there recently," said Oswald.

"Since you told her not to go in that shop, you mean."

"That was my mind, certainly. How did you know?"

Shaun's face had started to increase its blotchiness even before his mother said "I think he's got his eye on her on the quiet. Pity there's not fewer years between them."

"The one she's walking with is older than she is."

Shaun must have been encouraged by Oswald's tone; the redder patches of his face set about reverting to pink. "I've seen him, if that's a him."

"A conundrum, I agree. So what's my answer?"

The nineteen-year-old, as Oswald had now dated him, stared. "Scuse?"

"You haven't seen her go into that shop since I bade her."

"I haven't, Mr. Priestley. I can include it in my patrol if you like."

"I should think most folk would want you to. Were you about to say more?"

"He still hangs round that shop, her dope with the stuff in his face."

"I should have realised," Oswald said, wondering why he'd needed to be told. At that moment Amy turned towards the church, and her face hardened, which dismayed him so much that she was on her way to the gate before he called out "Amy, come here a minute."

"Merry Christmas," Jack said as though his loudness must provoke at least an echo.

"Yes, do join us. We're still yapping. We've already got one shy type here," said Hattie, nodding the pink whorl at her son. "Don't say you're another."

Something about this seemed to amuse Amy, who picked her way over the grass, her shadow catching on gravestones as it kept its distance from the spotlights that exhibited the church. "You know our Shaun, don't you?" Jack said.

"I know him."

Oswald didn't like her manner, nor the expressionless gaze she fixed on the youth, but Hattie took her attitude to signify the opposite of its appearance. "We were just going to say, weren't we, Jack, why don't both of you drop in over Christmas."

"We'll be delighted, won't we, Amy?"

"When?"

"Whenever's convenient," Jack said.

Shaun's chewed lips had started to admit to a grin. Amy stared at it and said "I'll be busy then."

"Convenient for you as well, we mean," Hattie protested. "Not just as well, as much. Shaun will put some records on for you, won't you, Shaun? It's not our style, all this Cliff Richard crooning, but I expect it appeals to you. I'm sure you'll find you've a lot in common if you get to know each other."

"I doubt it."

"No harm in giving it a try," said Oswald, keeping most of his anger inaudible. "I'd like to spend a little time with these good people when they've so kindly invited us."

"You go, then. No thanks," Amy said, and elicited a discouraging screech from the gate as she walked out of the churchyard.

"I'm sorry. I don't know what the problem is with her at the moment, but it's going to have to be solved damned quick."

"It must be a trial bringing her up on your own," Hattie said.

That made Oswald feel no less humiliated. He would have shouted at Amy to come back and apologise to their friends, except that would be to create more of a scene. Instead, as a kind of unstated apology, he stayed in the midst of the Pickles family as they trailed after her up Moor View. At Gorse Cottages he took an awkward leave of them, as a drunk began to rant somewhere ahead. "Peace on earth," Jack commented.

"There will be if I've anything to do with it," Oswald said grimly, and strode after his daughter. Once the Pickles family was out of earshot he spoke. "Wait there. I want to talk to you."

As Amy halted, an illuminated slab rose beyond her, filling the end of the street. It was part of the front of Nazarill, where the security lights had been triggered. Oswald overtook her and stared into her face, and saw only leaden resignation. "Perhaps you can explain yourself," he said.

"Shouldn't think so."

The drunk was still ranting, close to Nazarill. Had he wandered into the grounds and set off the lights? Oswald would have been finding out if he hadn't had to deal with Amy. "What were you hoping to achieve by such behaviour?" he demanded.

As her eyes waited for Oswald to go away the man's voice continued to rave, giving Oswald a confused impression that it was answering him. "I never imagined I'd see you so unmannerly," he said. "What do you suppose they thought of you?"

"Wouldn't know."

"You no sooner leave your mother's grave than you spurn my, not just my friends, my clients, on this of all nights." There remained far more to be said, but the man's voice was distracting him—its elusive familiarity was. "Come along," Oswald said harshly. "Don't think I've done with you by any means, but I want to scc what that is."

He'd halved the distance between himself and Nazarill before he heard her start to follow him. Once they were home where nobody could hear, he promised himself, they would have a proper talk. Spectators had come out of the end houses of Moor View to watch the grounds, somewhere in which the voice was repeating a few words over and over. Emerging onto Nazareth Row, which had produced even more of an audience, Oswald saw Alistair Doughty and Max Greenberg and Teresa Blake standing outside the shadowy cage of the oak. "What's happening, do you know?" Oswald asked the nearest onlooker, a burly shirtsleeved man who was sharing a can of lager with his wife.

"Some old feller's gone round the bend, looks like."

As though the words had focused the glare of Nazarill, Oswald saw a figure through the branches, a man in striped pyjamas and a dressing-gown who was clinging with all his limbs to the dark side of the tree. The man twisted his head round as Teresa Blake ventured towards him, and Oswald saw he was Harold Roscommon. "I'm not going back in there," he shouted yet again. "Keep off."

Oswald grimaced a rebuke at the audience while he crossed the road, but they gazed at him as if he was part of the spectacle. He strode onto the drive, and the gnashing of gravel drew the attention of those at the oak. The old man craned his head back. "Is that George?" he shouted. "I want George."

"The Goudges are trying to find him, Mr. Roscommon," the magistrate said.

"I don't know where he'd be at this hour," Max Greenberg said as though to use up his own preoccupation with time.

Both spoke so carefully it was clear to Oswald they were reining in their emotions. "Go inside, Amy," he said as she came abreast of him, having hurried after all. "No arguments. I'll be up in due course."

To his annoyance, Greenberg intervened. "Mr. Priestley, if I were you I wouldn't tell—"

"You're blessed with not being, Mr. Greenberg. I'm the father, and I think that gives me the right—"

"Nobody's about to contest that, only you mightn't want her going in by herself just at the present."

"Why not?"

It was Amy who asked, but the watchmaker persisted in addressing Oswald; he even lowered his voice. "Mr. Metcalf's door may be open, and you'd hardly want her seeing. He seems to be— he must have had the heart attack some of us were predicting."

If his murmuring was designed not to be overheard by Harold Roscommon, it didn't work. "No seems about it," the old man said, and louder "He's dead, and there was something in there with him."

"Children present, Mr. Roscommon," the magistrate said.

"I don't see any," said Amy, a protest that went unanswered as the old man cried "That won't shut me up either. I saw what I saw, and it'll take more than all of you put together to drag me back inside there."

"Stay where you are for the nonce," Oswald told Amy, and turned back to Max Greenberg. "What does he think he saw?"

"Nobody's sure. What he did see was Mr. Metcalf, which must be why he's in this state. He'd gone out of his apartment looking for his son and found Mr. Metcalf's door open."

"Has anyone called the police and ambulance?"

"The police will be here as soon as they can," Alistair Doughty said, "and the ambulance has to come from Sheffield."

"Well done, Mr. Doughty." The community of Nazarill was beginning to unite, thought Oswald. If only someone had cared enough to say to the photographer's face that his excesses were straining his heart! "Is anyone with Mr. Metcalf?" Oswald said.

"The medical lady from your floor is," said the magistrate. "She was the one who took his pulse."

"I suppose she must know what she's doing," Oswald murmured, only to provoke the old man. "What are you muttering about?" he cried. "Why won't anyone listen to me?"

"I will," said Amy, and before Oswald could prevent her she had ducked under the branches. "What did you see?"

As Roscommon shifted to face her, two large chunks of bark came away in his hands. "Somebody with a mouth bigger than this," he said, and shook his gnarled fist.

"Amy, will you please—" called Oswald, but the old man was louder. "I thought at first a dog had got in, because it was too thin for a person. Only it looked at me, and it used to be someone right enough, before all that happened to its face. Then it crawled off into the dark like an old spider."

"All right, Amy, that's quite enough." Oswald saw her and the old man staring at each other with a kind of recognition which he neither liked nor wanted to define. "Enough," he repeated.

Roscommon stretched out a hand to detain her, and the piece of bark hit a root with the sound of a gavel. "Have you seen it too?"

"I don't know."

"Of course she hasn't." Whatever game she thought she was playing, it infuriated Oswald. He made for her, to march her into Nazarill if necessary, but faltered as Max Greenberg spoke. "They've found— he's there."

There was movement at a window on the middle floor. One of Ursula Braine's curtains had been pushed back, revealing George Roscommon, naked from at least the waist up. The next moment he vanished, returning immediately to tug the curtain shut. "I hope he'll be quick down," Teresa Blake said, and with somewhat less disapproval "Mr. Roscommon, your son's on the way."

"Where was he? With that trollop, I'll wager."

"That isn't important," Amy tried to persuade him. "You were telling me—"

The magistrate frowned at her. "Morality is always important, miss."

"She knows that," Oswald said, and seizing Amy's elbows, turned her to face him. "And you've been told often enough to respect your elders."

Amy regarded him with a mixture of pity and disbelief as she disengaged herself from him. She glanced at the old man, but he was no longer looking at her; he'd redoubled his hold on the oak as if, Oswald thought furiously, what she'd made him say had aggravated his panic. As she reached the entrance to Nazarill, George Roscommon dashed into view, his untied shoelaces flailing the air, and held one glass door open for her. She went in slowly, then halted in the corridor. Before Oswald could move or shout, she pushed open the door of Dominic Metcalf's apartment and walked in.

Oswald sprinted across the lawn, skidding on the grass, and up the drive. George stepped back with a bewildered look to perform his doorman act again. As Oswald's footfalls were muffled by the carpet he heard Beth Griffin say "Don't worry, Amy, I'll be all right on my own." The next moment Metcalf's door swung wide open and Amy emerged, her gaze passing over Oswald as she headed for the stairs.

At first he thought she had seen nothing of significance, her expression was so blank. The homeopath was standing at the near end of a hall lined with framed photographs and additionally illuminated by the light of every room. She extended one stiff arm to push the door shut, and Oswald saw an object protruding from the doorway nearest to that of the kitchen. It was a man's clenched hand.

Its plumpness had apparently belied its strength. In its final convulsion it had ripped a thick brown fistful out of the carpet. Oswald found himself wondering distractedly how the Goudges might feel about that after they'd devoted so much care to carpeting the whole of Nazarill. Then the door blocked his view, and as he hurried to the stairs up which Amy had disappeared, the grotesque notion gave way to the thought he had been trying not to admit. Whatever Amy might have seen of Metcalf's corpse, her expression had seemed to imply she'd already seen worse.

8

NOT SUCH A GAME

Once the Goudges' families started to assemble on Christmas Day it became clear they felt bound to mention the carpets. "Good rich brown," Donna's mother said.

"Negro," said Donna's father from the kitchen, where he was placing cans of beer in the refrigerator.

"We aren't allowed to say that any more," Auntie Ethel halted on her two sticks in the hall to warn him.

"Don't hold up the traffic, sis. It's the other thing you can't say now," said Auntie Pen, fluttering her stubby fingers to shoo her onward.

Ethel swung round in the living-room doorway, prompting everyone to rush to her support until she steadied herself with twin triumphant thumps of her sticks. "I thought it was black you couldn't say these days, not good old brown."

"Not black or brown, the other thing." Pen turned her palms up and began to wag her fingertips as if to scoop the answer out of the air. "The *other* thing. En eye gee . . . that."

"Stopping talk doesn't change anything," Donna's father said. "It just lets folk pretend things have changed."

This provoked the general hoot of derision with which the family always greeted his profundities, and Donna's mother took the opportunity to put away the subject. "You look tired," she told Donna.

She often did, but this time the cause of any tiredness hadn't been a night of fun. Dave crossed the kitchen, having forked the turkey and fitted the plate back into the oven, and gave Donna's waist a squeeze. "We were in bed late and up early," he said.

Donna clasped his hand, in response and to hush him. While he was obviously not about to describe how they'd occupied the morning other than by preparing dinner—ensuring that every family item was not only on show but also not occupying more of a position of honour than any other, photographs and spectacularly inappropriate cushions and ornaments of a hideousness that had consigned them to the spare room until now—she hoped he wouldn't mention last night's events either. As if her thought of family had been overheard, the doorbell from the downstairs entrance rang. "Shall I have a go?" Pen, who was nearest, said.

"I expect it's my lot," said Dave. "Just—"

She had already poked the door release beneath the speaker with one adventurous thumb. "Ah well, it shouldn't matter," he said.

"Wasn't that the ticket?"

"I'm sure it was, only we usually check first who's there."

"You should have said," Pen reproached him, and leaned a knuckle on the other button. "Who is it?"

"I should think they'll have—" Dave began, but she shushed him with a hiss that rivalled the noise the speaker was emitting. Holding down the button, she lowered her head to the box. "I can't make it out," she eventually said, and straightened up. "They were singing."

"Waits," Ethel suggested, though nobody but Pen had heard anything but static.

"More like chanting. A long way off and too close into the bargain, if you know what I mean."

Nobody did, but Donna's father said "Maybe something's up with the rig."

"Picking up messages not meant for us," said her mother.

"A lady at the lunch club used to know someone like that," Ethel said. "She thought she was going mad because she kept hearing voices, until the dentist found it was her filling picking up the wireless."

"Shame they can't take a few more mad ideas out of people's heads that easily," Donna's father said.

Dave looked unhappy when the notion wasn't hooted down. "They used to think they could."

Donna hugged his waist as a promise of a reward later if he would just keep the peace, but the buzzer on the door intervened on her behalf. As soon as Pen responded to it, Dave's parents and his Uncle Rodney broke into "We wish you a merry Christmas," agreeing on approximately half of the notes. "That's what you must have heard, Pen," Ethel said.

"Wasn't," Pen said as she made way for the newcomers. "Sit yourself down for pity's sake, Eth. You look like a turnstile stuck in that doorway."

"Fine thick carpets," Dave's mother had been waiting to enthuse, which was sufficient not just to revive the theme but to set the guests competing to praise Dave's and Donna's professional taste and skill. By the time that was over Donna had managed to seat both families in the main room while Dave served drinks. Rodney brushed up his overhanging moustache with the back of his hand as a preamble to slurping the froth off his beer, then set the tankard down to be transformed into a variety of potions by the flickering lights of the Christmas tree. "I'm told you had some excitement round here while good Christian folk were tucked up in bed."

"Thought you were here. Saw your old heap," Dave's father was saying to Donna's, and turned away from him before he had time to retort. "What excitement was that?"

"It was people from here, wasn't it, Dave? Died and went crackers was the tale I heard from my friend who lives on the Row and came in the Scales for a festive pint."

"I don't think you could be mad if you were dead," Ethel said.

"Why not? Maybe that's what judgment day will be, a madhouse."

"Don't be so morbid, Pen," said Ethel, and raised the gin she'd dropped her stick for. "Here's to their memory, whoever they were."

Glasses were elevated, and agreement was murmured, before Pen said "What a day to choose for popping off."

"He didn't die at Christmas, the one who died," Dave told her. "The medics said it must have been days ago he had a heart attack. None of us had seen him for a week, not since he took everyone's photograph."

Up to this point Donna had avoided thinking that the photographer had lain dead for days as close to her as the tree outside the window, but now the thought felt like a presence that had lingered in the building to wait for the dark. When the families had finished expressing shades of dismay her father said "Will it come out?"

Donna shivered. "Will what come out of where?"

"Come out. Be any good. Develop."

"Oh, the photographs," Donna said with an attempt at a laugh. "I expect there may still be the negatives, but he'd be on them."

Some sounds of understanding greeted this, and Rodney seemed to feel it was left to him to say "So who went mad?"

"Those people who were playing whatever they were playing as we drove up looked a bit strange to me," Pen offered.

"Which bunch was that?" said Dave's father.

"They were spinning some old woman round and round down-stairs, and she didn't look too thrilled about it either."

"Nobody's downstairs just now," Dave said. "The old chap who lives there with his son found the, you understand, the photographer, which you can imagine would upset anyone, Uncle Rod. His son had to take him away to relatives in Manchester until he could find somewhere local."

"You nodded off on the motorway, Pen," Ethel said. "Too much sherry with your mince pies at mine."

"Are you saying there's nobody at all under you?" Pen demanded.

"Not as we speak. Not just at present," Donna said, though chang-ing the words didn't help much.

"I'm sure there'll be someone down there before you know it," said her mother. "Odds Pen had been thinking about the games we're going to play after dinner. Now I'm having a look at your bird, Donna, in case he's squawking to be let out before he goes up in smoke."

"Let's both look." As soon as they were in the kitchen Donna murmured "I was going to tell you and daddy what happened. I just didn't want it spoiling the day."

"We'll make sure nothing does," her mother said so lightly Donna almost thought she wasn't put out because Dave's family had heard first, and slid the turkey into view to perforate it with the fork. "Seven hours should do, even for such a plump feller."

"I'll start seeing to the vegetables."

"Don't talk about your aunts like that."

The clatter of plates started the families vying to help, and only the provision of more drinks persuaded them to resume their seats, apart from Ethel, who levered herself to a dining-chair and directed the servers like a sedentary housekeeper. Half an hour after Donna and her mother had repaired to the kitchen, everyone was seated at last around the laden oval table. As Dave flourished the carving-fork and knife, Pen appeared to waken from one of her dozes. "Is anyone going to say grace?"

"Grace," Rodney said.

Dave made the first incision, and then it was too late, though Donna would have taken up Pen's suggestion if she had been able to remember the words. "Couldn't have done better myself," her mother said after a mouthful, and surely those words were enough of a blessing. "To the chef."

"The chef," the guests chorused more or less distinctly, elevating their drinks, and Donna set about enjoying her own meal as much as everyone else was. Only the dance of flames on the pudding when Dave lit the brandy on it disconcerted her, or perhaps it was the way Pen's face jerked up beyond them that did, her face blinking and wavering as though the flames were as close to it as they momentarily appeared to be. Pen took refuge in another doze once the meal was over, various people having declared "I couldn't" before they did, and the families began to disagree over who was entitled to clear the table and wash up. A deal was ultimately struck by which all the men saw to these tasks, leaving the women to talk across Pen and speculate how long it would take her paper hat to slip off her lolling head. When Donna closed the curtains, the clash of wooden rings roused Pen to mumble in her sleep. Ethel thumped the floor with her sticks, which only brought the men to see if there had been an accident. "What's your weird sister saying?" Rodney wanted to know, or at any rate asked.

"Even less sense than usual."

Pen raised her head blindly, and the paper hat crackled as if her hair had caught fire. "Coming up the house," she announced.

"Good job we know her or we'd be having her locked up," Rodney said, projecting his voice at her. Perhaps in some way this caused her to protest "Don't want that bath." Nothing else she mumbled seemed worth a guess before the men returned from the kitchen again, looking virtuous. "Are we leaving Pen in her trance?" Donna's father said.

Ethel thumped the floor so hard it shook, and Donna imagined the vibrations invading the unlit empty room beneath. She was about to ask her aunt to stop when the sleeper blinked herself awake and blinked about her. "We're at Donna's. What were you dreaming?" Donna's mother said.

"Nothing at all. I just nodded off for a second. Are we going to play now? Let's have the game where we put bits of a body together."

"That's fun," Donna promised herself aloud, and went to fetch a foolscap pad and a handful of ballpoints from the spare room, which smelled of the glossy brochures she and Dave kept for consulting at home. The lack of a window trapped the smell, and so did the door as it crept shut, withdrawing the sounds of the families from her. She shoved a pile of brochures under one arm and snatched the door open, feeling as though she was releasing herself from a cell she hadn't known the apartment contained. "Here you are, everyone," she called as she hurried back to the party. She held out the pad for each person to tear off a sheet, and once the ballpoints and brochures had also been distributed, sat on the arm of Dave's chair. "You start us off, Pen."

Pen took her time with the face. She crouched over the sheet spread on the brochure until it seemed that rather than ensuring nobody could see what she was drawing, she was unable to straighten up from staring at it. Abruptly she folded the strip on which she'd drawn and thrust the page at her sister. "Shoulders," she said.

Her directing had been part of the game ever since Donna was little. "Chest and a bit of the arms . . . Belly and elbows . . . Hipbones and wrists . . ." Donna was in charge of feet for this round, and gave them hobnailed boots whose toes pointed in opposite directions. She handed the long thin wad to Pen, who unfolded it and held it up. "Oh," she said, not quite the cry of surprise with which she usually greeted the result of the game, and not all the other players laughed.

The various sections of the figure weren't supposed to match, but somehow the joke had gone wrong. The grinning wild-haired face seemed determined to ignore its elongated scrawny body, which was either performing a grotesque knock-kneed dance or dangling from the cocked head on the stretched neck. Even the hairy ankles protruding from boots far too large for them no longer struck Donna as amusing. "I used to go out with her," Rodney said, which allowed Donna to find a laugh within herself and Pen to propose another round.

This one was almost a success. The head Ethel drew with a bobble hat perched on top of its bald pate was sticking out its tongue, and most of the players guffawed at that, although Donna could have done without the dribble from a corner of its mouth where her aunt's ballpoint had slipped. Rodney started next, but the head he produced was so pop-eyed that nobody liked it much. "It's looking at me," Pen complained. "Cover it up." After that she found some aspect of each figure to dislike, and when she took issue with a pair of skinny hands which appeared to be digging their nails into the page in order to bestir the body they had patched together—hands which Dave's mother couldn't recall having drawn to look like that but which she must have—Donna thought it time to call a halt. "Let's play Consequences now."

"There can't be any harm in that," said Pen, and wrote the first line. "The man she met," she reminded her sister to write, and accompanied each passing of the folded sheet with a direction: "The time . . . the place . . . he said . . . she said . . . then she . . . and he . . . and the consequence was . . ." Donna wrote the most optimistic consequence she could think of and handed the sheet, now little broader than a wand, to her aunt. "The Queen met—" Pen said, and then "What's this wormy thing?"

"Napoleon," her sister interpreted, not without some pique at having her handwriting questioned.

"The Queen met Napoleon at thirteen o'clock on the blasted heath. She said 'I can teach you to fly,' as if she would, Rodney, and he said 'Shall we dance?,' I don't think. Then she ran three times round the oak tree, I expect that's the one outside here, and he, is there someone you'd like to do this to, Dave? He locked himself in the smallest room, best place for him. And the consequence was, I can't read this word either. They both lived . . . ever after."

"Happily," said Donna.

"I thought it said hoggily. They both lived like pigs for evermore."

"Well, they didn't," Donna objected, and heard herself making too much of a fuss. "Auntie Ethel, you start this time."

"Can't we play something else now? All this scribbling won't help my joints."

"Let's play the game where I'm always the old boot."

"That's Monopoly, Pen."

"I know what it's called. I haven't lost my senses yet, whoever else round here may have."

"We can be spectators," Dave's mother said to him. "We'll have to be homing before it's finished, or I'll never be ready for the family tomorrow."

"I'll see to the coffee," Rodney said as though he'd been given the excuse none too soon.

Dave fetched the game from the spare room, but it was less of a success than usual. Perhaps because she was tired, Donna found Pen's commentary chafed her nerves. "Better make sure nothing's living in those," Pen said when the plastic buildings started to appear on the board, and when she managed to buy some, shook them vigorously and squinted into their hollow interiors. A quirk of the dice sent her to jail three times in succession. "Back in my cell again. May as well lock me up and throw away the key," she complained, and as the other players moved their symbols around the track "Dance round, go on, don't mind me." Before she had a chance to release her miniature boot from jail she'd nodded off and was talking in her sleep again. "Round and round, stop it, you're making me dizzy," she mumbled, and "Keep it away, I'll be quiet, I will." When she began to moan on a rising note Ethel shook her awake, for which she was uncharacteristically grateful, and Donna's mother said "I think we should all be moving. Our hosts have had a long day. Let's say they've bought us."

Pen shoved the boot away with a fingernail, knocking over several raw red houses. "They're welcome to the lot of those squashed places."

Eventually all the guests had their coats on, Ethel refusing to be helped with hers and Pen following suit, and Donna's mother kissed Dave hard, then her daughter. "Thank you both for making the day special."

Once they'd seen their guests out and watched the cars up the drive, the two pairs of brake-lights flaring red as firebrands before swerving out of the grounds, Donna let go of Dave's waist and closed her hand around the icy metal bar of one glass door. "What kind of Christmas was that really, do you think?"

"It isn't over yet." He took her free hand in both of his, which were almost warm enough to counteract the chill of the metal. "Here's what I think. I think we shouldn't let what happened to those poor people ruin our first Christmas here."

"I know."

"You aren't having second thoughts, are you? Don't sit on them. I wouldn't want to live anywhere you don't."

"It'll be better when there are more people again." If the heat of the ground floor felt somehow illusory, that was only because the chill of the night had reached deep into her. The ruined carpet in the photographer's hall would have to be replaced, she thought, which touched off a memory as she hurried ahead of Dave to the stairs. "Do you remember when we came to measure?"

"How could I forget? Coldest day of the year, it felt like. So much for May."

"It was only cold in here though, wasn't it? I wonder . . ."

"So will I unless you tell me."

"Do you think that's what made us go wrong, the cold? We've never been that careless."

"We must be turning into an old married couple. We'll have to look after each other."

"We've always done that, haven't we? I still don't understand how we could have thought there were so many rooms in this place."

"Trying to be too clever. You remember, we figured since all the apartments had the same floor plan we could multiply one. I seem to recall someone kept saying 'God, it's freezing' and 'Get a move on.' Does it matter? We got it right in the end between us. That's what being together's about."

"One of the things." Donna was attempting to identify when they'd decided they would like to move to Nazarill themselves—surely not that cold confused first day here, and yet as far as she could tell it had been then the idea had entered her mind. "Let's go upstairs," she said.

"Yes, let's."

"I didn't mean for that."

"I just thought it might make you feel better after everything. We won't if you don't want to."

"I do," she decided by the time they reached their door. As soon as it was closed she showed him how much she did, pulling him to her and finding his tongue with hers as she lifted one thigh between his legs. When she and Dave parted for breath he said "Let me just unload some of the drink."

"I'll be waiting."

In the bedroom she closed the heavy curtains, beyond which the oak tree was groping for the light of the room, and lay on top of the quilt. She heard Dave turn off the bathroom light, and the kitchen light, and the one in the main room, and in the hall. It was their own dark, they would make it so by being together; she mustn't let herself feel as though he was inviting the darkness up from below them. When he came into the room she didn't speak until he went to the chest of drawers. "Dave . . ."

"Don't you want to?"

"It's my turn, isn't it?"

"Only if you like. It never has to be, you know that."

"I like." Putting themselves in each other's power only made them feel more certain of each other. "I do," she said as though repeating the marriage vow, and stretched her arms and legs wide as he brought the four silk scarves out of the top drawer. "Tighter," she said when he tied a scarf to her left wrist with a knot from which she could free herself with the merest tug. "Make it real," she insisted, and used her other hand to tie a knot on top of the first and haul it as tight as she could.

"Don't cut off your circulation."

"If I do you can get it going for me," Donna said, swinging her scarved wrist towards the bedpost for him to secure. She tugged at all her bonds when he'd finished tying them. "Now you can do what you like with me," she said.

A delicious tingling spread up her torso and down her thighs as he began to unbutton the front of her almost ankle-length dress. He kissed each part of her body he found, and each kiss made her feel a little younger and more eager for him. When he'd laid her dress open he snapped her bra open between its cups and lingered over kissing each of her breasts. Kneeling on the floor, his elbows on the quilt, he shuffled down the bed, tonguing her stomach. He popped the stud of her panties, and she felt herself open in anticipation of his mouth. At that moment the phone rang in the main room.

"Go away," Dave muttered, his lips and the day's worth of stubble tickling her above her hipbone, and stayed crouched beside her stomach. The phone delivered six pairs of trills and was halfway through a seventh when it fell silent. "Call again soon," Dave said indistinctly, and traced the outline of her hipbone with his tongue. He was hitching himself forward on his elbows when the phone recommenced shrilling, and he raised his head. "Shall I answer it?"

"Leave it. It can't be any of our folk, not so soon after we've seen them."

"Except if it was it would have to be something urgent, wouldn't it?" He slapped the quilt with both hands and stood up. "If I don't find out I'll worry. I'll be quick."

"The longer you are the older I'll be when you get back," Donna said, lifting her head to watch him hurry out of the room. She was just able to distinguish a flickering in the dark hall—a hint of the Christmas tree lights—as the door began to inch shut behind him. "Leave the—" she said, but it was more important that he reach the phone in time, and so she let her head subside on the pillow, which puffed itself up around her ears. She heard Dave switch on the light in the main room, making no appreciable difference to the visibility of the very little of the hall she could see, and then there was a clatter mixed with a curtailed trill. "Dave and Donna Goudge," he gabbled. "Hello?"

As far as Donna was concerned this was followed by silence except for the creaking of the mattress as she flexed her hands and feet, which were growing cold and stiff. "I can't make out what you're saying," Dave said at last. "Who are you?"

"It's nobody. Tell them happy Christmas and to go and bother someone else." Donna peered along her cheekbones at the sliver of dark hall, then closed her eyes to stop them aching. Through the enclosure of the pillow she heard Dave say "I'm sorry, I can't make any sense of this. You'll have to phone back."

"Not now," Donna pleaded, and might have repeated it loud enough for Dave to hear, except that he said "If it isn't urgent, make that tomorrow." His voice sounded more muffled, and she was assuming he'd turned away from her when she heard a faint noise beyond the foot of the bed. Her eyes widened just in time to see the door swing shut. As it did, the bedroom light went out.

Had she glimpsed a movement at the switch? Surely that must have been the shadow of the door. She sucked in a breath to replace the one she'd lost by gasping and opened her mouth to call to Dave. Instead she spoke. "Don't do that, Dave. It isn't funny, not after last night. I know you're there."

That brought no audible response, but she didn't need to hear him to sense the presence in the room. He was pussyfooting across the thick carpet towards her, perhaps even crawling over it, and she would never have expected him to be so stupid. She hoped he was able to see as little as she could in the dark that the curtains had closed in—she hoped he would fall over something. Nevertheless he was making her so nervous she might have wept with anger. "Dave, stop it now," she said louder. "You aren't turning me on at all." But her rebuke trailed off; she wasn't even sure if the last word passed her lips. The phone had emitted the single note it always released as the receiver was hung up. Dave was still in the main room.

She tried to cry out to him, but her tongue felt as though a weight the size of her mouth was pressing it down. He must surely be on his way to the bedroom. She jerked her hands towards the bedposts in an attempt to slacken her bonds and struggled to snag the knots at her wrists with her fingernails. They didn't reach, and she had succeeded only in clawing at her palms when she realised that by now Dave ought to have come back. Was he waiting by the phone in case it rang again? She dragged wildly at her bonds, and the scarf tied to her left wrist slipped off the bedpost.

Her fist thumped the mattress, and she was suddenly afraid of having drawn attention to herself. She opened her mouth—all at once she didn't care what noise she made to summon Dave—as she became aware that the rest of her bonds had remained unyielding. Then something trailed across her bare midriff.

It felt almost insubstantial enough to allow her to believe she was fancying the sensation. But something was there—a part of whatever had crept up to her in the blind dark and was leaning over her in a silence that was worse than any voice or breath. Before she could imagine what she might touch, her fist lashed out to ward it off.

The trailing substance was snatched away, and for a moment she was able to think it had only been the scarf which she'd been unaware of flinging across herself. The thought had barely offered itself when her fingers, opening in the dark, caught in the substance that was still dangling over her. It was hair.

It felt like thick cobweb loaded with grit. It clung to her fingers as she tried to flail it away, only managing to entangle them in it. She heard a sound that the removal of a sodden piece of sticking-plaster might have made—she felt the lock of hair detach itself from the scalp and settle across the back of her hand. She also heard Dave's footsteps in the hall, but he was too late; indeed, the prospect of his switching on the light dismayed her so much that she would have covered her eyes with her hand if it had been empty. Her arm shuddered in midair as he halted outside the door. "Who shut that?" she heard him wonder. "Are you up, love?" The doorknob turned with a faint squeak, and the door swung open.

The hall was illuminated only by the flickering of the Christmas tree, but to her eyes, which were famished for light, even that was sufficient to alleviate the blackness of the room. She was almost certain that she saw an appallingly thin silhouette leaning over the side of the bed. At once it retreated in a lopsided crouch to a corner of the room, into the alcove formed by the wall and the wardrobe, and shrank down as though shrivelling into the dimness. "What's happened?" Dave said, and slapped the light-switch.

The bulb under the fluted cut-glass shade lit up before Donna could wrench her gaze away from the corner. Except for the shadow of the wardrobe, which lent it some of the appearance of a gloomy cell, it was empty. That might have come as a relief if she hadn't been distressingly conscious of staring at it so as to avoid seeing the contents of her hand. "Sorry about that. Some maniac who sounded as though they'd got something in their mouth," Dave said, and then "What's wrong, love?"

She couldn't speak. She held up her fist to show him rather than look at it herself. "You want me to take them off," he said, and hurried to her. "Did you get scared? I wouldn't have left you in the dark if I'd known you were. I mustn't have put the switch right down, and the door closing knocked it off."

The hair was brushing the back of her arm now. She stared at him, willing him to see, and then, because there seemed to be no alternative, she forced herself to look. There was nothing in her fist, nothing in her trembling fingers when she stretched them wide, and only the scarf was trailing down her arm. "You're fit, aren't you?" Dave said, picking at the knot which held her other wrist.

"I will be," Donna told him and more importantly herself. "Only let's not tonight. Just hold me." As soon as he had freed her she retreated under the quilt, leaving her dress and underwear for him to wad up and throw in the laundry basket in the bathroom. She was about to call to him to hurry back when he did, and the opportunity was past for her to ask him to turn on all the lights. Besides, that would need too much explaining. She wanted to believe he was right to think she had just scared herself in the dark. "Open the curtains a crack," she told him, and when he joined her under the quilt she hugged him hard while she stared at the column of darkness in the corner next to the wardrobe. Nothing appeared there, and the feel of his familiar warm flesh against her was a comfort. Nevertheless it took her a long time to be able to close her eyes, and much longer before she could sleep.

9

THE SECRET OF THE TREE

When the oak began to tilt in the midst of an absolute lack of its own sound, Amy opened the window of the main room. Observing the workmen using chainsaws on the branches and the trunk had felt like watching a film of the event, but now it seemed as though someone had stolen the tree's voice. She dislodged the bolt that secured the twin sashes and pushed the lower one up just as the trunk fell. It uttered a groan of protest as its wooden jaw was forced wider and wider, and then there was a moment's silence like the absence of a breath before the remains of the tree struck the lawn with a thud that vibrated through Nazarill. A gasp of wintry air laden with smells of decay and old wood rushed through the window, flapping the Christmas cards strung up to the picture-rail on tapes. As they subsided her father hurried out of the bathroom, clutching a towel around himself. "For heaven's sake, child, what have you done now?"

"What does it look like?"

"What have you broken? Did you throw something from the window?"

"Like what?"

"Something you would prefer me not to see, perhaps. I wonder how much that's in your room that may apply to."

"You'll never know, will you? Because if you start poking in my room I'll leave home, and you won't stop me."

"Let's cease being idiotic," he said, but she knew he meant only her. The chainsaws went to work again, audibly now, and she saw him realise what the thud had been. He began to towel his greying chest with the hand that wasn't pinching the mantle shut behind him. "And shut the window, will you, please, unless you want me to catch an infection."

"Say you're sorry and I will."

"What am I expected to be sorry for?"

For her, she thought fleetingly, except she didn't want that from anyone. "For the way you keep treating me."

"Good heavens, what is that supposed to be?"

"Not even like a person sometimes."

"That's quite unfair, you know. I treat you as your behaviour warrants." He jabbed a finger at the window, and a drop of bath-water anointed her forehead. "And your behaviour just now—"

The door buzzed at the end of the hall. He waved his free hand angrily and clenched the other on the towel as he retreated to the bathroom. "Will you close the window and answer that, and if it's Miss Griffin, I should like a word with her. I'm sure the pills she gives you are partly to blame for your moods."

When she heard him bolt the bathroom door she felt as though he was locking her in. The problem was that she couldn't help doing as he'd asked: the snarl of the chainsaws was beginning to affect her with a headache such as Beth's medication usually cured, and she wanted to see who was at the door. She dragged the sash down, which was akin to thrusting a gag into a mouth; the chainsaws might as well have been switched off. She hurried through the aching silence to peer through the spyhole of the door at the end of the hall. A tiny man in black was loitering in the warped corridor.

Since he was nobody she'd ever seen before, her first reaction was to wonder how he'd got into Nazarill. She opened the door to replace his shrunken image with his six-foot self. He was either in his thirties or determined to appear that young, with a wiry frame and a flat turf of blonde hair and a spotless face which looked not merely shaved but planed, its long cheekbones squared off by the jaw. His suit proved to be blue, but so dark it might as well have been the negative of his white shirt—only his pale blue tie permitted itself more colour. "Afternoon, young lady," he said in not much of a Yorkshire accent. "Are your parents in?"

"My dad is. I wish—" She didn't want to admit that to herself, never mind to him. "He's just getting dressed," she said.

"Shall I come back? You might tell him it was Rory Arkwright of Housall."

"He wants you to wait." At least, she did: she had any number of questions for their visitor if she could think of them. "He won't be long," she said, as much a warning to herself as an invitation to the caller.

When she stepped back he eased the door shut with his finger and thumb on the latch, then granted the pictures along the hall a few quick blinks. "Are you the artist?"

"Not unless I'm older than your grandmother and a bit mad."

"I can see you aren't one of those." Having followed her past the eyes and into the main room, he found something else to say to her once he noticed the bookcase. "Are you the reader, then?"

"My mother bound all those."

"Is that who? I'm impressed. Can I sit anywhere?"

"That's what the chairs are for."

She sat on one to demonstrate, and was ready with a question as he perched on the edge of the sofa, but he wasn't giving up the subject without a contest. "They must be good," he said, bowing his head at the books.

"Why?"

"For your mother to have taken so much trouble to make them look special."

Amy could have argued with that and with his expression, which might have been implying some disloyalty on her part, except that she had a more useful response. "Like you did with here, you mean."

"Much like, now you mention it."

"You don't think sometimes people make things look good to cover up what they are."

"You can't be saying that about your mother."

"I wouldn't ever." Amy had tried to read some of the books once they were in Nazarill, only to be dismayed by how shallowly romantic and dated they were, but she wasn't going to admit that to him. "I was thinking of this place."

"Your home, is that? I'd say you should be proud of it too."

"Not the flat, this whole place."

"I'm afraid you've run ahead of me. Did you have a complaint about our building?"

"Don't you want to hear it if I have?"

"We want all our clients to be as happy as it's within our power to make them. That's why I'm here now." He drummed the start of a march on his knees with the flats of his hands, which he then used to push himself to his feet as the bathroom door opened, the bolt having emitted a sound like a trap. "Speak of the, well, I hope you don't think I'd dream of calling you that. Mr. Priestley, I believe? Rory Arkwright of Housall."

Amy's father was dressed all the way down to his slippers, only the unconcealed tag of his white polo-neck betraying his haste. He dealt his hair a swift comb in front of the nearest framed illustration before shaking Arkwright's hand. "Nothing to drink, Mr. Arkwright?"

"I wasn't asked, but if you're having one …"

"I apologise for my daughter. She used to be the little hostess, but now she must think she's too big. I'll have coffee, Amy, thank you, and Mr. Arkwright?"

"Straight coffee's my medicine too. I should tell you Amy was wanting to talk to me about Nazarill."

Was he offering that as an excuse on her behalf or informing on her? She couldn't judge for the fury which the men were taking turns to aggravate. "That's more than she's said to me," her father admitted. "Well, Amy, let us hear it if it's so important it makes you forget your manners."

She stood up so as to turn away from him, towards the Housall representative. "Do you know what this place used to be?"

"Offices, and I'll lay you a fiver you couldn't tell."

"Before it was offices."

He raised his eyebrows as though to persuade her it wasn't a quick frown that had wrinkled his forehead. "I couldn't say. Some kind of country house by the look."

"Not first a monastery and then a hospital."

"I can't see any signs of those, can you?"

"Where do you get such ideas, Amy? Who have you been talking to?"

Amy swung towards her father without glancing at him. "You don't think I can have any ideas of my own."

"I'd rather you had none like those if they can be blamed for making you act as though you wish we hadn't moved here."

"I'm sorry if you feel that, Amy. Is there some way I can help? With your father's approval, of course."

"Yes, tell me the truth."

"I assure you I—"

"I haven't asked yet. Are there any stories about Nazarill?"

"It'd be news to me. What kind of stories?"

"Like the one Mr. Roscommon told after he found Mr. Metcalf. Didn't you hear what he said he saw?"

"Why, Amy, that whole tragic episode is exactly why I'm here now, to put people's minds at rest in any way I can. We don't stop caring about our clients once we've sold them property. It saddens us that Mr. Roscommon and his son don't feel able to come back. But you surely aren't blaming your home for what tragically happened."

"Finding Mr. Metcalf was too much for his mind, that's all," Amy's father declared.

"And may I say this, Amy? You shouldn't be surprised if it has affected yours a little. Nothing to be ashamed of, just to take into account. I expect it feels as if what happened was too close, does it? But these things do happen, and it might just as easily have in the street where you used to live. If you laid all the flats in this building end to end you'd have a street, wouldn't you? Try thinking of it that way if it helps."

Arkwright sat back, obviously pleased with her response, although she had smiled only at the unpersuasiveness of his suggestion. "Anything more I can help with?"

He either thought he'd covered all she'd said or was pretending to, or did he have the nerve to assume she thought he had? "A couple of things," she said.

"Amy, the coffee."

"This is more important. What's strange about our windows?"

"Nothing I'm aware of," her father said at once.

"Listen for a minute. What can you hear?"

"Nothing much."

"Nothing at all, you mean. So why can't we hear the chainsaws out there?"

"Probably because the men are on their break," Arkwright said.

"No, that isn't it," Amy said, and strode to raise the sash. She'd taken hold of the chilly bolt when she saw that all three men had indeed stopped work. They were seated on the fallen tree, resting their victorious shadows on it too as they refilled plastic cups with the steaming contents of a flask, and she disliked them even more than she had for cutting down the oak. "I don't care," she said, and the glass threw her voice back in her face. "We couldn't hear them before either, not once I shut the window. You must have noticed."

"I didn't," said her father. "You may recall I was in the bathroom. And if the double glazing works so well it's hardly an occasion for complaint. We aren't all as fond of noise as you. Now if that's all that was keeping you—"

"Are you going to talk to him about security?"

"I suspect *Mr. Arkwright* and I may discuss that, so if you'd like to—"

"Ask him about Mr. Metcalf's flat."

"It's locked, Amy," the Housall representative said. "Try not to let it bother you. There's nothing to be afraid of, truly, and it'll stay locked until someone else moves in."

"How do you know?"

"How do I—"

"What makes you so sure it's locked? People kept buzzing it after he was dead, and they'd have noticed if it wasn't, but then Mr. Roscommon got in."

"The other people must have been mistaken, obviously, but I promise you I've checked it. It's locked up as tight as a, as a cell. You don't look convinced."

"If you say it's locked now I'll believe you, but suppose it was before?"

"You've run off again. You've left me behind."

"Suppose Mr. Roscommon was let in?"

"Don't waste Mr. Arkwright's time with such nonsense." Her father grabbed her hand to turn her towards him; his fingers felt hot and moist and swollen. "And stop thinking things like that as well," he said. "It can't be doing her mind any good, can it, Mr. Arkwright?"

Amy felt herself being held there to be judged. Even playing waitress would be preferable. She pulled free of her father and wiped her hand down the front of her sweater, and the doorbell rang. "Find out who that is, would you?" he said.

She was halfway down the hall when she heard him murmur "I apologise for all that. She used to imagine things about this place when it was derelict, when her poor mother was alive, but I'd assumed she had grown out of it. I'll deal with it, don't worry."

Through the snarl of her emotions one thought came clear: as far as he was concerned it was the Housall representative who needed reassurance. As she stalked past the paper eyes her fingers were tingling to poke them out, but she jabbed the button of the intercom instead, so viciously she almost broke her nail. "Who is it?"

"Me."

"You're early, aren't you, Rob? Or maybe you aren't, I don't know, but I want to get changed."

His voice sounded squashed into the metal cage by static. "Are you saying come back?"

"No, come up." She leaned on the door release button and then hurried to the kitchen, where she filled the percolator. "I'll bring the coffee when it's made," she called. "Let Rob in for me."

"Just tell me if I'm in the way," she heard Arkwright urge as she went into her room.

"It's my daughter's, I don't know if we're meant to call them boyfriends these days. It'll be the first time I've spoken to him face to face."

"Was there anything you wanted to raise while I'm here?"

"Nothing comes to mind. Please don't think we aren't happy here. It's just a pity that sad business had to happen while my daughter is going through a phase."

"Believe me, they go through plenty. I've got one who'll be older, and it gets no easier for me and her mother."

"That's all you think it is with mine, then, just her age. You wouldn't say she seemed . . ."

Amy had left her door open an inch, but the speakers must be lowering their voices, because she was less and less able to hear them. Or perhaps it was her rage which at this point deafened her to whatever they were saying, not that she was going to let herself care what they said. She pulled off her sweater and jeans and dumped them on the floor beside her plate and milk-smeared glass from last night's midnight snack, and having donned some black tights and her shortest skirt, sat on the unmade bed to wriggle into another black sweater. She was tying the laces of her calf-length boots when someone tapped on her door. "Don't bother with coffee for me," Arkwright said. "I'm off to finish my rounds."

Her father was in the hall too, though she'd heard neither of them emerge from the main room. By the time she'd finished tying up her boots he had ushered Arkwright along the hall. He opened the door as she stepped around hers, and Rob was outside. He gave a defensive blink and lifted his long face as if to level his sharp chin at her father, and the rings in his ear and nostril flashed. "One way to get yourself a magnetic personality," Arkwright quipped as he sidled past Rob and thumbed Beth Griffin's buzzer.

Rob blinked hard at him, then peered beneath his enviable eyelashes at her father. "Aim said come up."

"Step in and close the door."

"I just need to get my coat," Amy said.

"No panic, is there? Now I've got your friend here I'd like to acquaint myself with him," said her father, and made way for Rob so quickly that he appeared to be recoiling. "Do tell me all about yourself."

"Not much to tell," Rob mumbled. He looked nervous, and no wonder, Amy thought. His nervousness felt like a restless parasite in her stomach. She beckoned him into the main room, where she sat on the sofa and patted the space beside her, but he wandered over to the window. "Are the men still on their break?" she thought to ask.

"Sitting on their victim, looking pleased about stealing your oxygen."

"It had to be dealt with," Amy's father said. "It was starting to be dangerous. Its age, you know. Please have a seat."

Rob dropped himself next to Amy. A cushion separated them, and she left her hand there in case he wanted to take it, but he rested his fists on his thighs, protruding his knuckles at her father. "How did you and Christmas treat each other?" her father said, lowering himself into the seat opposite.

"Pretty fair."

"Something to celebrate?"

"I'd say so. Did Aim tell you my parents gave me a car?"

"I rather meant Christmas was an occasion to celebrate. Birth of our saviour and all that old-fashioned palaver. I'm not embarrassing you, I hope." When Rob released his fists from their apparent paralysis and tried to wave the suggestion away, her father said "A car, you say. Quite a gift, and a responsibility."

"My father sells them and my mother's an instructor."

"Fully insured, will they be?"

"Must be."

"You've passed your test, I take it."

"On my birthday."

"Weren't you too young to have learned?"

"They didn't think so."

"You're saying parents know their children best and hang the law."

Amy dug her fingers into the cushion. "He's saying they trust him."

"Which—"

"May I call you Robin? Please do continue, Robin."

"Maybe you should try treating Aim—"

"Don't damage that, Amy, please."

She forced her hand open and moved it closer to Rob's, but he lifted his to rub his forehead with his knuckles. "Maybe you should treat her more like they treat me."

"That must wait to be seen. She has more than a year before she can drive, though I must say I don't know why she would want to when she has me."

"Not driving. Trusting her."

Amy's father stared at him as though the words were remnants of a message, too little of it to be comprehensible. "And how would you have me trust her, Robin? Does it involve you?"

Rob's ring had flashed like a struck match as he wrinkled his nose at the syllable of his name he disliked. "It's up to Aim," he mumbled, not looking at her.

"I rather think at her age it's up to me, young man."

"Then let her go to Spain with her school."

Amy felt as though they'd both locked her in some hot cramped place in order to discuss her. "So my child has been talking to you about me, has she?" her father said. "Count yourself privileged. The reverse doesn't apply. You're one of her many secrets."

"Maybe if she felt you trusted her . . ."

"And letting her fly off to Spain would achieve that, would it?"

"It'd help, wouldn't it, Aim?"

"Might."

Her father was studying Rob's face. At last he said "I wonder why it should be so important to you for her to visit a country like Spain."

She'd had enough. He was determined not to let her go, and anything Rob said would only aggravate his distrustfulness. She had to escape the hot dark cramped cell he was making of the inside of her head. "Because he wants me to be happy, not that you'd know anything about that," she blurted, and grabbed Rob's hand to drag him to his feet. "Come on, Rob. Take me anywhere."

Her father stood up, closer to the hall. His face had turned blank, and appeared to have grown heavier; the whole of him did. "And just where might anywhere be?"

"Wherever Aim wants."

"Where's that, Amy? I'm sure we'd both like to know."

She turned to Rob, which left her father as a hulk on the edge of her vision. "Wherever you like."

"Shall we go for a drive and then back to mine?"

"Vital." As she headed for the door she was prepared to dodge her father if he tried to seize her, but he only said "Will your parents be at home when you are, Robin?"

"They didn't say. And listen, it's just Rob."

"You don't care for the name they chose for you."

Amy marched into her room to grab a coat from her wardrobe and a cap from the row of them before almost running along the hall, where her father appeared behind Rob. "Please make certain you're home by midnight."

"Why, what do you think I'll turn into if I'm not?"

"It's what you are already becoming that worries me."

If he expected a response to that, he could invent one for himself. Amy threw open the door and darted into the corridor, whose dimness seemed to narrow it, and down the stairs, which struck her as even more reluctant than usual to admit to their illumination. The light from outside only emphasised the gloom of the ground floor, on which the six slabs of doors gleamed darkly at her. The metal handles chilled her fingers as she emerged into sunlight cold and pale as the gravel of the drive, to be met by the renewed chorus of the chainsaws. She might have asked the men whether they had only just recommenced work, but the uproar was too oppressive to let her frame the question. She ran around the corner of the building to the car park, where Rob caught up with her. "Which is yours?" she said.

"Guess."

"The Jag," she said, though she'd deduced that the sleek black beast came with the Housall representative.

"No, the Microbe."

"It's a nice little microbe."

A blue respray had made the Nissan Micra look almost new. Inside it was redolent of car shampoo and faded upholstery, a homely smell. Once she ran the passenger seat all the way back she was able to stretch her legs under the dashboard. Her seat belt issued from its slot in a series of jerks, and by the time she'd fastened it Rob, having slammed his door a second and conclusive time, was saying "Where do you—"

"I don't care. Just drive."

Maybe once they were in the open she would want to talk, but for the moment everything beyond the windscreen felt like the oppression she was trying to leave behind: the chainsaws mutilating their prone victim in the midst of a spray of its substance, the locked marketplace whose lifelessness appeared to have spread into the streets which it brought to an end, the tics of the Christmas lights, even Partington itself, whose buildings seemed the exact colour of senile teeth. Rob steered the car to the main road and engaged fifth gear as the road began to unwind across the moors, and Amy opened her window a crack so that the wind could tug at her hair and cool her face. When her ringed nostril started aching with the chill she screwed the window tight, which Rob took as a signal to halt the car. "This is good, isn't it?" he said hopefully.

"Suppose." The sun had subsided behind a ridge, above which the sky was drawing into itself all the green of the darkening slopes and setting like a plane of crystal around the silhouettes of bare trees, slowing down their gentle dance. They were as black as the hem of the eastern sky, in which the first star was glimmering. She remembered loving to see that sight when she was little, especially at Christmas. But she couldn't ignore the sight of Partington like teeth in the broken lower jaw of the horizon; it had crammed itself into the wing mirror, where the smallness of its image only intensified its significance, so that she felt as if that was squeezing words out of her. "I don't know what's making him act that way," she hardly knew she said.

"Me."

"Not you, you you." She reached across Rob to switch off the engine before taking his left hand in both of hers. "I do know. He was never like that before we moved. It's that place."

"What about it?"

"I don't know yet. Something, and he won't admit there's anything, and that's why he's like he is."

"What way is that when I'm not there?"

"Same as when you were. No, worse."

"How? Tell me how."

"As if he doesn't know me any more. As if he wants to keep me a prisoner."

"Oh, right," said Rob, and his hand relaxed. "Mine are like that sometimes."

"Not like he is. Not trying to get you off with someone you hate because they think he'll keep an eye on you."

"Who, Aim?"

"Only the worst. Only Shaun Picknose."

"Antagonistic," Rob said, but then his concern made itself heard. "What's he been trying to do?"

"Shaun, what he's always trying, and he knows he can piss off. Why, did you think you'd got competition?" She leaned over and gave Rob's thin cheek a swift kiss. "My dad, though, he thinks Shaun's some kind of angel. Thinks he's what I need to turn me back into someone I never was."

"So long as you never are."

"Sometimes I don't know who I am," Amy confessed, and felt that the conversation was dissipating the subject she'd wanted to discuss. "I won't be who he wants me to be, I know that. You saw how he even stopped me working."

"That's bad, but that's parents. Martie gave me a present for both of us, by the way. And thanks for my CDs."

"Thanks for my hat and necklace. My dad gave me money I had to buy stuff to wear with, but you knew what I liked. What did Martie give us?"

"Can I have my hand back for it?"

"It's my hand too, so remember I'm only lending it back to you." Before he reached into the pocket of his black denim jacket she suspected what he might produce, and when she heard the crinkling of foil she knew. Maybe it would help her free herself of her lingering emotions, since talking had fallen short of them. "Do you want to smoke it now?" she said.

"Up here ought to be good, but I don't want to risk driving. Martie says it's phenomenal. Let's go to mine and I'll show you something else the car's good for."

Partington had begun to glow as if the jaw and all its teeth had been thrown into a fire. Darkness was welling up from the hollows of the moors, bringing with it a hint of fog, and Amy knew that if she allowed it, that would taste like tears. "Let's go down, then," she said. "Does the radio work?"

"Give it a finger," said Rob, switching on the engine and the dashboard lights. Amy poked the button as he set about turning the car, stopping well short of the unfenced ditches, and a mellifluous male Yorkshire voice soared out of the speakers. "I hope you got a big goose for Christmas like us. Oscar gave me all the stuffing I could handle. Replete, I was. Replete."

"Change the station if you want," Rob said in some embarrassment. "I was just listening for our weather."

"I don't mind Charlie Churchill. He's quite funny sometimes. My dad can't stand him."

The disc-jockey was announcing "Frosty the Snowman," a process which took him some minutes before he started the record. By that time the car had left the spiky dark behind and was reentering Partington, whose orange glow touched Amy without warmth, like an image of a fire. Rob swung the Micra off the main road opposite the entrance to the market car park and drove up the least modernised lane in town, a winding bumpy track that ended several hundred yards on, alongside six cottages above the reinforced wall of the main road. The drystone wall in front of Rob's house, the cottage farthest from the town, blushed as he reversed almost against it. "Nobody's in," he said.

"What a surprise."

"They didn't say they wouldn't be."

"So let's make the most of it."

"When we're up," Rob said as the song dwindled into oblivion, and gave her a slim round-bowled hash pipe to look after while he unfolded the foil and pinched off a moist lump of resin so aromatic she could smell it breaking. "I wouldn't want his icicle anywhere near me," Charlie Churchill was saying as Rob pushed the dashboard lighter into its socket and dropped the lump of resin into the bowl of the pipe. "Sends a shiver through my vessels, the very idea." When an inch of the lighter sprang out he removed it and inverted the bowl of the pipe over the red-hot disc, their circumferences matching exactly. He drew in a long toke and held it for some seconds before releasing it through his nostrils. "Wow."

"Let's see if it is." Amy reached for the pipe and thumbed the lighter into the socket. As soon as it protruded she brought it and the bowl together and sucked the brass stem with all her breath.

As the sharp hot spicy smoke overwhelmed the taste of metal, the world reinvented itself around her. Though the light didn't alter, the streets below her were no longer simply illuminated, they were luminous. An additional star came into existence over the eastern moors and winked at her to let her know it was the ghost of its long-dead self. She wouldn't exhale until she'd counted ten slowly, she vowed. While she counted, her awareness of Rob intensified as her senses extended themselves towards him: his long eyelashes like filaments of the night, glinting with each blink; the smell of denim and beneath it the clean cool scent of his flesh; the note of each of his indrawn breaths, very slightly higher than the sound of their expulsion; his pupils dilating with their eagerness to renew the sight of her. . . . "Christmas does linger though, doesn't it? I don't mind having the odd sprout in the midst of my festivities, but I feel as though I've been nibbling a parson's nose for weeks," Charlie Churchill said, and Amy had to exhale, because she felt she would otherwise have burst. She had just begun to giggle when the whole of Nazarill lit up.

For a moment she believed the light was searching for her. It wasn't just the effects of the pipe that made it appear so much brighter than usual. The crouching hulk the colour of a skull glared across the town at her, reminding her that she had to return to it, and she saw it squatting like a spider above its web of streets into which she would have to descend. Perhaps she took only a few seconds to grasp that the glare seemed brighter because the tree was no longer in the way of any of it, but that didn't explain why the security lights had switched themselves on; nobody had been visible in the grounds, and nobody was now. She felt as if the glare was trying to probe the depths of her mind. "You can't touch me," she whispered.

"Who can't?"

"Not you, Rob. Not anyone. Shush, I'm listening," Amy said, and caught up with Charlie Churchill's patter. "If me and Oscar hung around like Christmas we'd be arrested. What's that? Voices in my head. Oh, my producer's telling me it's time we let you tuner-inners use my channel. Anybody listening who wants to try my frequency, don't be shy. Call me if you've a Christmas anecdote to share. Oscar thinks it's time I put my legs up."

As he gave out the number to phone, the light of Nazarill seemed to enter a hidden corner of her mind. "A Christmas ghost story," she said aloud.

"Are you talking to me this time?" said Rob.

"You and anyone who'll listen." She released her seat belt, which slithered across her breasts and clanked against its slot. "I'm going on the air," she said, and assumed a cold cap of night as she ducked out of the car.

"Transmissive."

Given his enthusiasm for her proposal, she might have expected him not to take so long over ensuring the Micra was locked, unless it was the relentlessness of the elevated glare of Nazarill that made him seem slow. She walked over the chunks of garden path scrawled on by snails and waited for him to open the door, whose breasts someone had flattened before turning their rectangular frame on end. When he let himself into the red-eyed dark, she followed while he switched off the alarm and on the lights. An undimmed Nazarill appeared to lurch into the doorway until she shut it out and turned along the hall, which smelled as rosy as its wallpaper looked. At the foot of the fifteen thickened russet angles of the stairs and their fifteen opposites a telephone table stood on baby giraffe legs, its drawer poking out a tongue of supermarket tokens. Amy hoisted the receiver while Charlie Churchill's voice continued to repeat the digits on a loop inside her head. When Rob raised his eyebrows and opened his mouth each of the several times he lifted a cylinder of fingers and thumb to it, she managed not to laugh. "Whatever you're having," she told him, and dialled the number. She was preparing to wait or even to be mocked by the engaged tone when a woman's voice said "Charlie Churchill."

"He was asking for people with stories."

"If it's clean you're on."

"It's a ghost story."

"That's seasonal. Is it true? Did it happen to you?"

Amy saw Rob light up a picture of a kitchen at the end of the hall and step into it. The question, or her answer, which until this instant she hadn't been sure of, seemed to focus her mind like a telescope directed at the past, stripping away all her peripheral impressions. "Yes," she said.

"We'll put you on after this record. What's your name?"

Amy thought of offering an alias, but the only one she could find in her head was Hepzibah, which would sound like a joke. "Amy," she admitted.

"I'm putting you through to the studio now. Don't speak until you're spoken to," the woman told her, and at once a man's voice began to croon at Amy from two directions, from the kitchen and close to her ear. "May all your Christmases be white," it finished still more lingeringly. "As they sing at National Front Christmas parties," Charlie Churchill said, and rebuked himself with a stage cough. "I'm only pretending I'm not touched. Brings a lump to my pipe every time I hear it, that song. Reminds me of when I was in short trousers, my own, I mean, but I promised Oscar I wouldn't mention last night. Here's someone to tell us a funny instead. Amy, are you there at the end of my wire?"

"It isn't funny," she protested, and heard herself attempt to say so in the kitchen before her dislocated voice turned into a metallic screech.

"Oh, that went straight through my orifices. Have you got a radio on?"

"Someone has."

"Tell them to twiddle their knob or take it somewhere else and shut their portal."

Before she could tell Rob to do something of the kind, the kitchen had become a slab of pine. "He has," she said.

"That's more like it. Like ointment in my apertures, that is. So what were you saying, it won't be a joke?"

"Dead serious."

"Ghosts would have to be, wouldn't they? Now, now, Churchill. Stiffen the visage. Tell us all about it, Amy. Where are you from?"

"Partington."

"Fair little community. I've stuck my bum on a stool or two in the Scales & Bible. I didn't catch a glimpse of any ghoulies there, though.

No goblin available while I was in town. You're going to tell me what I missed, Amy, are you?"

"When you let me."

"I'll have Oscar come and gag me. The stage is yours. Tell us where we have to go in Partington if we want a scare."

"Nazarill."

"That's the big manor kind of place, isn't it, oop on t'ill."

"It's where I live."

"Lucky girl. I'd call that living. So what are you saying, something's popping up there that shouldn't be?"

"I think so."

"Great blessed blunderbusses, I can feel my vessels shrinking. Have you seen it?"

Amy felt as if each of his questions brought the memory creeping closer. "Yes," she said.

"My membranes are quivering. What did you see?"

She drew a breath which tasted like another toke. The brevity of her answers wasn't all the fault of his loquaciousness; she could hear her own locked-up muffled voice beyond the kitchen door, echoing or anticipating her. "It was through a window," she and her voice said.

"At least it was outside, eh? I thought you had it coming up behind me for a second there."

"No, it was inside. I was looking in." She still was; her inner vision was adjusting to the dimness of a corner of her mind. Her words were causing her to see more than she wanted to see, and she might have tried to outshout her locked-up voice if she hadn't had to broadcast what she'd seen. "It was in a room downstairs, in the dark."

"Does someone live there? Did you tell—"

"Nobody does now." All at once it was clear to her that the room she was remembering had occupied part of the area where Dominic Metcalf had lived. "Maybe nobody should," she blurted.

"Isn't that a bit—"

"I haven't told you what I saw yet. You tell me if you'd like to live there." She heard both her voices falter, and struggled to control at least one of them. "It was dead, but it was laughing, only it didn't make a sound. It looked as if it'd been locked away for a long time and forgotten about. It didn't have much of its skin left but it was reaching for me. Maybe it wanted to tell me something. And it hadn't any eyes left, but I think there were insects—"

"Were there. Creepy. Insects. Yeekh. Any more of that and my pudding won't stay down. I reckon after all that we need our cockles warming, so here's—"

"I haven't finished. That isn't all that's happened. Someone's cat was hanged in front of Nazarill, and I think—"

"*I* think we'll have a record." Immediately a brass band tethered by a disco beat struck up "Ding Dong Merrily on High," and then Churchill's voice, abandoning its camp modulations, pressed itself against her ear. "And I'll tell you what else I think if you'll pardon my frankness. I think your parents ought to take you to see someone if you're having such unhealthy ideas. Ghosts are one thing, nothing wrong with ghosts at Christmas, but the stuff you were saying goes too far. Cruelty to animals, as well. Have a thought for other people's feelings."

"Don't blame me. I didn't make any of it up." At this point Amy realised why she sounded wrong to herself: she was no longer audible beyond the door. She felt as if she'd been robbed of too much of her voice, especially since the dialling tone had flattened her last few words against her ear. She dropped the receiver in its cradle and gazed towards the kitchen. The door stayed shut, unmoved by the thumping carol, and she wondered if listening to her could have disturbed Rob. Being shut out made her feel shut into herself, which frightened her. "Rob?" she called.

The mechanical drumming might have been growing louder, the door appeared to shift, but she couldn't be sure what she was hearing or seeing until the kitchen opened its light to her. Rob paced into the hall, pausing to pick up from a shelf one of two glasses of Coke. She saw the air fizzing above them, and thought he resembled a solemn-faced wizard bearing potions. "What did you think?" he said.

"That maybe he should remember what it's like when people don't want to know you."

"Not about him, about the cat being hanged. Wait, I'll turn this off."

"Not yet. I want to hear if he says anything about me."

Rob handed her a glass as the record blew a final blast and drummed itself into silence. "Nothing like a brass band, is there? I love to watch their trombones going up and down," Charlie Churchill said. "Now here's a lady to tell us about her plum-duff that kept popping out of its container. I'll tell you, Flora, I've had problems like that myself. . . ."

"Switch him off," Amy said, and pressed the icy glass against her cheek. "I feel as if I don't exist."

"Well, you do. You must do. You think, and you're going to tell me what you thought about the cat."

Amy gulped a mouthful of her drink, which seemed to rise like a gentle firework through her skull as its cold wake plunged into her stomach. "I don't think anybody hanged it. I think the place made a sacrifice to itself."

"Might make sense."

"Think so?"

"Why not, if things got worse after that."

At first she wasn't sure if he was serious, and then she didn't know if she wanted him to be quite so amenable; she might have liked to be dissuaded after all. But he was fetching a sheet of paper that a green magnetic pig had held against the refrigerator door. "Here's a message for us."

AT YOUR AUNT'S, the small brisk felt-tipped capitals said. BACK BY MIDNIGHT. ENOUGH VEG LASAG FOR TWO IN FREEZER. "Do you want some?" said Rob.

"If you are," Amy said, and was suddenly hungry as well as weighed down by her cold hands and feet. She sat on a slice of the pine of the kitchen while Rob microwaved the lasagna and ladled half of it onto her plate before sitting on the opposite bench. "Good," she said once she'd fed herself a forkful, and was digging up another when he said "So don't you want to talk about it any more?"

"That place."

"Never mind, I'll put the CD with Clouds Like Dreams on."

"No, I do. He didn't let me say. What I said I saw, that was when I was little. I'd forgotten all about it. I must have thought I didn't really see it, but now I know I did."

"You mean the cat made you remember. The sacrifice."

She hadn't meant that, and she found the notion disturbing for no reason she could articulate to herself. She could only shrug and fork lasagna into her mouth. "So what are you going to do?" Rob said.

"I've done it." Once she'd swallowed she tried to sound more convincing. "I told people."

"You're going to stay there, I mean."

"Nowhere else I can go, is there?"

Rob lowered his head and turned lasagna over with his fork. "Maybe if I asked them . . ."

"Don't yet. I can't help it, I'm worried about my dad. I don't want to leave him there by himself."

"He isn't, is he?"

"He hasn't got my mum. That must be part of his problem."

"You mean you miss her."

"Of course I do, but that isn't going to bring her back."

"But if what you saw isn't alive . . ."

"That's different. I don't think that's ever been away."

"Since when?"

"That's one of the things I have to find out. Maybe someone who heard me will know. I wish they hadn't cut me off. There was more stuff I wanted to tell people about."

"You can tell me."

"You're just you," Amy said, and patted his free hand to reassure him that in some ways he was enough. Since he didn't look persuaded, she told him everything she could remember: how the old man had insisted somebody hadn't come out of Nazarill for the photograph; how something had let him into Dominic Metcalf's apartment, and what he'd seen there; how she was sure that was where she'd seen it too. Rob gave each new revelation a blink so lingering she could almost see his eyelashes catching on the air. When she shrugged to indicate she'd finished he said "I don't think I'd want to live there."

"It's only on the ground floor, and nobody's living down there now."

He seemed more heartened by this than Amy discovered she was, but she could see no point in admitting that aloud. They finished their meal, and were at the sink, admiring the rainbow bubbles while they washed up, when he glanced up at the flat square clock. "Back in a, have to record *It's a Wonderful Life* for my mother."

Amy recovered the plates and utensils from under the froth and having rinsed them, abandoned them on the draining-board. She followed Rob into the living-room, where six increasingly older and less fat-faced photographs of him adorned the chunky ridge of his father's homemade mantelpiece, in time to see the title of the film.

"Leave it on. I used to like it when I was little," she said.

At first she couldn't see why she had. She sat on the couch and moved over for Rob, which reminded her of cuddling up to her mother the last time she'd watched the film. Now she seemed to be watching people so dead they couldn't even make themselves be in colour, and the setting of a town where everyone knew everyone else no longer appealed to her. Though he was gawky and drawling, the hero married his girlfriend, apparently because she considered these qualities to be endearing, and Amy remembered how they fared: their luck turned so bad that he tried to throw himself off a bridge and had to have an angel show him the town needed him. That must have been the part she liked, his being able to see the future and transform it, but the significance for her of the scene had changed; she felt as though the darkness of the film was closing around her. She was living in the future her mother had been unable to take back, and she snuggled against Rob in search of comfort.

When he slipped an arm around her shoulders she settled closer to him and looked up at him. Her eyes were telling him how to continue, and less eventually and clumsily than the gangling character might have, he did: he found her open mouth with his and gently squeezed her breasts before slipping his hand under her sweater. When she disengaged herself so as to pull the sweater and her black bead necklace over her head he ran his hand up her back and, since she leaned forward, unhooked her bra. She peeled his sweater off and wrapped her arms around him.

The whole of her seemed focused where their bodies met—in the mating dance of their tongues, the same tastes in their mouths, the silky touch of his chest hairs on her nipples, the lump of him between her legs as she straddled his lap—yet all this felt distant, already remembered. Without warning she was afraid to imagine the future in which it would be a memory; worse, she felt as though she'd forgotten she already had. She thrust her tongue on his and pressed as much of herself against him as she could, but she could still sense the future lying in wait for her. As soon as the film announced its resolution with a flourish of an orchestra, and Rob groped for the video control, she lifted herself off him and picked up her bra from the carpet. "Better be going."

"Oh," Rob said, and flattening the disappointment out of his voice "Okay."

"I'm feeling a bit . . . Too much. . . ." That was vague enough to sound true, but insufficient as an excuse. She drew sloppy circles with her fingertips close to her forehead. "Maybe I should go to bed."

"There's one here." He must have decided that presumed too much, because he added hastily "Shall I drive you?"

"You don't want to do that. I'm all right to walk."

"Walk you, then."

"Another time, Rob, would you mind crucially? I want to think."

"I didn't know I stopped you."

"You don't," Amy said, and slapped his bare side. "Maybe not think, maybe remember. I don't want to talk about it any more yet, that's all I know."

"If you need to talk later . . ."

"You'd better be here." As she spoke she knew her fierceness was a substitute for admitting her instinct that whatever she was striving to recall, she wouldn't be able to speak to him about it while her father could hear. "If I don't phone you by midnight, call me in the morning."

"I was going to try and finish off Cromwell."

"Go on then." When he looked guilty she kissed his wounded side. "I don't want to be the bitch who messed your grades up. Call me when you're ready to."

That sounded like a sly rebuke, but all the explaining had begun to clutter up her brain. She flipped her cap onto her head as she led the way to the front door, where she held onto Rob's shoulders while she gave him a tongue-filled kiss, after which they gazed so awkwardly at each other they might have been auditioning for the old film. "Well," she said to move them, and opened the door.

"See you."

"Hear from you."

"I said."

"I know," said Amy, and that was the end of their words. She flashed him a smile with her mouth shut and picked her way along the ageing road. When she looked back from the bend at which it sloped down sharply he sent her the wave he'd been waiting to release. Then the door was shut, and she tramped down to the main road, only to learn that being alone wouldn't help her think.

Trees leapt about in windows on Moor View, houses muttered to themselves in television voices, and she wondered how many of the locked-up unseen people she was passing had heard her on the radio. Her hands and feet felt manacled with cold, so that she had to assume she was still experiencing some effects of the pipe. With every step she took, Nazarill inched a little more of its shadowy bulk into the frame of the top of the street to await her. She shoved her hands deep into her coat pockets and set down her feet hard enough to make the house walls ring, to remind herself of the town at her back.

An icy wind caught at her wrists and ankles and lips as she emerged onto Nazareth Row. A railing rattled in its socket, and beside the gateposts, in the additional but unreliable glow from the illuminations around the marketplace, ranks of spindly shadows were prancing on the grass. The drive bared its gravel at her all the way to the glass doors, on either side of which the ground-floor windows looked alive with darkness. She remembered telling Rob that nobody lived there, which seemed even less reassuring now that she was about to venture into the corridor. On reaching the gateposts she took a slow cold breath which she didn't intend to release until the security lights had tried to take her unawares. She stepped onto the drive and gasped as Nazarill glared at her.

It wasn't meant to do that yet. It was supposed to restrain itself until she was she didn't know how many yards closer. She felt as though it had been aware of her all the way from Rob's, and so eager to spring its trap that it was no longer able to pretend. She mustn't think that, or she wouldn't be able to go forward. Either the Housall representative had reset the lights or—of course—the oak was no longer blocking one of their sensors. "Nearly," she made herself scoff at the building, and kicked gravel in its direction as she marched herself up the drive.

A wind like an exhalation from a huge stone mouth came for her, and sawdust began to dance around the rooted stump of the oak with a sound like the faintest whisper of foliage. She watched it alight on the sprawl of sawdust that encircled the roots, and was about to return her attention to Nazarill when she came abreast of the patch. She halted, peering at it—at the blurred tracks in the sawdust. Some creature appeared to have walked several times around the stump.

It must have been a dog, she thought; the prints were about the right shape and size. It had gone to the remains of the oak and ambled three times anticlockwise, no doubt searching for somewhere to pee. The glare of Nazarill deepened all the prints that weren't overlaid by the black shadow of the stump, and showed her where they ended, between two roots that looked as though a convulsion of the tree had clenched them in the earth. Perhaps the animal hadn't been a dog; she could see how it had clawed at the niche formed by the roots, splintering it wider. An object that wasn't part of the stump was protruding from the niche.

She felt she ought to recognise it. It was black as a beetle, and appeared to glisten like one as she set foot on the grass. She would only go close enough to put a name to it, she told herself—and then she made it out. It was the corner of a book.

She padded across the lawn onto the sawdust rug. Her shadow reached for the book before she did, and then her fingers closed on the binding, only to find that the book was trapped in its hiding place. Even when she compressed the small volume with both hands it wouldn't shift. She worked it back and forth, trying to detect a way to ease it loose. All at once it seemed to squirm in her hands. She must have twisted it how it needed to go, because without further ado it flopped out of the stump.

It was exactly as long as her hand and as wide as the heel of it. Both covers were indented with a black cross, and before she turned it upright she identified the book. Squatting among the roots, she lifted the front cover gingerly, expecting the pages to have rotted. But the title page proved to be intact as it turned itself back, exposing words she'd once read: "In the beginning . . ." There was handwriting in the margins, a script so old that, along with the print, it was full of esses like worms. She leafed through the Bible, finding page after page that had been written on. Then a handwritten sentence seemed to focus itself for her, the spidery script turning a charred black in the light of Nazarill.

It had nothing to do with the Bible. Someone had used the margins as a diary. Perhaps it was a wind as well as the sentence she'd deciphered that sent a shiver through her; perhaps it was that, and her own state, that made Amy hear leaves rustling above her. She had to glance at the unobscured sky overhead before she could stand up. She wobbled to her feet and almost dropped her keys as she fumbled them out on her way to the entrance to Nazarill.

She tried to close the glass doors silently behind her, but they emitted a note like a stealthy alarm. As she hurried down the corridor the sunken eye of each door glinted at her, the light within it swivelled to follow her. Surely nothing had pressed itself against the inside of any door to watch her, but she tripped on the stairs in her haste to be at the top of the building. Wasn't the Bible supposed to protect you? She pressed it against her stomach as she clutched the clammy banister to haul herself around the first bend, and ran up the next flight, to be confronted by exactly the same corridor.

Of course it wasn't, but there was nothing to demonstrate that unless she went close enough to read the numbers of the apartments. She had an impression of too many rooms that were less deserted than they pretended to be, and she fled up two more flights into the corridor she'd fled. Except it wasn't, she could prove that by unlocking her door if her sweaty hands didn't drop the keys that felt warm as flesh and not much firmer. She ran to the end of the corridor that was oozing light from its panelled walls and jammed her key into the Yale lock, and twisted it so hard she was afraid it might snap. It turned, and the door fell away, and there was her hall full of eyes, and her father's voice beyond it. "Is that you?"

Who else could it be? She had to shrug off a shiver. She couldn't tell which room he was in; all of them seemed to be dark. "I'm going to bed," she called.

"That's sensible. Give your mind a rest. You see, it doesn't hurt to do as you're told now and then."

He was in the main room, which mustn't be as dark as the crack between its door and frame made it appear. She dodged into her bedroom and switched on her light with one elbow while closing the door with the other, and hung her cap next to the three already on the wall, and arranged her necklace over the other two adorning the dressing-table mirror; then she sat on the stretch of her mattress she'd uncovered when she'd got out of bed, and opened the Bible on her lap.

A hint of decay touched her nostrils and faded away as she bent her head to the book. The handwriting on the early pages was much smaller than the sentence she'd managed to understand, and even when she succeeded in locating that to remind herself how the handwriting read, it didn't help. Best to wait for daylight and copy out everything she managed to decipher. She closed the Bible and cleared a space for it next to the bed, and wished she hadn't reminded herself of the single legible sentence just as she was about to try and sleep. *Must survive until they take me from this place,* it said.

10

LIFTING UP THE VOICE

Oswald hoisted his briefcase out of the Austin and strolled across the car park of the Everybodys Shopping mall. A wind sharp as the cut-out edges of the clouds that were puffed up above the moors roamed the square mile of concrete, raising the blurred voice of the motorway and rattling trolleys outside the supermarket. One of the pairs of glass doors of the mall greeted him with a sigh and edged out of his way, releasing two storeys' worth of crowd noises and a giant jingle of bells accompanying the tune named after them. A security guard bade him "Many of them" and wagged a walkie-talkie trimmed with holly at him as Oswald crossed the chessboards of the floor to the escalators, beside which a Christmas tree towered to the roof.

Though it was New Year's Eve, most of the stores had begun their January sales, and there was hardly a group of shoppers in the mall without some kind of wrapped package. Children were challenging the directions of the escalators, and Oswald presented a tolerant smile to a little girl in a large mauve velvet hat, who was trying to race down the escalator that was carrying him upwards. "Look at the angels," he told her as he stepped onto the upper floor, and pointed at the muslined figures crowned with gilded lassoes and fluttering like moths the size of babies around the tree. He was expecting her to like them—Amy would have at her age—but as she clattered down the rising stairs she stuck out her tongue at the angels as though they made her sick. "Little devil," he muttered, and crossed the balcony to the offices of Pennine and Northern, where he worked.

It occupied a unit between a china factory rejects outlet and a remainder bookshop. Anybody passing could see whoever was working at the six desks, an openness presumably intended to tempt in trade, though Oswald suspected that was achieved by the sight of blonde bare-armed Louise behind the reception desk. "Mr. Daily Junior will speak to you himself early next year," she was promising the phone, and gave Oswald a pink-lipped smile and a glimpse of a frown as she returned the flat paddle to its recess. "Hello, Mr. Priestley. Happy, well, it isn't quite."

"I hope it will be."

"Oh, me too. I meant not new, not yet. Was your Christmas?"

"New? I imagine it was now you mention it. First of many in the new place."

"I wasn't really . . . I hadn't thought of it that way. So long as you do."

"Weren't you expecting to see me today?"

"I'm sure we were, at least I should think so. Why, was there some . . ."

"None at all as far as I'm concerned." Oswald had never before seen her flustered, and could only assume she'd encountered some problem in her private life. He patted her shoulder as he made for his desk in the middle of the left-hand row.

Derek Farmer was at the desk in front of him, Vera Winstanley diagonally opposite. Both greeted him a little cautiously, he thought. As he took his neighbours' proposal forms out of his briefcase and prepared to transfer the details of the Stoddard family onto the computer, Derek swivelled to face him with a loud creak of his overburdened chair. "So how did you fare with the Christmas spirit, Oh?"

Vera finished empurpling her mouth in front of her hand-mirror and pursed her lips, with what intention Oswald wasn't sure. "Derek."

Derek picked up the stubbly tweed hat he always kept ready on a corner of his desk and perched it on the upper bulge of his stomach. "Oh will tell me if I'm talking out of turn, won't you, Oh? Bravest chap in the whole firm."

"I can't see what I'm meant to be objecting to. Unless you mean we've forgotten the meaning of Christmas."

"See, I told you both. Nothing throws our Oswald. I should have put money on him. So you had a decent holiday, Oh, all things considered."

"Whatever they're supposed to have been, yes."

"I'd call that brave as they come."

Vera tugged her tight skirt over her knees before walking her chair around to confront the men. "Does it matter as long as he's happy? Isn't that the main issue?"

"It's one of them, Vee, wouldn't you say?"

"If you all know something I don't," Oswald said with the little patience that remained to him, "you might have the grace to tell me."

Vera's eyes met Derek's, and at once they had no more than half an expression apiece. Louise gazed out at the topmost angel, then seemed to reach a decision. "Excuse me, Mr. Priestley," she said, and was in the process of swinging her chair around when the phone rang.

"Pennine and Northern." She listened and turned away from her desk again. "Mr. Priestley," she said in a tone he couldn't interpret, "it's for you. A Mr. Arkwright of Housall?"

"I know him," Oswald said, and lifted his own receiver. "Mr. Arkwright, hello. If it isn't premature, let me wish you a happy new year."

"Same to you."

"And to your family."

"Likewise."

"So let me guess why you're calling."

Whatever response Oswald might have predicted would have been more than none. Perhaps the Housall representative was suffering the after-effects of too much festive indulgence. "Have you found someone to join us in Nazarill?" Oswald said.

"Surprisingly enough, Mr. Priestley, no-one has approached us."

"Do you think it would benefit from a little more publicity? I've seen none since we met."

"Or heard any."

"That's so. I meant that too."

"Or heard of any."

"I was including that as well, of course." At that moment Oswald became aware that while his colleagues had their backs to him, all three were pretending not to listen. "Why, has there been some I should be aware of?"

"You really don't know what this is about, Mr. Priestley."

"Spot on, I don't, so if you'd care to . . ."

"I'm sorry, I thought you would have heard by now, one way or the other." Arkwright emitted a muted grunt which seemed to be intended as aural punctuation and said "You did say you'd try and quiet your daughter down."

"I'm doing my best, I assure you. At least, I've made a start at it, but I don't see what that has—"

"She was on the radio the other night, spouting about Nazarill."

"On the *radio*, my daughter? I don't see how she could have managed that. Did you hear her yourself? How can you be sure it was my daughter?"

"I don't know of anybody else called Amy living there, do you?"

"Nor is there, but I can't understand how the radio . . ."

"They'll let anyone phone in who seems to have something to say. It's cheaper than employing people who have."

"That's one way of looking . . ." Oswald began, until he caught himself in a last attempt to contradict Arkwright. "You've the right of it. So what did she, my daughter . . ."

"Apparently the sort of thing she was saying to me when I visited you, only worse. She claims to have seen something herself."

"She can't have, or she would have told me. What night was she on? Was it the night of the day you very kindly came to visit us?"

"I believe it was."

"I'll lay odds it was, and I'll tell you why. We had a disagreement after you left, her demanding more freedom as if she hasn't already contrived herself far too much at her age. This performance must have been her little revenge. I can't apologise enough. I never would have expected such conduct of her."

"I hope you'll impress upon her not to play any more pranks like that. I've been asked to point out that we take defamation very seriously."

"I understand. I'm wholly on your side. I'll speak to her immediately."

"I rather think you'll find she's gone to the hairdresser's. I tried to have a word with her when I rang you at home just now, but that's all she would say."

"I can only apologise for her once again, Mr. Arkwright. Please tell anyone who should be told that I'll be taking the matter in hand."

"I won't ask how," said Arkwright. "Here's to a successful new year for all of us."

"Amen to that," Oswald said, and having rung off, dialled home. His fingers were shaky with anger, and he wasn't sure if he had misdialled, the silence that met each of the summonses of the phone was so absolute. He redialled more slowly, and imagined Amy staring at the phone, waiting for him to relent. When he'd relinquished the receiver at last he said "So may I ask who heard her?"

He might have thought his colleagues had lost their tongues until Louise admitted "I heard the tail end of her. I didn't realise she was yours."

"It sounds as if it was that end she was talking with," said Vera. "And—well, you won't want to hear that, Oh."

"I don't know what I want to hear."

"I was going to say if I'd done anything like that my tail would have known about it, even at her age. I know, you can't touch them these days for fear of the law. Used to be if you were dealing with a problem you were left to get on with it."

"I expect Mr. Priestley will if we let him," Louise said.

Oswald didn't know whether that was meant to rebuke Derek or to encourage himself. How responsible was he? Had he done anything Heather wouldn't have done and would have stopped him from doing? What mattered, he thought fiercely, was that since Amy had rejected everything he and her mother had made of her, she must be equally capable of changing back. The computer screen reminded him altogether too vividly of fog, and when he entered the Stoddards' details he seemed unable to key in their address. He erased the luminous green gibberish, though not before a careless keystroke had set it repeating itself like a silent chant, and managed to type Nazarill correctly. Once he had completed the proposal and sent it onward he called home again. As the ringing prodded the resilient silence he grew more convinced than ever that the phone in the apartment was being watched. When he'd borne the impression as long as he could he switched off the computer and pushed himself away from the desk. "If anyone calls I'll be at home. I just came in to process my neighbours."

"Give her hell," Derek said as Oswald reached the door, and the women uttered sympathetic murmurs—sympathetic to whom, Oswald wasn't sure. He stepped onto the escalator and closed his hand around the rubber banister, which felt like a weapon restless with eagerness. The tethered angels rose beside him, and all at once they seemed false, absurd as his nostalgia for Amy and her mother, which wouldn't help him deal with Amy as she was now. That was his task, he thought as he strode out of the mall—only his.

The moors had pulled the sun down. The motorway was busily stringing its lights. He joined them for two miles to the Partington exit, from which he saw that the town had begun to glow like a fiery tribute to its highest building. As the Austin nosed between the gateposts, the building lit itself to greet him. The gravel kept up its welcoming sound all the way to the car park, where Lin Stoddard and her daughter were unloading their Celica. Oswald had climbed out of his vehicle when Lin rested a carton of bottles on the roof of hers and half turned to him. "Mr. Priestley . . ."

"All secure. Your endowment policy's in the system, and the money to keep you when you go to university, young lady, younger lady. I had to spell your name the way you were christened, perhaps I ought to mention."

"I wasn't christened," the girl said indignantly, and tried to hitch her loaded carton higher on her chest, only to bump a corner against the underside of the tailgate. "And I'm Pamelay now."

"There can't be much left for her," Oswald said to Lin, which earned him the merest glimpse of a smile, and to the girl "Here, let me take that."

She let the carton fall into his hands so readily he only just caught it. Lack of sleep had thumbed darkness beneath her eyes, he saw. "Little Miss Sleepwalker, is it?" he said to her mother. "Season of excitement and late nights, I suppose."

"That's some of it. Pamelay, would you like to let us in and run up to open the door?"

"Mummy . . ."

"Just do it, please. Mr. Priestley and I will be right behind you."

The girl sucked in her lips and hesitated until Lin nodded sharply at her; then she unlocked the glass doors and held one open. "I've got it," Lin said.

The heat of the building embraced Oswald as she let the doors meet behind him. As the girl sprinted along the corridor and up the stairs the subdued light appeared to make her part of itself. He hefted the carton, setting bubbles swarming in the plastic bottles. "Are you entertaining tonight?"

"Librarians and a couple of our daughter's friends. Feel free if you aren't booked."

The invitation seemed polite rather than enthusiastic. "I'm not sure what my child's doing," Oswald said.

"Are you not?" Before he had time to answer this reproof or even to acknowledge that he didn't know how, Lin said "I've got to tell you, Mr. Priestley, she was why I sent ours on ahead."

"We're speaking of Amy. You're saying she was the reason . . ."

"The reason why ours has been losing her sleep." Lin went to the foot of the stairs to ascertain that the girl's running footsteps had reached the top corridor; then she propped a corner of her carton against the banister and fixed her quick eyes on Oswald. "She's imaginative enough without having it encouraged."

"What has Amy been saying to her?"

"Don't you know? Didn't you hear?"

He was beginning to sweat with the heat and his burden, which thumped him under the chin as he tried to settle it more comfortably in his arms. "When she went on the ether, do you mean?"

"Ah, so you do know."

"This afternoon was the first I heard of it. I've come home to take it up with her. What did she say?"

"I've really no idea, Mr. Priestley."

"But I understood you to—"

"I know our daughter's friends told her yours said she'd seen a ghost down here. Not just a ghost either, like something out of one of the videos we won't have in the library. I wouldn't have thought you'd let her watch that sort of thing, but it must be where she got the idea." Lin raised her tall body into its usual stoop and lifted her carton away from the wall. "We'd better be making our way up. I don't want another panicky scene."

Oswald felt unreasonably accused of having delayed their progress. At the first bend he said "I can't tell you how much I regret Amy's behaviour. What would you have me do?"

"Pamelay's friends nearly wouldn't come tonight, they'd been got so worked up about this place. Leonard was for keeping them away, except that might make her think there was something to the nonsense." Lin tramped up to the middle floor and murmured "It's got her hearing noises in her room."

"What manner of noises?"

"Noises she can't be hearing when there's nobody below us."

"She couldn't even if there was anyone. We have Mr. Kenilworth beneath us, and I've never heard a note. You can't hear us, can you?"

"I don't think so."

"You'd know if you could. The way Amy listens to what she calls music, it's a miracle she still has all her senses left."

"I suppose Leonard and I have that to look forward to."

"Nothing quite so diabolical, I hope."

For the moment they were united by the complicity of parents, and he was trying to frame another promise or apology to strengthen it when instead he had to pant after her to the top of the stairs. "Pamelay?" she called. "Pam."

The girl appeared from the apartment at once, tying a pink bow on the crown of her head as if she was making a present of herself. "I was coming to find you."

"Mr. Priestley has something to tell you," Lin said, and tramped along the corridor to shoulder the door wider, broadening the mat of brightness on the dim carpet. "Haven't you, Mr. Priestley?"

Oswald risked holding the carton with one hand long enough to backhand moisture from his forehead. "Pamela, Pamelay, rather. If I've any control over it, and I intend to have, she'll tell you herself she's sorry for whatever poppycock she dreamed up, and I hope you'll also accept my sincere—"

"About not being able to hear." Lin dumped her carton on a kitchen surface and marched back along the hall. "Mr. Priestley was going to explain to you you can't hear a sausage through these floors. It's as your dad and I said, it must be your hamster. Take that from Mr. Priestley, there's a girl, don't leave the poor man staggering."

The girl dug her fingers between the carton and Oswald's chest with such force it drove his gallantry back into him, so that he let her load herself. "Ufe," she said, and "It wasn't Parsley. It wasn't just a scrabbly noise. I heard someone laughing like a witch."

"Then you were dreaming, or thinking too much when you should have been asleep," her mother said. "Shall we take Parsley out of your room if he won't let you sleep?"

"Don't. He'll be lonely all by himself in the dark."

The girl sounded close to tears, not a spectacle Oswald was anxious to watch. "Let's see if we can find the one responsible. She can tell you she was being foolish, telling fairy stories they shouldn't have allowed on the wireless."

"Give me that before you drop it," Lin told her daughter as Oswald flexed his aching arms and unlocked his door. He was about to call to Amy, despite the lightlessness of all he could see of the apartment, when he noticed she had covered up the nearest picture in the hall. Had she blotted out the eyes so as not to feel watched? In that case, what had she been doing? He switched on the light and saw that the sheet of paper taped to the glass was a note to him. *Gone to hairdressers then Rob's. Don't make me any dinner.*

"Well, after all that, she isn't even here." Oswald felt disobeyed and made a fool of. "She must know to keep out of the way, mustn't she?" he said, and when the youngest Stoddard didn't so much as nod "I'll bring her to you as soon as she deigns to return. I'll see to it she gives you back your sleep."

As the girl darted into her hall she was clearly taking refuge from the dimness of the corridor, and Amy was to blame. Oswald hung his overcoat on his bedroom door, then stood absolutely still while he tried to remember her boyfriend's last name. Robin, Robin, Robin—he clenched his hands prayerfully together and had it: Robin Hayward. Now he had to find the phone number.

It seemed that as well as leaving schoolwork strewn across the dining-table and three mugs, not to mention several plates, drowning in the sink, she'd hidden the directory. When at last he found it, face down beside the hi-fi and with an empty cassette box on its back, he felt as if she'd blinded him to its presence. At least its Haywards were few, and only one in Partington was listed. The paper gave beneath his fingernail as he dialled the number.

"Defy me as long as you wish. I shall be here when you tire of it." The ringing seemed to take him at his word, and he'd begun to wonder whether Amy could have lied to him about her whereabouts when the bell made way for the voice of her accomplice. "Hel," it said before it disappeared into a trough between syllables and had to raise itself. "Lo?"

"I wish to speak to my daughter."

"Is this Amy's dad?"

"This is he. That's who I still am."

Silence was the answer, and he imagined Robin miming, especially when he heard Amy let slip a giggle that infuriated him. Without further preamble her voice arrived at the phone. "What do you want?"

"Where shall I start?" Oswald demanded, and controlled himself. "When are you coming home?"

"Don't know."

"I can quite see why you would prefer to keep away."

"What do you mean?"

At first he couldn't understand her tone, which sounded close to hopeful. Of course, she must be hoping he'd been impressed by her balderdash. "After your play-acting on the radio," he said.

"Oh, you know about that."

"You'd rather I stayed ignorant, would you? That shows your lies for what they are, that you didn't want your own blood to hear them."

"You wouldn't have believed me."

"You're right in that, but someone you chose not to consider did. Your young friend from next door. Was it too much for you to spare a thought for her age?"

"I was younger than her when I saw what I saw."

"How young? If you mean—"

"Right, when I was little and you tried to throw me in a window of that place. Seems like you wouldn't be happy till you got me in there."

"Don't you dare tell such lies about me for your friend to hear. I remember exactly how it was. I was lifting you up because you wanted to look in, and you leaned too far and nearly fell. I'm not saying I shouldn't have had a better hold on you, though I would have expected you to know I was sorry. But if you imagined you saw anything in here that shouldn't be, that was you taking after—"

He was on the verge of saying too much before they were face to face with nobody else to hear. "You ought to have spoken up at the time," he went on quickly. "However, that's by the way, and no excuse for broadcasting such claptrap now."

"I've only just remembered what I saw."

"What you imagined, if even that, and why didn't you confide in me instead of displaying yourself to people who don't know you and won't understand?" His anger was fading; he wanted to reach her before it might be too late. "Come home so we can talk."

"I may in a bit."

"See to it it's no longer, will you, please? I've undertaken to your follower that you'll speak to her."

"What do you think I'll say?"

"It's your duty to make her see there is nothing to fear."

"That's what you think."

Her tone was so flat he couldn't judge how mocking she intended to sound. "At the very least be certain you're home before midnight," he said.

"What's this thing you've got about midnight?"

"It's the start of the forthcoming year."

"Oh, that, right. New year." Her voice retreated while it added the explanatory phrase, then returned. "You're staying there, are you?"

"Most certainly, for our first New Year in our best home."

She released a sound that was little more than an expulsion of air and cut him off, leaving him to wonder if her question had been meant to establish he wasn't planning to go to her. What might she be up to where he couldn't see? For the moment that troubled him less than the memory she'd roused. If he had frightened her as badly as she claimed the day he'd lifted her up to look inside Nazarill, it had been in the process of demonstrating there was nothing inside for anyone to fear—that she couldn't scare him.

If she was still trying, it wouldn't work. So long as he kept the apartment spotless, his fears would have nowhere to breed. He fetched dusters, a cloth and a bunch of bright green feathers on a stick from the cupboard under the sink, having decided not to cook just for himself: an evening's fasting would do him no harm. He dawdled along the hall, flicking at the tops of the picture-frames, and pushed his bedroom door open. Before he could switch on the light he glimpsed an object in the left-hand bottom corner of the window, a twitching many-legged silhouette.

He'd let that happen, he thought. He hadn't prayed hard enough—perhaps hadn't really prayed at all. His mind seemed to shrink around the idea as he groped for the light-switch. The bulb came on, and the spider froze. Its body was withered, its legs were haphazardly splayed, yet he'd seen it move just now. He thought it was shamming until another flicker of the illuminations around the marketplace twitched it again. He crossed the room quickly, and had grasped two soft handfuls of the curtains to shut out the sight when he saw what the spider had done. Beside it, trapped within the double glazing, was a small round white shape that reminded him of the pills Beth Griffin supplied to his daughter.

Even if the cocoon hatched, he told himself, anything that might emerge from it would die between the panes. He forced his head towards the window to convince himself there was no movement in the glass prison. He didn't realise how close to the pane his face was until the edge of the fog of his breath spread to the spider's forelegs as though they were drawing it towards the shrivelled mouth. The cocoon appeared to shift wakefully as the illuminations ran through their sequence yet again, and he hauled the clammy curtains together before retreating from the window to grab the feathered wand and poke it into every crevice he could find in his room. "Please God," he heard himself repeating, "please God," as he progressed into the hall, where the pictures goggled at him.

He was being irrational, he managed to think. He'd cleaned only yesterday, and nothing had been added to the main room since then except, on the table, the chaos of Amy's schoolwork. Surely that wasn't a strand of web joining a corner of her foolscap notepad to the volume of Shakespeare; it must be a strand of hair, even if it looked greyer than it should. He brushed it off the table and frowned at her work.

ARE WITCHES SUPERNATURAL? must be a question on *Macbeth,* or at least a summary of one. Her answer was in a scribble so minute it might have been designed to be illegible to him, and was surrounded by doodles in the margins—pentagrams in circles, and long-haired laughing wild-eyed bearded faces. His gaze trailed down the page and snagged on a group of words that appeared twice, or almost. "Insane root that takes the reason prisoner," he read, and then "InʃAne root that takes the reaʃon priʃoner." He gripped the edge of the table and squinted at her notes until the elongated letters which she must have written as some kind of secret joke writhed into a dance, having become suddenly visible all over the page. He straightened up with a jerk and tidied her schoolwork into a pile, and was dusting the table when a prayer broke out of him. "Please God don't let me lose her. Please don't let her go like her grandmother."

He could barely hear himself, and made himself speak up. "Please, if she's starting, let me be able to get her back. You should know if anyone does what it's like to lose a child." He seemed to remember having sensed long ago—when he was younger than Amy, perhaps—whether his prayers were reaching their destination, but how could he expect that if he wasn't devoting all his attention to praying? He laid the duster beside Amy's heap and having drawn the curtains, switched off the light and fell to his knees. Since moving to Nazarill he'd found he prayed best in the dark.

The floor felt harder than it would have looked. Along with his fasting, that ought to help him pray. He wouldn't move until he sensed that he was—not answered, that would be presumptuous, but heard. "Please God don't abandon us," he said at the top of his voice. "I only want You to do anything I can't. I wouldn't ask more of You than I'm asking of myself. If I have to change I will. I'll be anything I need to be to save her...."

He didn't know how long he knelt there, shouting. When his thighs began to shiver he pushed his knees apart to steady himself. By now the floor was so hard it might as well have been uncarpeted, yet the sensation seemed inextricably bound up with the imminence of peace. At some point he had closed his eyes, and now he felt he was in a dark place no larger than it had to be. His voice was too big for it, and so he quietened his voice gradually, until he couldn't even hear what he was saying. That was surely unimportant, given the promise of peace that surrounded him, a peace such as he'd never experienced. His whispered undertaking was a part of the peace, and he reiterated it until a thought intruded on his consciousness. He'd become so immersed in praying on Amy's behalf that he had forgotten about her. His eyelids fluttered, and the green digits of the clock on the videorecorder swam into focus. It would be midnight in less than five minutes.

His hands began to throb as he pulled them apart, his thighs burst into prickling as he sat back on his haunches. When he gripped his knees and shoved himself up in the dark, his legs and lower body proved to have been holding so many aches in reserve that he gasped. He staggered to the light-switch, and as soon as his eyes had stopped trying to blink away the light, limped to the window.

He didn't know if he was hoping that his prayer or just the hour had brought Amy home. When he parted the curtains, however, he could see no sign of her. Beyond the drive the illuminations danced above the marketplace as if to invoke the year that would snuff them out. For a moment they held his attention, and then he noticed movement close to the building. He craned towards the window, his body shrinking away from the spidery corner of the pane, just in time to glimpse a thin bald figure in clothes as black as the shadow it was dragging across the gravel. Then the figure vanished into Nazarill.

Oswald limped rapidly to his bedroom and grabbing his keys, managed to run along the hall. As he emerged into the corridor, a confusion of voices met him, and he thought they had something to do with the intruder until he saw that Lin Stoddard was shooing a boisterous family—twin pink plump-faced girls followed by their ruddier and even more rotund parents—out of her door. "Quick march or we'll miss it," she cried. "Mr. Priestley. This is Mr. Priestley, our next-door neighbour, I expect you figured that out. You're coming down to let the new year in, aren't you, Mr. Priestley? You'll dance with me even if old misery won't."

Leonard lurched after her, his hands on their daughter's shoulders. "I never said I wouldn't dance when it gets to midnight. You know I always do."

It was clear that all the adults had devoted some time to drinking, and Oswald saw it would be quickest to follow them downstairs without describing what he'd seen. He was locking his flat when Beth Griffin appeared in the doorway of hers, nervously fingering her high forehead. "We didn't know you were in, Ms. Griffin," Lin declared. "You should have wandered over. Come down with us for the ceremony."

The homeopath responded with a hasty smile which she then covered with her fingertips, and Oswald left her to the revellers. He went fast but quietly down the stairs to the middle floor. There was no sound from below, nor from the corridor ahead, all of whose doors stayed shut. Eight people who sounded like far more came downstairs faster than he had, and he was turning to hush them when Lin stared beyond him and gaped.

Oswald swung round. The bald figure in black had come upstairs behind him and was waiting to be recognised. Having recovered, Lin said "Why, Amy, you look—"

"She looks good," said Beth.

"Different, I was coming to."

"She looks that," Oswald said, and clamped his teeth together. Amy wasn't quite bald—her scalp and the back of her neck were covered with enough stubble to retain the colour of her hair—and yet he felt there could be no repealing what she had done to herself. He gazed at her until Lin said "About turn, Amy, if you want to celebrate with us. We're going on the lawn."

"May as well," said Oswald's balding alien child, and led the way downstairs. As she pulled the glass doors open, the town began to clamour as though it had been waiting for her. Cars hooted, a rocket hissed up from the market car park to explode into glittering above the moor, the church commenced ringing its bells or at least playing a tape of them, so amplified they sounded softened by rust. Nearly every door on Nazareth Row opened, discharging celebrants, as Lin urged the Nazarillians onto the grass. "Hands," she directed, stretching out hers to be caught, and as soon as an arrangement with ambitions to be a circle was complete, led the singing while she danced with a vigour that shook her words almost to pieces. "Should old acquaintance be forgot . . ."

In the rush Oswald had ended up between the twins. Beth Griffin was opposite him, dancing close and retreating, with Amy on her left. He kept trying to catch Amy's eye as she glanced first towards the stump of the oak as if she thought the dance should be taking place around it, then at the windows of the ground floor. People were pointing across Nazareth Row at the ring of dancers, but he couldn't shake off the impression that they were pointing at her. The song speeded up as it reached its final chorus, the dancers rushed at one another across the tangle of their inky shadows and fell back and collided again, their feet drumming on the turf that glared with dew. A second rocket whooshed up its trail of sparks above the market as the dancers cluttered to an end. Amy let go of Beth and Leonard, and stared at the building again. "Are we everyone?"

"Everyone else must be out with their friends," Lin said as her daughter peered at the dark windows. When the twins copied their friend, their moist plump hands clasping Oswald's for reassurance, Lin's voice sharpened. "Nobody is in there, that's for sure."

"That's so, Amy, isn't it," said Oswald, staring hard at her. "You once thought you saw something in there when it was an old ruin, but you were years younger than any of these young ladies. Now you're of an age to know you imagined it, and I'd like you to begin the year by making it clear that you did."

"I imagined it," she said as tonelessly as she might have read a stranger's words out loud. "If that's all you wanted me here for, I'm going in. Good night, or good morning, who cares."

"Amy. Amy!" When she carried on walking away from him, Oswald squeezed the twins' hands before letting them go and darted after her. He had just reached the gravel when she arrived at the doors and fished her keys out of her canvas handbag, along with an item which a key had snagged. The black object struck the doorstep with a flat thud. She stooped swiftly and crammed the object into her bag, and had barely straightened up when she unlocked the doors and was through them.

Oswald let her go. Time by herself might help her find her way back to the right road. The possession he'd just glimpsed had to make a difference. The church bells toppled into silence as though rust had overtaken them, but as he followed the Stoddards and their guests into Nazarill he continued to hear the peals. He was imagining Amy alone in her room with the Bible she had seemed embarrassed to let anybody see. She could hardly be lost when she had that. He needn't decide yet whether to mention it or wait for her to acknowledge she had it. For the present it was enough for him to know that their lives were on their way to improving in the new year.

11

A SUMMONS IN THE NIGHT

When the notes of the church bells finished tumbling over one another Ursula took her hands away from her ears, and Harold Roscommon favoured her with the nearest to a smile she'd had from him. "His mother used to do that," he said.

"What else was she like?" Ursula risked saying.

"Like someone who couldn't stand summat, just like the rest of us." His arthritic hands grabbed the wheels of his chair and turned it expertly round on the narrow pavement of the main road, and she thought he was dismissing her along with the subject until he said "Are you coming back in for another glass of wine? It'll have to be drank now the bottle's opened."

"Anything I can do to help, I told you that."

He peered at her over his shoulder, his slack unsunned face having reverted to its standard loose-lipped petulant expression. "Don't go straining yourself," he advised her, and wheeled himself rapidly into the hall of the nondescript cottage discoloured by traffic.

As George made to follow she laid a hand on his wiry arm. "What sort of an impression am I making, would you say?"

"Better than he's letting on."

"No need to look so surprised," she told him, though his pale-eyed round face habitually did. She had time to soften the set of his mouth with a swift kiss before his father began grappling two-handed with the knob of the living-room door, leaning his weight on it until the chair was in danger of propelling itself away from him. "Blasted thing's shut itself with the wind now," he complained. "Won't stay shut when it's wanted and now it's the other way."

"Here, father, let me see to it before you—"

Ursula thought the old man looked too stubborn to relinquish his hold, but at the last moment he shoved the chair backwards, almost running over George's toes on its way to thumping the opposite wall. George twisted the knob and shouldered the door open, and as soon as he'd switched on the light which his father had earlier sent him back to extinguish, the old man sped into the room.

It didn't feel to Ursula as if they were living there. Apart from the dining-suite and the sofa and matching chairs, many of their possessions were waiting to be produced from the cartons stacked against the indifferently coloured wallpaper. Only the wheel-tracks crisscrossing the thin rucked brown carpet seemed to have staked some claim on behalf of either of the men, and George was engaged in surreptitiously treading the carpet down as his father swung round by the nearest armchair and levered himself into it. "I've had sufficient," he said when George attempted to refill his glass. "You youngsters see it off."

Ursula resigned herself to a final glassful of the sweet red German wine he'd insisted George bought. She was hoping George might join her on the sofa, but when he sat in the remaining armchair she fed herself a fast swallow of the wine. "May I take it you aren't in any hurry to move in?"

The old man let his lip droop further. "We aren't."

"Aren't . . ." When that brought her no clarification Ursula said "Aren't moving in."

"That's what I said. I thought he'd have told you renting this is only temporary till we find a place."

"I wasn't sure if that was still the plan."

The old man peered at her from beneath his unkempt eyebrows. Eventually he said "What's the idea?"

"Father . . ."

"If she's got a better one, let her spit it out."

"I just think it's a waste, Mr. Roscommon, you spending your savings on renting, please don't be offended, somewhere so inferior to where you were."

"Owned by a friend of his mother's, this house is." It was unclear whether this was meant to abash criticism or to suggest he was being charged a favourable rent, and Ursula was silent until he said "On top of that, once we've sold our piece of that joint on the hill we can afford somewhere even a woman should be proud of."

"You wouldn't consider moving back."

Both men's expressions became self-parodic, and George lowered his glass so hastily from taking a sip that a spot of red bloomed on his shirt-front. "Ursula, I think that's a bit too—"

"I didn't mean into the same flat. Even the same floor, I can see that wouldn't be very attractive. Only there's an empty flat next to mine, and I don't think the Housall people would dare to object if you wanted to exchange that for yours. They were round the other day to find out if there was anything we wanted doing. We could get them to put a ramp down one side of the stairs. They should have in the first place, or a lift for people with difficulties."

"You mean what us cripples call cripples."

"Father, Ursula's only trying—"

"I don't know what she's trying," the old man said, then lowered one eyebrow as though to be ready to wink. "Or maybe I do," he said to her. "Can't you stand having that next door?"

"What, Mr. Roscommon?"

"Whatever you think's there."

"Why, I don't think I think—"

"Fair enough, I don't want to scare you out if you can live with it," he said, though he sounded at least as impatient as reassuring. "But I know what I saw, and I hear I'm not the only one who did."

"You couldn't have heard that about me."

"Not you, the girl. The one who talked to me after I found the photographer and that thing with a mouth you could stick your whole hand in."

"Don't get yourself worked up just before you go to bed, father."

"Not being heeded is what works me up. You weren't even there, you were up with your lady friend."

"I did try to tell you I was sorry, Mr. Roscommon, but we weren't to know . . ."

"Nobody wants to know owt these days, seems to me. If they can forget it they will. Not that girl, though. She was on the wireless saying what's up there."

"The way I understood it, father, what she actually said—"

"Was she saw something moving about in one of the rooms downstairs that shouldn't have been alive and maybe wasn't, either. You were there when Lottie said she heard that on whatever show it is with the music-hall style of feller she likes. If they strung him up in public I'd help pull on the rope, but that's by the way just now. If you want to hear what the girl saw, Miss Braine, you know where to find her."

"She mightn't want to, father. She's still living there, remember."

"That wouldn't be why I'd worry. If the place is acquiring that kind of reputation, won't it make it harder for you to sell your flat?"

"Maybe. Don't fret." The old man turned on her an unexpectedly sympathetic look. "Like as not I'll run out before my savings do, and then he can keep you all the company he wants. He can do it now, I'm not stopping him. I'm old enough to see after myself if I have to."

"Mr. Roscommon, I hope you know if there's any way I can help—"

"Thanks anyway. One fussing round me's enough. And don't put that face on, you look like his mother when I raised a hand to him. Can't stand slop, never could."

Ursula lifted the glass to her mouth, then stood up instead, not only to hand the drink to George. "This can be yours to finish. It's time I was heading for bed."

"You'll be round again, I reckon," the old man muttered at his shoes.

"I'm glad you think so." To repeat her seasonal wishes to him now would seem like sarcasm, and so Ursula preoccupied herself with donning her heavy overcoat while she made her way out. A passing Astra stuffed with merrymakers blew a fanfare at her as George followed her onto the token doorstep and eased the door shut. "Try not to take any notice," he murmured. "He knows he's said too much, only he can never take it back."

"Which are you saying was too much?"

His round face appeared to be trying to sort out an expression. "Well, if you don't—I think I'd have felt—"

"Come here." She dug her fingers into his shock of blond hair and pulled his face close to hers. "I can put up with worse if I have to. Like he said, and I wouldn't if he hadn't, it won't be forever." She gave George a fierce kiss and then a long soft one that reached deeper into his mouth and earned them a cheer from a carload of revellers. "That's your first of the year," she eventually told him, and stepped back. "Don't leave it too long to collect your next install-ment."

"I'll be up one evening this week."

"Just for once, bring me some flowers."

"I would have. I always thought you'd have had enough of them at work or you'd have felt insulted that I'd bought any somewhere else."

"They're an insult I can take. And if you grow some for me that certainly won't be an insult."

"That's what I'll do," George said in a voice almost as pleasantly surprised as his face.

This seemed an ideal moment for her to be on her way, while they'd arrived at an understanding that felt like the start of their fu-ture. She crossed the road and smiled at him until he closed the door, and as she walked up the nearest lane she sensed the smile rest-ing on her lips. Even when a thought penetrated her euphoria, her mouth shrank only gradually. George's father had suggested more than he knew. It might indeed have been possible for him to have heard that she'd encountered something odd in Nazarill.

George mustn't have found it worth mentioning. Most probably he didn't even remember by now, but she did. She remembered telling him as they came downstairs from Oswald Priestley's get-together that she thought she'd seen Teresa Blake's cat roaming the corridors—but while waiting to be photographed in front of Nazarill she'd learned that the animal had never been let out by itself until the day it had died.

Someone blew a party hooter in a house on the lane, and she imag-ined the mouthpiece poking out its puffed-up tongue. Perhaps she would encounter some of her fellow tenants celebrating in the cor-ridors, and she could join them for a drink. There was no sound from Nazarill as the alert facade responded to her approach over the gravel, but then nobody would have their windows open when it seemed to have turned so cold that, despite the illumination brighter than day and her heavy coat, she'd begun to shiver. When she un-locked the glass doors, however, there was silence within too.

Surely someone was awake in the building, but she couldn't think who would be. She was suddenly aware how little they knew one an-other—how ready everyone was to close themselves into their rooms once they were home. The doors sounded their hollow note behind her, and she hurried along the corridor, which she might have thought was dimmer than usual. No doubt it appeared so in contrast to the brightness she'd just quitted, and that explained why the gloom was patching her eyes, obscuring the sight of the doors she was passing. She didn't need to see them clearly to know they must be shut, and she was ashamed of herself for wishing she could.

Her feet collided with the lowest stair, and she almost fell before locating the handrail. The stairs faded into visibility as she stumbled up them, and by the time she reached her corridor she was able to see all six of its closed doors. There was no point in wishing George still lived downstairs, never mind living up here; she ought to have known that his father would never agree. The wish only made the stretch of corridor between the stairs and her apartment feel like the ground floor: empty of people yet not quite deserted enough, and altogether too dim. She pulled her keys out of her coat pocket, then grabbed them with her other hand to muffle them. It must have been an echo that had caused their rattling to seem to have wakened a similar noise, although she hadn't previously noticed an echo. "Stop being daft," she told herself furiously, and dashing past the unoccupied flat, twisted the key in her lock and snatched open the door.

The scents of her house plants came somewhat feebly to meet her. She'd left the hall light on, and so was able to close the door behind her at once. The corridors and staircase had laid a chill on her despite the central heating. Usually before bed she would have a pedal on the exercise machine in the spare room followed by a shower, but tonight her walk would have to be enough. She tugged the heavy wooden buttons of her overcoat out of their fat holes and hung the coat on its personal hook on the skeletal pine cylinder next to the reproachful exercise machine, then she made for the most perfumed room.

She didn't stay in there any longer than was absolutely necessary, and she couldn't help blaming George's father for making her so conscious of how the plumbing sounded. The water running out of the sink aroused a sympathetic mumble in the plughole of the bath, as if something under her floor was attempting to address her with very little, although just too much for comfort, of a voice. When she began to be tempted to listen for words she rushed herself across the hall to her bedroom, having wrested all the taps tight. The abstract white rectangles of the wardrobe and chest of drawers, and the pastel green one of the bedspread, looked no better than disinterested, but she could live without more of a welcome if she had to. "Get your head down," she advised her triplet selves in the winged mirrors of the dressing-table, and watched them begin to obey as she sank back, relinquishing the light-cord once it had released the dark.

At first she couldn't sleep for listening. Once the plastic weight at the end of the light-cord had finished tapping against the wall above the pillow, she had to overcome a tendency to hold her breath. As she fell into a fitful doze, she thought she should have left the inner doors open to confirm there was silence throughout the apartment. She was just too drowsy to leave the bed, and in any case, she reflected with a slowness that was close to merging with sleep, what she would most like to have heard wasn't silence but George on the phone to tell her that he and his father had decided to return to Nazarill—indeed, were already downstairs. It seemed to her that this series of increasingly less wakeful thoughts was why she dreamed she slipped out of bed to go down and look.

Since it was a dream, she didn't need to get dressed. She was mildly surprised to find herself padding into the spare room, to fetch not her coat but her keys, which she would hardly need in a dream. They felt like a not especially detailed lump of metal in her fist as she moved to unchain her door. While the chain persisted in swinging against the doorframe with a small vague distant clank, she stepped into the corridor.

She knew she'd shut the door behind her only when she remembered having let go of the outer handle, but she didn't have to be aware of all her actions; the dream would look after her. If the corridor appeared to be withholding even more of its light than usual, that was because she was dreaming it. The carpet under her bare feet couldn't be bothered to feel any different from the one in her bedroom, though perhaps it never did. What was it again she was clutching in her fist? Keys, of course, despite her momentary notion that should she examine her handful she would see a bunch of flowers, a peace offering to George's father. When she glanced at her hand she was somewhat bewildered that the dream hadn't produced them. Still, she couldn't control her dreams, and here were the stairs, to which she apparently had to devote some attention.

She wondered why she had to hold onto the banister in a dream.

Perhaps, she was just able to think, the need was a residue of some uneasiness which she wouldn't suffer if she reminded herself why she was going downstairs. It felt as though she had been called down, though she was unable to remember having heard a voice. Of course she mightn't in her sleep, and by the time she turned the corner of the grudgingly illuminated stairs she was happy to follow the dream to its end.

It was growing impressively detailed. As she descended the last flight of stairs, with each step she saw an extra portion of the dark grey drive extending itself past the splash of sawdust on the lawn to the gateposts, beyond which the jumpy Christmas illuminations around the marketplace were lowering themselves into view. Between her and the vista the trios of doors faced each other across the corridor, which would have been brighter with the security lights. She could see well enough that every door was shut, and in any event there was nothing to fear, not in this dream.

As she stepped off the stairs she had the odd idea that it wouldn't matter which door she approached. Even in a dream that made no sense, especially given her impression that she'd been summoned to George's flat. If all the dead eyes of the doors seemed to be aware of her, that needn't trouble her as long as she kept to the middle of the corridor. She padded almost to the exit before veering with hardly any hesitation to George's door and thumbing the bellpush.

She couldn't hear the bell, and because this was a dream it took her some indeterminate length of time to recall she wouldn't have been able to do so. All the same, the button she'd pushed felt less than entirely convincing, insufficiently present, as she stared at the pink fingerless lump of the back of her fist protruding its thumb horizontally as though attempting a secret sign. Clearly that would achieve nothing by itself. "Abracadabra," she told the door, and then "Open sesame," which proved as ineffectual. Then she found herself pronouncing another formula, a bunch of words which she hadn't known before they were put into her head somehow and which she forgot in the process of uttering them. No doubt they would have revealed themselves as nonsense once she was awake, and so she didn't miss them. She pushed the door with her thumb, and it swung inward.

Plainly this was the stage at which the dream became more of a dream. When she reached into the hall for the light-switch, just to the right of the door as hers was, it wasn't there. If this hadn't been a dream she doubted that she would have ventured into the dark, particularly when, in a clumsy attempt to sidle past the door, she bumped it shut behind her.

That didn't just trap her in the unlit hall; it robbed her of her sense of where she was supposed to be. At first she was relieved when her eyes began to adjust to the dark, for all that she considered this to be an unnecessarily realistic detail. Before long she was able to identify that the hint of illumination, so faint it made the walls appear to glimmer with moisture, was seeping through a doorway a good few yards ahead to her right. Though it didn't much resemble any doorway of her own flat, and so oughtn't to be here either, she seemed bound to head for it. The sooner she dealt with this part of the dream, the sooner she hoped she would be off this floor, which felt like cold damp stone. So did the wall when the knuckles of her left hand brushed it, and she had to remind herself not to drop her keys. They jangled as she renewed her grip on them, and she thought she heard a sound that wasn't quite an echo beyond the doorway she was approaching. She padded forward, grateful that at least the dream was keeping the sensations of a stone floor at a bearable distance, and looked in.

She was at the entrance to a cell. At the far end smudged black clouds were dragging themselves past a high narrow glassless window, and patches of the stone walls of the cramped rectangular cell appeared to have turned that movement on its side. If the patches were of damp, it was also crawling over the solitary object in the cell, a shape which, as she began to distinguish it, Ursula took at first to be a large plant or small tree that had withered after thrusting itself up through the floor and against the wall to the right of the window. Then she saw the remains of hands at the ends of both branches fastened to the wall on either side of a shrivelled lolling head. There was no question they were hands, because as she located them in the dimness they began to writhe all the fingers they had left, beckoning her into the cell.

Knowing this was a dream, she had no reason not to obey—indeed, every incentive to finish with the unpleasantness as soon as possible. The figure was jerking its fingers at itself and drawing its contorted legs up towards a rib-cage patched with skin, all of which activity communicated its requirements without its having to speak—not that it seemed likely to with the very little that remained of its mouth. Once she released it from the shackles she'd heard rattling in the dark, she thought, surely she herself would be released from the dream. She went to the left-hand manacle, keeping her gaze well away from the incomplete face and in particular the glistening contents of the eye sockets. Holding her keys between her teeth, she gripped the iron ring with both hands.

It would have seemed reasonable of the dream to let such a rusty manacle snap in her grasp at once. Failing that, it could at least have dispensed with any taste of metal in her mouth. The fleshless legs were clacking against the wall, the torso and the hairless skull were straining towards her; the left hand was continuing to twitch its fingers, and the dream was having trouble in distancing her from the notion that they might touch hers. She wrenched at the manacle with all her strength, hurling herself backwards, and lost her grip before finding it again, at which point something broke.

She saw what that was, and retreated, her hands fumbling at her mouth. The left arm as far as the elbow was dangling from the manacle. The figure swung against the wall, wagging the half of its arm, then sagged towards the floor. Its weight tore most of the right hand through the other manacle. Fragments of skin and bone flew away from the ring, and it was free.

At the moment when it rose from its crouch as though discovering that it could extend itself to its full height, which was a head taller than Ursula, she found she could move. She was able to withdraw in time only to glimpse the figure groping across the wall to fetch the rest of itself. As she backed through the doorway she saw a vertical thread of light away to her left. The outer door hadn't closed as tightly as she'd imagined.

Her sense of dreaming was secure again before she emerged into the familiar corridor—so secure that as far as to the stairs the carpeted floor felt like stone. She trudged up to the next level and admitted herself to her flat, where she dropped her keys in her coat pocket. At least the dream ended there rather than conducting her all the way back to her bed.

When she awoke, it was still dark. An unpleasantly metallic taste was in her mouth. She wobbled upright to grab the light-cord and kept on going, out of bed. In the bathroom she made to cup a hand beneath the tap, then washed her hands instead. Once they felt clean she scooped up a palmful of cold water and gargled with it before drinking a handful. This done, and the toilet used, she plodded back to bed and fell asleep almost at once, exhausted beyond thinking. The taste was out of her mouth, the gritty sensation of her hands was washed away, and in honour of the new year she resolved that by the morning she wouldn't even remember the dream.

12

FIRST WORDS

"I'll be off out now then, Amy. You'll be forging ahead with your homework, will you?"

"Looks like it."

"So it does. Getting up to date for going back on Monday, eh? I'll just be a couple of hours with some clients. I shouldn't be long."

"Fine."

"You'll be all right then, I take it? Is there anything you need?"

"Like what?"

"I don't know exactly. Anything I can bring you back."

Amy thought of the evening before the Sunday he'd lifted her up like an offering to Nazarill. She'd played Snakes and Ladders with her parents until she'd grown so tired the ladders had begun to wriggle, and she'd been unable to distinguish them from the snakes. When she'd started to nod over the board her father had carried her upstairs to bed, where her mother had sat beside her and told her a story Amy couldn't now recall. She felt her lips part and her tongue move. "No," she said.

"I'd best be off, then. Can't be back until I've gone, can I? I'll see you when we're older. Let's hope we're wiser too. It looks as if you ought to be, at any rate, with all that reading."

By now Amy was wondering how much of this speech and the preceding dialogue was simply his method of keeping himself there, and if he was just uttering as many words as possible, what he was actually thinking. She gazed at him across her notepad surrounded by

Shakespearian material and saw a furtively anxious old man in an out-of-date grey overcoat and black scarf. His face seemed to have devoted its recent years to producing more of itself, its lower cheeks bellying on either side of the jaw and pulling down the corners of the mouth, while the underside of the chin had settled for adding itself to the throat. His eyebrows had always been prominent, but their greyness made them appear heavier, and to be weighing down his eyes. At that moment he reminded her too much of the old man who'd refused to be coaxed back into Nazarill, and she didn't want to aggravate his condition. "Go on then, before it gets dark," she said, which sounded more like a covert plea than she'd intended. "Don't worry about me."

He gave a laugh that sounded closer to the opposite of one. "I'm afraid that comes with the job."

"What, insurance?"

"The job your mother left me with."

Even if he didn't mean her to, Amy felt accused. "Never mind," she said, "you won't have to do it much longer."

"Only until I die." He rubbed his forehead hard, flattening his eyebrows, and frowned, not necessarily at her. "Don't let us become ensnared in another argument. You carry on improving as you have been and I'll have no grounds to worry. Carry on, there's a good, a good teenager," he said, swinging one upturned hand to indicate her work, and buttoned his collar over his scarf as he strode into the hall.

He hadn't meant her schoolwork to begin with. When the door at the end of the hall slammed, shaking its chain, she listened to be sure he hadn't lingered in the flat for any reason, and then she took the Bible out of her canvas handbag. It had been what he'd meant, but he wouldn't be so pleased if he knew why she had it. She opened it to Genesis and turned her notepad over. Maybe this time her attempts to transcribe the writing in the margins of the book wouldn't give her such a headache.

She lowered her head until her nostrils filled with the smell of old paper and she could see nothing but the cramped script. She shaded her eyes with her left hand, pinching her brows together with finger and thumb, and ran the tip of a pencil under the writing, a fraction of an inch short of marking the page. "I," the writing began, and repeated that a few words further on, where it was once again followed by—never mind the raised wand of the third letter—"must." That seemed to unlock the handwriting for her, and all at once her pencil was dodging between the Bible and her notepad as though lifting the words off one page onto the other.

"I must set down my thoughts that they keep firm. I must not count myself abandoned by God as well as by my family in" (so said the top margin, and Amy had to lean still closer as she turned the right-hand margin upwards) "this place. That there were such places I knew; that they were such as this I could not have dreamed in my worst fits. Certes no other book would be" (Amy inverted the Bible) "allowed me by the fiends my captors, yet to use God's word as concealment for my own until the day comes for them to be read—"

Amy straightened up in order to turn the page, and wished she hadn't moved. Her headache had been waiting to be noticed as she emerged from her trance of concentration. Her forehead felt as though she'd clamped a metal band around it, her cropped scalp felt raw, her neck not merely stiff but stretched. She closed her eyes until the aches dwindled a little, then she read what she'd written. She couldn't help being pleased with her achievement, especially with having deciphered "certes," a word she understood only now she had written it down. More to the point, the passage was evidence that something had been wrong with Nazarill in the past, and she had to read on to discover what that was.

Not today, however. When she tried to read the first words in the next margin, her headache closed around her brain. She sat back, working her shoulders in an attempt to relax, and leafed through the Bible to see how much she had to transcribe—page after page. As well as writing in the margins, the owner of the book had underlined parts of the text. "Saul had put away those that had familiar spirits, and the wizards . . ." These words were underlined shakily three times, and so were fragments of another sentence: "There shall not be found among you . . . a witch . . . or a consulter with familiar spirits, or a necromancer." The underlining had left alone a reference in the midst of this to "any one that maketh his son or his daughter to pass through the fire," but Amy had an impression she couldn't quite grasp that the words ought to have some significance for her. A third underlined passage appeared with a whisper of stale paper. "Thou shalt not suffer a witch to live."

She copied that and the rest of the underlined words, and gazed at them. What had they to do with anything? All that she was aware of knowing about witches derived from Shakespeare and from rhymes she'd read half her lifetime ago. When her headache began to renew itself in proportion with her attempts to think, she flipped the pad back to her schoolwork notes in case her father came home early, and buried the Bible in her canvas bag as she stood up. For several reasons it made sense for her to get out of Nazarill.

She zipped herself into a black suede jacket that came down to her hips, and let herself into the corridor. She wasn't going to allow its insinuating glow to daunt her, not the dimness nor the rest of the place. She went quickly downstairs, scowling hardest at the doors on the ground floor, daring the rooms to be other than empty. By the time she began to wonder how that could have any effect, she was out of Nazarill.

Clouds had drawn a stained white sheet over the sky. Beneath it, at the end of Little Hope Way, the Christmas lights flared doggedly, doing their best to celebrate their last day. Children of about the age she'd been when her father had lifted her up to Nazarill were riding new bicycles around the perimeter of the market. One jingled a bell at her as she dodged into a gap in a haphazard parade of shopping trolleys and hurried whenever she could to the bookstall.

From a distance the bald bearded stallholder's face reminded her of a trick illustration which you could invert and still have a face. She saw that wasn't possible as he straightened up to give a female customer a smile which involved producing the tip of his tongue between his teeth. "Nowt wrong with romance. I could do with a bit in my life," he said, and noticed Amy. "I haven't forgotten you, girlie. Haven't turned it up yet."

The woman included Amy in the frown she'd been aiming at him, then dumped her parcel of books done up in second-hand gift-wrapping in her wheeled basket and sped it away. "Might have been on there," the bookseller complained, then let Amy glimpse a grin not too far from apologetic. "Get many books for Christmas?"

"Not since I was little. I'm looking for some now."

"Cart away all you can carry with my blessing. How about some of these fat individuals? *The History of Mattresses*? *Secrets of Town Planning*? *Slimming Through the Ages*? Not much call for that with you young bonesters. *Insects, Our Household Companions*? *Character Analysis Through Clothing*?"

By now Amy was sure he was inventing at least some of the titles as he tapped spines with an increasingly dusty fingertip. "Something about witches," she said.

"Ah, you've heard about them."

"About . . ."

"The Partington Witches."

"What about them? I mean who, what . . ."

"Weren't they supposed to dance up on Nazareth Hill?"

He sounded convinced she knew more than she did. "I don't know anything about it," she insisted. "When did they?"

"Must have been before your place was a hospital. Just a ruin, there'd have been."

"Why didn't you tell me about them last time?"

"You never asked."

He was gazing at her as though one of them was joking, but Amy's gaze more than equalled his. "I'm asking now. What else do you know?"

"Same as I already told you. They used to go there to dance and whatever else they got up to at night. If they were doing it that close to the houses you'd have to reckon they thought the hill was some kind of special place. That's if you believed in them."

"You haven't got any books with them in."

"Aren't any that I know of. If your witches ever existed, they didn't last long. Maybe someone made them up to put the fear of God in kids, that's when you could."

"How about books about witches?"

"None of those either. I've got none at the moment, that's to say. Pretty popular, they are. Hang on, girlie," he said, though Amy had made no move, "there might be this."

He extracted one of a pile of books that were doing duty as a bookend and throwing open the faded red cover, leafed through until he found a plate. "Take a look at these," he said, twisting the volume towards her. "That'd put the fear of God into you all right, what they used to do to them. Swung them around till they couldn't stand up, stuck needles in them, chucked them in the drink, and is it water they're shoving down her throat through that funnel? And when they'd had their fun with them they hung them on a tree."

The plate reproduced several small woodcuts depicting these activities. The faces of the torturers and of their victims bore exactly the same look of grim determination. The title of the book was *The*

Joys of Torture, Amy saw. Somebody had added breasts to all the male victims with a blue ballpoint. The bookseller was watching her reactions; for a moment she felt enclosed with him and the book. She straightened up, and the sounds of the market seemed to explode around her. "This isn't your book, is it?" she said.

"Wouldn't have it in the house. Only in the garridge," he said, and in some of this playful tone "Are you taking it? Christmas special. Going cheap for a scarce book."

She was about to clap it shut and wave it away when he glanced past her. "Shift over so this chap can get at the Westerns," he said, then his voice blunted itself. "Oh, you're with her."

The possibility of having been caught out made Amy feel as defensive as he sounded. When she swung to confront the newcomer, her revived headache reached for the top of her spine. "Oh, it's you," she said, but not for the reason she'd prepared to, because it wasn't her father. "Still interested in books, I see," Leonard Stoddard said.

She was considering a retort along the lines of hoping he was too when he leaned his large skewed face over to examine the book which the stallholder had defiantly left open where it was. "What's this? What are you getting mixed up with now?"

"He was showing me how they used to treat witches." Amy pushed the book away and waited for the librarian's face more or less to line up with hers. "Do you think you'd have any—"

"We'd certainly have no books like that in any library we're connected with. That sort of thing may have gone on once, but it's time we forgot about it if we want to progress. Digging it up does nobody any good, particularly not at your age."

"Any books about witches, I was going to say if you'd let me finish."

"Only in the little children's section. I should think you'd be too old for fairy tales. Pamelle is."

Maybe his daughter was too busy devising names for herself to have time to read, thought Amy. Could the libraries be quite as useless as he wanted her to believe? The stallholder closed the book with some force to remind his possibly potential customers he was still there, and she transferred her attention to him. "Shall I put witches on your wants list?" he said.

"Wants list."

"As well as the book about where you live."

"I live there too," Leonard Stoddard said, "and I think I'd be aware of anything about the place."

"Good job someone else is, then. Get her to give you a lend when I come up with it."

"Perhaps you should tell him what you said, Amy."

She was tempted to take this request at face value, but instead she told the bookseller "You don't know I said anything, do you?"

He shook his head once slowly, and after a heavy pause the librarian said "I hope we can keep it that way. Are you going home now?"

"No."

"I should, to hide this," he said, showing her a small package wrapped in gold paper and tied with a silver bow. "Pamelle's birthday next week."

Amy didn't know if he was hinting she should buy a present or making her aware of not having been invited to the party, nor did she care. She'd thought of someone who would be able to help her in her search for information: Martie always kept books on the occult in stock, and surely that wasn't so far removed from whatever Amy needed to know.

A van was parked outside Hedz Not Fedz, where several women were hefting cartons out of the back of the vehicle. They looked too permed and overcoated to be customers of Martie's, and in a moment Amy recognised that they were carrying their burdens into Charity Worldwide next door. She stood back for two women before dodging past the van, whose reflection was making the window of Hedz Not Fedz appear to be boarded up. She was at the doorway when she saw the window was indeed obscured, its inside covered with plasterboard, and the glass was smashed in two places. Down in the nearer bottom corner was a handwritten notice on which a great many stars surrounded a very few words. SORRY! MOVED TO MANCHESTER.

She tried the door anyway, then stepped back to gaze at it with all the reproach she was feeling for Martie. The women had stopped unloading the van to watch her. Though none of them gave the impression of being especially sympathetic, one took pity on her. "What's the woe, love? Hadn't you heard she was gone?"

"No," Amy admitted, and instantly wished she hadn't, because Shaun Pickles had strayed out of the marketplace to overhear both question and answer. His bony face looked less productive of hair than ever, and had intensified its mottling as a crackle of his walkie-talkie betrayed his presence. He shrugged his shoulders or squared them and stuck out his chin above his tight uniform collar. "Not much of a loss if you ask me," he said.

"Nobody did," she snapped, and walked so vigorously at him that one of the bystanders gasped. Once she was out of the space cramped by the van and the abandoned shop, she rounded on him. "I'll bet you had something to do with it, didn't you?"

"Didn't need to have. I couldn't stop folk smashing her windows and posting what they did through her slot while I wasn't there, could I? Waved my hank right enough when she drove off in her bus painted all over with the Lord only knows what crap."

Amy remembered the minibus covered with images of flowers from a different and presumably better world. "Not missing her, are you?" the guard said. "She can't have been much of a friend if she didn't tell you she was off. Unreliable all round from what I hear. Always late with her rent and the rest of her bills."

"Is that why they told you not to look after her shop?"

She saw him considering how to answer, and wondered if he was stupid enough either to agree or to claim the decision for his own. Abruptly she didn't care. She was thinking of heading for Rob's when Pickles said "Heard you the other night."

"What an honour for me."

"Don't listen if you can't be bothered. I just thought it was interesting."

Amy halted by a butcher's stall. Could she afford to reject anyone who would listen to her, however unappealing they otherwise were? "What sort of interesting?" she said.

"Well, I'll tell you." He paced up to her and put his hands behind his back. "My mam called me down when she heard it was you, so I got nearly everything. I heard whatever you want to call it."

"I don't know. I'm not sure."

"I could tell you."

"You know about things like that, do you?"

"Too bloody much."

"You mean you believe in them. Are you saying something like that happened to you?"

"Me? *Me?*" He displayed his fists before using all his fingers to indicate himself. "Hang on," he said with an effort she was meant to notice. "What do you reckon we're on about here?"

Amy saw her mistake, and couldn't suppress a giggle. "I thought we were talking about what I said I saw."

"That's a laugh. I hope you don't think I swallowed any of that. Maybe your dad ought to be wondering what you were on when you saw it. I'll bet he'll be glad to hear that shop's closed down."

Amy felt she'd had more than her portion of him. She was retreating alongside the butcher's stall when the guard said "Don't you want to hear what I was going to say?"

He was holding his hands apart in front of his chest as though to demonstrate some measurement. "What you thought was interesting, you mean," Amy said, and waited.

"Just how you seem to get on so well with, you know, people who aren't what God made them. The one who ran the shop and that one on the radio." With each sentence he took a pace closer and lowered his voice. "We were discussing it at home after you were on. My mam said it was a phase some of us go through at your age. Only the feller you hang around with, him with all the hair and the ring in his nose, he should have gone through it by now if he's going, shouldn't he? I'll tell you something though, I never went through it. So if you want to try a real man for a change, how about it? I don't like to see someone like yourself going to waste when you could be someone."

The butcher grabbed a gutted rabbit that was dangling head down from a hook. A smell of raw meat invaded Amy's nostrils, and she could have taken it to be the smell of the inflamed patches on Shaun Pickles' face. She felt sick, then furious, then hysterically amused. "Speak up," she said loudly. "I can't hear you."

"Course you can." Nevertheless he raised his voice a fraction, at the cost of some further mottling to his cheeks. "What didn't you?"

"Go through it again and I'll tell you, only speak as loud as this."

"Keep it down. You're disturbing people."

"Just this loud, then. That's not too loud when there's so much noise already."

"You're making a scene. I'll have to ask you to move on if you don't quiet down."

"That's it, like you're speaking now. Go on, say what you were saying to me before, unless you're ashamed to repeat it in public."

Several stallholders and at least as many shoppers were watching

them, and now the staff of a video library came to the shop window.
Pickles stared at the audience, then snatched the walkie-talkie from
his belt and wagged its plump black aerial at her. "Move along,
please. You're causing a disturbance."

"What else do you think you just did to me?" Amy reminded herself that she'd had enough of him some minutes ago, and began to
stroll away, wishing that tension wouldn't stiffen her legs. When she
saw him following, however, she called "You stay back or I'll tell
everyone what you were saying to me. Stay right back."

She had to shout at him again more than once before she reached
Little Hope Way. While she took her time over walking up the brief
street he stood at the end of it, thumbs stretching his belt. He wasn't
worth another shout, although he made her feel as if she was being
returned to Nazarill. She strolled between the gateposts and shook
her head at the security lights as they flattened the facade against
the sunset above the moors.

Her anger with Shaun Pickles and with Martie saw her through
the ground floor and up the stairs. Once she'd slammed her door she
was able to keep the rest of the building out of her mind. Beyond
the window of the living-room the market stalls were toppling with
as little noise as distant pins. Amy played an Abnormal Smears video
to distract herself from the silence and sat at the table with a glass
of fizzy Zingo, trying to rub some ideas either out of or into her forehead. She hadn't conjured up a single word to write on her pad when
the tape relented long enough to allow the buzzer in the hall a
chance.

A glance through the spyhole let her open the door. She knew the
large-boned woman's amiable face and her blonde hair that fell
about as far down the back of her white silk blouse as her terse skirt
extended down her black-nyloned thighs. She offered a smile with
her wide lips shut and a wave that kept her elbow pressed against
her rib-cage. "Amy, isn't it?"

"Hello, Mrs.—"

"Mrs. Nothing. Donna will do. We're both girls, aren't we?" She
widened her eyes as those members of Abnormal Smears who sang
abandoned it so as to apply themselves to extracting more volume
from their instruments. "Is this a good time? I was just after a word."

"I was only listening while my dad's out."

"How long will he be, do you think?"

"Probably a while yet, knowing him. He likes talking to his customers."

"A bit lonely, is he?"

This interpretation hadn't occurred to Amy; she'd assumed loquaciousness was a requirement of the job. "Maybe," she said, not wanting to consider the issue now.

"Old enough to know his own mind and sort himself out if he wants to," Donna took her to mean, which Amy supposed she might have, given the opportunity for reflection. "Do you think you've time for a little chat and your music afterwards, or just turned down a smidge?"

"I expect."

Donna closed the door and lingered in the hall. "I'd forgotten your big eyes. I don't think I'd like to find them waiting when I got up in the wee hours for a sprinkle." She must have realised Amy might feel the same way, even if not previously, because she darted to another subject. "Do I take it since your mother—I mean, there hasn't been anyone else."

"I don't think he's bothered."

"I'm certain I would be."

She could easily have said that Amy would think differently when she was older, and Amy switched off the television as a token of appreciation. "You don't need to turn—" Donna protested. "Well, whichever you like."

Amy recognised that politeness was assumed to involve this kind of pretence as you grew up, and so she let it pass. "Drink?" she said.

"If you are. Oh, you already are. I won't then, thanks. Let's just gab while we've the chance."

Amy curled up in an armchair and Donna sat opposite, exposing more thigh with a whisper of tight skirt and nylon. Seated, she seemed less certain how to proceed. "So," she began, only to follow that with a smile no words could slip through. After some seconds she said "I don't know if you heard a few of us were talking to your father."

"When? What about?" said Amy, and with resignation "Oh."

"That was it, really, your moment of fame."

"Who was saying what?"

"Mr. Shrift thought it could attract the wrong kind of sightseer. Mind you, I should think any kind is wrong so far as all of us are concerned. Mr. Greenberg, I'd have to say he was angry because according to him you shouldn't talk about the kind of things you went on the air about, they only distract people from what's actually bad in the world. Ghosts are, how did he put it, a way of romanticising history is what he said. And Mr. Sheen, he mightn't have said, but I think he was mostly peeved you hadn't gone to him if you thought there was a story."

"Maybe I will when there's more of one. I just had an impulse to go on the radio."

"I heard him promising your father he wouldn't touch the story now. It's yesterday's news if it was news at all, he said."

"And what did you say?"

"To him? To your father, not as much as I might have. Dave, you met my husband, told him you were just imaginative because you're an only child and, it's true, isn't it, rather a loner."

"Most of my friends live in Sheffield. I don't like the people round here from my school."

"You must be looking forward to being old enough to drive. Anyway, about—you don't mind talking about it, since you talked about it, do you? Your father said you were very young."

"He thinks I still am."

"You should hear my mother sometimes. But you were half your age, weren't you? What made you bring it up now?"

"I'd forgotten about it, but that doesn't mean it didn't happen. Even he remembers the day it did."

"If you forgot something that bad it means it was traumatic. Do you—well, never mind."

"Don't do that."

"I was only wondering if you're sure you remembered everything."

"I think so. I must have," Amy said, growing less convinced in proportion with how certain she declared herself to be. "Why are you so interested? You know there's something, don't you? Have you seen it too?"

"No, no. Nothing. I'm sure there's nothing solid here, let's say nothing you could photograph. Maybe some places can make you see what happened in them or feel how they felt when it did. Only people should be able to make that go away by living in a place and being happy there, don't you think?"

"Depends what it was that happened." Precisely because Donna was appealing to her for reassurance, Amy was unable to provide it. "What have you felt?"

"When we were measuring—I've been trying to think how it seemed. Older than it looked, but older than it would have been before they got it up like this, I'd say as well. And maybe . . ."

"Maybe's almost as important."

"Maybe I've felt sometimes as if something that old is, I don't know if living here is the right phrase."

"Where?"

"Down below, all the way down. You don't sense anything up here, do you?"

"Not yet," said Amy, then wished she hadn't. Donna's impressions had clearly required some effort to communicate, yet she wondered if they were the whole truth. They were enough for now, since they were a good deal less comforting than Amy would have liked, and so she said quickly "Did you find out what this place used to be?"

"I haven't asked."

"Wouldn't you have expected them to say when they hired you? I don't think they want to say, or maybe they really don't know. Don't care either. I'm trying to find out all about it," Amy said, only to realise how much more systematic than it was she'd made her research sound.

"More power to you, Amy. I want you to know—"

She pressed her lips together, this time with hardly any of a smile, and stared towards the hall. Amy too had heard the outer door— the sound of its closing. In a moment her father called "Hallo?"

"Hello, Mr. Priestley. It's Donna Goudge."

"I gathered as much." With very little noise he was almost at once in the doorway of the room, where he opened his fist to let his keys jangle into a pocket. "Do please continue. You were telling my daughter what you wanted her to know."

Donna opened her mouth and thought better of speaking, then apparently decided that not to do so might look worse. "Just that it isn't everyone who thinks she's been fibbing. At least one of us is of the opinion she may be on to something."

"I doubt our next-door neighbours would care to hear you say so. I've this moment come from speaking to them, and now I'd like a word with my daughter, if you'll excuse us."

"Oh dear. I hope it isn't anything too—"

"Good day to you, Mrs. Goudge."

As soon as Amy heard the outer door close she said "Do you know how rude you are?"

"It isn't rudeness to a woman of her sort."

"You heard she believes me, and I'll tell you someone else I bet does—Beth."

"It would tally with the rest of her old wives' nonsense. What a pair of supporters you have, a charlatan and a trollop. God be thanked you've better people who care about you."

"Like who?"

"Mr. Stoddard for one. He informs me you're trying to dig up even more unholy nonsense about our home. I warn you now on behalf of all the good people here, finish. Stop at once."

"And if I don't?"

"I'll stop you." As he spoke his hands gripped the doorframe, which creaked, and his shoulders broadened to block more of it. Then a look of slow realisation settled on his face, an expression so heavy she could have imagined it was its weight that was nodding his head. "I know how," he said almost to himself. "I'll show you what there is to fear."

13

FACE TO SOME FACE

The bus to Sheffield was smaller than last year's, and it was almost ten minutes late. When Amy had arrived in good time at the brick bus shelter by the Scales & Bible it was full of Bettina and Deborah and Zoe pronounced Zoh, or at least they behaved as if it was. They had made grudging room for her, though not on the cigarette-scarred bench under their names scratched on the wall, and once they'd each said "Hi" to see whether she would respond three times they had set about pretending to ignore her. Whenever any of them glanced at her they all giggled behind their hands, and so she knew they were saving extra for the journey. She might have stood outside the shelter except for the rain that was weaving its way through the town. While she gazed at the dance of water in the air she was able to persuade herself that her three schoolmates had ceased to exist, until the sound of the bus chugging up through Partington roused her from her trance.

The vehicle was less capacious than her bedroom. It smelled of upholstery faded by last year's sun and of a recent presence that Amy identified after some reflection as wet dogs. By then she was seated immediately behind the driver, whose neck put her in mind of a joint of pork encircled by several grooves incised by string, and the three had spread themselves across the back seat. As the bus laboured onto the moor and the sky lowered a smoky chunk of itself to meet the headlights, she was tempted to hope the other passengers had for-

gotten about her. Then her left ear grew hot with a breath which at
once turned into a shriek of "Boo!"

She couldn't help jumping. She stiffened herself at once and
clamped her hands between her knees, but her reaction was good for
a few shrieks of laughter from the girls at the back of the bus as Bettina returned to it. At least Amy had resisted looking back. She readied herself for the next onslaught of wit, signalled by silence from
behind. "Boo!" screamed Deborah, almost precisely when Amy expected her to, but in her right ear.

Amy wasn't about to let it affect her this time, any more than
whatever her father was planning would. "That's brilliant," she said.
"That's really imaginative. Did you think it up all by yourself?" She
was preparing to continue along these lines until Deborah either retreated or was goaded into a response as stupid as her joke when the
driver turned one cratered ruddy cheek but not his eyes towards
them. "If you're going to play, sit at the back where I won't be irked."

"I'm not playing," Amy protested, and heard how she sounded:
not just as petulant as her choice of words but years younger than
she ought to feel. She twisted round so violently that Deborah shied
into the aisle. "Come on, Zoee," Amy called. "Your turn. Get it over
with. Say boo and then the three of you can fuck off."

"Eh. Eh. Eh," the driver said, the high-pitched syllables as terse
as the pauses between them. "I won't have language on my bus. Any
more and you'll be put off."

"You can't put her off out here in this," Bettina objected.

Even if this wasn't slyly designed to cause the event it purported
to be forestalling, Amy didn't want her tormentors to side with her.
"I don't care," she said. "I don't give a, what you are."

Since she'd faced front, perhaps the driver thought she meant him.
"Just you remember I know which school you go to. I know your
headmistress."

"We know about you and all," Zoe told him. "We've seen you
looking at us in your mirror when we sit down."

At that moment the blurred speeding lights of the motorway
swam into view ahead, and the driver braked. He was going to turn
everyone off the bus, Amy thought. While she might resign herself
to being left alone out here, might even perversely welcome it, being
stranded with three of her least favourite people was another mat-

ter. But the driver had decided against this, unless he'd braked as a final warning. He set the windscreen wipers sweeping faster as the bus rushed along a mile of open road.

When the vehicle found itself space on the motorway it proved to be capable of as much speed as most of its competitors, even if it shook as though its nerves weren't up to the situation. Amy's weren't, not once she found herself thinking of her mother. It had been fog that had taken her, and the spray from all the traffic very much resembled fog. A watery taste kept trying to gather at the back of her mouth, and she knew that if any of the girls tried to torment her again she would say worse than she had. They confined themselves to bursts of giggling, however, renewed when necessary by muttered comments. They didn't stir from the rear seat until the bus was out of the drowned race and in sight, or as much of it as the fleetingly clear windscreen admitted, of the school on the outskirts of Sheffield.

Amy let them dash between the puddles in the schoolyard and into the elongated building, which was at least twice as dark a brown as usual, before she allowed herself to run. At least none of them was in her class. She shed her cap and hung it over her coat in her tin locker just in time to join her classmates as they were herded to the assembly hall.

That delayed her having to answer the questions and respond to the comments she could see had been stored up for her. Nevertheless she felt conspicuous, especially once the headmistress had given her cropped head a sharp look while delivering her customary New Year speech with all the enthusiasm it exhorted from the school. Some of the teachers went further than looking. "I see we've a novice among us," the maths master remarked at the beginning of his class, and the English mistress said "Dear, dear" before "Dear," perhaps a lofty endearment, as a preamble to informing Amy "You make my head feel cold." All this was only a prelude to being surrounded when the bell at the end of the morning let everyone loose.

As it turned out, Amy wasn't surrounded for long. Her friends lost a good deal of interest in her encounter at Nazarill once they learned how dated it was. Neither the uproarious dining-hall nor the classroom to which the rain confined them afterwards seemed the place to discuss her subsequent impressions, even with those of her friends whom she would expect to be sympathetic, and so the conversation drifted onto the subject of horror videos that had left people unable to sleep, and the parties the films had been viewed at, and the boys who had been at the parties.

The final lesson was religion. Last term's supply teacher had applied herself to raising ethical questions, but now Mrs. Kelly was back, two sizes thinner and the more intense for it. As she marched with a limp into the classroom her eyes, which shared more than one quality with slate, sought Amy out and shot her a rebuke. Long before the end of the period crammed with sharp questions about Biblical punishments Amy was wishing the lesson could be like every one she'd seen in films, lessons that lasted two minutes at the outside before being terminated by a bell. At least she proved to know more of the Bible than she'd realised, which might have been the reason why she became the target for more than her fair share of questions. After longer than she would have believed it possible for a lesson to drag on, the bell was unable to restrain itself. She thought she was succeeding in concealing her relief as she headed for the door when Mrs. Kelly said "Who'll carry my bag to the staffroom for me, Amy Priestley?"

Despite their tone, the last two words had ceased to be a question. Amy picked up the battered leather briefcase stuffed with books and moved towards the corridor again. "No fire, is there, that I know of?" Mrs. Kelly said. "That's not the bell we heard."

"I have to go to the library in town."

"That's good to hear at any rate. I'll be driving that direction, so."

If anything her last word made it even less clear whether she only now would. Apparently the delay on which she'd insisted was to enable her to watch everyone other than Amy out of the classroom. "Tell me now, Amy Priestley," she then said. "Do you enjoy my lessons? Shame the devil."

"Sometimes. A bit."

"That's what I asked for, so," Mrs. Kelly said, looking as though she was bracing her face against an unexpectedly chill wind. "You can be honest when you want to be. A girl like you who reads her Bible, I'd think she would be proud of what she could achieve."

By now Amy had little sense of being alluded to, and less of how to respond. "Mm," she said, and having heard the inadequacy of that: "Mm hm."

"You can't just read the book and put it away from you. You're the intelligent one. You know that, don't you?"

Amy had to guess what she was being asked; even by the standards of most of the teachers she knew, Mrs. Kelly appeared to feel entitled to use language as loosely as possible. "Thanks," she said.

"Too intelligent to—yes?"

The last word was aimed with no little force at a third-year who would otherwise have tapped on the open door. "Excuse me," the girl said, and hid her inky hands behind her back. "Excuse me," she repeated, apparently for having paused. "Excuse me, is she Amy Priestley?"

"Oh." The syllable summed up so much disapproval that for a moment the teacher seemed prepared to restrict herself to it. "Has her reputation travelled all the way down to you young ones?"

"I don't, I don't think so, Mrs. Kelly. Has it?" The girl was confused enough to ask Amy the question, not that Amy felt able to help. "Are you her?" the girl then said.

"She is she. Perhaps now you could have the grace to address yourself to me and explain—"

"Miss Sadler wanted me to find her and send her to the office."

"Well, now you have, and you may tell the headmistress we are on our way. What class are you in, and your name?"

"Gillian Fairbrother in 3A, miss, Mrs. Kelly."

"I shall look forward to taking you next year."

Perhaps the girl had been hoping for praise. The implied threat sent her away trying not to look dismayed. Mrs. Kelly gave a sharp nod to indicate that Amy should follow the girl's example, which she did to the extent of stepping into the corridor, briefcase in hand and her own bag strapped over her other shoulder. "So what do I hear?" Mrs. Kelly said.

Though Amy had worked that out, she saw no reason to admit it. "I don't know," she said, which was a pronoun more than she would have offered her father. "What?"

Mrs. Kelly waited until Amy had held open the fire doors to the staff corridor and the doors had closed with a slow attempt at a thud. "You know you did wrong."

"No, I don't. I didn't."

"We've talked about false witness in my class, and worshipping false gods. A girl like you knows what those mean."

Amy couldn't tell whether that was an accusation or a claim made on her behalf. "I don't know what they have to do with me."

Mrs. Kelly either limped hard or stamped her foot, halting a few yards away from the open door of Miss Sadler's office. "Worshipping false gods, I remember you were there the day we spoke about that because you tried to make out capital was one. What were you, busy with your own thoughts when I counselled you all against spiritism? That's one of the paths to the false gods, no better than witchcraft. And bearing false witness is lying."

"I didn't lie."

"The other's even worse." Mrs. Kelly jabbed a hand at her, but only to seize the briefcase; then the fierceness of the gesture transferred itself to her voice. "You aren't telling me you believe in the things you told that, that fellow on the radio."

Amy felt she had already answered this, and so nothing was left except to look forthright. "Dear heaven, what a stare you have about you. You're giving me a headache," Mrs. Kelly complained, and glanced past her, towards Miss Sadler's office. For a moment Amy felt triumphant, even though the distraction was presumably the headmistress. But when she turned she saw her father.

The surprise wasn't pleasant, and gave her no time to choose her words. "What do *you* want?" she demanded.

Mrs. Kelly uttered a sound between a grunt and a gasp, to which Amy's father responded with a smile suggesting he was having to employ a habitual saintly patience. "I've come to run you home," he said to Amy. "We don't want you catching a cold in the rain and having to miss school."

"I need to go to the library."

"Not today, young lady."

"Yes, today."

Mrs. Kelly produced her sound again, and this time she followed it up. "I'm afraid, Mr. Priestley, you've a girl there that in my childhood we'd have called wilful."

"You'll be which of her teachers?"

"Religious."

"I'll do my best to ensure you see an improvement next time. Amy, look at me."

Amy did so, earning herself more of a grunt and less of a gasp from

Mrs. Kelly, who then stalked askance into the staffroom. "Now, Amy," her father said, "we both know you don't want to visit the library for your schoolwork."

"You don't know anything about me."

"Oh, now, Amy." This was the headmistress, emerging from her room and folding her arms as though to ensure her large breasts wouldn't draw attention away from her small solemn face. "If I had a day off for every girl who thought that . . . We folk whose job it is to help you grow up do have the odd insight you might find useful if you slowed down long enough to listen. We've been you, after all."

Amy liked her enough not to want to antagonise her, and so extended her a smile as far on the way to agreement as she could force it, to which Miss Sadler responded "Your father and I were just saying—"

"What's he been saying about me?"

"Amy!"

"Thank you, Mr. Priestley. I was *about* to tell you, Amy, we were saying you're usually a conscientious girl who can be relied upon to produce good work, and if you've any problems at the moment either of us can help you with, that's part of what we're here for."

"Then tell him to let me go to the library. That's me being conscientious."

"I can't intervene between you, of course. You must see that isn't what I had in mind. Was there anything else you wished to say?"

Even if this wasn't just an invitation to apologise, it felt like one to Amy. "No," she said.

"May I leave her in your hands then, Mr. Priestley? Work never done and all that. Same for you, I'm certain, as long as we're both doing our best to look after those we're responsible for." She unfolded her arms, freeing her breasts in a gesture Amy found disconcertingly maternal. "You know where I am, Amy," the headmistress said.

Amy did indeed: at least a generation distant, and far less understanding of her than the headmistress imagined herself to be. As though to demonstrate this, Miss Sadler said "Before you trot off to make peace with your father, there was one thing I had to say to him."

"Don't mind me."

"I have," said the headmistress with a look which hoped Amy had genuinely misunderstood her, "and now I'm saying it to you. Please don't be so severe with your hair. Moderation in all things is the way to social harmony."

"Your headmistress means she doesn't want such hair at her school."

"I'm prepared not to go quite so far this time, given Amy's previous record. Let it grow out as soon as nature provides, Amy, if you would. In most ways she has shown herself an agreeable girl. I'm sure this is just a token rebellion," Miss Sadler said, and even less to Amy "May I leave further discussion to you? Please do feel free to contact me at any time within school hours."

She'd taken hold of the inner doorknob when Amy said "Did you hear me on the radio?"

Miss Sadler looked disappointed. "I'm glad to say I didn't, Amy," she said, and closed the door.

Amy hadn't expected much better. She marched at the fire doors and held one open with her foot just long enough for her father not to have a reason to accuse her of having let it swing in his face, then she walked fast through the school. By the time she reached the next pair of doors he was too far behind for her to bother holding one. She heard them repeat their creak behind her, and her father calling "Amy. Amy" low and sharp. He sounded as though he was summoning a dog and trying not to admit to his attitude, she thought. She could keep walking, out of the school and away to the central library; how could he stop her? Surely the library would be one where you still weren't supposed to make a noise, and so he would have to leave her alone to research. But the long windows overlooking the corridor had started to rattle and crawl with tendrils of water, and as soon as she let herself out of the heavy front door of the school she couldn't see for rain.

She was knuckling her eyes in a fierce attempt to clear them, and feeling infuriatingly as though some of the moisture was or might soon be tears, when her father took hold of the arm she was using. "Don't stand there, you're getting drenched. This way, now. Our vehicle is over here."

She had to give in. The Bible from Nazarill was in her bag, and long before she reached the library it would be soaked, its message illegible. Yet she couldn't help feeling that her eyes had been affected in order to trap her. She suffered herself to be guided across the swimming concrete, which appeared to be emitting jabs of rain, to the blotchy reddish lump that proved to be the Austin. Her father held onto her until he'd unlocked the passenger door and handed her into the car, and then she was alone for a few seconds with rain trickling down her face, a trickle she didn't manage to palm plopping on the bag she'd transferred to her lap. By the time she'd finished wiping her face her father was beside her and the doors were locked.

He switched on the headlights to catch the rain and set the wipers sluicing the windscreen, and waited while three girls dashed shrieking out of the gates before he advanced the car to the road. As he accelerated cautiously along the road out of Sheffield Amy demanded "Did she call you?"

"There was no need. I had to be here."

That was about as clear to her as the smudged street beyond the side windows. "What were you saying to her about me?"

"Let's pass over who said what. The issue is that we agreed you're having problems that require addressing. We decided what I already thought, they have to do with your view of where we live. Mend that and we're sure you'll improve."

Amy stared at the wipers as they wagged mindlessly at her. "What. Were. You. Saying. To. Her. About. Me?"

"Carry on as you choose, you won't wear me down like—" He braked as the underwater beacons of a pedestrian crossing inflated their glow ahead, but nobody was waiting to cross. Once the orange blobs had floated by, drawing the edge of the city with them, he drove faster towards the motorway. "I may tell you we heard your teacher facing you with your reputation," he said.

Amy held herself silent and still almost to the motorway, but as the Austin sped up the ramp she burst out "Who did you mean I wore down?"

He sent the car into the discoloured wake of an oil tanker, peered in his mirror, swung the car into the middle lane. Settling into the speed of the traffic ahead of and behind him appeared to give him a chance to reflect, since he then said "You exasperated me. I wasn't suggesting you wore anybody down, just that you might have if our situation were different."

"You were talking about my mother."

"I was, yes. That is, I am."

At once Amy knew what he'd stumbled over. "You talked to Miss Sadler about her."

"We may have exchanged a few words on the subject."

"About how I killed her?" Amy had to rage, or she would have wept. "How I got on her nerves so much she crashed her car?"

"You're imagining horrors again. You weren't like that." Instead of adding "then" out loud he said "If anyone ruined her nerves, it was her mother."

"You're not saying there's something that wasn't my fault."

"You're being unreasonable. You're just indulging yourself." He eased the car into the inside lane before frowning sidelong at her. "You haven't really been blaming yourself for the accident all this time, have you?"

"Not that long."

"Truthfully, I can think of no reason why you should, so please don't. It can't be helping your state of mind. You'll hardly remember her mother, will you?"

"I don't remember yours either."

"My parents fell out with me once they found I was set on marrying Heather. I should point out we were both considerably older than you. Her mother was the cause of the trouble with my parents. She already had a history, you see."

"Oh, I thought you didn't believe in history."

"You're going to hear this. It's time you did." He swerved into the middle lane so abruptly that she thought the wind laden with rain had taken control of the wheel. "By the time you were old enough to travel she and Heather's father had moved down south. They kept inviting us, but we always managed to find some excuse."

"You never lied. Not *you*."

"We did it for your sake, perhaps you should realise. That ought to show you how seriously we regarded the problem. She was forever seeing things and hearing things, but when they were getting ready to move she turned worse. Wouldn't stir out of the house until she'd read all her daily horoscopes and consulted her tea-leaves and laid out her cards. And after the move, every letter we had from Heather's father contained some new tale of her. She wouldn't leave the house because everyone she met knew she could see the future and was out to stop her, and if it wasn't that it was her thinking she could prevent the future she'd foreseen if she kept still enough.

Heather went to visit her a few times, but it only distressed them both, her mother trying to convince her God knows what was in store for her and having hysterics when Heather tried to calm her down."

"I remember being left alone with you when I was little," Amy said, but she didn't have time for nostalgia. "What's all that supposed to have to do with me?"

"In my view she scared herself out of her wits with her tripe. Scared herself, as they say, to death."

"I'm not scared."

"Maybe you should be a little more than you are in some ways."

"You mean of you."

"That wouldn't hurt." His eyes flickered as the sign for Partington swam out of the grey depths of the downpour. Once he'd rejoined the cortege in the inside lane he turned to her for as long as he could bear to keep his eyes off the red lights that were being dragged ahead of him. "Can't you see *I'm* frightened for *you?*"

"Well, don't be. You needn't be."

"If I weren't frightened *for* you—" His left hand jerked towards her face and raised the lever to indicate he was about to quit the motorway. "I wish your mother were with us," he said, barely audibly. "She might have handled this better."

"So try and be like her."

"You imagine you could get round her, do you? I think she would have had to agree with me." If it had occurred to him to allow Amy some concession, he had clearly changed his mind. He drove up the exit ramp, beyond which even more rain was waiting to assault the car, and reverted to talking mostly to himself. "I'm the one who has to live with it and it's my task to deal with it. If I'm wrong in my course, God forgive me."

Amy felt as though the chill of the sodden moors had found the dampness of her clothes. She'd assumed that his reminiscences about her grandmother had been the source of fear with which he was determined to confront her, but now— She shivered and said angrily "What are you ranting about?"

"Action that should have been taken some time ago."

The Austin sped up the crest of the Partington road, and Amy saw the glow of the marketplace repeatedly flickering as the windscreen wipers scythed the rain. It looked as though someone was failing to douse a fire under the pale blotch of Nazarill. The idea made her feel feverish, as hot as she had just been cold. "Don't tell me, then," she said almost as indifferently as she wanted to sound. "See if I care."

"You'll see soon enough. If this doesn't cure you, God only knows what will."

If he was as uneasy as he seemed, thought Amy, perhaps he would leave the threat unresolved, to be revived whenever he didn't approve of her behaviour. She wasn't going to ask any more questions, in case they revealed her own nervousness. The car plunged downhill between the streaming banks of the road as the wipers toiled to sluice away the town. Of course Partington wasn't smaller than usual, yet as the car dredged it towards the windscreen Amy felt as though the streets were closing in. Each time another grey wash of rain inundated the glass fewer houses were visible beyond it, and she could fancy the view being cleared to show that the town had dwindled to a former size. When the car crossed the town boundary the streetlamps looked dimmer and less numerous than usual. The streets were deserted, and so were the lit shops apart from their staff, who turned one by one to watch the passing car. Their faces were so blurred, wads of flesh under glass, that she imagined all of them knew what she was bound for—were wishing it upon her, perhaps. Then the car halted by the massive drooling cross that reinforced the wall under Rob's lane. Amy was thinking of making her escape, and telling herself her father was capable of nothing that could frighten her enough to justify her flight, when the Sheffield bus to which the car had deferred sloshed away and the car swung up Moor View.

Cottages slithered through the rain on the side windows. The street was fleeing Nazarill as fast as she was being borne towards it. They cut off the glow of the marketplace, but although the security lights were dormant for the moment, the building shone with the pallor of something kept for a long time in darkness. At each sweep of the wipers the pale hulk wavered in order to reform larger and more solid. Only the railings stood between her and her father's destination for her—the railings and the gates that had been erected since she'd left for school that morning. Except that surely nobody could have worked outside on such a day, and as she realised that she saw there were no gates.

The railings and the gateposts writhed, then they and the emptiness between them steadied. Her cold hands and colder feet stiffened as her glimpse made her feel vulnerable to seeing worse than gates which didn't exist, or existed no longer. She rubbed her fingers against her palms to render them controllable, she wriggled her toes until she felt the skin chafe against the damp toecaps of her shoes as the car crossed Nazareth Row and veered onto the gravel drive.

As Nazarill magnified its pallor and lurched at her, the rain redoubled its attack on the roof of the car. With that she could have imagined the illumination was lightning, but instead of flickering out it grew more relentless. It froze her thoughts as the car pulled up at the entrance. "Run in and wait for me," he said. "I'll be with you as soon as I'm parked."

"I'll be upstairs."

He turned his head and stared at her. Any emotion in his eyes was hidden by the glare of Nazarill. "No," he said. "Not upstairs."

"Wherever. I don't care," said Amy, and tried not to as she groped in her bag. The backs of her fingers slid down the cover of the Bible, snagging her knuckles on a cross. She couldn't tell which way up it was. She closed her fist around the keys and dragged them free of the tangle in her bag.

In the seconds it took her to dash around the car, the rain jabbed at her eyes as though the ashen blaze of Nazarill was acquiring substance and splintering into the air. The car screeched away, water and gravel spraying from beneath its wheels, as she landed on the massive doorstep and searched with her key for the lock. It seemed she had barely felt metal slide into metal when the door yielded. She stumbled inside, dabbing at her eyes, trying to rub away more darkness than the corridor ought to contain.

She heard the doors meet behind her. They still sounded like glass. Perhaps it was the rain on them that made the corridor appear gloomy and flickering, but how could that be? As if in response to her thought, the view ahead stabilised, although not to any very reassuring effect: she could have fancied that the three pairs of doors facing each other in the sly light were sharing a silent message. If her eyes rather than the light had been flickering, that didn't reassure her either. She felt that Nazarill had somehow changed or was poised to change, and having dropped her keys into her bag, she reached for the door-handle. At that moment a hooded figure loomed beyond the glass, a figure whose outline crawled in and out of shape.

The doors parted and took their watery crawling with them. The new arrival was her father; she'd known that despite not having heard his approach over the gravel. He threw back the hood of his raincoat and wiped his eyebrows with the side of his hand, a gesture which made him look to be surveying the prospect ahead. Then his gaze lit on Amy, and his eyes widened a little as though to make room for more than the determination they held. "Would you like to go up first and get changed?"

"Before what?"

Either he wanted to be done or believed she was pretending not to know, because his gaze hardened. "On second thought, never mind. You aren't as wet as your father, and this oughtn't to take long. Besides, it's never cold in here."

Amy thought it was, or was about to be; certainly her hands and feet were. She had an unhappy impression that their stiffness was keeping her captive as she watched his fingers vanish into his coat pocket. She heard a metallic rattle, and he pulled out a bunch of keys—not those he habitually carried. "What are they for?" she demanded. "Where did you get them?"

"Why do you suppose I was in Sheffield? As to their purpose, that's up to you. You tell me." This sounded threatening enough, but Amy could make nothing of it until he said "Which room did I nearly deposit you in that you are unable to forget?"

They were the keys to the ground-floor apartments. He'd borrowed them from Housall—by undertaking to do what? "You're not locking me in there," she said.

"I didn't say I would," he said, but his expression didn't waver. "I simply want you to see once and for all that there is nothing to be afraid of."

"All right, there's nothing."

"No, that won't do. You have to be shown. I want to see you realise," he said, and jangled the keys. "Which was it?"

"Can't remember."

"As you wish. I've as much time as is required. We'll go through them all."

"Try and make me," Amy almost said, and then she saw the chance she would be missing. If she saw anything this time, he would have to see it too. "Don't *you* remember?" she said.

"It was at the front, I know that." He frowned as though he suspected her of trying to trick him into more of an admission than he was willing to concede, then he pointed with a key. "I believe it was in that area. Where the old gentleman who was starting to imagine things lived with his son."

"It must have been if you say so. In there, yes."

It wasn't, Amy knew. The room had been across the corridor, where the photographer had died and the old man had found him—not only him. Abruptly the notion of venturing in there, even with her father, was not at all enticing. For now she would be satisfied with convincing him that he'd persuaded her she was wrong, and surely there was indeed no reason for her to be scared of the apartment where even the old man had found nothing to fear—so far as she knew, came the unwelcome modification, to suppress which she said "Go on then, open it up."

Perhaps she oughtn't to have seemed so eager. When he held up the keys in front of his face she thought he was taunting her with them until she realised each key bore a number. He identified the one he needed and inserted it in the door which had briefly belonged to the Roscommons, and Amy heard a faint clawing sound which she told herself was being emitted by the lock. He pushed the door inward and withdrew the key with a swift harsh scrape. "In you go," he said.

It struck Amy that the reluctant illumination of the corridor didn't reach as far along the hall as it should. "You aren't going to . . ."

"I said I wouldn't. Hop to it before I change my mind." He glanced into the apartment and sighed, and knuckled the light-switch before returning the fistful of keys to his pocket. "Now you can see. I pray that's the end of any foolishness."

Amy gazed along the hall, which was maintaining its resemblance to a panelled corridor in a country house. All five doors, two in each wall and the kitchen door at the end, were shut, and she was beginning to appreciate how much effort and nerve it would take her to open any of them. At least she wouldn't be alone. She made herself step over the threshold, and shivered, at which he uttered a harsh terse breath. "Have you begun?"

He was close behind her, already in the hall. There was no use telling him what she'd sensed too late—that the apartment had been waiting for them, and now it had them. Its mockingly unchanged appearance made her want to cry out, to batter at the walls until the panels cracked, but all she said was the least of the truth. "It's too cold in here."

"The chap from Housall must have turned the heating down while the floor is empty. Quick march and you won't notice it so much."

She heard the rattle of a chain at her back, and whirled round. He was closing the door to the corridor. "Leave it open," she pleaded. "Let some of the heat in."

He grasped the latch and held the door where it was, more than half closed. "I'll leave it if you open one of those."

Amy made herself turn to the hall. Neither her hands nor her feet were eager to function, and their cold stiffness seemed to have infected her mind. On one side of her lay the main bedroom, on the other the room that was the equivalent of hers, but she'd lost the ability to judge which would be which. The prospect of opening the door to the windowless room and having to reach in to switch on the light dismayed her so much she couldn't think. At least the main bedroom shouldn't be entirely dark, or had the curtains been shut when her father had driven up? She reached for the left-hand door, then stretched her other hand towards the door opposite, only to be brought to a standstill. "What ceremony's that?" her father said roughly. "Are you supposed to be on a cross?"

"Can't you hear that?" Amy said, jerking her fingers, as much to move them as to indicate. "What is it?"

"Good God, child, we won't get far if you kick off like this. Of course I can hear it. In my day it was called rain."

She screwed her torso round and stared at him. "How can we be hearing it? I couldn't even hear the tree being cut down."

"Because, because it's . . ." He waved a hand at the outer corridor, and she saw him grow aware that the slow hollow dripping was somewhere within the apartment. "Keep that look to yourself," he said, and shoved himself away from the door. "If it isn't rain it must be a tap."

Amy grabbed at the door, which the force of his movement was closing, and having pushed it wide, propped her canvas bag against it. He'd brushed past her to stride to the end of the hall, where he flung the kitchen door open and slapped the light-switch. The colourless glow of a double fluorescent tube snatched at the surfaces of the fitted kitchen before gathering itself to fasten on them, by which time Amy's father had arrived at the sink beneath the silently inundated window and turned away. He tramped back into the hall and held up his hands, miming uncertainty as to which side of him the bathroom was. He lurched leftward to seize the doorknob and disappeared into the room, where Amy heard a light-cord being tugged almost simultaneously with the cessation of the dripping of liquid. As she tried to find some reason in that to relax at least a little, he rushed into the hall. "Happier now, are we?"

To an extent she was, since she knew the bathroom had to be next to the other windowless room. She made herself step to the door of the main bedroom and grasp the chill brass handful of the knob. She needed to add her other, equally unwieldy, hand before the knob would turn. Then it did, and she could only push the door away.

The windows were uncurtained. The Roscommons had taken the curtains with them, of course. Except for the abstract indentations left in the carpet by the furniture, there was no sign that the large square room had ever been occupied. Yet she faltered on the threshold, because the walls on either side of her appeared to be streaming with damp.

She ducked her head just far enough into the room to locate the switch, and fumbled the light on. The walls, which were papered in a discreet leafy pattern, betrayed no movement at all. She must have been seeing shadows of the rain, she told herself, even if the glimpse she had driven away could have been of bare wet bricks. She managed not to start as her father's breath stirred the hairs on the back of her neck. "Now," he said. "Show me anything in there that could frighten a child half your age, let alone a big girl such as you're supposed to be."

Amy switched out the light. The walls began to shift at once, shadows appearing to soak the paper off, though not yet exposing the brick. "Are you going to show me?" her father said, crowding her into the room.

It felt colder than she liked—as cold as a room composed of bare wet bricks would feel. "I can't," she blurted.

"Of course you can't. I could have predicted as much. Have you seen enough?"

"Yes, oh yes."

"Come along, then." When he stepped back she felt liberated until she saw that he was heading not for the outer corridor but for the main room. He must have thought she was dawdling as she trailed after him, because he threw open the door with some impatience as she arrived beside him. "Well?" he said.

The chill of the crawling walls reached for her. Since the room was larger, it felt colder than the bedroom had, and was darker. "Same thing," she told him.

"Put on the light so you're sure."

Amy clenched her fists and forced herself across the threshold. She punched the switch, and the light seemed to inch the walls back as well as renewing their paper. For the instant between her finding the switch and the blaze of illumination the space in front of her had felt constricted, as if it had been divided into more than one room. Her father was staring into it with a pained expression, eyebrows high. "Satisfied?" he said.

"Nothing to see."

"That's satisfactory, isn't it? Or were you hoping for the reverse?" When she didn't answer he sidled past her and switched out the light in the room. "Please don't turn destructive because you can't win me over. You might have broken that switch. Next time use a little restraint, if you don't mind."

Amy might have pointed out that she was restraining herself more than a little, except that arguing would delay her escape from the apartment. She retreated along the hall while he shut the three doors he'd opened. "That's it, go on," he said.

She'd passed the door to the windowless room when he called "Not out. Don't try on your cleverness. It's time it was your turn again, otherwise I shall be bound to doubt you're cured."

He wanted her to open the last door. Amy halted closer to it than to the corridor. It was almost within her arm's length, which was why she pressed her arms against her sides. As she'd come to a stop, arrested less by her father's words than by her sense of how unreasonable they were, she'd heard movement inside the windowless room.

Not long before they'd taken up residence in Nazarill, she'd encountered a mouse in their old kitchen. She'd heard it in the dark and had switched on the light in time to glimpse it scurrying into the wall. Now she'd overheard a noise like the one in the kitchen—the sound of something which had been discovered in the dark and which was preparing itself—but its source was audibly much bigger. She dragged her gaze away from the door to see how her father had reacted, and found he was squeezing his lips together, turning them the colour of the exterior of Nazarill. He opened them only to say "What are you waiting for?"

"Didn't you hear?"

"I heard nothing. There is nothing, you keep saying so." Without warning he stalked at her, so violently that she shrank back. "Don't you dare leave this apartment," he said. "Stand here."

He'd halted opposite the unopened room, and looked ready to shove past her so as to slam the outer door. At least while she could see the corridor she was able to remind herself that someone might come home at any moment, when she wouldn't be alone with her father and his single-mindedness. She went reluctantly to stand beside him, but that was the most she could do. When he jabbed a hand at the doorknob she dug the knuckles of her fists into her hips. "Deal with it for the Lord's sake," he said. "It's only a door."

"Then you open it."

She hadn't said three words before she wished she hadn't even thought them. Her father glowered at her, then he jerked forward. She was afraid he meant to capture one of her hands and use it to turn the doorknob, but instead he grabbed that himself. There was silence beyond the tall wooden slab—a waiting silence. As he twisted the knob and thrust the door inward a dead smell crept out of the room, and Amy flinched against a panel of the hall. Then she gasped, and her father swung around to glare at her. "What the devil is it now?"

She couldn't speak—couldn't move. The back of her right hand had touched the wall, and felt not wood but cold bare brick. That was why she had gasped and stumbled away from the wall, but it wasn't why she was paralysed now. The dim walls of the windowless room were peeling and patchy with moisture, and so was the face of the figure that had reared up beneath the unlit bulb.

It was taller than her father, and thinner than anything except bones could be. Through a gap in the rags which might be the remains of its skin she glimpsed a shrivelled slit which meant it had been a woman. A mass that looked composed as much of cobwebs as of hair dangled from its brownish piebald scalp. Its left eye glittered, or at least the contents of the socket did, before flying round the head to the other eye. Even if the figure couldn't see Amy, she could tell it was aware of her, because its right arm wavered up to gesture at its face.

The arm was appallingly long. One finger wagged at the cracked brow, where it might have been describing a cross or some less angular sign. Perhaps Amy would know when it spoke, because a blackened object was starting to protrude between the lipless teeth. Then the jaw fell open against the stringy throat, miming a laugh or else a scream as soundless and as desperate, and the object tumbled out to crawl between two exposed ribs.

Amy's father was scrutinising her face and muttering with dissatisfaction. All at once he raised his voice as though to penetrate some barrier between them. "Don't put yourself out. Don't say a word if it's too much of an effort to speak to your own father." He sucked in air, and she thought he'd become conscious of the smell from the room behind him until she saw he was replenishing his breath. She was struggling to utter a sound, even if it was only a cry, when he turned away from her and poked a hand into the room.

He was leaning through the doorway when the light came on. Amy saw the eyeless figure with the yawning withered mouth fling up its impossibly long arm. It was more than one arm, she realised as the other brandished the torn stump of its elbow. The hand at the end of the composite limb collided with the light-bulb, and the light vanished amid a muffled tinkling of glass. Darkness filled the room as if the glistening walls had exuded it, and the figure scuttled to the corner farthest from the door. The next moment it had gone through the wall which the apartment shared with its neighbour—gone through a door where no door should be.

Amy's father was still confronting the room. His shoulders had writhed and hunched themselves up, but otherwise he hadn't moved. She couldn't see his face. She was wondering whether to touch him or otherwise remind him of her presence—wondering how hysterically he might react if she did—when he spoke. "I trust you aren't proposing to make anything of that."

Amy thrust her lips, which felt stiff and swollen, open with her tongue, but even when she'd moistened them and rubbed them together she was able to produce only one word. "Of . . ."

"Of the damned light going pop. Shuffle in if you think there's anything you haven't seen. I'll even come in with you if you wish it."

Amy could think of no response. He'd looked straight into the room while the light was on and had seen no figure, no hand with half an arm in it, no partial yet animated face. She felt as though his inability to see had settled on her mind to crush her thoughts. When he leaned further through the doorway she shrank into herself, but he was only flipping the switch preparatory to closing the door. He turned to her, and determination took over his face. "Let's be shaking a leg," he said, and dug in his pocket. "We're going to look in every room down here."

14

SEEN FROM THE OUTSIDE

Sheffield Central Library was the grey of a wide expanse of sunlit fog. As Oswald came up from the subway under Arundel Gate, several dozen little girls in uniforms of almost that grey were drawn up outside the library by two nuns to be lectured by the bulkier of them. Buses of various colours and sizes went rumbling over the subway, which lent them its hollow amplification, so that Oswald wondered how the soft Irish voice was making itself heard. She had the respect of the children, of course, a respect founded on faith in God. As the two foremost girls held open the doors for their classmates to file into the library in pairs while the nuns stamped their feet in unison to control the pace of the march, he strolled towards the Housall office, thinking and deciding. He'd taken only a few paces when a voice detained him.

He had just passed a house with a doorway whose arch resembled rays of flame turned stony and with windows surmounted by symbols altogether too occult for his taste, not least a sun with eight spidery rays. He'd thought someone had left a sack of rubbish outside to be carted away, but now he saw it wasn't the chill darting wind that had made the bundle stir. The bundle raised a head capped with a black woollen lump and produced a face which looked resigned to its straggles of discoloured hair and its sagging yellowish porous skin. "Care in the community," she repeated in a voice that was Oswald's only reason to assume her to be female, and gave a nod which shook her cheeks at the plastic cup beside the blanket he'd taken for a sack.

His hand went to his pocket, where one fingertip poked through the ring that bore the keys to the ground floor of Nazarill. By the time he'd shaken off the ring he'd had a chance to reflect. "That's an organisation for which you're collecting, is it?"

She nodded energetically three times and then shook her head thrice with just as much vigour. That done, she lowered her hairy chin onto the blanket, from which she disentangled one fat-veined hand to point across the windswept flagstones. "I went there."

The last schoolgirls were being shepherded through the doors by the hinder nun, and Oswald couldn't tell if the woman was referring to the library or the school. "Threw us out, they did," she said, apparently not about either.

"I wasn't refusing to help you," said Oswald, finding some change in his pocket. "Just because one organisation has let you down doesn't mean you can't see if another may do you some good, don't you think?"

She crossed her hands over her chest to clutch at the edges of the blanket as if she'd begun to suspect he might try to snatch it. "Who are you? Where are you from?"

"I'm nothing to do with it. I mean, what I am isn't, what I do. I was just thinking you might see if one of the churches could sort you out something."

The woman turned her eyes down until the pupils were almost hidden by the lower lids, and appeared to be addressing some concealed part of herself. "He's one all right. If it's not nurses trying to dig in your head it's the God lot, and the worst kind are both."

"Excuse me, madam, but I sell insurance."

She jerked her head up, slamming it against the house wall with a thud whose softness Oswald fervently hoped belonged to her cap, and began to shout with her eyes shut. "He wants to sell me a policy. Can I get some home insurance on my blanket? This on top of my nut, does it count as a roof?"

"I didn't mean to say, I didn't say— Please, madam, for your own good. You'll be getting someone called if you carry on like that." As his attempts to calm her only provoked her to grow louder and more incoherent, Oswald started to panic. He dragged his hand out of his pocket and dropped the contents in the cup—three pound coins, much more than he'd thought he was donating. He stepped back before he could be tempted to retrieve them while her eyes were shut, and waited until she had to pause for breath. "I pray I've been some use to you," he said, and hurried away as she protruded one carpet-slippered foot to hook the cup.

He didn't think he had been—not in the right way. "Charity begins at home," he reminded himself, and wasn't aware of having spoken aloud until a woman wheeling a toddler protected from the world by a plastic shield on the front of the push-chair glanced sharply at him. He dodged around several corners, beyond each of which the wind renewed its chill, and past a cathedral some centuries less mediaeval than it appeared at first sight. By then the rumble of traffic behind had made way for its twin ahead on Fargate.

The Housall office was there, beneath a gargoyle whose grimace appeared to be propped open with a rusty pipe. Silver letters spelled HOUSALL—PROPERTIES FOR SALE along the wide plate-glass window, through which he saw, amid the photographs strung up to catch the passing eye, the front of Nazarill. He remembered the shadowy afternoon when Dominic Metcalf had taken the picture of Nazarill and all its tenants. Now the lawn was deserted even by the oak, and for a moment Oswald felt disoriented, unable to imagine when the building could have been photographed. Arkwright must have snapped it during his last visit, he thought as he let himself into the office.

At the far side of an expanse of carpet as green and as springy as moss, the receptionist lifted her head to examine him. With her black polo-neck concealing her throat, her hair confined so severely to the upper reaches of her head that she might as well have been wearing a glossy black hat, not to mention the sharpness of her chin and cheekbones and the overstatement of her pencilled eyebrows, she looked as fearsome as ever. "Ah, Mr. Yes," she commenced by apparently naming him. "You'll have the keys."

"That's why I'm here." Oswald reached in the pocket he'd emptied of coins and ventured across the room. Since she didn't extend a hand for the keys he laid them on her impeccably white desk, where she separated them with a fingernail to check they were still six. "Thank you," she said, or at least the end of it, which made him feel so dismissed that he blurted "Nobody wants a word."

She looked unprepared to hear the question he intended. "Mr. Arkwright," he said.

"I knew whom you meant." She gazed at him as though to impress her grammar on him. If he could live with Amy's looks, he thought, a receptionist's eyes couldn't daunt him. After not so very many seconds as measured by a timepiece she reached for the switchboard, which it was his impression she regarded more like a set of servants' bells. At that moment the door beside her opened. "Save your power," said Oswald. "Here he is."

It was indeed Arkwright, his blond scalp as flat and clean as his long smooth cheeks and square chin. "If you're happy I'm happy," he was assuring a middle-aged couple while they buttoned up overcoats that looked even heavier than the carpet. "Every time I find someone a home I feel that's another tick in my personal book." He saw them to the door, and having waved them through it, turned to Oswald. "Mr. Priestley, not even a day later. Good to know there are still some folk who can be relied on. Step through a minute."

Having preceded him into the office full of twelve desks, each in a three-sided cubicle whose backs joined down the middle of the long room, Oswald said "Someone for us?"

"Second on the, ah, you remember. For who is that?"

Oswald lowered himself onto a leather chair which seemed to have been holding its breath and waited while Arkwright sat, driving a gasp out of his own chair. "The couple you showed out, I wondered if they might be for our ground floor."

"They're moving up from apartments. First house at their age, would you believe, and just married into the bargain."

Oswald remembered the day he and Heather had chosen their only house—remembered sitting hand in hand with her before such a desk. The memory of her squeezing his hand as they'd said almost in unison that they'd decided on their home caused his stomach to draw into itself. She'd gone, he thought, and so he had to be two people for Amy, as strong and as wise as two and if necessary as impervious to argument. This impressed him as so crucial to fix in his mind that it took a throat-clearing from Arkwright, followed by more of a cough, to remind him where he was. "Sorry," he said, and when that proved insufficient "Sorry?"

"Were you going to give me your report? About yesterday's whatever you would call it. Yesterday's experiment."

"It worked. I'll be making sure it did."

"That's reassuring to hear. Anything more I can pass on to my boss? Any details?"

"No less than I promised. We went through every room, and there was nothing to see."

"That's what your daughter says, there was nothing."

"Exactly. I asked her and she did."

"And meant it."

"Well, you know how they are at her age. I expect they're all the same. If you ask them for an answer they behave as if you're forcing it into their mouths. But as I say, I had her answer. Twice, to be certain."

"You'll know if that's enough, obviously, being her father."

"She's aware she has done wrong, that's the main thing."

"If you say so, Mr. Priestley."

Oswald felt rebuked for not having done enough. Perhaps he hadn't yet, but surely it was up to Arkwright to help rather than simply disapprove. "I'm presuming you don't know of anything that could start her off again," Oswald said.

"I'm not sure I understand."

"I think she's clear how angry I would be if she tried to turn up anything more to make a fuss about. Old bits of history, say. You and I would know they're nothing more than that, but I was wondering if anyone who might have heard her on the radio could have reason to think otherwise, if there might be anything they would be able to tell her."

"I can't foresee anybody saying anything."

"Just to clarify the situation, that means there's nothing to know, does it? You saw how her mind works. There's nothing she could make into more than there was in the first place."

"That's correct. I was thinking along your lines myself after I met her, so I checked back. I don't think even your daughter—no, I don't see how she could when it was so long ago. All the same, perhaps you shouldn't tell her."

"I hope I may be the judge of that."

"Of course, no question. I wasn't trying— We're talking hundreds of years back. Two hundred at least, going on for three."

"You don't need to persuade me that's ancient history. Tell me straight, man to man."

Arkwright sat forward on his chair, which had already given vent to an inadvertent exhalation. "How much do you actually know about Nazarill?"

"That it's my home and my daughter's."

"Good man. Before that, though, perhaps you've heard it had been offices in the Victorian era. And before them, nothing much."

"It must have been something, surely."

"Oh, right enough. Not for a while, I meant. For a long while there was just the shell of the place. There'd been a fire, you see."

Oswald supposed he did, but felt he ought to see more or was expected to. "All right, a fire. I don't think she can make much of that."

"Just of a fire, I shouldn't think anyone could."

"You sound as if there was more to it."

"Well—yes. What happens more often than not when there's a fire in a property, though let me assure you there's never been a single one to my knowledge in any property we've sold."

"You mean someone died."

"That's the size of it. To be totally accurate, not that it can make any difference so long after, I'm sure you'll agree, a few."

"What do you call a few?"

"I couldn't tell you that in terms of numbers. Quite a few, my understanding is. As far as I can make out, all the inmates and the staff."

"All the . . ."

"Of the hospital. Not a hospital as we'd use the term, you understand, not back then. I expect we'd hardly believe how unsafe some of those places were with nobody going round to check, nobody such as yourself trying to see they were safe."

"Some things have improved." Oswald's thoughts hesitated momentarily over that, but it wasn't the issue he felt bound to raise. "Inmates was the word you used, wasn't it? I'm only asking so I'll be prepared in case it somehow gets to my daughter, but what sort of place are we discussing?"

"I don't know what they would have called it back then but, you know, the closest they'd have come to an institution."

"A mental hospital."

"That's the sort of area, only maybe you're aware they used to treat them nothing like we treat people with a mental history today."

"Too many of them are wandering the streets instead of being looked after."

"I'll give you that. Maybe they weren't treated badly at Nazarill. They must have got out of hand to finish with, but I don't suppose some of them needed anything we'd regard as an excuse to set the place on fire."

"That's what you think happened, or you know?"

"That's as much of a story as my nephew's fiancee could find in the vaults at the paper where she works."

"It wouldn't be easy to unearth."

"It wasn't. The nephew says I owe them each a bottle of good plonk. Oh, I follow," Arkwright said, lowering his eyebrows to demonstrate his comprehension. "The files aren't on computer, they're on microfiche. Unless someone knew what they were after and how to look, they'd never find it while they had breath."

"It can't be common knowledge, this old story."

"Nothing like. I don't mind telling you we hadn't so much as a sniff of it when we took over the property."

"I hope it would have made no difference if you had."

"You've my word on that," Arkwright said, and gazed at Oswald.

"You've mine that my daughter won't learn about any of this from me."

"Thank you for that."

"And supposing anyone who knew of it had heard her, they'd have contacted her by now if they were going to, wouldn't they?"

"You'd think so."

"Not that I can imagine any reason why they should."

"I'm sure there's not, but if by any remote chance we're both wrong, perhaps I can ask you to do your utmost to head off any trouble."

"Here's my hand."

Arkwright considered it before accepting it, having stood up. Perhaps Oswald's choice of words had thrown him, though Oswald didn't think them too old-fashioned. "Thank you for stopping by," Arkwright said to end a quick loose handshake, "and for all your efforts."

"The least I could do."

Arkwright paused as if he thought the words were truer than intended. "I know we can rely on you to take any action you find necessary," he said, and sidled from between his desk and the partition. "After all, you won't be doing it only for us."

"Appreciated," Oswald said, and shook hands again, gripping Arkwright's until it responded with equal firmness, which felt as though Arkwright was either satisfied for the moment or exhorting him to do more. Oswald didn't need to be exhorted. Perhaps he'd hoped the meeting would convince him otherwise, but he already knew he hadn't done enough.

As he let himself out of the Housall office, the wind struck him in the face and thrust its chill inside his collar. Until he pulled himself together he felt as cold as he imagined the woman in the blanket must feel. At least he knew he wasn't quite alone. He'd overheard enough to be aware that someone had insights into Amy that might help him—her religious teacher.

He turned to breast the wind, and the photograph of a deserted Nazarill came into view. Whatever Amy might invent about the place would be preferable to her discovering that it had once, no matter how many years ago, been an asylum. How could he have been so weak that he'd allowed her to annoy him into telling her the truth about her grandmother before he was sure it was time for her to know? It wasn't Nazarill that was at fault, it was himself.

The wind urged him round the corners to the house carved with secret symbols. The woman in the blanket had gone, but he had far too little difficulty in remembering her eyes, locked into themselves and glistening with a sheen of fear. Arkwright's revelations had made him anxious to see Amy, to reassure himself she was all right or at the very least no worse. He hurried through the subway, which hooted like a huge stone owl as a racing ambulance halted the traffic, and up to the car park.

The traffic was as headlong as ever by the time he drove under the barrier that had raised itself in a mechanical salute. Once he succeeded in joining the rush it carried him towards the edge of Sheffield. Soon he caught sight of girls in the dark red which Amy resented still having to wear. As he steered the Austin into the side street the last few ran across the schoolyard into the building which appeared to have lent their uniform its colour. Rather than use the parking area within the grounds he drove until the wall hid him from the school.

He didn't care if Amy saw him, for all the trouble that might cause, but he wanted to observe her before she knew she was being observed. He walked to the point where the wall became railings, through which he saw a schoolmistress appear in Amy's classroom and begin to address the girls seated invisibly beneath the tall windows. The gale hastened him into the yard, raising his hood as it did.

The school secretary, a long-faced woman with a great deal of red hair tugged back from her high forehead and tied at the nape of her neck, came to her window inside the panelled lobby. "Mr. Priestley. Back so soon?"

"Can't get rid of me."

"Is anything . . ."

"I wanted a chat about Amy's religious progress. I didn't have a chance last time to speak to Mrs. Kelly, is it not?"

"She'll be marking in the staffroom. Along the corridor from Miss Sadler's office. You know the way."

Oswald did: it led past Amy's classroom. The sound of a choir rehearsing in a hall floated to meet him. The pure young voices sang "Amazing Grace" as he passed rooms full of girls working, their faces upturned to their teacher or lowered to their books. The fire doors next to Amy's classroom bumped shut behind him, and three more paces gave him a view of her class through the glass half of the door. He found her at once, and his innards grew cold and hollow.

She was seated two rows back, her head bent over an exercise book—her cropped head shorn of the hair Heather had loved to brush. It looked wholly inappropriate among her classmates, as if she had strayed in from some quite different place. As he saw her pen speed across the page, he couldn't help wondering if this was a show she was putting on for the schoolmistress. The fire doors shuddered as the wind insinuated itself into the building, and he was suddenly afraid she would glance up at him—afraid not of being seen but of how her eyes might look. He retreated to the opposite wall and dodged past the room before even the teacher could notice him.

Mrs. Kelly was watching him from the next classroom. She opened the door at once and raised her eyebrows as high as they would go. "May I help you?"

"I was on my way to see you. I apologise for not making an appointment, but I found myself in the vicinity."

Her face hadn't relaxed when she eventually said "You're Amy Priestley's father."

"I hope that's a compliment."

The desperate hope was close to a prayer, and the teacher turned away from it. "If you'll close the door," she said, limping to her desk piled with exercise books, "we won't be disturbed."

Oswald eased the door shut and leaned against the desk in front of her. When it emitted a sharp creak Mrs. Kelly frowned at it and him. "Do sit down if you wish."

Oswald managed by protruding one leg into the aisle. Having watched his struggles to arrange himself, Mrs. Kelly said "If I may say so, Mr. Priestley, you looked worried."

Her voice echoed in the empty room. He thought it capable of penetrating the wall, and spoke low to drop her the hint. "Do you think I should be?"

"Frankly, yes."

Oswald was shocked to discover that deep down he'd been willing her not to say so—shocked by his own weakness. "Please tell me your thoughts," he said, feeling like a not especially able but cooperative pupil. "I want to hear."

"I sense you're of the mind I am, Mr. Priestley. Girls of that age need firm direction, and we've been charged with providing it."

"That's my belief."

"Most especially where unhealthy influences are involved."

"Do you mean any in particular?" he said, and heard himself sounding worse than stupid—dishonest, reluctant to admit to his own knowledge. "I heard the tail end of you talking to her yesterday. That's why I'm here, to find out what you meant."

"I should have hoped you would know."

"I'm sure I do, but to hear someone else who cares about her put it into words . . ."

"I was telling her that some of her interests seem not just unhealthy, unholy. I wonder if you know how far that's gone."

"You mean that ghost business. It's been nipped. I took her where she claimed she saw it and showed her there never was anything."

"So she believed there was."

"She never said so at the time. She wasn't much past half her age, you understand, the fairy-tale age. Maybe she dreamed it and thought she remembered it, but now she's come round to seeing she couldn't have."

"I suppose that must count for something."

"You don't think much."

Oswald saw at once he should have put a preposition in there, but apparently that wasn't the source of her dissatisfaction. "I'm afraid I think if she was able to believe it at all she must be well on her way down the wrong path, so."

Once again Oswald found himself wishing she'd said the opposite. "Have you any suggestions?" he demanded with a roughness aimed entirely at himself.

"I'll tell you something now I've told very few people."

"Well, thank you," Oswald said before wondering if it would turn out to be an occasion for gratitude. "What would that be?"

"When I was their age," said Mrs. Kelly, raising her eyebrows to indicate the classroom behind him, "I came under the spell of somebody unsuitable. A boy, it was."

Unsure how much surprise he was required to express, Oswald nodded. "Ah."

"And my parents dealt with it as you did in those days."

"Ah hah. How was that?"

"I was locked in my room until I swore on the Bible never to go anywhere near him again."

"That's certainly a thought."

Perhaps Mrs. Kelly felt he was taking her self-revelation too lightly; she pursed her wrinkled lips, rendering them virtually colourless. "Maybe our rights aren't what they were, but can't you keep her home at night until you see a change?"

"I don't see why not."

"Then I should, Mr. Priestley, before it's too late."

This sounded to Oswald like a welcome release. He was painfully unbending from behind the desk, having scraped the tops of his thighs on its underside, when he heard a girl's voice raised in argument behind him. "Is that . . ."

"I think it might very possibly be."

If Amy was questioning, perhaps that wasn't objectionable in itself, but the shrill aggressiveness of the voice beyond the wall dismayed him. It took him a few seconds to realise that she would be looking up from her desk. "Is there another way out I could use?"

"Another?" said the teacher, and with some disbelief "Oh, I see."

"I don't want to begin by handing her an excuse to flounce out when she comes home."

Mrs. Kelly let that hover for an uncomfortable length of time. At last she said "If you slip along by Miss Sadler's room you can sneak out of our door."

Oswald thanked her with, he hoped, sufficient vigour to encompass the entire interview, and stole into the corridor. A draught helped him close the classroom door with more of a slam than he intended. Once in the passage reserved for the staff he felt somewhat less panicked, but hurried to the imposing door opposite Miss Sadler's office. As he dodged around the far side of the school from Amy's classroom and past a succession of glassed-in voices, the wind kept leaping in his face.

He shut himself into the Austin and wound his window tight to exclude a thin chill blade of air. He had the impression that he'd learned all that he needed to know if he could only piece it together, but no thought seemed able to pass through his mind before a bell tuned to the wind made itself audible, heralding the afternoon break at the school and sending him away as fast as he could start the car.

On the motorway gusts of wind did their best to force him out of whichever lane he was struggling to follow. At the exit he encountered a gale which for quite a few seconds felt capable of shoving him back. It kept relenting and then ambushing him while he clung to the steering-wheel and drove across the moor. Then Partington heaved into view ahead, and his foot faltered on the accelerator.

The car had been struck by a gust so fierce it shook the windscreen, but that wasn't why he felt suddenly uncertain. Nazarill had risen above the huddled streets as though the town was thrusting it out, and against all his expectations the sight made him wonder if bringing Amy to live there had been a mistake. Now that he'd told her of her heredity, how might she feel if, despite the efforts he would make to prevent it, she discovered that Nazarill had once been an asylum?

The car shivered almost to a halt, and he grabbed the gear-lever. He jerked it through its positions, describing some kind of a cross, and having descended to first gear, trod on the accelerator. For the moment there seemed to be nowhere to go except forward into the forbidding wind. He couldn't just move himself and Amy out of Nazarill, not least because that would be to go back on promises he'd at the very least implied to the Housall representative. But wasn't Amy's welfare more important than anything else?

The road dipped and then soared to find the town, which brandished its speed-limit disc at the car. The first houses cut off not only his view of Nazarill but also, it seemed, his ability to reach a decision. He turned the Austin along Moor View, where a slate from a cottage roof lay shattered in the middle of the road. Just as one of his wheels crunched a slate fragment, Nazarill reappeared at the end of the lane. Instantly he knew without question that he had been wrong.

The windscreen trembled again as the car emerged onto Nazareth Row, but the railings in front of Nazarill stood firm. There was no longer any oak to bow and thrash and fling its leaves about; perhaps that was why the grounds appeared so still. When he drove onto the gravel the wind dropped as though the building had breathed it in. Once he'd found his plot in the car park, a new wind raised his hood for him while ushering him around the corner. He slid his key into the lock and took refuge in Nazarill.

Warmth and silence and light as soft as the glow of candles in a church were there for him, bringing him immediate relief from any doubts he might harbour. This was his and Amy's home, and he need only find a way to make her feel as he was feeling. Praying ought to help, and he began to murmur to himself as he climbed the stairs. He met nobody to interrupt him en route to his door. Beyond it the great eyes of the framed pictures looked awed by his willingness to be shown the right path. He left the lights off and moved through the dimming rooms, eventually falling to his knees at the foot of the bed. "Please help me keep her here. I know it's the best place for her. I thought it mightn't be, but I see now I was confused. Only if she should find out it used to be what we know it was, please let me think what to do."

He sensed the cold stone beneath the warmth of Nazarill. Together they suggested a life held in balance. He thought he could detect truth gathering like the darkness; soon it would be clear to him. But there was still a residue of light in the sky, and he was praying drowsily and patiently, when the phone rang.

He dug his elbows into the mattress to lever himself to his feet and ran to grab the receiver. "Priestley."

"Dad."

"Yes, Amy. What do you want?" said Oswald, and immediately knew.

"One of my friends wants me to stay at hers tonight so we can do our homework together."

Not only had he been right, but he was sure he heard untruth in her attempt to sound casual. He closed his fist on the receiver, its plastic stem as thin as her wrist when he had lifted her to Nazarill. "I think not. Let your friend come home with you."

"But she lives here in Sheffield."

"All the more reason for you not to stay with her." As Oswald heard the plastic crack he relaxed his grip. He didn't need to be violent, just firm. "Come home now, please. Dinner will be waiting, and so will I," he said, and cut her off.

15

THE WHISPER OF THE PAST

Halfway through the first lesson of that afternoon the English mistress said "Miss Priestley?"

Amy was gazing over the thoughts she'd written about illusions in *Macbeth,* a dagger and Banquo's ghost and the blood on the hands of, as she'd scribbled it, Mrs. Big Mac. Her attention had been hovering somewhere between the blackboard and a similarly flattened image of Carolyn Henderson's hair piled up to expose the freckly nape of her neck above her broad shoulders at the desk in front. "Yes, Miss Burd," Amy said.

"Can I be of any help?"

She'd raised her head enough to halve her chins and opened her mouth until it was almost as round as her face, all of which signified that the question wasn't just an offer, more the threat of a rebuke. "I was thinking about the witches," said Amy.

"Do tell."

"They make him see stuff, don't they? They get into his mind and then he starts not knowing what's real and acting mad."

"I take it we're referring to the weird sisters and the way Macbeth is prompted by the supernatural."

"Them, yes."

"Interesting thoughts, best developed in a different essay, perhaps on the question of how much the characters use predestination as an excuse for what they do."

Until Amy had spoken she hadn't known she had the thoughts;

they didn't represent what she'd been thinking. Some doubt must have escaped onto her face, because the teacher said "You disagree?"

"I'll save it if you say." Amy thought that was sufficiently agreeable, but Miss Burd looked as though she hadn't heard an answer. All Amy could produce now was the truth. "I'm still thinking about witches."

"By all means speak up if it's an insight the rest of us should have."

"Shouldn't think so," Amy said, and saw that wouldn't be enough. "I think there used to be some where I live."

"I've an unhappy suspicion you aren't talking about insight."

"I only just heard about them," Amy protested. "The Partington Witches. They're supposed to have used to go up on the hill where I'm living at the moment. Have you heard of them?"

"I'm quite relieved to say I haven't. It's hardly my area of—"

Amy felt close to the panic she was trying to fend off. For a moment the dark in which she'd lain awake until she'd switched her light on seemed to have entered the classroom. She half rose in the trap formed by her desk and its seat, and twisted round. "How about any of you?"

Most of her classmates shook their heads and gave her varieties of smile, some of these amused or worse. There was silence until Miss Burd cleared her throat at the pitch of chalk on a blackboard. "Miss Priestley."

Amy subsided behind her desk. "Sorry," she mumbled.

"I was about to say that the person to consult is presumably Mr. Berrystone."

"I suppose."

"So if you're content with that, perhaps we can return to our theme for today."

Amy didn't know how she could have felt less content, not least because the history master was the teacher she most disliked. She bent her head to her work to hide her feelings, and when she could think of nothing further to write, began to lengthen all the esses. The door of the adjoining classroom slammed, and she was touched by a draught as though the secret stony cold of Nazarill had come to find her. The night, far too imminent in any case, lurched nearer. She had to discover all she could, in the hope that she would learn something even her father would have to take notice of, and so at the end of the English lesson she went in search of the history master.

He was in the schoolyard, keeping an eye on the girls. His expression, which opined that he was watching a spectacle staged for his benefit, almost made her turn away without approaching him. As he noticed her dawdling towards him he withdrew one hand from the pocket of his green suede jacket and fingered the point of the beard that further sharpened his small neat face. "Yes," he said in the tone of responding to an offer which, although perhaps only in the circumstances, was acceptable. "Yes."

Amy hugged her breasts as the wind flapped the lapels of her blazer. "Miss Burd said I should see you."

"And here you are," he said with the unnecessariness that was one of his traits she particularly disliked. "I take it she said why."

"We were talking in class and she said you'd be the person to ask."

"As is frequently the case," he said without humour. "About."

The curtness of the word suggested he was patronising her question in advance, and only desperation made her blurt "Some witches there were supposed to be. The Partington Witches."

"That's your territory, is it not? That's where we have you from."

"Partington."

"That cosy retreat," he agreed, and pinched his beard as a wind set it bristling. "Well, my winged colleague has me right. I do know something about them."

"What?"

"All there is to know, I dare say."

Amy was silent, suspecting this to be the preamble to a poor, hence unbearable, joke. At last she said "Such as . . ."

"Thirteen individuals whom the people of your village when it was half its size didn't like to encounter after dark, especially on some nights of the year."

"Why, what did they do?"

"Some, probably no more than concoct old remedies. But some had a reputation for making anybody who crossed them ill with just a look. What they did when they all gathered together, well, how could anyone know? If the villagers were so afraid of them, nobody would have risked spying on them, would they?"

That seemed to Amy much more logical than helpful. "So what happened to them, the witches?"

"Little enough by the standards of the day. One or two may have been strung up from a convenient tree, and the rest seem to have taken the hint and made themselves scarce. You should appreciate all this was supposedly occurring after the official witch-hunts had been ended and something slightly more like sanity was creeping into fashion."

It was suddenly apparent to her that the emotion he experienced while surveying either history or the present was resignation fending off despair, not that she felt better for the insight. "That can't be all," she protested. "Someone must know more than that."

"You're assuming there's more to learn and not less."

"How can there be less?"

"Perhaps your witches never existed. I only heard about them from a grandmother who was half past knowing what she was saying. Perhaps they were no more than a story to frighten small children, the kind of tale I hear you're good at."

His words let Nazarill at her. She might as well have been back there, trailing after her father through the downstairs rooms, terrified of what else she might see and yet willing him to be confronted by some sight he would be unable to deny. Once she'd heard a series of effortful breaths beyond a door he was about to open, noises suggestive of a throat trying to clear itself of some of itself. Once she and her father had been preceded through an apartment by a shuffling which had changed in ways that made her think the feet had been wearing themselves closer to the bone with every step. She could tell he'd heard none of this, nor the sound as he'd switched on a light in a room of someone scuttling away on too few limbs, withdrawing spiderlike out of sight through an exit where none was visible. The denizens of Nazarill had been hiding themselves for the moment, so that by the end of her enforced tour so much anger and frustration had been mingled with her fear that her sarcasm had sounded all too indistinguishable from the truth as she'd declared there had been nothing, oh no, nothing even remotely wrong. She'd wanted her father to hear how little she meant it, but she had failed to take into account his need to believe that she did.

And now Mr. Berrystone had elected himself spokesman for her father—for almost everyone she knew. "Have a care," he said. "Watch out or you'll finish up frightening yourself."

Rather than respond as she thought he deserved, she was turning away quickly when he said "Before you rejoin your peers, some words along the lines of *thank* you, Mr. Berrystone, for racking your brains might seem in order."

"Is that what you did?" she was about to retort when she saw in his eyes that he had. "Thank you for telling me what you knew," she said, but any sincerity she intended was swamped by her realisation that now she was unable to avoid remembering last night, she couldn't bear the prospect of going home.

She wandered through the crowded windswept schoolyard until she located a friend who would surely be able to help. "Lorna, is your Cathy back at university?"

"Went on Monday. I've got the bathroom for all the hours I want again."

"Is her room spare?"

"Till Easter. Come and stay soon if you like."

"How about tonight?"

"I don't expect they'll mind. They won't have to, will they? Is it your dad, why you want to stay?"

"It's just something I have to work out," Amy said awkwardly, wondering how she would deal with going home tomorrow. Time enough to decide that when tomorrow came, she thought, only to spend the afternoon trying. At last school was over, and she was on her way to Lorna's, stopping at a phone box by the school to call in case her father was at home.

The bell began to pulse as though the heart of Nazarill was stuttering into life, and she had the sudden awful thought that it wouldn't be her father who answered. Then his voice said "Priestley."

"Dad," she said with more warmth than she had for a while.

"Yes, Amy. What do you want?"

Amy pressed a knee against the door, which she'd already closed firmly to keep out the wind, so that Lorna wouldn't overhear her lying. "One of my friends wants me to stay at hers tonight so we can do our homework together."

"I think not. Let your friend come home with you."

His tone hadn't been particularly welcoming to start with, and now it was sharp and chill as the wind that was probing beneath the door. "But she lives here in Sheffield," Amy said, shivering.

"All the more reason for you not to stay with her. Come home now, please. Dinner will be waiting, and so will I," he said, and left her with a hollow droning that merged with the moan of the wind around the booth.

More would be waiting than he knew. She didn't have to go home just because he said so; he wouldn't be able to find her until she returned to school. She snapped her purse shut and let it fall into her bag on the metal shelf by the phone, then she sucked in a breath which hurt her teeth, and heaved the bag wide open. She'd left the Bible in her room.

She'd fetched it during the worst of the night, not knowing whether she meant to search its margins for an explanation or to hold it as a defence against whatever might have been making its way through the dark of Nazarill. Eventually, in the midst of one of the dozes into which she'd been unable not to lapse, she had allowed the book to slide down the quilt onto the floor, which was presumably where it lay now.

She felt as if she'd tricked herself, or Nazarill had. The writing in the margins of the Bible was evidence that she couldn't risk leaving in Nazarill, even if she wasn't sure what danger it might be in. At least with her father waiting she wouldn't be alone when she went home. She stuffed the bag under her arm and heaved the shuddering door open. "You were long enough," Lorna complained, brushing her brick-red hair over both shoulders with her fingertips to clear her periodically spotty face. "Let's run. Listen to my teeth."

"Sorry about them," said Amy as her friend displayed their chattering. "And sorry, but I can't come after all."

"Why not?"

A harmless lie was less complicated than the truth. "My dad's not well. He's just got me."

"See you Monday, then," said Lorna, and dashed off.

Amy turned from the phone box in time to see the bus pull up, halted by Bettina or Deborah or Zoe, all of whom were flashing their passes at the driver. The next bus wasn't due for an hour, if then. She displayed her laminated rectangle containing herself from last year, a pressed specimen, and as the doors fluttered shut she levelled a glare at the three girls on the back seat before sitting diagonally opposite the driver.

The bus shook itself along the motorway and struggled onto the moor. Before long Amy couldn't ignore the sight of Nazarill squatting above the town. Ten minutes, and the building ducked behind the houses to await her while the vehicle entered Partington. "Here we are," Deborah advised Amy as a wind cold as stone flapped the doors open, and Zoe said even more helpfully "Home."

A wind sent the giggles of the trio and bits of their words after Amy up Moor View. Not much less than a gale, which felt as though Nazarill was drawing an inhumanly protracted icy breath, was carrying her forward. Under a sky crawling with darkness the lane resembled a corridor whose ceiling was unstable with damp. At its end the pale bulk of Nazarill forced the gap between the cottages wider with each involuntary step she took. She saw her destination waiting in its cage of railings, and remembered the day her father had made her look in the windows, and was dismayed to find she preferred the memory. At least back then nobody had helped the place to pretend it wasn't as she'd seen it, hollow and rotten and yet full of secret life.

It crowded the rest of her surroundings out of her vision as the gale marched her across Nazareth Row. As she stumbled onto the drive a railing rattled, then another, suggesting that eagerness to confine her was shaking the bars of the cage. Beneath the darkening sky the facade appeared to tremble with the imminence of its own light, which in a moment leapt on her, erasing her shadow from the gravel. She saw the ground-floor windows pinch themselves thinner against the glare, the better to watch her. Sawdust had begun to dance in a ring on the flattened patch where the roots of the oak used to be, scraps of bark raised themselves and crept over the grass, and she knew at once that if any witches had been hanged in Partington it would have been from the oak. Perhaps they had danced around it when they were alive—perhaps not only then. As her thoughts and impressions, no more under control than the dancing sawdust, teemed about her head, the gale hustled her to the steps of Nazarill.

As the livid stone reared above her and closed on the edges of her vision, the glass doors showed her the dim corridor pretending that the ground floor was deserted. Her chilled shivery fingers fumbled in her bag, only to leave her keys where they were. If she was admitted to Nazarill rather than letting herself in she mightn't feel quite so alone. She closed her fist to reduce its shaking and knuckled the doorbell.

The glass doors quivered as though Nazarill was preparing to open them itself. She was about to ring the bell a second time when the grille beside the twin columns of nine buttons emitted a hiss that turned into a cold thin version of her father's voice. "Amy."

"How did you know it was me?"

"You may be surprised what I know," he said in a tone she couldn't identify for the distortions of the microphone. "Come."

As the grille went dead the front doors buzzed, a sound that made her feel a trap had been sprung. She took a breath which the gale did its best to snatch from her and strained her hand towards the doors. Its palm had barely met the icy metal plaque of the lock when the doors yielded. The next moment she was fleeing through Nazarill.

She heard the wind falter, and the low tolling as the doors shut, and then she was surrounded by an unnatural silence invaded by the subdued thuds of her feet on the carpet, a noise she wished were either louder or not present, because the ground floor was no longer bothering to keep up any pretence for her. She could sense more rooms around her than the apartments were supposed to contain, an impression that made the corridor seem unbearably prolonged and rendered the already muffled illumination unequal to it. She thought she glimpsed the door beyond which the photographer had died beginning to creep open—she thought she heard a scrabbling at the doorknob. She hurled herself at the stairs and fell up them, bruising her knees, and was almost at the bend when she became aware that a large object was thumping slowly down towards it. As she reached out a hand to the wall for support and jerked her arm back for fear of how unlike their appearance the panels might feel, Donna Goudge appeared, lugging a suitcase.

The sight of her wasn't nearly as much of a relief as it ought to have been, especially since her husband was following her with more luggage. "Where are you going?" Amy said, too dismayed to care if she sounded childish.

"We're off for our dose of sun," said Donna with a smile sufficiently lopsided to be apologetic.

"How long for?"

"We won't be much more than a couple of weeks."

Amy might have asked her to be precise, but Dave Goudge was looking less than pleasantly surprised by the urgency of the questions. "Will you come and see my dad," she said to Donna in some desperation, "and talk to him?"

"What about, Amy?"

"What we talked about. You know."

"Remind me when we get back."

"Couldn't you now?"

"We have to be out of here. We haven't much time to the plane when we reach the airport. Don't worry, I won't forget you. I'll send you a card."

"You won't be able to say much on that."

"The rest will have to wait," said Donna, and more gently "Remember, things you only see can't hurt you."

Amy remembered the elongated arm putting out the light in the Roscommons' room. She watched the Goudges bump their luggage down the stairs, and called "Have a good. . . ." As Donna hefted her suitcase into the ground-floor corridor with no indication that she found the place daunting, Amy heard her murmur "I'll tell you about it when we're in the car."

That referred to Amy, who couldn't help feeling discussed like a patient who mustn't be allowed to realise her condition. She trudged upstairs, trying to be aware that each step put more distance between her and the ground floor, though as the Goudges left the building she felt a huge cold breath pursue her. She had just reached the top corridor when her father stepped out of the doorway at the far end. "You were long enough. What kept you?"

"Talking to Dave and Donna. Donna, anyway."

"And what did Mrs. Goudge have to say for herself this time?"

"They've gone away."

"What's the old saw about sinking ships? Except we aren't sunk by any means. That's been seen to."

Or were his words "being seen"? She had an unsettling impression that although his gaze was aimed at her, he was talking less to her than past her to an audience. His gaze sharpened as he said "In you trot. Don't loiter in the corridor. Dinner won't be long."

Amy closed the door behind her and tried to judge how much that excluded of her sense of Nazarill. When her father turned away from his continued scrutiny of her, she made herself lay one hand on the nearest panel of the wall. It felt as it looked: like wood. That might be moderately reassuring, but it couldn't change the whole of Nazarill. "I'll have something later," she said. "I'm not hungry now."

Her father pivoted in the kitchen doorway. His gaze was as oppressive as the rectangle of dark sky vacated by the branches of the oak. "I've cooked your favourite. All the vegetables you enthuse about are in it. There's nothing wrong with fasting to a purpose, but we don't want you starved."

"I'll have it another time. I expect I'll be eating with Rob."

"I think not."

The hand with which she'd touched the panel was suddenly cold and moist. "What's going to stop me?"

"I spoke to him earlier."

"So?" When that only produced a look as patiently triumphant as his answer she demanded "Saying what?"

"What was the burden of his message, do you mean?"

"Right, that kind of stuff."

"The usual. The standard formula. The ritual. And when I informed him that he couldn't because you weren't here, he exerted himself to vouchsafe that you won't see him tonight. I gather he has fallen in with the wishes of his family for once and is dining out to celebrate an unexpected visit by a distant relative."

Amy felt suffocated by so many superfluous words. "When did he call?"

"While you were in the process of returning to the bosom of your family."

All at once she was convinced that meant while she'd been talking on the stairs. He'd known she was in the building but hadn't asked Rob to hold on. She threw her bag on the nearest chair in the front room and grabbed the phone to poke Rob's number out of it with her fingernails. When it had trilled long enough for anyone who was in any part of his house to have had more than enough time to stroll to it she recalled the number, and having listened as long again, gave up. The instant she cradled the receiver, her father leaned his ostentatiously patient face around the kitchen door. "When you've taken the opportunity to calm yourself, perhaps we can be about our dining."

"I'm as calm as I'm going to be, and I already said I'm not hungry."

"Amy, for heaven's sake, child. You're making no sense to me. I don't think you know what you're saying, or you're saying it just to make a noise. First you were going to stay with a girl in Sheffield, and yet at the same time you proposed to eat with your friend who lives above the wall that's falling down."

"I'd have called him from Sheffield. He'd have come, or if he wouldn't, I don't care." She felt suffocated by her own words now. "I'm not eating, I told you. I'll be in my room."

"To cleanse it, I hope."

"Reading."

"May I ask what?"

"Would you believe a book?"

"That depends on its nature." His voice had grown as thin and cold as it had sounded through the grille. His gaze tried to hold her, but she shoved her door open and scraped the light-switch on. "I'll inform you when the meal is ready in case you change your mind," he said.

Amy's only answer was to close her door. She took off her uniform and dropped it on a pile of her schoolwork, feeling that the chaos of her room was some kind of a defence, some assertion of herself. She pulled on her holeyest jeans and her Clouds Like Dreams T-shirt, which bore a softer version of the portrait on her poster, and dug her notepad out from beneath the pile. Having retrieved the Bible together with the pencil that was nestling against it on the carpet, she sat on the bed. She was going to read the writing in the margins, however badly doing so made her head ache.

"—yet to use God's words as concealment for my own until the day comes for them to be read likens me in my own mind to the very wretches for one of which I am mistaken."

That took Amy over the page at last. As she scribbled on her pad she felt committed to a race between her understanding and whatever was waiting to happen in Nazarill. At least for the moment her head was light rather than constricted, and she'd begun to grasp the next words when her father's voice pressed itself against her door. "Do you remember this, Amy? *The Four Seasons* by Vivaldi. You used to like it as much as your mother did. You used to dance to it for her."

He must have been holding the remote control, because the music started at once. It had become the soundtrack of far too many films and advertisements. "I shall listen to it while I dine," her father said.

"I won't." Amy was wondering if it might have been composed close to the time of the writing in the margins. The notion that the anonymous writer could have heard the bright swift music as they wrote disturbed her, but suppose it helped her understand? She held the Bible so tight she smelled musty paper and turned it sideways.

"I must pray that God will understand. I shall supplicate forgiveness and to be returned to my room where my possessions render my world small. Merciful God, allow me to shut Thy welkin from my sight lest it burst my brain. Now must I make myself plain and terse to fit the space God has allotted me in His margin."

A clatter of cutlery and plates had joined the dance of music in the air. Her father was making all the noise he could; he might even be wafting a vegetarian aroma towards her door. She swallowed her saliva and turned the inverted Bible the right way up.

"Sick for a day. Thank God, now I have found space between the bricks to conceal my pencil. Yesterday, upon hearing Clay's approach I could devise no ruse other than to close it in my mouth as he looked in. God grant my sickness save me from their purging me!"

This was preceded by a cross, and followed by one—the writer's way of separating entries, Amy saw. The lower stretch of the second cross was fractionally shorter than that of the first. She omitted the crosses from her copy, instead starting a new paragraph.

"I am dressed and allowed into the grounds. At first I thought this was some new torment devised by my captors—God help me, I fear them more than I fear the wretches among whom I find myself numbered. But I am guided beneath a shade into the shelter of the spreading oak, whose aestival foliage masks the empyrean. There I may sit for hours, companied by this guard or that, for I alone of the women am let loose. Perchance the mockery of freedom which Clay accords me is merely my reward for pattering the Lord's Prayer to him, the which Hopkins would require as proof of their faith from those he hunted down, but I pray that this concession signifies the imminence of him to whom I must prove I am unfairly judged a wronghead."

All this occupied the margins of three pages, and was brought to an end by a cross whose upper bar was just shorter than the lower. The last word bothered Amy even more than the rest for some reason. She didn't realise how long she'd spent in poring over the word and transcribing the passage until she heard her father tramping into the kitchen to rattle objects and then dull their sound with water. The music fell silent in the middle of a phrase, and at once he knocked on her door. "I'm about to deal with some of my clients."

Amy pushed herself off the bed and stumbled, employing the

prickly lumps of her rudely awakened feet as best she could, to open the door. "Going out, you mean?"

He and the bulging eyes on the wall behind him stared at her. "Why, would you wish me to?"

"Don't care."

"Are you asking me to stay in?"

She couldn't quite admit that, not until she was absolutely certain what she had to show him to read. "Asking what you're doing, that's all."

"I'm establishing that I want to speak to people without having to compete with noise from your room, or anywhere else in the home for that matter."

"So speak. I won't be listening."

"That will be a blessing," he said, having presumably deduced that she meant listening to music, and glanced past her. Something in his eyes appeared to flatten until they reminded her of the eyes under glass. "May I know what you will be about?"

"Reading. Writing."

"So I observe. What, may I ask?"

"For school." She would have to take the lie back later—she hoped she would have to. "For religion. For Mrs. Kelly," she said.

"That good lady." For a moment he seemed about to say a great deal more. Then the lack of expression spread from his eyes, and he was turning away as he muttered "We must do whatever is required."

It was unclear to Amy how this included her. He jerked his head over his shoulder, so sharply she could have imagined he was trying to imitate somebody hanged, and settled his gaze on her for as long as it took him to say "It will do you no harm to stay in for a change."

That served to remind her not only how little he understood but also that it was Friday, when she would ordinarily celebrate the weekend. Reading the margins had driven that awareness out of her head. She closed her door tight and stamped her feet to revive them as she returned to the bed. She found it hard to recapture her concentration, not least because she felt as though her feet, grown swollen and leaden, were pinned to the bed. She wriggled her toes until the sensation of their being jabbed with needles became less unendurable and very eventually faded, and then she bent her mind upon the writing, larger and more careless now, that followed the previous cross.

"One of my fellow sufferers has addressed herself to me. Often I hear their screams as they are bled, or swung, or held in the bath of surprise, but never before have I seen the face of a single poor wretch. She must have within her some strength she has contrived to hide from our tormentors, for this afternoon she made shift to drag herself to the limits of her shackles, and that without attracting the attention of my keeper. She bore her head, as shorn as mine, above her window-sill while her eyes and bleeding lips pronounced words which caution forbade her to speak aloud. She is Alice, daughter of Hepzibah Keene."

Amy's head rose as though it had been caught in a noose. Should the name Hepzibah mean something to her? She stared around the room, her attention catching on her four caps lined up on the wall, then finding her reflection behind the three black bead necklaces presently worn by the mirror. Her neck looked too slim to support their weight, and her face was as confused as she felt. When her gaze began to twitch she dropped it to the page.

"—daughter of Hepzibah Keene. The surviving Keenes are within these barbed monstrous walls, as the Crowthers also are, the Whitelaws too, the Elgin family besides, and Jane Gentle and her girls. Those who had fled Partington returned to be captured by worse than they had fled. Such places as our prison are refuges not for the sick and the vagrant, but for the tortures of the witch-finders re-christened treatments. This and her name she conveyed to me, and that now I have heard her voice within me I shall do so again. Then she lowered herself into her cell, her face bespeaking the agony of her stealth."

Amy laid the pad and pencil down beside her. Her fingers had begun to twist against each other, with strain and with the memory of the figures she'd seen rising up in the dark of Nazarill. The notion that they'd suffered—were perhaps still suffering—made them more dreadful, not less. When the pencil rolled against her she retrieved it and the pad, though she was growing uneasier about the revelations she might encounter. Indeed, the next sentences almost caused her to relinquish the pencil.

"This morning, as my keeper brought me victuals no dog would swallow, I heard them bleed Moll Keene. Before they drowned her shrieks with hymns she cried that they were putting leeches to her eyes. I think Ben Clay is half lunatic himself. Certes they would never have allowed him to prosecute such tortures in Bedlam, but since he came into his father's inheritance and erected Nazareth Hill Refuge he is lord of all within his walls. His brother Joseph may declare himself a surgeon with impunity, while Clay's wife, Liza, is responsible for the filth in which we are kept and on which we are fed, through the funnel if need be or for her delight. I pray God that they will not be able to conceal so much from the Commissioner."

Amy closed her eyes and opened them again, which failed to stop the flickering of her vision. The writing in the margins appeared to be performing feeble leaps, trying to regain her attention by raising itself higher than the printed text. She was no longer sure she comprehended all that she was transcribing, but it seemed more important to write it while she could. Across the hall her father was talking, presumably on the phone, though he sounded as though he was muttering to himself. She turned the flimsy page, on which the pencilled scrawl was terminated by a cross whose four bars were equal.

"Moll Keene is blind, and Alice can no longer reach the window, her hands and feet being mortified by rusty manacles and fetters. This I know and more, because Alice has been true to her vow that I should hear her. In the night her whisper comes to me between the bricks, for none of our tormentors to hear. Clay blames her and her sister most grievously, she whispers, not merely for keeping old beliefs alive but for the state of every lunatic in his private-madhouse. He dreaded Moll's eyes, and Alice fears her own may be subjected to his mercies. On occasion he has burned her and her sister with torches, declaring these to be a foretaste of hellfire. Yet I sense that Alice awaits some deliverance, and what could this be save the Commissioner's visit?"

Amy's gaze skipped past the cross to the next words. The events about which she was reading had occurred centuries ago, yet her heart sank as though her innards had turned to quicksand—as though the events were happening, or about to happen, to her.

"God help us, all is lost. The Commissioner has made his visit. It was my design to convince him first of my sanity before recounting the horrors which are our lot, but every proof I gave him of the soundness of my mind he dismissed as my delusion. At the last my words eluded my control. Mayhap I have no words to call my own, but only those I learned from the books my father would read aloud to us until I grew incapable of restraining my arguments against the falsehoods called natural law, that system which maintains that God created lunatics for his own purposes and hence that they deserve their plight. Alas, my parents! They have vowed never to visit me until I am cured, but why should Clay declare me so and relinquish his fee? After the visit Clay stalked through his domain to inform us that the Commissioner cannot withdraw the licence, no matter what conditions or mistreatment may have been apparent, but is confined to displaying a report in the Royal College of Physicians, a world away in London. Clay's triumphant shouts were audible in Partington, and from my window I saw folk grin at them as they do at our pleas and screams."

The cross that ended this passage appeared to be flying apart, and Amy closed her eyes as its fragments stirred. Only the aches that the pencil and her thumbnail embedded in her forefinger made her look again and, however shakily, write.

"The visit has increased Clay's fiendishness an hundredfold, and Alice no longer has a tongue; yet still I hear her whisper to me in the night. He has promised her that she will suffer the great fire by Candlemas, and raves of purifying every woman in his charge. Howbeit Alice and her disciples seem almost to encourage and to welcome their fate. Clay thought to raise their prison and their tomb close to their sacred place, not knowing that he built upon the place itself, just as the monastery was built to crush it. This is their hill of celebration and renewal, Alice whispers, and there is a power in death not to be found in life. Yet how may I believe such stuff, or even trust that I am hearing it in truth? Has she or my treatment turned my brain? Why must I drudge at scribbling so? Does that not prove me wrongheaded? I should deface these pages no more, but seek solace in them."

Amy turned the page, which felt barely substantial to her awkward fingers. Contradicting the previous sentence, the scrawl continued, so large now that each margin could contain only a single line of writing. It was preceded by a cross whose upper bar was significantly longer than the lower.

"Candlemas is come, and with it fire. I hear those scream who have the means to scream, and smell their burning. Clay must mean to put it to me, believing me tainted by the old beliefs, for I am fettered. Should I have heeded Alice's exhortation to discover the old powers within myself? I can find it in me to be comforted by the antics of her pet Perkin, the cat with the face of a Keene. I shall write until Clay comes to me, that someone may read of his monstrous handling of the wretches in his charge. Then Perkin will bear away—"

A capital letter showed that the writer had interrupted herself.

"The fire is at my door. At least Clay cannot delight in my death, for the flames have proved greater than he. The Clays have gone up like chaff on a bonfire, and now the inferno consumes his refuge. Did Alice and the others find the power to turn the flames on our tormentors? May the fumes stop my breath before I burn!"

The writer had made a last mark on the opposite page, which bore the opening verses of Matthew. It was a defiantly inverted cross, drawn so savagely that the pencil had ripped deep into the succeeding pages, and so broad in its outlines that the vertical bar could have been used as a niche for the pencil itself. No pencil was there, however. Perhaps, thought Amy, it had been dislodged when the writer had flung the Bible out of her window, if she had. She hardly knew what she was thinking. She dropped the pad on the quilt and placed pencil and Bible on top, and lifted her head. The headache which had been awaiting that moment exploded at once.

She stood up very gingerly and wobbled to her door, from which she wavered across the hall to fetch her forgotten bag. When she managed to locate the pills Beth Griffin had prescribed for her, she found just two in the stubby plastic tube. They would have to suffice until the morning. It was past midnight, and at some point her father had gone to his room. She sucked the minute herbal tablets as she groped her way to the bathroom, and swallowed them before brushing her teeth. All she wanted now was to close her eyes; there wasn't even room in her head for fear. Nevertheless she took time to lodge the pencil in the niche inside the Bible, and stored the Bible and her pad beneath her pillow. Then she switched off the light and let her eyelids add to the darkness, which welcomed her like an old friend and led her into the last untroubled night's sleep of her life.

16

THE PAST DECIDES

While Amy pored over her Bible Oswald spoke into the phone, but soon discovered he had no more calls to make. "If there's anything further I can do for you, Mrs. Kay," he found himself saying before long, "anything whatsoever you can bring to mind. Your home or your car or your children or your old age. You can never be too safe. If you're absolutely sure there's nothing . . ." He already knew there was: not so much as a voice in his ear, or even a dialling tone now that he'd switched off the receiver to shut up the mechanical exhortation to replace the handset and try again. All he could hear apart from himself was a series of monotonously shrill electrical noises not unlike an incomprehensible message in Morse, and he no longer knew why he was pretending to carry on a conversation, nor why he'd invented that name to address. "Miss Key is more the way of it," he muttered as his grimace tried to form itself into a grin.

He had no reason to be amused, and his cleverness only distressed him. Cleverness wasn't needed here, hard cold thinking was. He shoved the receiver into its housing and made himself sit down again. However much he wanted to storm into Amy's room, there was no point until he was certain how to deal with her and her behaviour.

He'd found the evidence after she'd attempted to persuade him to let her stay in Sheffield overnight. Her call had betrayed that she wasn't as resigned to living in Nazarill as she wanted him to think. While awaiting her return he'd looked into her room in case it contained anything that might suggest a way to reach her, and at once he had seen the Bible next to the bed—indeed, it had been the sole item on which he'd been able to focus amid all the untidiness. But when he had turned to the first verses he'd groaned and cried out to God.

She'd filled the margins with nonsense in a scrawl that hardly even resembled her handwriting. He'd been able to distinguish the occasional word: fiends, captors, books, father—more than enough to show him that far worse was wrong with her than he'd had the courage to admit. He had been ready to confront her with her unholy scribbling as soon as she came home; had it been a further lack of courage which had impelled him to make the book appear untouched after he'd admitted her to Nazarill? Now she must be scribbling in the secrecy of her room, a vision from which his thoughts retreated in search of occasions when he should have known all was not right with her. Almost at once his memories halted as though Nazarill had reined them in. It had been here she'd first upset her mother.

She ought to have known he wouldn't drop her through the window. He had only been lifting her up so that she could see, the way fathers always lifted up their children, and she would have known she was safe if she had been a normal child. Instead she'd behaved as if he hadn't rescued her. He saw the truth now. His child secretly enjoyed believing in the things she purported to fear.

Even if he'd realised at the time he mightn't have told Heather, who had already been distressed enough. "She'll be all right, won't she?" she'd kept trying to reassure herself after they had seen Amy off to sleep. "Do you think we'll need to take her to the doctor?" That had been less a question than a plea, which she'd repeated as though guilt was forcing it out of her mouth. The situation hadn't been her fault, he thought fiercely, but perhaps she had continued to blame herself despite all his efforts to comfort her; perhaps in the darkest depths of herself she'd concluded that given her heredity, she should never have had a child. Suppose it had been her concern for Amy that had distracted her on the night of the murderous fog? There was no question that if it hadn't been for Amy he would have been with Heather at the end.

Perhaps it was unfair to hold a child of that age responsible, but he certainly felt justified in doing so at the age she was now. She wasn't even acting it; she was behaving like a small destructive child.

She mightn't be so ready to destroy the reputation of their home if she spent more time in it, which would at least place out of her reach some of the temptations to do God only knew what damage to her mind. That mind was his responsibility, and he had to save it while there was time, if it wasn't already too late.

"It mustn't be," he said aloud. "Please, I'll do anything. Just show me what has to be done." He heard his voice reach out, and felt as though the very rooms around him yearned to answer him—almost all the rooms. The thought of the mess in Amy's bedroom made his skin feel as grubby and infested as a dusty cobweb in a dark corner, sensations which seemed designed to distract him from praying, so that he flung himself out of his chair, muttering "Get away." Rubbing his hands and arms and torso hard enough to hurt them, he gave Amy's abandoned bag a conspiratorial glance before hurrying into his bedroom.

He closed the door and without switching on the light fell heavily to his knees by the bed. He clasped his aching knuckles with his aching fingers and squeezed his eyes shut until they throbbed, but Amy or his fears for her seemed to be preventing him from praying. Eventually he managed by concentrating on key words which, like handholds, helped him through the fraught dark. Father. Heaven. Kingdom. Will be done. Trespass against us. Temptation. Evil. "Amen," he said, and began again at once.

Each time the word came round it felt stronger in his mouth, more of an acceptance of the course on which he was set. When his commitment was absolutely secure, incapable of being reversed or modified for any reason, he rose from his bruised knees and hobbled to the bathroom to cleanse himself inside and out. "You can never be too clean," he said, sharing a grin with himself in the mirror. Then he remembered Amy's room, and saw his face stiffen, pressing his lips together an instant before he felt them meet. He tugged the cord and stared at the glazed picture of himself in the dark. When it had communicated all its implacability to him he went back to his room. He changed into his pyjamas, whose stripes always put him in mind of both a convict and a businessman, and having slipped the keys under the pillow, climbed into bed.

He was by no means asleep, although his thoughts had at least begun to melt into a doze, when he heard Amy emerge from her room. Even when he realised she was going to the bathroom, he couldn't relax. He made himself listen until she finished, then he strained his ears to reassure himself that she hadn't simply closed her bedroom door as a preamble to wandering the apartment. Thank God, she was safely shut in. Sooner or later there would no doubt have to be a confrontation, but he was glad that wasn't now, before he'd a chance to sleep. He was able to soothe himself into slumber with the knowledge that she wouldn't be going anywhere, not when the mortice-lock of the door to the outer corridor was locked with the key on the ring he'd taken from her bag and was keeping safe beneath his pillow.

17

A PUBLIC DISGRACE

The instant Amy opened her eyes she was fully awake. She remembered everything she had deciphered, and now she understood. She had to tell someone: not yet her father—someone who wouldn't take so much persuading. She raised her hand to where she knew the light-cord was, and closed her fist around the plastic knob, and pulled. The illumination brought all the chaos of her room to life, a sight which for the present seemed irrelevant, and revived the threat of last night's headache. As she sat up and kicked off the tangled quilt, the whole of the inside of her skull felt like the back of her eyes. Beth would give her more tablets, but first she needed to talk. She rubbed her cold feet, then let her hands attend to each other as she padded from one patch of uncluttered carpet to the next. She eased the door open and came face to face with her father.

He was sitting on a dining-chair in the doorway of his bedroom. His hands were clasped in his lap, but as he saw her his fingers rose from gripping his knuckles and stretched in her direction like the tendrils of a plant with animal ambitions. Several repetitions of a momentary smile which appeared to express or at least to pretend surprise hoisted the corners of his lips and let them drop. His gaze was far steadier, so resigned it might as well have been blank. "This is not like you," he said.

Amy sidled within reach of the plaque which held the phone. "What?"

"Up before noon of a Saturday. Was your sleep troubled?"

"It was fine. How about yours?" Amy retorted, because he looked as though he had been dressed for hours in the business clothes he was wearing. An untouched mug of coffee squatted beside him, its surface muddy with scum. His eyes grew almost as blank as that before he said "The sleep of the just."

She couldn't tell whether he was referring to his own or making a less straightforward comment about hers. She was reaching for the phone when he said "May I ask what you are planning?"

She might have said to use the phone, but she couldn't help reacting. "To get older and buy a car and live in my own flat when I go to university."

"Attempt to confine yourself to the next few minutes."

"Phone Rob."

"You don't consider that you might be disturbing him."

"If he isn't up he'll get up for me," Amy said, her eyes on the day beyond the window. Weak though it was, the external light felt like a promise of release from Nazarill. "It isn't that early," she told her father, and freeing the receiver, tapped Rob's number.

Two pairs of rings and the first syllable of the third were enough to bring her a response. "Hello?"

"Rob?"

"He isn't about just yet. In fact, I heard him very definitely going back to sleep. Is that Amy?"

"Hi, Mr. Hayward. Could you tell Rob—"

"This is his mother."

"Sorry. Mrs. Hayward. Tell him I'll be round in a bit."

"If he ever joins the living I will."

Amy had said as much as she could have to Rob within earshot of her father. She housed the receiver and turned to find her father watching her as though he hadn't even blinked. "Problem?" she demanded.

"They sound somewhat of an odd couple to me."

"How would you know? You've never met them." Amy was readying herself for an argument when she saw that would only delay her. For a moment she had a nervous impression that Nazarill had manufactured it for just such a reason. "Whither now?" her father said.

"Over to Beth's."

"To what end?"

"The usual." His questions had begun to close in on her, and she was heading for the outer corridor until she became more aware of her state. "You didn't think I was going dressed like this," she said.

"I had to wonder."

He sounded so grim she was sorry she'd bothered to joke. She dodged into her room to grab a handful of clothes for carrying to the bathroom, where she pulled off the T-shirt she wore in bed and doused herself in a quick shower before dressing herself. As she unbolted the door she was suddenly nervous of finding her father outside, but he was still sitting where she'd last seen him, his gaze waiting for her. She slung the wadded T-shirt onto her bed and closed the door. "I won't take my keys," she said.

"Quite so. I shall be here. The mortice is unlocked."

Amy hadn't time to judge his tone, because as she arrived at the end of the hall she glimpsed movement through the eye of the door. Beth was emerging from her flat. Amy seized the latch and pulled the door open, and found her mouth emptied of words. An ominously large bag was lolling against the wall next to Beth. "What's that?" Amy managed to ask.

"Why, hello, Amy." Beth swept her blonde hair back from her high forehead. "Just my overnight things. Well, a couple of nights."

"You're going away too."

"Only to see an aunt I haven't seen for too long. As well as Miss Braine, you mean."

"No, as the Goudges. You're seeing Miss Braine on your way out," Amy assumed, and then a worse interpretation suggested itself to her. "You don't mean she's going as well."

"Mr. Roscommon has had a stroke and she's moving in with his son to help look after him. What's wrong?"

"You're all leaving. It isn't just a coincidence."

"What else would you like it to be?" Beth said with untypical sharpness before she regained the sympathy into which her profession transformed her shyness. "Amy, don't let it worry you. Some of us will be coming back, and there are still the Stoddards, and Mr. Greenberg, and Miss Blake. Mr. Shrift and Mr. Inky Doughty, and our musician is Mr. Kenilworth, isn't he, and what's his name, whatever his name is, the newspaper man."

All this merely served to remind Amy how little she knew of these people or they of her. Nazarill was half empty now, at least of living occupants, and she thought she sensed the emptiness rear-ranging itself below her, rooms growing smaller and darker and more numerous and, worse yet, more inhabited. "Something *is* wrong, isn't it?" Beth said. "I'd locked up, but can I help?"

"I was coming to see you for some of my pills. I've got none left."

"Oh dear." Beth started a gesture that looked as though it was going to bare her wristwatch, but which led her hand to the keys in her bag instead. "Our usual trouble?"

"I was up half the night reading and gave myself a headache."

"Not the best idea to keep yourself awake reading, I find. Artificial light, you know." As if to demonstrate the drawbacks of that, Beth peered at her keys in the dimness of the corridor before inserting one into her lock. "What was the book? Something spicy, dare I guess?"

"A kind of—" The harsh sound of the key gave Amy time to reconsider how much she would have the opportunity to explain. "About the witches who used to be here," she said.

"Ah." It wasn't obvious how much of that Beth had heard or had wanted to hear over the noise of unlocking. She darted into the flat, from which Amy then heard the opening and shutting of two kinds of door, and out again. "Pay me when you see me next," she said, and placed a tube of pills in Amy's hand as she wielded the keys again. "Take two whenever you need them and less of what hurt you."

"Maybe some writing has to hurt."

"Maybe," Beth just about conceded, and having dropped her keys into her handbag, stretched a hand towards her luggage. "About witches where, did you say?"

"Here. Here in Nazarill when it was a mental place. They must have been locked up because people thought they were only mad."

"I suppose that makes sense."

Now Amy found she wasn't sure she wanted it to do so. "What kind?"

"People stopped torturing witches around the time they started building asylums. I did hear this place used to be a hospital. The poor creatures who were locked up probably couldn't tell the difference from being tortured. It was reading the history of medicine that got me into alternative treatment," Beth said, and fingered a sudden wrinkle in her forehead. "Did you say people thought these witches of yours were only mad?"

That was a great deal for Amy to explain, and she was considering how to start when Beth's gaze flickered past her and tried to look casual. "May I intervene?" said Amy's father at her back.

"Oh, Mr. Priestley. We were just—"

"I heard you."

"Oh, you did." Beth was as thrown by his abruptness as Amy was by his having sneaked the door open unnoticed. "And—"

"I should be most obliged if you would refrain in future from discussing such subjects with my daughter."

"Actually, Mr. Priestley, it was—"

"Besides which, may I enquire what you passed to her?"

"Just her tablets." When he seemed to be awaiting some clarification Beth said "The ones she takes."

"Perhaps you can tell me what they are meant to achieve."

Amy gripped the container in her fist. "They make my head better. You know that."

His stare wasn't letting Beth go. "What I don't know, or perhaps I do, is what made it worse to begin with."

"Mr. Priestley, if you're implying—"

"It's something bad she has been putting into herself, I know that much. If not from you, then from that evil shop that should never have been allowed to open, though I shouldn't be surprised if it were a combination of both."

Amy saw Beth start to lose her confidence. "I'll walk down with you, Beth," she said. "I'll get my coat."

As soon as she was in the hall her father moved between her and the door. "Walk where?"

"Rob's."

"He won't have risen."

"How do you know? I don't." Amy raised her voice and shouted in his face "Coming, Beth."

"Actually, Amy, I'll have to be rushing. I said I'd be on my way by now." As she spoke she was, her words dwindling along the corridor. "I'll be back next week," she called, and was gone

Amy dashed into her room and threw back the pillow. She tore off the pad the pages containing the material she'd copied and wrapped the Bible in them, and was stuffing the package into her bag as she grabbed a coat out of the wardrobe. "Wait, Beth," she shouted, and slammed her door behind her in the process of thrusting her arms through the sleeves while she juggled with her bag.

Her father was still between her and the corridor, his faint regretful smile as fixed as his stare. "She's well away. She seems to have found some discretion at last, so there's no further cause for haste that I can see."

Amy jerked her coat around her and strode towards him. "How long were you listening through your crack?"

"More than long enough," he said, and stretched his arms wide. He might have been waiting for her to run to him for a hug as she so often had, years ago, except that his face had never been the stony mask it was now. He was backing towards the door to shoulder it closed. She threw herself at him and at the last moment ducked under his right arm. He flung out a hand which struck a pop-eyed illustration, and she heard glass creak and almost splinter as she fell into the corridor.

As her free hand slapped the opposite wall for support the evasive illumination appeared to well up and subside like the flaring glow of smoky torches. She shoved herself away from the panel, which at least felt like wood, and fled along the corridor.

Her father's voice pursued her. "Come back, Amy. I want to speak to you. Come back here this instant. I forbid you to leave this house." He was in the corridor, which amplified his shouts like a huge stiff mouth. They faded as she ran downstairs, though she continued to hear them on the middle floor, and had the dismaying sense that they might rouse the tenants of the abandoned rooms. She forced herself to run down through the clinging dimness to the worst floor, where she threw herself at the exit doors. Dragging them apart, she skidded onto the gravel beneath a sky sealed with cloud, into a dull light that was far too similar to the illumination within Nazarill, and raced along the pale facade to the car park.

Beth had gone. Amy glimpsed the tail of her white car flourished like a flag at the upper end of Nazareth Row before it disappeared. There were people by the few parked vehicles, however; Paul Kenilworth was taking his leave of Peter Sheen and preparing to climb into his Honda, in the back of which Amy saw a suitcase and a violin-shaped black box which put her in mind of a little coffin. "You're off too," she said, in a despair so deep it was close to resignation.

"On a welcome concert tour."

"Welcome how?"

"I think it's a sin not to use any skills you have to the full," the violinist said, and having shaken hands with the journalist, shut himself into the car and drove away with a chorus of gravel.

Amy watched the brake-lights signify an invisible gate before the car swung onto Nazareth Row. Some of her longing to be understood must have shown in her eyes, because Peter Sheen said "I'm still here."

"Can I talk to you?" Amy said, straining to hear any sound that would betray the presence of her father.

"I'd say you were."

"About something you might want to put in the paper."

"My ears are up," said the journalist, but for once seemed in no hurry to reach for his pen. "If it's news, tell me."

"It's history nobody knows about. That ought to be news, shouldn't it?"

"The history of . . ."

"Here. Where we live."

"Oh, that. I don't think so, sorry, not at all."

"But you haven't heard it."

"I've heard enough. It could have been news before you went on the air with it, but that put the lid on it as far as we'd be concerned at my rag. And I may as well be honest with you, your father's made it clear to various of us in the building that he wouldn't be at all elated for any of us to be your, what word did he use, your dupe."

Amy felt the shadow of Nazarill, pale though it was, inch more of its chill over her. She stared at Peter Sheen, who at least had the grace to look away, then she whirled on the gravel. A fragment of stone clacked against the facade as she bolted for the gateway, and she felt as though she had alerted Nazarill to her flight—not, she thought wildly, that it needed to be told.

She sensed it looming at her back as she hurried beneath the deadened sky into Little Hope Way. The growing distance seemed unable to reduce its presence. She turned up her collar and pinched it about her throat to fend off the cold that was trying to seize her by the back of the neck. In the marketplace several of the stallholders turned to watch her, none of them favourably. She ran past the bookstall, the proprietor of which was too busy serving a customer to acknowledge her, and down Market Approach, where the sight of the boarded-up frontage of Hedz Not Fedz struck her as one more triumph for Nazarill. Until she clenched her imagination the thought made the place feel capable of lowering the sky towards her, of narrowing the already narrow street or even walling off the far end. "Balls. Bollocks. Crap. Garbage. Shit," she declared, and more of the same, to convince herself she would arrive at the main road.

She ran across it, well in front of a lorry that nonetheless honked, and up the crumbling road to the cottages above the wall restrained by a cross. Her elevation only raised Nazarill to confront her across the too-small town. It appeared to be lending its pallor to the corpse of a sky, and she imagined it closing the sky around her like a cup over an insect. She turned her back on it so as to run up the path of the last cottage and ring the doorbell.

She had to press the button again—to lean her hand on it—before she saw movement beyond the whorled glass that occupied much of the middle third of the upper section of the heavy door. The colours under the blotch of a face were too bright and various for Rob, and the opening of the door confirmed it was his mother, a short grey-haired woman in a housecoat whose padded shoulders emphasised her angularity and breadth. The height of the hall relative to the path enabled her to look Amy straight in the eye, if with some visible reluctance. "Amy. We thought it might be you."

"Is he up yet?"

"I've not heard him stirring." Rob's mother kept her gaze steady while she raised her square-jawed face, then blinked. "I'll be candid with you, this is awkward. We've had your father ring up asking us to send you home."

"You won't, will you?"

"It's between you and your father. I don't think we should get involved."

This impressed Amy as little of an answer, but the way Mrs. Hayward didn't shift her posture was one. Amy felt paralysed by it and by the weight of the sky stretching from Nazarill, so that only the sliding of a sash allowed her to lift her head. Rob had opened his bedroom window to display his torso cloaked in a quilt. "Hey, I didn't know you were here."

"Some people didn't want you to know." Amy couldn't stop her mouth from quivering, and her anger with her inability only aggravated it. "Well, I am, and I need to talk."

"I'll be downstairs in five."

"I don't know if I'll be there," Amy said, and looked at Mrs. Hayward, who heaved a sigh that bulged her housecoat.

"He can walk home with you, Amy. Wait there for him if you like. Excuse me if I close the door to keep the chill out," she said, and did so at once.

Amy crossed the road to lean on the wall and challenge Nazarill over the huddled roofs. When she felt a shifting beneath her elbows she thought the bricks were about to topple into the main road, as if the solidity around her was being undermined, but the looseness was only of moss. She glared at Nazarill until the streets appeared to twitch, to edge jerkily towards it as though it was drawing them in, reducing the distance between her and itself. She couldn't watch that for long, and so she occupied herself with stamping her feet and chafing her hands together until Rob hurried down his path. "What have you been doing?" he said.

This sounded so accusatory that at first she couldn't speak. Since he couldn't have meant to be accusing, she wrapped her arms around him and the long black coat he'd bought in Charity Worldwide and pressed her cheek against his warm one. Her temperature must have shocked him; his cheek flinched, his long eyelashes fluttered. As she hugged him with all her strength to make him reciprocate, she saw his mother watching, masked with the net curtains of the front-room window like a yashmak. "Let's move," she said, freeing him, "and I'll tell you."

They were on the steep downward track before either of them spoke again. "I got most of it from my mother," Rob said. "Is it me? Doesn't he want you seeing me?"

"It isn't you, Rob. I don't think even he could blame you for this. He can't, he doesn't know yet. I haven't told anyone."

"Lateral."

"He won't like it when he does know. It's all about Nazarill."

"Tell."

"I found an old book, a Bible. It must have been around the place for, you'll see how long." Amy halted at the foot of the slope. "I'll show you. Wait, look."

"I will when we're across," he said, squinting at the battered cover as she handed him the Bible, and stepped into the road. A pale hulk like a dislodged chunk of Nazarill rushed at him.

It was a furniture van. Amy dug her nails into the inside of his elbow through his coat and dragged him back against the rusty cross that held the wall. "Thanks," he said, and gingerly rubbed where she'd pinched. "Close."

"If that's all." She held his arm more gently while she looked both ways twice before hustling him to the opposite pavement, where she rested a moment, clinging to him. "Why are you looking at me like that?"

"Wondering what else you thought it was than close."

"Maybe nothing if you think so. I don't care now, it's gone. Let's get away from the road."

"Like where?"

"Anywhere but home. I'm not going back there, not yet anyway. Maybe not ever." Amy found that as difficult to conceive as it might have been if Nazarill wasn't allowing her room to think. "I know, the bookstall. There may be things I can ask him now I've found out more."

Rob paced into Moor View and held up the Bible. "You mean in here?"

"Open it and see."

He did, at Genesis. He narrowed his eyes at the margins and brought the book close to his face, and having turned the Bible three ways, blinked at her. "I can't get it, Aim."

"I wrote it all out, look." She pulled the folded pages out of her bag and showed him the topmost sheet. "You can read that, it's me."

He let his eyes widen but seemed otherwise no more enlightened. "I'll need to be sitting to read it if it's that much."

"The pubs aren't open yet, are they?" Amy was reflecting on how few places to socialise Partington offered. "We'll have to go in the tea place by the market," she said.

It wasn't just its proximity to Nazarill she disliked, it was Tea For You itself. All the most intolerant old ladies of Partington congregated there, eyeing the market with inexhaustible disapproval out of faces like tissue paper that had been crumpled and smoothed as best it could be and then powdered, especially in the wrinkles. Even a stranger of their own generation would have been made to feel like an intruder, and as Amy set foot on the polished floorboards she became conscious of her thinness and her cropped head and every bit of metal in her face. The younger of the two waitresses in milkmaid's outfits looked prepared to repel the invaders, but Amy had noticed an unoccupied though cluttered table for two in a corner, towards which she pulled Rob through a shaking of severely hatted heads and a clucking of tongues which put her in mind of an insect hopping from table to table, emitting its call at each one. "You can read while we're waiting," she said loudly to Rob.

Several faces twisted away as though she'd slapped them, and began to murmur for her to hear. "Who do they think they are, I'd like to know." "What do they think they look like?" "What can their parents be thinking of?" The last comment affected her in more than one way, so that she rounded on Rob. "Ignore them," she said through her teeth. "Just read."

"I'm trying." He'd cleared a space among the lipsticked cups and the plates sticky with crumbs and jam, and was turning pages and swivelling the Bible on the pink-and-white checked tablecloth. When she flapped the sheets torn from her pad he only glanced at them. "I don't need those. I'm getting it."

"Fine," Amy said, regretting that she hadn't saved herself a headache if he found the margins easier to read than she had. She caught the eye of the younger milkmaid, who looked away. "We'd like two coffees when you can spare the time," Amy said.

The request for coffee had earned a disparaging blink all by itself. "You're not the only people here, you know," the waitress told her.

"We'd noticed," Amy retorted, and became more aware of the girl's profile, which appeared to have devoted itself mostly to producing a sharp nose. "I know you. Weren't you a prefect when I was in the second year? You wanted to confiscate a book I'd brought to show how my mother bound them because you said I must have stolen it."

Silence had gathered around her voice, but then she heard a comment which might have floated over from any of the surrounding tables. "Like as not she did."

Amy might have reacted so that the entire clientele would hear, but that would be to let her mind be shrunk to the size of Partington's pettiest attitudes—the kind, she thought, which must have permitted the activities at the asylum to continue unchecked. Before she could speak, the waitress intervened. "She didn't. It looked so expensive, that was the mistake."

In a tone of support for the offending comment a woman in a helmet white as marble and bristling with pearly knobs said "Perhaps you could serve us our cakes."

Amy gave the waitress an encouraging grimace and glanced at Rob in case the incident had distracted him, but he seemed unaware of it; he was twirling the Bible and peering at the margins, his frown of concentration now transformed into a frown of some uneasiness. She glanced towards the market as the bell above the door allowed itself a modest ping. Her body jerked, clattering the china on the table. In the doorway were Shaun Pickles and her father.

Pickles saw her first, and pointed. His scraped face looked blotchier than ever, no doubt with righteousness. "I knew I'd seen her come in here, Mr. Priestley. I'll wait, shall I?" he said, and all but sneered at Rob. "We don't want any trouble."

"I foresee none. She's still my child," said Amy's father, striding between the tables. "Come along now, Amy. You were instructed to come home."

"It's the wrong kind of home."

"Even if your friend encourages you to talk nonsense, please don't do so to me," he said, and further acknowledging Rob: "Did your parents ask you to escort my daughter?"

"Something like that."

"I thought not," Amy's father said triumphantly, and his gaze fell on the Bible. His face writhed, and Amy saw his eyes redden. "What are you about with that?"

"Reading it," Rob barely admitted.

"I had no need to worry where she was. This is a Bible reading," her father called across the tearoom to the guard at the door, then relinquished his irony and more of his self-control as he turned to her. "Have you no shame, displaying that in public? If it isn't still a crime it should be, defacing the word of God. Perhaps before you leave us you would like to tell me how you're involved."

The last part was addressed to Rob, who said "I've only just seen it. Aim brought it to show me."

"Which is to say she could rely on you to indulge her and encourage her."

"You haven't read it," Amy said. "Rob has. You'll tell him, won't you, Rob? You can tell him what it says about that place."

"God forgive you, and me for letting you stray. I've read enough of your crazed unholy nonsense."

"You haven't even looked at this, but Rob—"

"I saw it yesterday when you abandoned it in the midst of the rest of your leavings. I saw how you've scrawled in the Bible you had deluded me into thinking was for the good of your soul."

"You went in my room." She hadn't time to pursue that now, not least because the elder milkmaid had emerged from the kitchen and looked poised to intervene. "You should have read it properly, then you'd have seen it wasn't my writing. And you'd have read the truth about Nazarill. Rob has, haven't you, Rob?"

Rob was gazing at two pages of Lamentations. He'd read more than enough to be able to answer, she thought, and stared at him until he raised his head and blinked slowly twice at her. "Don't know," he said.

"How can't you know? What did you read?"

"All sorts of stuff." He seemed uncertain whether to address her or her father, and let his gaze sink to the Bible instead. "About witches, and how it used to be a mental hospital, and how there was going to be a fire. But Aim—"

Amy was watching her father, who was visibly taken aback; some of this had got to him. "You ask them at Housall. I bet they'll have to say there was a fire," she said. "Or if they won't let on they know about it, there'll have to be something about it somewhere. I'll look."

"Aim."

Rob had lowered his voice, and that made her inexplicably nervous. "Yes, what?" she almost snapped.

"Maybe all that happened if you say it did, wherever you got it from. But—"

"I got it where you just did."

"You can't say that. I don't know why you're saying it. It doesn't help, it screws things up."

That brought a disapproving murmur from the adjacent tables. "What are you pussying around?" Amy demanded. "What are you trying—"

"It's no use telling him you didn't write it when he can see you did."

All the sensations of the room seemed to close in on her: the heat laden with the smells of powder and desiccated flesh and pierced by a thin aroma of too-sweet tea; her surreptitious observation by everyone who wasn't openly watching her; the scrape of a spoon within a teacup, a sound like the turning of a rusty key in a lock. "I didn't," she said as though the words could fend everything off.

"Look, Aim, this is you. It doesn't start off like your writing, but that's how it ends up. See, the writing round these pages is the same as on the sheets. Why did you write it twice? So that ..."

As soon as he trailed off she knew why he had. He must think and not want to admit thinking that she'd set out to pretend to have transcribed the secret journal. She stood up with a screech of her chair on the boards and folded the sheets around the Bible, which she shoved into her bag. "Thanks I can't tell you how much, Rob," she said into his face, so close her breath fluttered his eyelids. "You've really helped."

"It wouldn't have been much use if I'd said I couldn't see it, would it, Aim? Anyone else could too."

"I used to think you weren't anyone else."

"Tell me what else I can do."

He must have seen her answer in her eyes, because the hand he was holding out wilted. "I believe we are finished here," her father said.

She supposed she was. The smells and metallic sounds and neurotically shadowless light of the tearoom were drawing themselves into a headache which was about to render them unbearable. She moved around the far side of the nearest table from her father and picked her painful way towards the door. The guard opened it, letting in the hubbub of the marketplace, and stood outside looking smug. Rob had followed her, his eyes pleading for a second chance to aid her. She hated him more than Pickles now. Not much more than conversationally she said "Just fuck off, Rob."

There was a chorus of shocked cries and gasps from the customers, and a stifled giggle from the younger waitress. The elder advanced purposefully on Amy as Rob faltered. Amy's father was closest to her, however, and taking her by the elbows, steered her out of the tearoom. "I apologise for my daughter," he said away from her. "Please be assured that you will never witness such a scene again."

Pickles waited until the door shut, springing the hammer against the bowl of the bell. "I don't want to worry you, Mr. Priestley, but why I had my eye out for her in the first place besides looking out for her generally was I'd had a complaint about her going down the street using filthy language to herself."

"That will be seen to, you can tell anyone who heard her." Amy's father relinquished her right arm so as to close both hands around the other. "God bless you for your help in her hour of need."

"Do you want me to help you take her home?"

"I've the impression that she won't be any further trouble now she has had to acknowledge the error of her ways. That's so, isn't it, my dear?"

Amy managed, agonising though it was, to focus on the market-place. Everyone in sight was watching her. She ignored Rob, who was standing inside the tearoom like a trophy stuffed by the customers, and turned her throbbing stare on a butcher whose attention looked especially voyeuristic. Soon he glanced away, but only to lift half a raw rib-cage off a hook and remark to a customer "That's the crazy girl who went for that guard here last week. She's from the place on the hill, wouldn't you know."

Amy supposed he was right: she must be crazy—Rob had shown her she was. That, and his having let her down, felt like the worst that could happen to her, so that it no longer mattered where she went, not that she appeared to have left herself any choice. The headache was lowering itself like a massive stone to crush her thoughts, and she was almost glad when her father steered her towards Little Hope Way. At least in a few minutes she would be able to lie down in her room.

Shops wavered by like ill-hung pictures in a gallery. The voices of the market, all of whose comments seemed to be directed at her, turned into a stony wind along Nazareth Row. A dog ran out of the grounds of Nazarill, carrying a ball a boy had thrown for it to catch, and Amy saw it silenced by a rubber gag. The gateposts nodded towards her to greet her, first one and then the other, as the gravel bit into her feet—as Nazarill fitted itself into her vision as though it had made itself a niche there as wide as her head. Although it was too early in the day for the security lights to be more than dormant, she saw Nazarill brightening jerkily as it lurched towards her with each step she took.

Perhaps it was borrowing the dead glare from the sky. She had to close her eyes against it as her father brought her to the doors. She looked again as he halved his grasp on her arm so as to twist the key in the lock, and found that the dimness beyond the twin glass rectangles coated with a reflection of the drive seemed actually welcoming. That dismayed her, and so did being grateful for her father's presence, perhaps even grateful to have her choice of direction taken away. As soon as the doors tolled behind her she headed for the stairs so fast her father lost his hold on her. Let him think she was anxious to be home—let him think whatever he liked. If she told him what she was feeling he would only think she was mad, but she sensed figures pressing themselves against the inside of each door along the corridor to greet her, peering through the spyholes at her if they had anything left with which to peer.

18

AN ANSWER TO A CALL

By the time she reached her room Amy's headache was so savage that she could only take it to bed. She even swallowed the brace of paracetamol tablets her father offered her, which allowed her to fall into a fitful doze. Whenever she awoke she found him sitting at her bedside, watching her. Once, when she was delirious, her mother had sat all night by this very bed, and his presence made Amy feel as she'd felt then, little and ill and cut off from a world which resembled a dream. If everything was as distant as it seemed, it surely couldn't harm her, in which case only she could do that, and perhaps by not thinking she could avoid doing so. Perhaps her mad thoughts were the source of her headache; if she tried to make any sense of them the ache redoubled itself. She could only retreat behind her eyelids from the blaze of the room.

At some point her father turned off her light and sat in the patch of illumination from the hall. The first time she awoke to see his faceless silhouette watching her she flinched against the pillows so hard the glow through the doorway appeared to flare twice as bright, but soon she grew so used to his being there that she didn't even speculate about how his face might look. Sometimes when she turned over in bed, moving with infinite caution so as not to rouse her headache, he leaned close to her and asked if she wanted anything. Since all she wanted was for his hot breath on her face to go away, she mostly answered no, except when he brought her more paracetamol. That happened twice, but it didn't occur to her to measure the passage of time by it; even such meagre thinking might hurt. It was incalculably later, on the far side of at least one prolonged sleep, when he stooped to her in the changed light from the hall and murmured "Do you feel up to walking?"

She found she'd been expecting his face to have changed while it was invisible—hoping it had lost some of the grimness with which he'd confronted her over the Bible. To some extent it had, but its blankness looked grim. She shifted her head gingerly on the rumpled pillow and watched him step back beside the dining-chair for which he'd somehow cleared a space. "Where to?"

"Why, to church."

"When?"

"In a few minutes. As soon as you can be up and dressed."

"Why now?"

"Because it's past ten of a fine Sunday morning. The Lord's Day. Can you not tell?"

Amy wondered how she was expected to tell anything of the sort without windows, then saw that wasn't the kind of awareness he felt she ought to have. Besides, the quality of light in the hall should have shown her it was day. That by no means attracted her; it was the threat of everything she'd managed not to remember while she was asleep. "I still don't feel right," she said, truthfully enough.

"I see that. Would you like anything to eat brought to you? There should be time."

"Before you go, you mean?"

"Before we both do."

"I'm not going. I want to rest my head," she told him, and let her eyelids fall shut to terminate the discussion. When she heard no movement she peered through her eyelashes at him. He was exactly where he had been, digging the fingertips of his right hand into the back of the chair hard enough to pale the upholstery. "I see you spying, Amy," he said. "Church is the best medicine to cure you."

"Not now. You go," Amy said, and identified another chance she might have to escape if she had the energy and could think where to head for. "Maybe I'll go later."

"In that event we both will, and meanwhile we can pray together. That should remind you of the benefits."

"I just want to be quiet."

"Quiet comes from prayer, Amy, you ought to remember that. Either God sent you your headache or it must be something you've visited upon yourself. Whichever is the case, prayer is the answer."

"Pills are better. Can't I have some more?"

"Perhaps when we've prayed, if you still feel the need. Come along now. Our Father . . ."

"You do it for me."

"Don't you think I have?" There were tears in his eyes until he rubbed their gleam brighter. "I want to hear you join in. You used to when you were small, before you started your foolishness about our home. It will help to bring us back together apart from anything else. Don't you want that?"

"Suppose," Amy said, no longer knowing.

"Then let us be about it, and no more nonsense. Your mother liked Gracie Fields singing it, if you recall. Our Father . . ."

By now all she wanted was for him to go away or at least to shut up, and the quickest way to achieve either seemed to be to respond. "Our Father," she mumbled, feeling embarrassed and trapped and absurd, and kept her next few words to herself. "It hurts," she protested instead.

"How can praying hurt?" The gleam in his eyes grew momentarily cold and suspicious. "You aren't applying your mind to it. Just remember how. Close your eyes and put your hands together and concentrate on what you're saying. Remember the idea you used to like, that your fingers are an aerial sending your prayers up to heaven."

None of this soothed Amy's head. Both the effort of trying to pray and the strain of suppressing the words that insisted on suggesting themselves were hurtful, and his shouts certainly would be if she uttered the version which had lodged in her brain. "My father who fart whenever, horrid be thy name . . ." Perhaps he was making her think these things by refusing to leave her alone, but mustn't she expect to suffer such thoughts if she was mad? "Doesn't work," she mumbled.

"Of course it works. All that can get in the way is wilfulness. Eyes shut and hands together and submit yourself to God. Feel your prayer go up like a flame to Him."

Amy closed her eyes as tight as they would go without setting off the flicker of her vision, and pressed her hands together as if to crush some insubstantial prize. She felt smaller than ever, but that was no longer comforting: she seemed shrunken around the core of herself, which was a charred aching useless lump. She couldn't prevent her father's voice from probing into her head. "Our Father ... speak up now so He can hear you. Our Father who art in heaven ... I still can't hear. There could hardly be a lesser reason to be shy in front of your own father. Our Father who art in heaven, hallowed, which means holy if by any unfortunate chance you have managed to forget what you were taught, hallowed be Thy name ..."

"My kingdom come, my will be done." In a moment Amy thought she might say the words out loud, and the hell with whatever followed. She had a fleeting notion that the result mightn't just be yet another argument but some event she was unable to conceive—another mad idea, she concluded. She felt her lips parting, and her eyes strayed open. Before she could speak, the buzzer chirred in the hall.

"Who's that now?" Her father dragged his fingers apart to brandish them. "If it should be that wretched interfering woman with her quackery ... You stay there, Amy, seeing that you're too unwell to get up for church."

"Leave my door open, though."

He hesitated outside the doorway, staring rather blankly at her, so that she wondered if he meant to shut her in. He tramped away without touching the door, however, and a jingle of keys denoted that he was unlocking the mortice after rattling the chain back. "Why, Mrs. Stoddard," he said, "and is it Pamela again? Bound for mass?"

"We are soon, yes."

"We would accompany you, only my young blessing is sick in bed."

"That's a pity," said Lin Stoddard with no sympathy that Amy could distinguish. She didn't need it from the Stoddards, and was lowering her head onto the pillow when Lin added "We were hoping for a word with her. I wonder if we could still have it."

"What would it concern?"

"I'd like her to finish the job you said she'd do."

"I'm certain she will if I said so. Remind me if you would."

"Persuading this one there's nothing to be scared of."

"Good heavens, most assuredly. Why, did she not?"

"Not the way this poor little girl was last night."

"Then come in by all means. Mine isn't so ill as she acts, I suspect.

Perhaps exerting herself to perform good works may help her back to health."

The muffling of the pillow was allowing Amy to pretend that none of this had much to do with her, but when she heard an assortment of footsteps bearing down on her she pushed herself up with her elbows, fitting her head into a tight dull ache. She'd propped her spine against the plump headboard when Pam, which was all of whatever her name was now that Amy intended to acknowledge, appeared in the doorway with her mother holding her shoulders. She was more beribboned and trimmed with lace than ever, but these apparently weren't the only reasons why she looked fragile. When her mother gave her an enlivening shake her face prepared to crumple. "Go on, Pamly," Lin said. "You tell her."

"You."

"It's you it was supposed to have happened to, young lady," Lin said, then sighted across the topmost ribbon at Amy. "She was upset for a start. Her little Parsley died last week."

Amy felt unfairly accused. "Sorry," she nonetheless said.

"No fault of yours, that wasn't. He was ancient for a hamster. But then—your turn now, Pamly. Up to you to say."

The girl bit her lip, then clasped and unclasped her hands in front of her as though trying to choose which of them to rub with the other. "I thought I heard him in my room last night. It woke me up, and I was going to put the light on when I remembered it couldn't be him."

"And now you know it couldn't have been anything," Lin said straight at Amy.

"I did hear it, I was sure I did. Running about like him when I had his cage in my room, only it was too big to be him, and it sounded like it kept falling over." The girl's stare dodged about, but that failed to rid her of the memory. "It sounded . . ."

However much Amy didn't want to know, she had to. "What?"

"Excuse me, Amy, but you're supposed to be telling her—"

The girl mustn't want to be alone with the memory; she raised her voice to interrupt her mother. "It was making noises with its mouth. It sounded like it wanted to be fed."

Lin breathed out loudly through her nose. "You'd have been thinking about Parsley when you went to sleep, of course you were, and that's why you had a bit of a nightmare. That's all it could have been. Amy will tell you."

"Did you see anything?" Amy asked Pam.

"No, oh no."

"I should think not," Lin said. "We all of us know, don't we, Mr. Priestley, there was nothing to see."

Presumably the group referred to was meant to include Pam, but Amy had seen that it didn't—had seen Pam's face writhe at the notion of having had to watch the thing she'd only heard. "You know that, Amy, don't you?" Lin insisted.

"I don't know what I know."

"Not much of a way for someone who's supposed to read so many books and want to go to university to be."

"If you don't believe I know anything, why do you care what I say?" Amy was tiring of the contest of words; she wanted to be alone, to see if she could think despite the ache. "I don't know if she heard anything or not. I wasn't there."

"Your influence was." Her father's face sidled into view beyond Lin's shoulder. "Do as you are asked for once."

"Better listen to your mother, Pam," said Amy, "if you want some peace."

"But do you think there was anything?" the girl pleaded, clutching her left hand with her right to keep them still.

"Maybe."

Pam's face attempted to decide how that made her feel as the faces of the adults hardened. "She's saying that because she isn't well, because she can't be bothered," Lin told her daughter, firming her grip on her shoulders to emphasise the point. "I hope her room's like that because she's ill, don't you? It's not like yours, is it? An untidy house means an untidy mind, my mother used to say. We shouldn't have expected to get any sense."

As she began to pilot Pam along the corridor Amy's father lingered in the doorway, glaring at her. He turned away when Lin said "Thank you, Mr. Priestley, for at least trying to help."

"I wish I could have been more. Perhaps I shall. In the meantime, may I ask you while you're at your worship to pray for us?"

"Well, ah, yes," Lin said, audibly embarrassed by so direct an approach. "You can, Pamly, if you like."

Amy heard the door shut after the Stoddards and the chain

dragged across, and then her father must have as good as run along the corridor. "I hope you're satisfied," he said, blocking her doorway, "now you have succeeded in distressing a young girl."

"I shouldn't think you'd want me lying when you keep going on about all this holy stuff."

His face grew mask-like, forcing more of the gleam into his eyes. "I prefer not to know you while you are like this."

"Fine. So take your chair out of my room, and after you've done that you can close the door."

His initial response was to push the door open wider; then he advanced into the room, so slowly and purposefully that without knowing why, Amy reached up and pulled the light on. The brightness seemed to flatten his eyes, so that they resembled the pressed glazed eyes of the picture behind him in the hall. He took hold of the chair by its back and raised it from the floor, and she was reminded of a circus trainer facing a dangerous animal. He didn't turn away from her until he was out of the room and depositing the chair beneath the pop-eyed gaze of the old woman being tossed in a basket, and at once he swung to watch her. "I shall leave you to ponder your ways for a little," he said, and shut her in with her thoughts.

She gazed at the faces of Clouds Like Dreams, but they were no more use than the helpless old woman. Whatever the truth about the writing in the margins of the Bible might be, Pam had reminded Amy she wasn't alone in having seen something on the move that shouldn't have been. Old Mr. Roscommon had, and he'd read in her eyes that she had too. Dominic Metcalf must have seen it, and the sight had stopped his heart. Now the desertion of so many of the apartments was giving the unquiet tenants the run of the building, or had Amy's and her father's exploration of the ground floor attracted them? She was tempted to open her door, because she no longer knew if her room was a sanctuary or a cell, but first she wanted to examine the Bible again while she was unwatched by her father.

She leaned gradually over the side of the bed and let her hand trail to the floor. Her fingertips encountered the round moist toothless mouth of a coffee mug before touching the rough porous skin of a misshapen object. This was her canvas handbag, which she hauled onto the quilt so as to fumble out the Bible wrapped in the pages torn from her pad. The book fell open halfway through Genesis, and immediately she saw what Rob would have been unable to realise. He'd never seen much of her handwriting until yesterday, and so how could he have judged the evidence she'd shown him? But as she spread out the sheets from her pad she became aware that although the handwriting in the Bible wasn't hers, hers grew more like it as the transcription progressed.

She felt as though the past she'd dreaded for so long had crept deep into her while she was distracted by the events within Nazarill. The ache forced her head down, trapping her gaze on the pages until she leafed to the pencil embedded in the upright of the last and biggest cross. She dug out the pencil and resting the final, mostly blank, sheet from the pad on the back cover of the Bible, set about writing her name.

Her signature had changed so much over the years that she found herself struggling to recall how it was meant to go. Eventually she thought she remembered how she had most recently decided it should look. Trying consciously to reproduce it stiffened her hand, however, and even when she'd covered the blank paper with her name, none of the dozens of signatures looked quite like hers. Besides, hadn't her signature changed since she'd moved to Nazarill? She didn't want to reflect on that, any more than she liked the appearance of all her signatures; she'd been unable to make any of the esses small enough to reassure herself, and each of the pair of e's resembled eyes spying on her. She crumpled the pages and stuffed them together with the book into her bag, which she kicked onto the floor. She didn't want to see them any more, and especially didn't want her father to do so; he would only think she was going mad. He could think so all he liked once she had convinced herself that she was nothing of the kind. There was one person she could talk to, and as soon as her father was out of the way at church she would.

She wouldn't be comfortable staying in her room until then. She squirmed out from beneath the quilt and stood up. Feeling the paracetamol coming to an end, she swallowed two of Beth's tablets before pacing to the door and edging it open. Her father was muttering to himself somewhere out of sight, presumably praying. She dodged into the bathroom and turned on the bath taps and the extractor fan that was the only break in the outer wall. The water had hardly started to rumble into the fibreglass bath when the doorknob rattled, followed by a harsh knock. "Amy."

"I'm having a bath."

"Best unbolt the door in case you need help."

"Maybe you didn't notice, but I was bathing myself before we ever came near here."

"In case you take a turn for the worse was my meaning."

"I'm fine. Just leave me alone," Amy said, peering at the door to confirm it was bolted. Once the bath was full almost to the trunks of the taps, the way she liked it, she turned the water off and listened at the door. She was unable to sense him, and so she padded to the bath and plunged her hand in. She didn't realise she had braced herself until she recognised that she was trying to be prepared for the possibility that the water would be icy cold. It was hot, only just bearably so on first contact, and she lowered herself by degrees into it and closed her eyes.

Usually she enjoyed letting herself float in the bath. When she was little she used to imagine herself in a sea with the sun on it, on her way to a magic island. Now, however, she felt in danger of somehow drifting too far if she lost awareness of herself. Every so often a wind caught the fan, which responded with a noise like claws scrabbling to get in. Of course the water was cooling, but several times she emerged from a doze with an unpleasant start at how suddenly chill it felt. Each time she unplugged some of it and replaced it with hot water, a process which had grown not so much automatic as obsessive when her father rapped on the door again. "Are you still in there, Amy? Are you likely to be much longer?"

It was a familiar enough enquiry, but there was a new cold sharpness to his voice. "Why?" she said.

"Because it's nigh on time for church."

That so many hours had passed without her noticing came as a shock, but surely it was to some extent welcome. "You go," she said. "I'm staying here."

"I should like to come in there myself if that's not too inconvenient."

Presumably it was his attempt at sarcasm that made him sound as though he was reading an old script, playing at being himself. Amy climbed out of the bath, slopping water on the chubby linoleum, and wrapped herself in a towel from the rail before sliding the bolt back.

If her father had been standing any closer his fixed face would have been against the door. He stood back barely far enough for her to sidle by; indeed, she felt the towel begin to slip as it brushed against him, so that for a moment she thought he had seized it. She was fleeing into her room when she noticed that he hadn't followed but was staring into the bathroom. "Have you done wallowing?" he said.

"Don't know. Why?"

"I suggest the water is let out. I doubt you would relish a cold bath."

She couldn't help shivering at that. She heard the plughole utter a choking sound, eventually followed by a cackling which took rather too long to fade. By that point he'd emerged from the bathroom, and soon he knocked on her door. "You will be staying in, then, since you aren't fit," he said.

"If you say so."

He muttered a few words and moved away, continuing to talk to whomever he was addressing. The door into the corridor opened and closed, and she found she was still listening. When there was no further sound she leaned out of her room to gaze along the hall, which was empty but for eyes. Having returned the towel to the bathroom she pulled on a clean T-shirt, then she removed the phone from its niche and carried it to the main room, dialling on the way. "Directory Enquiries," a woman said almost at once. "What name, please?"

Amy told her, and a likely initial, and the town. Shortly an announcement composed of samples of a female voice gave her the number. She keyed it and heard it ringing out there in the dark. It sounded far more distant than the other side of Partington—as though she was hearing it along a passage so lengthy and narrow she rubbed her forehead hard to rid herself of the idea. She was trying instead to think how best to convey her message when a man said rapidly "I will in a minute. Let me answer this first. Hello."

"Mr. Roscommon?"

"One of them, but sorry, if you're selling anything it's not convenient right now."

"I'm not. I—"

"Bear with me," he said, and withdrew to answer a mumbling. "That's what I'm about to find out if you'll allow me, father. Hello? Who are you, then?"

"It's Amy. Amy Priestley. I used to be on the top floor from you. I mean, I still am."

"I remember. We met you at the photo. What can I do for you?"

"How's Mr. Roscommon?"

"It's kind of you to ask, Amy, very thoughtful. The girl who used to live upstairs on the hill, father. The daughter of the chap who brought us all together, yes, you unfortunately excluded, I was about to say if you'd given me the chance. He isn't as well as he might be, Amy, but as you can hear, he's still able to talk."

"Could I speak to him?"

There was a pause during which she felt her heart thump. "That rather depends," George Roscommon said. "Bear with me a minute, father. What about?"

"Something both of us saw."

A longer pause ensued before he said "I don't know."

"It's important. I've nobody else to ask."

This time there was no reply, so that she thought her desperation had driven him away until she heard his father's mumble in the background. "She's after you, father," he said. "You heard her on the radio. It'll be about that kind of thing."

Mumbling ensued—the same phrase more than once. "Pardon? You—" said George Roscommon, and brought his mouth to the phone. "He'll speak to you. It's against my advice, but I'm just the son."

A silence which Amy took to express more of his reluctance was followed by an outburst of creaking. He must be bearing the phone to his father. A sharper creak apparently indicated the old man's grasp on the receiver, because in a few moments she heard what he had of a voice. It sounded as though he was forcing it out of one side of his mouth. "Who," he said.

Since it was also very slow, she waited for more of the question, only to have him repeat it in a fury at his state or at her lack of response. *"Who."*

"Amy. Amy Priestley. Like Mr. Roscommon said, your son, I live—"

"Help you."

That might have been a promise, except that it had been preceded by a mangled syllable which Amy suspected was "God." She'd fallen silent when he began to heave more words out. "Know you. Saw you outside. Should've stayed there."

"Because of what's in here, you mean. Nobody but me believes there's anything."

"Heard you on the wireless. Would've rung except I wasn't talking to that, that . . ."

His voice was grinding slower; perhaps his thoughts were too. "What would you have said?" she prompted.

"Get everyone out and burn it down. It's crawling."

"Father," his son protested.

"I can't do that," Amy said.

"Then just get out."

"My dad won't. He can't see what we can."

"Get out yourself."

"I've seen more since I was on the radio," Amy said, and then his advice caught up with her. It wasn't at all the sort of advice she would have expected a parent to give her. "Why just me?"

The old man drew a breath which she heard rattling in his throat. "If you can see these things," he said, slower than ever, "they can see you."

"Father," the son repeated, closer now. Amy was afraid the younger man might take the phone away, though that was by no means all she was afraid of. The old man's answer had made her feel both watched and overheard. She stared about, first at the window with the night adhering to it, then through the doorway at the largely unseen hall. She was about to speak, with nothing much to say but yearning to have another person hear her, when the old man demanded "What's that? What's she saying?"

"Shall I take it, father?"

"Crossed line. Some crazy woman saying—that's never a prayer. Tell her to get off. Giving me another stroke. Feel it in my face."

Some or all of this might have been addressed to Amy, but she was unable to respond. She could hear no other voice, and knew it wasn't a crossed line. She was forcing her mouth open to tell him, though that rendered being overheard more of a threat than ever, when his son took over the phone. "My father can't talk to you any more."

His tone made it obvious that he blamed her for the old man's aggravated state—perhaps assumed that the voice responsible had been hers. Before she could argue, the connection was broken, so abruptly she wasn't sure he'd done it. The receiver hummed smugly to itself until she silenced it. Holding it like a small fragile club, she made herself look out of the room.

The hall was deserted, but she felt no less observed. She glared at the kitchen before she remembered there was no longer a tree for anything to climb. The flattened eyes along the walls led her gaze to the dead eye of the outer door, beyond which she was almost sure she glimpsed movement. "Can't get in," she said as loudly as she dared, and tried to feel encouraged. Squeezing the receiver in her fist, she was able to take the first step. She trudged along the hall and hugging herself with both arms, leaned her face towards the spyhole.

At first she thought all the lights in the corridor had failed. Then the object which was pressed against the door retreated far enough for her to see a hole in it which might have been a puckered mouth to which shreds of the lips still adhered. As it withdrew another few inches, a similar hollow in the shrivelled brownish surface became apparent next to it, and below them the stringy gap where the nose had been. The head reared back further, and the gaping jaw came into view. Perhaps it was so wide with a scream at the contents of the mouth, which were swarming over the cracked fleshless chin. Amy stumbled away from the door, the phone in her hand scraping a panel of the wall, and the image shrank, but not soon enough for her to avoid seeing the shape outside the door raise on either side of the remains of its head the handless sticks of its arms.

She retreated until the movement in the lens was no larger than an insect wriggling in a spider's web. "Can't get in," she heard herself repeating, almost as often as "Can't touch me." The eyes on the walls watched her like spectators at an asylum. Eventually the writhing vanished from the bulbous glass, but it took her a considerable time to venture close enough to determine that as much of the corridor as she was able to spy out was empty. That only meant the figure she had seen was somewhere else, and her repetition of the things it couldn't do no longer seemed so powerful. She flung open all the inner doors and switched on all the lights, then she grabbed the remote control of the television, having abandoned the phone on a chair, and searched the channels. Three sitcoms and a congregation swaying and singing and clapping in church, a spectacle she left playing on the basis that television might be modern enough to help fend off the past, one of the few thoughts her headache hadn't pinched out of her skull. On that basis she played a tape of Resurrection Merchants as well, and then there seemed to be nothing to do except sit at a kitchen bench with the phone on the table in front of her and stare along the shaky hall, willing the door to stay shut and impregnable. The spyhole was too distant to betray any movement beyond it, but she kept imagining a handless stump poking about the outside of the door in search of the bellpush.

The tape was at its loudest when she thought she heard a scrabbling at the door. She seized the phone before she realised there were better weapons in the kitchen drawers. She was shoving herself away from the table, the bench digging into the backs of her knees, as the door swung open.

It was only her father, but at once that was bad enough. He covered his ears for a moment as though fitting his mask of grim resolution to his face, then shouldered the door closed and thrust his keys into his coat pocket. "So this is how you conduct yourself when you should be praying," he said, and frowned at the scraped panel. "Good God, what have you been doing to this wall?" He strode towards her, turning off the room lights as he advanced, and stalked into the main room. "Dear Lord preserve us," he muttered, and more that she couldn't distinguish as he killed the stereo and television. As he lurched into view his blank gaze swung at her, gleaming as it came. "We shall put an end to your devilry," he said.

19

KEPT IN THE FAMILY

Oswald was observing how the arched roof of the church resembled saintly bones pressed together and upraised, and so he didn't notice that the Pickles family was following him until they caught up with him in the small stone porch. "All on your own today?" Jack Pickles said.

"As you say."

"Where's the daughter?" Hattie asked from beneath an outbreak of headgear reminiscent of a rockery.

"I'm of a mind to send her away for the good of her health."

Oswald had lit upon this notion in the midst of his prayers, but Jack appeared to think it betrayed some weakness. As they emerged from the porch into a wind as cold as the stones in the churchyard he passed a hand over his freckled scalp imperfectly crossed by failed hair and peered up at Oswald through his square tortoiseshell spectacles. "We hear you had a bit of a to-do yesterday."

"Just some behaviour that should never have been seen in public."

Hattie pushed her son forward in order to refer to him. "Might have been worse if one of our tribe hadn't been there to lend a hand, would you say?"

"I was glad of him."

"What was it all in aid of, anyway?" Jack asked. "Something to do with a Bible, weren't you telling us, son?"

"She'd been writing things she oughtn't in it."

"No need to draw us a picture," Hattie said at once.

"Mam, I wasn't going to," Shaun protested while his cheeks developed a few additional patches of red.

"She was scaring people in the street, wasn't that it too?" said his father.

"And the old biddies in Tea For You," his mother said. "One of them was telling me just now before church."

"You'll take this how it's intended, Mr. Priestley, but your girl's getting a reputation. I'm sure you wouldn't want that."

"I didn't think at first old Miss Clay could be talking about her," Hattie said and glanced around before lowering her voice, though there were only gravestones near. "What's making her behave like that? Is it drugs?"

A thought lanced Oswald's shame. "Let me undertake before you that no poisons will ever be allowed near her again."

"It's a pity there isn't a school here in town so you could keep more of an eye on her. The bigger the place, the worse the influences. Stands to reason."

"I shall be taking that in hand too." Oswald followed her through the gate, which Shaun closed behind his father. "I am grateful to all three of you," Oswald said.

Only Shaun looked as though he felt entitled to be thanked, and Oswald had to resist a compulsion to explain. They'd helped him clarify the course of action he must pursue, but there was no need to publicise his methods. He watched them turn downhill with their son towering between them. They'd kept Shaun under their control, and now it was time for Oswald to do more than they had, before it was too late. He crossed himself while he gazed across Heather's grave at the church, then he drove to Nazarill.

Had she really been too ill even to be driven to church, or could she have been wary lest her behaviour there might betray her? He remembered the last time she had entered the churchyard, remembered her muttering at the grave as if to resurrect her mother. Thank God her mother wasn't here to see how their daughter had gone wrong, nor to hold him back.

No gates, he thought as the Austin passed between the gateposts, nor any need for such so long as there was a keeper. As the light saluted him, Nazarill appeared to expand the better to embrace him. When he admitted himself to the building, the quiet and the subdued light put him in mind of a church. Though he saw nobody on the stairs or in the corridors, he felt welcomed home. He paced along the silent passage to his door and let himself in.

Amy was rising to her feet from behind the kitchen table. She subsided at the sight of him and dropped the phone she was holding. Though he saw it strike the table, he couldn't hear the impact for the uproar in the apartment. As he covered his ears, the keys in his hand stung his cheek. He rammed his shoulders against the door and shoved the keys into his pocket while he breasted the sound, which immediately began to retreat. "So this is how you conduct yourself when you should be praying," he said, and saw as his senses recovered from the onslaught that out of vandalism or worse she had scratched a panel by the door. "Good God, what have you been doing to this wall?"

She'd done more; she had left all the lights on. What had she been about in his room? As the tape held its breath, trying to take him unawares with its next outburst, he marched along the hall, clawing at the switches in the rooms. He had to flail at the air in front of his face as he dodged first into his bedroom, where nothing appeared to have been touched, and then into Amy's; he thought he'd felt a tickling on his skin. Before he could identify the cause, the stereo recommenced its pandemonium, in the midst of which he was just able to distinguish a voice yelling "Let's dance while we die." He stalked into the main room to do away with it, and saw that Amy was using it to drown out the sound of a hymn on television.

"Dear Lord preserve us, are you afraid of a hymn? Thank God your mother—" He pressed his lips together as he switched off the cacophony and then, to allow himself to think, the television. He thought he felt the tickling again, as if his nerves were about to escape his control. He wouldn't allow her to do that to him. He dragged a hand over his face, pinching his eyes with finger and thumb on the way, and stepped into the hall. "We shall put an end to your devilry," he said, and strode at her.

She might at least have had the grace to flinch, he thought. When he turned from replacing the phone in its nest, he found her watching him as if he was the one who'd changed, not her. "I'm what you made me," she said.

"Never dare suggest that, even to me. What you have become is none of my doing, nor any of your—" The reference to her mother caught in his throat as he lowered himself onto the bench between Amy and the hall. "Perhaps it isn't entirely your fault either. I want to know whom you have been talking to."

"Myself."

"Don't say that, even as a joke."

"It's what you think, isn't it? You think I made up all that stuff that's written in the Bible."

"As it happens I think nothing of the kind. Perhaps now you'll have the goodness to tell me where you learned it."

"Learned what?"

"Don't play the innocent, child. You forget your friend gave me an account of it while you were entertaining all the ladies in the tea-room. How did you know there was an asylum here, and a fire?"

Her stare fastened on him. He wouldn't look away from his own child, but he couldn't help rubbing a hand over his face. She appeared to have more than one question to ask, and the one which emerged was "How did you?"

"I made it my business to find out in case it could cure you of your fancies."

Her attention strayed past him. That might have been a relief, except that she gave the impression of seeing or expecting to see more than the empty hall. He felt the crawling on his skin again, and clenched his fists rather than touch his face. "No chance of that," she said, and brought her gaze to bear on him. "You're saying it's true. That's what this place was and that's what happened."

"Amy, please don't try and make me sound as though I've fed your maggot. You know it's true, and I insist on being told who took it upon themselves to give such information to an impressionable girl of your age."

"Can you hear yourself? What do you think you sound like?"

"Your father. Whether you like it or not," he said while his face mouthed outside the kitchen window as though it was prompting him, "that is who I remain. You're playing games, but you shall not be the victor. You're the subject of this discussion, not I."

"So discuss me."

"I believe you have been using this tale of an asylum to behave as if you . . ." He couldn't quite say it—having to think it was bad enough—but other words crowded out of his mouth. "Telling wicked stories on the radio for the world to hear, uttering foul language in the marketplace, going for people in the street as well, I understand. And defacing the Bible, God forgive you, and now damaging our home. Do you realise the whole of Partington knows about you? In the past they would have had you locked up, and perhaps . . ."

"Go on. That's what it wants."

"I have no idea what you mean, nor any wish to know. Is it not possible for you to attempt to listen for once instead of saying the first thing that strays into your head? I'm attempting to confront you with the truth we need to see."

"You are."

"Staring so won't silence me, and I suggest you give it up. Answer me this, a straight answer if you have any within you. Some remedy has to be found for the way you've grown. What do you think it should be?"

He saw her thinking rather than blurt out an answer, and thought she was taking him seriously at last. Then she said "When do you think I started?"

"Becoming as you are? Pretty well since we moved here. I think you decided at the outset to dislike it. I know you were sorry to leave our old home, I appreciate that it had memories for you, but you must see it was too big for just the two of us. We would have moved sooner if I could have found somewhere smaller that was suitable."

He was offering her an excuse for herself, but her concentration seemed to be lingering on his last word. His face began to itch even before she responded. "Do you know what you're saying?" she said.

"I know to the letter."

"You said I started when we moved here, but I didn't know it was an asylum then."

"Which simply means that once you were told about it you used that as a pretext to worsen your behaviour."

"I wasn't told. I read it in the Bible."

"Amy, if you persist—"

"I didn't write it. I wasn't even sure it was true till you said it was."

"Enough. Finis. You won't muddle me. You can stay in your room until you are ready to talk sense, and that means until you tell me who supplied you with all this harmful information I committed myself to keeping from you."

Amy stood up at once, blotting out his night face. "You'll have a long wait."

"Take all the time you can bear. You shall find me waiting."

She stepped around the table, and his face glowed out of the night. It gave him the impression of being her guardian angel until he noticed her keeping as far away from him as there was space. "Cease trying to make me into a monster," he said. "Perhaps you should appreciate I am restraining myself. As soon as you decide to behave rationally—" He was watching her faint shape opening a fainter door, which slammed so hard it would have shaken the wall which contained it had that been less firm. Feeling as though at least some of his speech had been a pretence he'd had to maintain in order to convey her to her place, he turned out the kitchen light and headed for his room.

As he came abreast of her door he felt the tickling on his cheeks. He went swiftly into his bedroom and threw himself to his knees, bruising them, but he wasn't swift enough. Even when he dug his fingernails into the knuckles of his clasped hands, he couldn't pray—couldn't rid his mind of the thought of Amy's room full of crawling things, swarming away from her head and over her quilt and into the mess that covered the floor. He dragged his knuckles over his cheeks to drive away the tickling—the sensation of cobwebs in the air—but couldn't drive away his thoughts. In the past the heads of the unhealthy had been shorn when they became infested, and perhaps that had been Amy's secret reason for having hers cropped. As he shuddered at the threat of the sensation which had invaded the air of his home, it seemed clear to him that she hadn't succeeded in disinfesting herself.

If that hadn't proved successful, what would? This was a question with which he didn't feel able to cope by himself. He was clasping his hands again, bruising his knuckles with his fingertips in an attempt to distract himself from the anticipatory itching of his face, when the phone summoned him.

In one movement he was up from his knees and through the gap he made with the door and snatching the receiver from its perch before it had completed its second pair of rings. A voice he recognised said "Hello?" He let it repeat itself twice while he closed his bedroom door behind him and sat on the end of the bed, at which point he said "Yes."

"Can I speak to Amy, please?"

"I fear not." A sense of calm, of having had at least part of his so

far unspoken prayer answered, let him use the caller's name.
"Robin."

"Doesn't she want to talk to me?"

"I imagine that to be the case. She has given me no contrary impression. Besides, that isn't quite the issue," Oswald said, and permitted himself a smile at the whiteness of his imminent lie. "She isn't here."

"Where is she?"

"Gone away."

"Where?"

Though the boy's voice was beginning to cause him to itch with annoyance, it was at least encouraging him to work out details to tell anyone else who might ask. "To an aunt's."

"I didn't know she had one."

"You scarcely knew she had a father, did you? Little wonder that she failed to mention her Aunt Alice," Oswald went on smoothly as the name presented itself in his head. "I trust you recognise that a retreat is what she needs. She may have told you how upset she was that she couldn't go away with the school."

"How long's she going to be away?"

"As long as need be. I shall be clearing it with the school."

"Have you got her address?"

For an instant that seemed wily of her ill-chosen friend; then Oswald was more in control than ever. "Not even I shall be in contact with her until she improves."

He was assuming that must silence his listener, but he'd omitted from his reckoning the stubbornness of the young. "If she gets in touch," the boy said, "could you tell her—"

"I thought I had made clear that is impossible. Please refrain from calling here again," Oswald said, and cut him off for good.

He listened to the almost monastic drone of the dead line for a few moments before restoring the handset to its place, beside which Amy's door was shut. Was she asleep, or had she heard the phone and ignored it? He rather hoped the latter was the case. Her wilfulness might have some merits after all—indeed, already had. He remembered coming home along the peaceful corridor only to be greeted by her crazed uproar. She had shown him more by that than she could have intended. Whatever had to happen in their flat would be inaudible outside its walls.

20

THE GUARDIANS

Amy was awakened from the latest of her restless dozes by a stealthy sound beyond the foot of her bed. Her eyes snapped open, and she saw the door creeping ajar to let her father peer in at her. His face didn't change as her eyes met his; it seemed as set in its expression as any of the pictures in the hall. It was blank as a sketch waiting for its details to be filled in. His gleaming pupils fixed on her, and then, apparently having seen nothing he wanted to see, he stepped back. As the door began to swing closed she knew she had to get out of the room.

It no longer felt like a haven. Though she'd kept the light on all night, that hadn't helped her sleep; only her exhaustion had. Whenever she had jerked awake she'd felt compelled to survey her surroundings for evidence of intrusion—for any sign that her father, or something less alive, had invaded the room while she'd nodded in her vigil. Once she had opened her eyes to see a denim jacket sliding off a pile of clothes in a corner of the room, and for a moment she'd thought the headless handless shape was about to launch itself at her, to wrap its arms around hers and pin her to the bed. The idea had pursued her into her sleep, where worse nightmares were waiting, all of them set in Nazarill and an increasing number in her room. Now the door was about to shut her in with them, away from the daylight, however feeble, that was levering itself almost imperceptibly more vertical in the hall. "Wait," she called.

The door halted, framing the right side of her father's face. That eye found her again, and the half of a mouth parted its straight lips. "Have you decided to tell me the truth?"

There was only one answer she could give him. "Yes."

"All the truth?"

She might have been trapped in a fairy tale where some evil gate-keeper kept requiring more questions to be answered before she could pass through. "You just wanted to know where I got the history from before."

"Very well, let us make that the beginning. Who was your source?"

"It wasn't a who, it was a what. A book in the market. I read it there, I didn't bring it home." Neither his face nor the door showed any inclination to stir further, and she was searching her abruptly empty mind in some desperation for a title in case he asked for it when he said "After you were expressly instructed not to pry into the past."

"I wanted to know why I saw—the kind of place we're in." Her changing the explanation halfway didn't influence him, and so she forced out another word. "Sorry."

"That at least is welcome. It has been far too long since I've heard that word from you." He pushed the door, revealing all his face. While the door was on the move he looked as though he might be about to turn back into the father she'd had when her mother was alive. Then his gaze strayed to the top of her head, and his face reverted to twice the mask it had been in the narrower gap. "We shall attempt to build on your contrition. Can I trust you to restrain yourself while I go out to work?"

Amy couldn't remember when she had last consulted her watch, but now she did so, having located it on the floor. "Why didn't you wake me?" she cried, raising herself against the headboard. "I've missed my bus. I wanted to go to school."

"I hardly think that is appropriate."

"Why not? What do you mean?"

"Why, so soon after your condition was supposed to have rendered you incapable of attending church."

"I don't feel so bad now," Amy tried to assure him, despite sensing that her headache lay in wait behind her eyes for any number of excuses to constrict her brain. "I can still go. I'll just have to be late."

"No."

He took hold of the edge of the door so swiftly that she heard a fingernail scrape on the wood, and turned his head towards the kitchen. Was he looking for some object with which to wedge her door shut? "All right," Amy called, and had to suck in a breath to steady her voice. "All right, daddy. I'll stay at home. I can work there instead."

His eyes seemed to close around her words and grow brighter for the sustenance. "Where?"

"Here," Amy said, recognising that she ought to have used that word to placate him. "In the flat, I mean. On the table, the dining one. I can't spread myself out in my room."

"No doubt you plan to pollute the air of our home with your diabolical clamour."

"I won't," she said, and saw his eyes narrow further: she shouldn't have seemed so eager to please him. "Only low. I'll have it, my music on low."

Perhaps she had reminded him of some notion he found positive; he nodded to himself before allowing his eyes to grow almost indulgent. "Listen to your dance music, though God knows what kind of dance it is meant to promote, if it will help to keep you here until I return."

"Oh, it will," Amy said, and met his gaze with all the innocence she could muster.

When he finally moved away from the door she threw herself out of bed at once and began carrying schoolwork into the main room. She was on her second trip when he reappeared from his bedroom, buttoning his overcoat. "When are you back?" she said, squaring the pile of books in her arms.

"When I have seen those of my charges I must see."

"Your trade, you're saying," Amy said, less to clarify than to do away with his usage, only to have him look angry, even bewildered. "When about, do you think?"

"As soon as is practicable, I assure you."

She might have concluded that the idea of quitting the building confused him. Nevertheless he strode to the door and unchained it. "For the moment I have responsibilities beyond these walls."

He was hauling the door shut behind him when, having dropped the books on the table, she ran along the hall and grabbed the latch. His face swung towards her, his eyes bright as the spotlights of Nazarill. "What are you bent upon now?"

"Just wanted to say goodbye."

His face shifted, but she had barely glimpsed a reminiscence of affection before it vanished into blankness. "Goodbye for the present."

"I'll close it."

She wasn't holding the door open only to make certain he was really leaving; she wanted to see him looking like her father. From the back, trudging away down the corridor narrowed by dimness, he did. The sight reminded her she was about to be alone, and she had to remind herself that she needed to be. She was biting her lip so as not to call him back—any company was beginning to seem desirable—when his head turned to her as it set about jerking downstairs. Even at that distance she could see the gleam which substituted for compassion in his eyes. She retreated into the flat and slammed the door, telling herself that she wasn't afraid of him, only anxious to be sure he left the grounds.

She had been standing at the window of the main room for some minutes when the Austin nosed into view. As its distorted oblique shadow dragged it to the gateway, she thought he was driving more slowly than usual. The brake lights flared as though the wind that was shivering the grass had kindled them, and then the car edged between the gateposts. As soon as the dead lights disappeared around the curve of Nazareth Row, Amy dashed into her room.

She flung off her T-shirt and fumbled some underwear on before covering herself in the first socks and jeans and sweatshirt and trainers and jacket that came to hand. Some of her fellow apartment-dwellers must surely still be in the building, and even if she didn't meet them in the corridors, their presence should be enough—had to be—to let her reach the outer doors. She strapped on her watch and grabbed her bag and ran between the crowd of pressed fixed goggling eyes to release herself into the corridor.

It was deserted and silent and barely illuminated. She took a step into it and pulled the door after her, let it drift further, saw it shut her out of the apartment with a stealthy thud and a click. Ought she to lock the mortice? Her hand was moving to her bag when she wondered if she should ring Beth's doorbell to ascertain whether she was home from her weekend—except that should Beth not be there Amy wouldn't just have wasted time, she would have robbed herself of some of her determination to brave the way out. Clutching her bag shut in her fist, she sent herself towards the stairs.

Two blurred thin figures paced her, doing their best to mimic her actions. Whenever one came to the edge of a panel the wood pinched it thinner before letting go of it. She had to keep recalling that the figures were herself—versions of herself that the walls wanted her to see. Each time she passed a door she glimpsed movement in its pupilless eye, and that was her too, or part of herself that the constricted squeezed-out globes were attempting to trap.

The secretive dimness clung to her like centuries of grime, and yet it was impalpable as the stifling heat. They seemed to conspire to render her footsteps inaudible on the marshy carpet, and she had to restrain herself from tramping hard to convince herself that she was indeed on the way to making her escape. She had grown so preoccupied with her own lack of sound as she reached the stairs that she wasn't sure whether she heard a door opening beyond them.

She grasped her bag tighter, it being the only weapon she was aware she had, and felt her held breath trembling in her nostrils. Just before she had to gasp it out she heard the door shut gently, and a rattle of keys. Someone had come out of an apartment on the middle floor. "Hello?" Amy called. "Who's down there?"

There was silence from below while she breathed again, followed by a renewed sound of keys, sharper and quicker. The door was being locked. Amy raised her voice to be sure she was audible over the metallic clatter. "It's Amy. Amy Priestley from the top floor. Hang on, I'm coming down."

This time there was no pause. The rattling turned into a harsher sound and reverted to itself, then ceased. The keys had been snatched out of the lock to be shoved into a pocket or a handbag, and the muffled rapid padding that ensued meant that whoever was below was making for the stairs. It took Amy several seconds—long enough for the footsteps to start descending—to understand that the person was anxious not to meet but to avoid her.

Amy faltered, then she hurled herself at the stairs. It didn't matter who was down there or what they thought of her, only that she kept them in sight long enough to help her flee through the ground floor of Nazarill. At least now she was able to hear the thuds of her own feet, but she could also hear those of the other person speeding up. She seized the clammy metal banister and swung herself around the bend in the stairs, and took the lower flight two at a time.

As her heels dealt the middle floor a united thump, the footsteps she was pursuing came to a halt. She hadn't had time to draw breath to call out when she heard a subdued glassy clang. The other tenant had opened the exit doors.

Amy heard the world let in: the generalised murmur of Partington augmented by the slow roar of a lorry passing through the town, a repeated single note of a birdsong chipping at the icy air, a child's high voice calling "Mummy, come and look at this." A hint of the chill of the January day touched her, and she didn't think there could be any sensation more welcome. The next moment the deadened note of the doors tolled, shutting out the world.

"Wait," Amy cried without thinking—without knowing whether she was trying to arrest the person who'd abandoned her or to hold on to a sense of freedom beyond Nazarill. The latter was enough to make her reckless, and she launched herself onto the next flight of stairs, slapping the banister as she missed each second tread. She almost collided with the glowing wall at the bend, where a faceless parody of herself floundering in amber loomed up to meet her. She shrugged off the image and caught at the banister, which was thrumming dully from her slaps, to swing herself onto the last flight. Her heel struck the second tread down with an impact which seemed to jar her brain, and then she was teetering on the edge of the next but one. Not only her precariousness made her clutch at the banister so hard that pain surged through her wrist. She could see the ground floor, and it was going to be worse than she'd feared.

The spectacle of a vehicle shrinking along the drive distracted her from immediately seeing the worst. The car was a shiny black Honda—Max Greenberg's car. So it had been the watchmaker who'd fled upon hearing her voice. She would have expected better of him. Scarcely aware of her actions, she descended a step to keep the car in view. As she did so it flashed its brake lights at her between the gateposts. Then it was gone, and she was alone with the vista of gravel stretching to the distant road.

The glass doors seemed almost as distant. Perhaps that was one reason why the view beyond them appeared less than entirely convincing, more like a photograph projected on the glass and framed by the dim elongated corridor. It was all too easy to imagine herself trapped in a former time with which the outside world was insufficiently real to connect. That couldn't be, any more than it was possible for the corridor to have extended itself; the tinge of daylight seeping across the carpet towards the stairs was enough to refute both these fears. Indeed, the daylight was strong enough to cast a thin shadow of the edge of each apartment doorframe onto each door—except that her innards were tightening as though to retreat deeper within her, because she knew she was deluding herself. None of the doorknobs cast a shadow, which meant that the vertical lines of darkness weren't shadows either. Every one of the six doors was ajar.

The sight froze her and, it seemed, everything: even the advance of the feeble sunlight across the floor. Perhaps when the light reached the stairs she would be capable of moving—and then she realised it never did. If someone, anyone, came downstairs she could walk through the ground floor with them, though it was late enough by now for everyone except her to have quitted the building. She strained her ears for any hint of company while she stared in panic at the gaps between the doors and their frames. Staring only made the doors appear to creep wider, so that she had to blink away the impression, and suppose any sound she managed to hear came from beyond them? Her clenched hands were being transformed into bruises, one containing sensations of metal and the other of rough canvas, and her ankles had begun to throb from pressing her heels into the angle of the stair. If she moved now it would only be to bolt upstairs, but if she did that she thought she would never leave Nazarill. She was struggling to derive some impetus from that thought—enough rage at her helplessness to inflame her to action—when she saw movement beyond the glass.

While she kept glimpsing traffic on Nazareth Row, none of the cars seemed to have any function other than to mock her plight, but there was more to this. A small truck emblazoned with a crossed fork and spade had pulled up outside the railings. She recognised it, and almost cried out to the driver to come on, but succeeded in restraining herself to a choked gasp. In a moment the truck turned along the drive and halted a few yards inside the grounds. She didn't dare step down yet, but she stooped to watch as George Roscommon climbed out of the cab.

She would wait until he saw her, and then nothing would deter her from sprinting for the exit—nothing that she wanted to imagine. She saw his heels strike the gravel, and he gave the door of the truck a hearty slam. She heard neither impact, but perhaps she was wholly preoccupied with feeling in danger of losing her balance, having stooped too far. She clung to the banister while she lowered one foot to the next stair and planted it so gingerly her leg quivered with the strain of being careful. George Roscommon reached through the open window of the cab and fished out a clipboard before turning towards Nazarill.

She had to go down further to ensure she was seen. She made her grip on her bag more uncomfortable to assist her in relinquishing her hold on the banister, and took a jerky tentative step which froze in midair. Hers had not been the only surreptitious movements within Nazarill. While she had been intent on the gardener, both of the doors closest to the stairs had opened at least another inch.

That almost paralysed her again, but not quite. George Roscommon was gazing along the drive at Nazarill as he strolled past the truck, and she would never have a better chance of being seen by him. She flung herself away from the banister and down the stairs, six of them between her and the ground floor which she must see only as her route to liberty. Five, four, and now he couldn't avoid noticing her; he was gazing straight at her. She risked another stair—though that made it impossible for her to ignore the gaping inhabited darkness on both sides of the corridor—and waved her arms, agitating the contents of her bag. George Roscommon was shading his eyes as he passed the front of the truck. The next moment he turned, his face making clear that he'd observed nothing unusual, and headed for the nearest flower-bed.

"Wait," Amy cried, her voice tearing at her throat. "Don't go away. I'm here." The gardener continued walking, no more aware of her than she had been able to hear the slam of the door of the truck. Before she had time to fill her lungs again, he moved out of the frame of the doorway. At once the view was no more than a picture of a freedom she couldn't attain. The gaping doors were altogether more real, and she knew her pleas had been heard beyond them.

Her panic seemed to darken the corridor almost to blackness, and then she found herself shaking with rage. She was letting herself be rendered helpless while daylight and companionship and release were practically within her reach. "You can't stop me," she shouted, "I'm going to him," and started down the last three stairs, not so much setting her feet down as allowing them to fall of their own weight. They took her to the beginning of the corridor, but that was as far as her body was willing to go. At each of her steps the nearest doors had crept further open, and now an object was visible just above the knob of the left-hand door.

It might have been a set of legs on one side of a spider, legs emerging from the trap that the creature was widening in anticipation of its prey. Only their size told Amy that the four long thin crooked members were the fingers of a hand, which was displaying itself to notify her that it was ready to throw the door wide if she ventured nearer. Amy hugged her bag with both arms in case that gave her strength, but it simply made her feel even more crushed into herself. Her lips had begun to tremble, drawing so much of her awareness to them that it was partly to control them that she spoke. "What do you want? I've never done you any harm."

The fingers hitched themselves forward on the wood, and then the forefinger raised itself, tatters of skin at the knuckles peeling away like bark on a rotten twig. Though it had no nail and very little flesh, there was no mistaking its intention. It was pointing straight at her.

Amy had to respond, because she'd thought of a ruse. "Well, you can't have me. I never wanted to live here in the first place," she said with the very little confidence she could summon up, and as she spoke she was forcing herself to be prepared to move. The moment she fell silent she made herself start tiptoeing towards the doors.

She had never considered how vulnerable that posture felt—as though she was about to lose her shaky balance with every step. All the same, her plan seemed to be working. The remains of a finger were continuing to point at the foot of the stairs, where Amy had last been audible. So long as none of the doors was open wide enough to allow her to be seen as she crept past, or to let her see whatever remnant of a face lurked there—but she was several paces short of the nearest doors when she was addressed by a voice.

It was toneless as a sound of husks rubbing together in a wind. She wasn't sure that she was hearing it outside her brain, where it felt like webs settling over her consciousness. "None of us did," it said.

You can't blame me, I wasn't even alive, thought Amy, trying to stand still on the tips of her trembling legs. In a moment she saw that her efforts were useless. Her response, though silent, had betrayed her. The finger raised itself almost to snapping like a twig and pointed in her direction, then it beckoned, twitching more than ever like a spider's leg.

She'd had enough of its games. If she couldn't conceal her presence she wasn't going to act afraid, however much she was. Surely there was nothing in the rooms that would be capable of overtaking her if she sprinted for the doors. She dropped herself to her heels, causing less noise than she'd feared, and poised herself to run. They couldn't scare her by opening the doors, she tried to convince herself: she had already seen how they looked.

Her pretence of reassurance might just have worked, except she had forgotten that it could be overheard. It brought an immediate response. The fingers flexed as though recalling how to exert themselves; then they pushed the door away and sent their body tottering to meet her.

Perhaps in answer to her thought, it appeared to want her to see it as it had once been. If anything, this worsened its looks. The grey wispy coating of the skull was certainly not hair. The figure still had some of a face, or had somehow reconstructed parts of one, which looked in danger of coming away from the bones, as the scraps of the chest were peeling away from the ribs to expose the withered heart and lungs, which jerked as though in a final spasm as Amy's gaze lit on them. It had taken her only a couple of seconds that felt like forever to distinguish all this—not long enough for her to back away, supposing she could. Then the shape took another staggery step towards her and raised its cobwebbed head against the sunlight. Enough tatters of its lips survived for her to be able to see it mouth the words that entered her mind: "Remember your dream."

Amy almost understood, and that was why she resisted understanding. She felt close to a terror even more dreadful than the sight in front of her. The figure stretched its arms wide, so slowly and unevenly it might have been tearing them free of an enormous web, and she saw light between the bones. She thought it meant to wobble forward and embrace her, and despite its slowness she wasn't sure that she would be able to back out of its reach—but she had misinterpreted its intentions. When it began to curl what passed for fingers on its right hand, she knew it was summoning a companion from beyond the door.

Amy heard movement in the dark—a scuttling over the carpet.

It sounded crippled but rapid, and smaller than its summoner. Despite guessing its size, she wasn't prepared for how low down it presented itself around the door, hardly a foot above the carpet. The face might once have been almost human, and even now the hole too large to be called a mouth was doing its best to counterfeit an expression, rendered yet more grotesque by the shrivelled blackened lolling tongue. Though its eyes were long gone, it cocked its head around the door towards Amy, and the scrap of skin between its ragged nostrils fluttered in and out. It lurched into the corridor on members which had never been entirely hands nor paws, and dropped to its haunches, its incomplete sides heaving. It was waiting for instructions from its mistress.

Amy's body had taken over from her thoughts. As the hands jerked to point at her, she wasn't aware of retreating until the backs of her ankles struck the lowest stair. The shrivelled creature hobbled quickly at her, its head wagging like a puppet's with each unequal step, and she whirled round, not knowing which way she was turning or which hand her bag was in or whether it was that hand she had flung out for the banister. It was not, and as it struck the metal she hauled herself upstairs almost faster than she could breathe.

Was the light growing dimmer? She was almost certain that it had begun to flicker. In the midst of all her terror she found she was afraid to touch the wall. She swerved around the first bend and glanced downwards. Her pursuer was already halfway up the lowest flight, its enlarged mouth writhing over the bared display of more than teeth. She practically fell up the stairs to the middle floor, and only just saved herself from sprawling helplessly onto it by clinging to the banister. As she let go of it, she heard a door opening along the corridor.

If she had been thinking—since she had no time to establish which door it was, and no means of knowing who or what had opened it—she might not have called out. "Quick, come and see," she cried. "It's on the stairs. You have to see it, then you'll believe me."

She was indeed addressing one of her fellow tenants. That was immediately clear from the way the door—Peter Sheen the journalist's, she realised now—slammed, shutting her out. The silence was broken by a muffled scuttling which sounded so close below her that she dared not look. Grabbing almost blindly at the banister, she floundered upstairs, trying to open her bag with the hand in which it was, to have her keys ready by the time she reached her door.

All she achieved was to risk both dropping the bag and losing her grip on the banister. In her panic she hardly knew which hand was which. She hitched herself around the bend and up the last handfuls of banister. When it came to an end she had to remind herself that now she had both hands free to deal with the bag. As she fled into the unreliable twilight of her corridor she supported the bag with one hand while she picked at the drawstring with the other. Her earlier attempt to loosen it seemed to have pulled it immovably tight. She was nearly at her door, and sobbing with rage and loss of breath, when she felt the mouth of the bag give a reluctant inch. She wrenched it wide with all her fingers and thrust them in.

The stiff cold rectangle of her bus pass, a crumpled five-pound note and a scattering of coins, an open pack of towels which yielded to her groping, a birthday card which she'd forgotten to send one of her friends and which she was saving until next year, the Bible and the pages in which it was wrapped, a lump of rock she'd thought resembled a baby's smiling face when Rob had found it for her on the moors, her tube of pills from Beth, some scribbled bits of paper, and—at last, at the very bottom of the bag—a chink of metal against metal. She closed her fingers around her keys. They almost pierced her skin, the tines did, because the object she'd located was her comb, which had knocked against a stray coin. Her keys weren't in the bag.

She hauled it open to the limit of the drawstring and peered desperately into it, but could see little of its contents in the dimness. She upended it and shook it empty in front of her door. Everything she'd felt in it spilled out, and nothing else. She flung the bag at the glinting eye of the door and dug her hands into all her pockets, but there were no keys. As her thoughts began to circle helplessly in search of when she'd last had the keys and what she could have done with them, she heard a movement at the far end of the corridor. Her reluctant eyes turned towards it, dragging at their sockets until the ache forced her head round. A shrivelled eyeless head was poking above the top stair, awaiting her next move.

Amy stooped so fast the rush of blood to her head seemed to drive all the meagre light from the corridor. She knew what she was reaching for, and before she could see she'd straightened up again with the comb in her hand. She'd known when she bought it that the pointed handle could double as a weapon if she ever needed to defend herself, and now she had a use for it. She imagined rushing along the corridor to stab wildly at her persecutor, but she couldn't bear the prospect of touching any of the denizens of Nazarill. Instead she began to gouge at the door where the wood concealed the lock.

Splinters flew, and she heard and felt the chunk of metal cutting into wood. Fewer than twelve blows, however, and the handle of the comb started to bend. She dug the point between door and frame and tried to catch the bolt of the lock to chivvy it out of its socket, only to find herself unable to thrust the comb deep enough or, once she'd given up, to pull it out either. She lurched across the corridor, her eyes refusing to glance in the direction of the stairs, and leaned both hands clenched together on the doorbell in case Beth had come home before Amy had left the apartment. When there was no response for longer than she wanted to imagine, she snatched up her bag to protect her hands while she hung onto the comb and threw all her weight backwards. The comb sprang free, and she almost cannoned into the opposite wall, but crouched away from it and renewed her assault on the door, trying to straighten the comb with her blows. She failed to recognise how her chipping at the wood was overwhelming all her senses, narrowing them down to itself, so that she didn't immediately notice when she ceased to be alone in the corridor.

When she heard movement closer than the stairs she whirled round, raising the comb like a knife. Her father was halfway along the corridor, staring at her and the debris around her with no expression she could name. As she saw him he strode forward and grabbed the wrist of the hand that was holding the comb while he slid his key into the lock. He twisted the key viciously and shoved her against the door so hard that she staggered several feet along the goggling hall. She recovered in time to see him kicking her bag and its contents into the apartment as he retrieved the key. In a moment the door was shut, and he was locking the mortice. "You don't need to do that," Amy said with the little breath she was able to summon.

"Yes," her father said in a voice she hardly recognised—didn't want to recognise. "Yes, I must."

21

THE LAST MESSAGE

The key was withdrawn and inserted in his trousers pocket, and as he turned towards her Amy had time to realise how afraid she was of him—too afraid to venture within his reach to pick up her belongings from the floor. She couldn't help retreating a step as his face came into view, though she wasn't quite able to define what she saw. Some quality she might not have appreciated while it was there had gone out of his face to be replaced by the unyielding gleam of his eyes. If she let her fear take over her mind she would imagine that he was only pretending to be her father, that the eyebrows she'd seen growing bushier and greyer throughout her childhood, and the cheeks and chin that had sagged with the burden of those years, were the most convincing aspects of a mask. She didn't want to hear his voice again, not now it had become as cold and heavy and oppressive as the old stones walling her in. Still less could she bear the silence, however, and she saw him waiting for her to speak. Perhaps there was some way to move him. She made herself breathe evenly despite the shivers that kept passing through her, but she couldn't think of much to say—just the truth. "I lost my keys."

His gaze closed around that, but she couldn't read the gleam. Maybe more of the truth might appeal to him on her behalf, if he truly wanted to protect her. "I was frightened," she said, and fought another shudder. "I couldn't get back in."

"You should not have been out. You undertook not to be."

"I know what I said, but when you'd gone I couldn't—I had—"

The truth hadn't worked, but she was incapable of manufacturing a story that might convince him. "Didn't you see anything when you came in?" she blurted, though if these terrors hadn't been so recent she would have kept them to herself. "Didn't you hear something on the stairs?"

"I heard someone causing damage to the property, and I prayed it was not my daughter. Perhaps you yourself can tell me what I saw."

"I told you, I was trying to get back in. I'd have thought that would please you," Amy said, and realised she sounded crazy even to herself. "It's like I said, I lost my keys, and I wasn't expecting you back so soon."

"You hoped I would not be, rather."

"Why would I have felt like that," Amy said, so confused she no longer had the least idea whether this was true, "when I needed you to let me in?"

It was clear that he thought she was trying to trick him; the blankness hardened on his face before his mouth shifted. "I have your keys."

"Where did you find them?" Amy said, and held out her hand.

He stared at the gesture with a weary disbelief which he then raised to her face. "Where you left them."

"Why didn't you just give them to me?" she said, and kept her hand out. "Can I have them now? They're mine."

"I should not have taken them if you might have them."

Amy felt in danger of shivering again, but instead the cold which had suddenly invaded her body held it still. "Taken them from where?"

"I fear your untidiness has proved to be your downfall," he said, and poked her bag with a foot. "You may remember leaving this unattended after you had sought asylum with a friend in Sheffield."

"I don't believe you," Amy said unevenly, meaning his behaviour. "You stole my keys."

"Perhaps you should remind yourself you had them by my sufferance. This home is your only refuge, and I was making sure of it."

"A refuge from what?" Amy demanded, seeing her chance.

"From the eyes of everybody who has seen what you've become."

"If you hate me so much, give me my keys back and you'll never need to see me again."

"I think not. I shall not shirk the responsibility I have been given."

Amy's headache was pressing against the backs of her eyes, and she cared less and less what she said. "If it hadn't been for mummy you wouldn't have had me. Try and think how she'd have treated me. She'd never have behaved like you're behaving."

"Your mother's dead."

A disgust so total it looked capable of extinguishing any other emotion that remained in him had filled his eyes, but that wasn't enough reason for the fear which Amy sensed awakening in her. As though weighed down by his contempt, his gaze sank to her bag and its scattered contents. "Clear away this offal," his stony voice said.

At first Amy didn't think she could—didn't think she dared venture within his reach while her new dread remained unspecified and yet so close to definition—and then she saw the Bible and its attendant pages at his feet. If she lost that material, the nearest thing she had to evidence was gone. She made herself stoop to recover her bag, the foremost item, and felt as though his contempt was dragging her head down by the neck. "Mind out," she managed to say, more timidly than she wanted to. "Give me space."

Perhaps her gaze had revealed her intentions. When he moved it was to lumber at her, sweeping the strewn objects with the sides of his feet, except for the Bible and its papers, which he left behind him. "Stop kicking my stuff," she cried. "I thought you didn't like things being damaged."

"That is no longer your Bible," he said as if she hadn't spoken. "There will be no more desecration here."

"I found it. It's mine." As she spoke Amy was shoving her comb into her bag to prevent herself from jabbing at him with it. Changed though he was, she mustn't let her desperate panic cause her to attack him; what would her mother have thought of her? "You don't want it now it's been written in," she told him, staring her hardest at him.

"It is my duty to acquaint myself with your ravings," he said, and brushed at his cheeks with his fingertips, exposing more of the gleam in his eyes. "You have kept your last secret from me."

"I wanted you to read the writing in there, don't you understand?"

"I'll hear no more of your lies." He swiped his cheeks again, enlarging his eyes so that they rivalled the eyes squeezed huge by the glass of the picture-frames, and this time his fingernails left marks. "God help us, I think you believe them."

Amy bowed her head and fell almost to her knees as if he'd got the better of her. She scooped the rock that had lost its baby face into her bag, and followed it with the pack of towels. Now the Bible was within her arm's length. If she had been able to think more clearly she might have seen that pretending to ignore it only betrayed her plan. She darted a hand out, and had touched the wad of loose pages when her father planted one heel on her forehead and shoved.

It was the brutality of the gesture as much as its force that sent her sprawling. The heel felt rough as a brick, and she caught a whiff of decaying vegetation. As her elbows struck the floor she clenched her teeth so that he wouldn't see her wince. For an instant too brief for her to be certain she'd glimpsed anything he appeared dismayed by her fall and by his own action, then his eyes renewed their blankness. They looked as if they were forgetting how to blink. "Don't require worse of me," he said. "Do as you were bid and clear—"

His voice rose to a shout. Amy had used her aching arms to heave herself upright and was retreating along the hall. She flung her bag through her doorway onto her bed, to have both hands free, and dashed across the main room to the window.

Beneath a sky like ice on a lake George Roscommon was scrutinising a flower-bed near the railings. Amy wrenched at the catch of the sash, bruising her fingertips. It wouldn't budge. Even when she succeeded in digging the side of her left hand behind that end of the semicircle of metal while she rammed the heel of her right against the other dull point, nearly breaking her skin, the catch didn't stir in its groove. She heard her father tramping towards the room, and each of his footsteps felt like the threat of another bruise to her forehead. She freed her hands from the catch and began to thump the window with her fists. "Help," she cried. "My father's hurting me. I don't know what he'll do."

The pane vibrated with her blows, and it seemed the view beyond it did, a phenomenon which rendered the presence of the gardener even more distant and unconvincing. He had paused to scribble on his clipboard, but despite all the noise she was making, close to deafening herself, he didn't so much as glance up. She should have kept hold of her bag—she might have been able to smash the glass with the rock. She swung around, desperate for something else she could use, and found herself staring instead at her father.

He was watching her from the hall, his hands clasped in front of him. At first she couldn't understand why his remaining there should frighten her, and then she saw that he knew he needn't approach—knew she wouldn't be able to open the window or make herself heard outside Nazarill. Her forehead was throbbing as if her earlier headaches had been a premonition of her injury, but she hung onto her thoughts and swallowed a sour taste, and spoke. "What told you he couldn't hear me through the window?" she said, and fastened her stinging gaze on her father.

She wouldn't have believed his expression could grow blanker, but it did. It was no answer, she thought—it was a pretence, even if he didn't know it was—and so she held his stare with hers. Soon he began to jerk his head from side to side as though to dislodge the idea she'd planted there. When her gaze didn't leave him he unclasped his hands and clawed at his cheeks, and she had a sudden terrible impression that she was about to see him drag his face into the shape of someone else's. Before that could quite happen he let go of it and stalked into the room. Rather than argue with her question or even consider what it implied, he meant to turn his confused rage on her.

He was halfway across the room when she darted for the hall. She had to dodge around the table to stay out of his reach, but she hadn't realised how much time that would give him to head her off. He took just three deliberate steps to match her effort and was between her and the door, his hands stretched out negligently on either side of him. His face seemed to have abandoned all interest in wearing an expression until she seized a chair by its back and overturned it in his path. As he saved himself from toppling over it, his teeth bared and his blank eyes bulging, she fled into the hall.

Her first, thoughtless, instinct was to run to the corridor. That made no sense until she found her keys, if she ever had a chance to find them. She was sprinting to her room and thinking how to barricade her door when another course of action suggested itself—the only one that might work. She snatched the telephone out of its plaque and dashed into the bathroom, hurling her weight against the door as her father leapt over the chair and flew across the hall. She was jamming the bolt into its socket with her left hand, which seemed to possess by no means enough strength, when he crashed into the door.

The inch or so of bolt that had penetrated the socket almost sprang out again, and she thought she saw it start to bend. She tried to dig her heels into the linoleum, and felt them slither out from under her as she failed to wedge the door with herself. Then its pressure against her slackened, and she was able to ram the bolt home as the door shook with a blow from his fist. "Return that instantly," he shouted.

Amy took hold of the receiver with both hands to quell its trembling. She thumbed the talk button and waited, but there was dead silence in the earpiece. She'd begun to think Nazarill had cut her off from phoning when the receiver established contact with a line, just as her father dealt the door a series of thumps that made her forehead throb. "Unbolt this now," came his voice like a sharp blade through the wood.

His noise was driving out of her head every number she might call. For an unbearable few seconds the only person she could bring to mind was old Mr. Roscommon, but she couldn't remember his number, and what use would he be in his state? It occurred to her to consult her watch for some sense of who might be at home now. Her watch had stopped for the first time ever—stopped close to, or perhaps exactly on, her emergence from the flat. The period since then felt as though it reached deep into the night, but her last view from the window implied some stage of the afternoon, surely late enough for people to be home. Her father battered the door again, so hard she saw it quiver in its frame, and as he shouted "This is not your door. Open it at once" she keyed the only number she'd left in her head.

The phone rang five times as if to discourage her from waiting before it greeted her with a wholly impersonal hired message. "Hello. Nobody's here at the moment. Please leave your name and number and we'll get back to you as soon as possible." In its modernity it struck her as the sound of a future from which she was being excluded. "Rob?" she pleaded. "Are you there? Be there."

The receiver emitted a shrill beep and then fell silent. If she didn't speak the tape would switch itself off. "It's me," she said awkwardly. "I—"

It wasn't only the memory of how she had dismissed him in Tea For You that made her hesitate. She had a sense of being overheard—by Nazarill, or by her father, or both? She mustn't let either silence her. "I'm sorry I told you to fuck off," she said as another blow rattled the door in its frame. "I felt like everyone was against me. You aren't really on my dad's side, you can't be, he isn't my dad any longer. Come here and you'll see. Please don't just call."

Was there a faint sound along the line—a hint that someone at the other end was listening? If her father spoke someone else might hear his changed voice, but he was busy throwing his weight at the door, which looked as though it wouldn't last much longer. She pressed the receiver against her face so hard the earpiece amplified a creak either of plastic or of bone. "Come and fetch me," she said unsteadily. "He won't let me out. I tried to get out while he was at work, but—I couldn't. He came back before he would have normally. I think it called him back, this place did."

She'd restrained herself from mentioning why she had been unable to leave, but perhaps she had still said too much. "I mean . . ." she continued, to retain her presence on the tape while she searched for an explanation that wouldn't demand too much faith of Rob. "It's like . . ." she added, and had conceived nothing further to say when a woman's voice revealed itself in her ear. "Amy, I think that's enough."

She sounded even less welcoming than when she had refused to admit Amy to her house, but Amy couldn't let herself be put off now. "Is Rob there, Mrs. Hayward?"

"He is not. He's at school, where I'd have expected you to be."

"When is he home, do you know?"

"I couldn't tell you."

"Don't you really know?" Amy pleaded, and when the only answer was a silence which she had no doubt was offended, said not much less desperately "You'll let him hear what I said when he comes home though, won't you?"

"I'm afraid I won't be doing that, no. I'll be wiping the tape."

Amy felt as though her forehead had received another blow, and sat down hurriedly on the edge of the bath. "Why?" she heard herself protest.

"For a start, I won't have language like the word you used in my house, and I hope Robin never uses it anywhere else either."

In that case, Amy thought, she didn't know her son as well as she was implying, but the perception was no help. "I was saying I was sorry I did," she said with all the contrition she could muster.

"I'm glad of that at least."

"So will you—" Amy closed her eyes tight and vowed she was going to sound reasonable. "Will you say to him I need to see him as soon as he can come over, no later than tonight, so I can tell him to his face?"

"No, Amy. Forgive me, but no."

"Why not?" Amy cried, and her thin shrill voice in the earpiece seemed to penetrate her brain.

"Because it isn't Robin you need to see, and I hope your father's taking care of that."

"Didn't you hear how he's trying to take care of me?" Amy almost screamed, and realised she could no longer hear him—couldn't judge when she had ceased to do so or where he was now. "What do you mean he should do?"

"Oh, Amy, if you're going to force me to say this I will. Just from what I heard when you didn't know I was listening it's clear you need medical help, you poor child."

"You should talk to my father," Amy said bitterly, "you'd get on with—" and clapped her free hand over her mouth. She'd told herself how to distract her father, perhaps even how to persuade him to take her out of Nazarill. She let her hand drop, uncovering her resolutely artless face in the mirror, and said "I mean it, you should talk to him. He needs someone to tell him I ought to have help. Wait and I'll—"

At first it was the noise outside the room which cut her off—a wrenching that resounded through the wall. She thought her father was attempting to dig out some of the bricks that were keeping him away from her. Then the wrenching gave way to a splintering crash, and the phone went terminally dead.

It took her a good few seconds of jabbing buttons and trying to be certain she hadn't somehow switched off the receiver before she could believe that he'd ripped the housing of the phone off the wall. She hugged the useless receiver to her midriff and stared, her eyes feeling shrivelled with lack of sleep, at the door. She was bracing herself to see it quiver, but her father only spoke. "What more will you have me do?"

The chill of his voice seized her whole body. The aerial of the receiver tapped against the mirror, then scraped it, and she reached to push the metal rod into itself. The back of her hand touched the back of a hand cold as glass, and she saw herself holding a weapon. She firmed her grip on it without interfering with the aerial and did her best to hold herself as steady, along with her speech. "If you go away from the door I'll come out," she called.

She'd taken two deep breaths which tasted not quite pleasantly of soap before she heard a response—a crunch of plastic. He'd trodden on a fragment of the housing, not many yards along the hall. "I have moved," the wall said in his voice.

"No, where I can see you. Go in the big room. Go right across and keep talking."

"Let my words enter your soul." As he spoke she heard another snap of trodden plastic, and his heavy steps returned along the hall. She thought he was loitering outside the bathroom door until she heard him commence praying in the main room. "Our Father . . ."

Amy ventured almost to the door, but only so as to understand what was happening: he no longer sounded as though he was in the room she knew. Even when she grasped that he was speaking louder with each pace he put between them, she had to convince herself that she would see nothing unfamiliar if she opened the door—nothing except the man who was shouting his prayer as if to falter might rob him of the ability to pray. He was more than halfway through a second repetition of the prayer by the time she finished sneaking the bolt out of its socket and edged the door open a crack.

He was standing at the window, his shoulders against the pane. Beyond the glass the shadow of Nazarill was encouraging the night, a darkness which Amy thought she saw solidifying around his face, like a liquid capable of eating away its outline. "Deliver us from evil," he roared as she inched the door towards her. Their eyes met, and he gasped himself silent.

He'd run out of breath at last, Amy thought, but it was immediately apparent that he didn't think so—that he blamed her for his faltering. He scratched at his face on either side of his mouth, which he had clamped shut so hard its lips virtually disappeared, and stepped forward as his dwindling image sank into the night. Amy stood her ground and brandished the receiver, wagging the aerial at him. "Better not touch me again," she said.

He held out his upturned hands, then let them drop as though the spectacle they were indicating was too much for them. "What kind of creature have you become that you offer violence to your own father?"

Despite everything, that affected her—forced her to imagine how it would have made her mother feel. "It's no worse than you did to me," she cried.

"That was my unhappy obligation. I am your father."

"Then act like one. If I'm supposed to be ill, take me to a doctor."

"I heard you."

She thought she'd managed to fasten on his words at last until he said "I need no outsider to tell me my duty. It is plain to me the shame of it is best kept within these walls."

He'd overheard her talking to Rob's mother. Amy felt as though his responses were walling her up, compelling her to pace an area bounded by the same few cramped ideas over and over again. She'd let the receiver droop in her grasp, but now she raised it as a warning. "You won't," she blurted, and dodged along the hall.

The pressed eyes appeared to be gawping at the mess she and her father had left on the floor. Glancing back to ensure that he wasn't in sight, she darted into his room. She was barely over the threshold when she halted, too confused even to think of closing the door.

The neatness of the room was daunting enough: the disciplined ranks of items on the dressing-table, their symmetry doubled by the mirror; three pairs of shoes supporting one another, toes upturned, on the floor at the foot of the bed; the pillow innocent of the slightest trace of a head, the pale quilt smoothed flat as a slab. The room felt lifeless, no longer inhabited by anyone she knew, and cold enough to make her shiver all the way to her teeth. Her keys must be somewhere in it if they weren't on him. She was glaring about, feeling as though the indefinable unfamiliarity of the room was helping hide the keys, when she heard footsteps enter the hall. She ran to the wardrobe and flung open the panelled doors.

To the left his shirts, a flattened mass of white, were dangling their many arms; to the right his suits had drawn their legs up. All the contents of the wardrobe seemed to represent her father's absence. As she leaned into the stifled dimness a faint musty odour snagged her throat. She hadn't time to search the pockets individually, but she gave the suits a fierce slap that would have rattled any keys. She'd heard only a jangle of hooks on the rail when her father stalked into the room. "What cursed thing have you planted in there?" he shouted.

As Amy swung away from the wardrobe, her forehead pounding

with the threat his appearance constituted, the aerial of the receiver in her left hand whipped the air not far short of his face. "I've put nothing," she said, snatching the aerial out of his reach. "I'm looking for my keys you stole."

"If I were a wronghead that is where I might have left them for you to find," he said, and fished the keys out of a pocket of his trousers to display them.

Couldn't it be an old dialect word he'd picked up from his grandparents? For as long as it took the keys to catch the light twice they seemed less important than the question, and then only retrieving them mattered, however she achieved it. "Thank you," she said, holding out her empty hand, though not far.

"This is my room and I want you out of it."

At least he hadn't pocketed the keys. As he stepped backwards through the doorway with a jingle of them, she followed. The flattened eyes looked astonished by her behaviour, unless they were mocking it; she couldn't interpret the gleam in his. "Close the door," he said as soon as she was through it, and once she had: "Right away from my room."

He was backing towards the kitchen and holding up her keys, which kept emitting a hypnotic glint. He meant to lure her to her room. As he retreated past it she saw he was intent on closing the kitchen door, perhaps to deny her access to all the knives beyond it. He groped behind him for the handle, and at the moment when his attention flickered, Amy lunged at him. The door slammed, a plastic fragment which she'd failed to avoid cracked beneath her heel, and he lifted the keys like a flame above his head. "These are no longer yours. Go to your place."

"I'm not going in my room till you give me my keys."

"I think you are," he said, and came at her with a swiftness that made clear her weapon no longer deterred him.

Amy fled into the main room. At the end of the drive the gateposts were stained red. She dashed to the window in time to see George Roscommon's truck hesitating at the road. She stared wildly around her in search of an object she could use to break the pane. A dining-chair might do, and she made herself drop the receiver in order to seize one. At that moment the gateposts turned grey as a doused fire, and the truck drove away along Nazareth Row.

Her father had restored the keys to his pocket and was advancing on her, hands outstretched. "Calm yourself now," he said. "You see you cannot beat me. Come to your room."

Amy ran around the table, placing it between them. Once again she had the impression that she and her father were doomed to keep repeating the same actions, the same words. "I'm not staying anywhere in here," she cried. "Can't you see it's making me worse? You let me out or take me out, I don't care which, or you'll see what I do."

He backed to the doorway and folded his arms. "You can do nothing that will turn me aside from my duty," he said.

Amy felt her hands distort themselves into claws, eager to find something they could rip apart or smash. The furniture, the hi-fi, the television or the videorecorder—and then she saw what must surely affect him if she could bring herself to do it. She went to the bookcase along the wall that contained the door. Whispering "Sorry" so quietly she scarcely heard herself, she made herself trap between her hands a clump of the books her mother had bound and hurl them to the floor.

Not even his face moved. Amy dug one hand behind the next book on the shelf and stared accusingly at him. Dismay was gathering in layers on her consciousness: dismay at her own actions, at his unresponsiveness, at her mother for having abandoned her forever—worst of all, at the realisation that the lovingly bound books meant as little to her now as their banal contents did. In a rage that made her forehead feel swollen and throbbing she pulled the book off the shelf and wrenching back the leather covers, held them creaking in her left hand while she gripped the wad of pages with the other. "You take me to the doctor or I'll rip this to bits," she cried.

She didn't know if it was the threat or her stare that reached him. She saw his hands fumble at his cheeks, and the gesture put her off guard, so that too much of her attention was concentrated on the book in her hands when he flew at her, covering the distance between him as she gasped out a breath. "You devil," he said in a low cold monotone. "You're mad, and you're staying here in Nazarill."

He grasped her shoulders, bruising them, but his words had already caught her. She'd heard him say them once before, in her nightmare after he had raised her up like a sacrifice in front of Nazarill, and she felt as small and helpless as she had been then. Before she could make up her mind to struggle he'd dragged her across the hall.

To her bewilderment, he didn't throw her into her room. Instead he pushed her relatively gently across the threshold and slackened his grip on her shoulders, resting his hands on them while he gazed blankly at her forehead. She was about to duck free and dodge around him when he spoke. "Whatever must be done," he said, and drawing back his right fist, drove it into her face.

22

PREPARING FOR THE WORST

As the girl's face fell away from Oswald's knuckles, its intolerable eyes turning up their whites to meet their sagging lids, he experienced such a surge of relief that he crossed himself in gratitude. He had time to complete the gesture as the backs of the girl's legs struck the end of the bed. The body encased in black swayed as if it was about to execute a staggering dance, and then it toppled backwards onto the quilt and was still.

He had to make himself advance into the room. He didn't like the clutter—didn't care to think what might be breeding underneath the heaps of clothes and books and cassettes and schoolwork and unwashed plates, breeding like the maggots that infested her mind. He dreaded to think what he would have smelled had it not been for the scent of unholy incense. He might have kicked himself a way to her except for his fear of disturbing something alive. He picked his way across the stepping-stones of bare carpet until he was beside the bed.

For the moment her face was peaceful, unless that was a trick. The book she had threatened to destroy lay next to her as though she'd fallen asleep reading it—as though she was enacting a wicked parody of the child she used to be. His fist clenched at the notion, but he mustn't let himself be overcome by wrath, however righteous. He should do no more than had to be done, and he had no reason to be distressed by the print of his heel on her forehead: her face bore far worse that she'd done to herself. Perhaps that had been the start of her madness—perhaps all the metal she'd inserted in herself had poisoned her. No sooner had this occurred to him than he was stooping to twist the rings out of her ears and nose and shy them, seven unwholesomely warm bits of metal, out of the door. He felt as though he was casting out evil, or rather beginning to learn how to do so. As the last ring clinked against the glass of the picture opposite her room, leaving a red speck above her nostril, he wiped his hand fastidiously on his sleeve and took hold of her wrist.

Finding her pulse was a more unpleasant task than clearing her face of its disfigurements had been. The mindless stirring in the bony wrist felt too much like an infestation of her flesh, some parasite which her unhealthiness had encouraged to breed. The moment he was sure of the pulse he flung the arm away from him, and her fingers rapped the wall before her hand dropped to the pillow. If her unconsciousness had been a pretence, the pain would have caused her to betray herself. She could be left while he ensured she stayed where she would do no more harm.

He rescued the book before retracing his steps out of the room. He switched off the light and closed the door, and having laid the book on the shelf, hurried to the airing cupboard opposite the bathroom. He grabbed the topmost pair of the pile of her sheets—God alone knew when she'd last changed the ones on her bed—and tied them together with all his strength. He knotted one end of the improvised rope around her doorknob and hauled it taut while he tied the far end to the bathroom doorknob. That must hold her if she regained consciousness before he prayed she would.

"I shan't be long," he said aloud, and refusing himself the luxury of a grimace at the litter strewn about the hall, stepped out of the apartment. He turned the key in the mortice-lock and ran downstairs. Halfway down he thought he heard a door creep shut, but since it couldn't possibly be his, it didn't matter. He hurried past the six locked-up apartments of the ground floor and let the night in.

The security lights pointed his shadow along the drive, and he had the impression that Nazarill was urging him onward, undertaking to keep his charge locked up until he returned to her. That would be as soon as possible, not least because he felt unprotected with only the black ice of the sky cracked by stars overhead. When he took refuge in the car its roof seemed flimsy and a good deal too close to his skull. His hands and feet saw to their tasks, swerving the vehicle across the empty car park and sending it in pursuit of its shadow tattered by gravel.

No traffic was moving on Nazareth Row, and so his foot stayed off the brake. The car sped straight across into Little Hope Way, towards the scrolled iron gateway beyond the few shops before the marketplace. Then a uniformed guard stepped into the path of the vehicle and held up one hand. "No further if you don't mind, sir."

Oswald reminded himself of the location and use of the brakes before he clambered out of the machine. "That was never my intention, Shaun."

"Oh, Mr. Priestley. I didn't . . ." The youth glanced away from whatever had confused him and discovered another excuse to do his job. "Don't you want to switch your lights off?"

Oswald had apparently been distracted by his yearning to return to Nazarill. He leaned into the car, and as he identified the switch he heard the rattle of a shutter being pulled down on a shop-front. "Not too late," he pleaded.

"Which shop are you after?"

"Joinery. Carpentry," Oswald said, and nearly called it the Lord's work. "Work about the home," he said with some vehemence.

"Die," Pickles seemed to advise him, not least by explaining "Do it yourself. I'll ask them to keep it open if you're quick," he then said, and marched across the concrete scoured by spotlights, glancing back to encourage Oswald to keep in step. "And house . . ."

Oswald thought he was being offered some further advice until he grasped what he was being asked. "She is receiving treatment," he said, and overtook the guard beneath the sky, which was no more reassuring for having been squeezed smaller overhead; the pallor it derived from the glow of the market suggested it was about to shatter. He was first through the entrance of the Handypersons' Haven, but it was Pickles who spoke. "We've a gentleman here who needs help."

The eldest of three men in yellow overalls on which two letters H were supporting each other indicated with a tilt of his head that he might be persuaded to glance up from the paperwork at which he was frowning. "Tell us what and we'll fetch it."

More than the profusion of skeletal shelves, the metallic smell of the large room was confusing Oswald, reminiscent as it was of the smell of blood, and so he named items as they occurred to him. "A hammer by all means. Nails, I think not. A chisel might prove useful, and of course a screwdriver. They come to a point these days, do they not?"

The youngest of the overalled assistants was ranging about the shop on his behalf. He halted, having added a pointed screwdriver to his handful, and regarded Oswald with a patience so visible it was its own contradiction. "There is what I most need," Oswald said, and took it off the shelf.

His insistence on paying cash earned him a glance of disfavour from the manager, presumably for adding to the paperwork, but some instinct made Oswald reluctant to sign his name. "Call it thirteen," the manager said, saving Oswald a few pence and himself the necessity of disturbing the change in the drawer. His assistant bagged the purchases and preceded Oswald to the door, where he handed him the bags as a preamble to bolting the door after him.

Pickles was outside, and tugged his peaked cap lower on his forehead by way of greeting. "All set? Don't mind if I hurry you along, do you? It's time for the gates."

Oswald needed no encouraging; indeed, he was wishing he could have stepped straight into Nazarill out of the shop. He was so intent on reaching his car that he'd unlocked it before he noticed that Pickles had followed him and was speaking to him. "What I meant, Mr. Priestley, is I do all the fixing things round our house if you wanted a hand."

"You think you would have the chance to see the girl."

The guard's face instantly doubled its blotches. "I wasn't, that's to say, if there was anything I could . . ." He took a breath which only gave him more to babble. "I don't mean to slip myself in, but seeing as the other feller, the one she was going round with . . ."

"I want him nowhere near my property. There is no longer any cause for him to be." Oswald had fitted himself into the vehicle, and spoke over the lowered window. "You could bar him should it become necessary."

"Trust me, Mr. Priestley," Pickles said with a vigour which immediately deserted him. "And she's, is she . . ."

"She is with a relative who knows how to handle her," said Oswald, and wound the window tight, only to have the guard crouch down to mouth "Will you tell her I was asking after her?"

"Who knows when I shall have word from her," Oswald murmured, and swerved the car backwards to receive an urgent slap on
the roof from the guard. A forward swerve came within an inch of
scraping the bumper along a shop-front, and then the car was carrying him to safety. It sped across Nazareth Row in front of a home-
bound boxy vehicle whose angry flare of headlights meant infinitely
less than the way Nazarill lit itself up to greet him. As he drove into
the light he seemed to feel his eyes brighten all the way to the car
park.

It was no longer empty. Three cars had settled there, and one was
disgorging a woman whom it didn't take him much thought to identify as the magistrate. All that he had to do was lawful because necessary, and so he experienced no qualms at the sight of her waiting
to walk with him. When he and his clanking bag arrived beside her
at last, Oswald having turned back once he remembered that not all
the light within his headlamps emanated from Nazarill, the question
that passed over her shadow to him was unexpected. "Something
amiss?"

"What should be?"

Though she looked taken aback by his curtness she answered
civilly enough. "I assume you're planning some kind of repairs."

He might have retorted that he assumed she was planning her customary inebriation, given the muffled colloquy of bottles in the carrier nuzzling her breasts. Instead he responded "Nothing that should
disturb my fellow tenants. I imagine it will go unheard."

"I'm sure I shan't be listening," the magistrate said, and panted
after Oswald as he hurried to bring the entrance to Nazarill in view.
"I expect you've your share of worries without anybody setting out
to add to them," she said with an effort which fell short of the final
consonant as Oswald reached the doors.

He was already inside Nazarill, he saw. He turned one of his keys
in the lock and pushed the glass away so that he could become the
man he'd seen in the discreetly illuminated corridor. Once across the
threshold he ceased to feel driven, and lingered to hold the door
open for the magistrate. "What worries arc we speaking of?" he
prompted as the doors glazed the night.

"None, I suppose, if you feel you've none." The magistrate peered
at him as though less than certain what she was seeing in the dim-

ness. "I only wanted you to be aware I do know people who ought to be able to help you if you felt the need."

"What help do you imagine me to lack?"

"Just tell me if I'm speaking out of turn." When Oswald kept his peace she said "My job brings me into contact with professionals who deal with, in your case would you call them mental problems?"

"That would require me to identify the subject under discussion."

"Mr. Priestley." The magistrate sounded so accusing Oswald thought she'd presumed to give him his answer until she said "Aren't we talking about your daughter?"

"Ah, I see the misunderstanding. She is no longer a problem."

"If you say so."

"I do indeed." That ought to suffice, but he saw it made sense to do away with her inquisitiveness. "She is receiving the appropriate care," he said.

"Forgive me, you were ahead of me. Can I ask where . . ."

"She is in a place where such problems are attended to."

"Oh dear. I'm sorry. I don't think any of us realised the situation was quite that bad. When do you think we can look forward to seeing her again?"

"Whenever she is fit to be seen," Oswald said, reflecting that he'd given Pickles a different version of events. It was unlikely that the versions would be compared, and in any case nobody had the right to demand the truth or to interfere. He stared at the magistrate to indicate that he wanted the subject dropped, and saw her withhold a further question. Instead she murmured "Let's hope there are more people for her to come home to."

"By which you intend to imply . . ."

"I thought she was bothered by all the empty rooms."

"I doubt they will concern her any further."

"That's good." The magistrate sounded less than entirely convinced, but when Oswald didn't deign to acknowledge this she said "Shall we go up?"

"To what end?" For a space between heartbeats Oswald thought she must be entitled as a magistrate to inspect the arrangements he was making, and then he saw that she was eager to be in her rooms. "Let us by all means," he said.

Her bottles betrayed their presence all the way to her floor while the contents of his bag audibly anticipated being put to use, and he was ready with a pointed answer if she made any comment. She turned to him as she stepped into her corridor. "You could tell her when you see her, this is if you think she is, that she shouldn't blame herself any more for my Pouncer. I've seen a kitten I like."

"I am glad that too has been resolved."

The magistrate frowned, and her mouth opened, but only to say "Good night."

"Indeed so," said Oswald, and strode purposefully upward, feeling both triumphant over her and encouraged by the desertion which met him. The top corridor was as quiet as any hospital should be—so quiet that the peace might almost have persuaded him that his task was done. Of course it was far from discharged, and he braced himself to be reminded as he unlocked his door.

But the apartment was silent too until he sidled through as meagre an opening as would admit him, when his foot struck an object on the floor with a soft thump. His nervous glance showed him the Bible, which he'd kicked into the hall earlier, and his disrespect caught up with him. He'd let himself be manoeuvred, however briefly, into behaving as the girl might. He would be doubly alert for any more of her tricks. He eased the door closed and set the bag down soundlessly, and crept along the hall to her door.

He could hear nothing beyond it, even when he leaned an ear against it. He hung up his coat and mounted his jacket on the back of a dining-chair and rolled up his sleeves in preparation for his task. As he picked at the knot on the girl's doorknob with his fingernails he remembered trying to free the cat from the noose on the oak, and wondered if she might have hanged the animal as a first stage of her madness. He brought his bag of purchases to her door and poked the screwdriver into the convolutions of the knot, which gave at once.

He cast the rope of sheets towards the bathroom, where the other knot would have to wait, and then he laid out his tools on the hall carpet. He took hold of the doorknob and lifted the hammer. Before he set to work he ought to satisfy himself that no interruption was being planned for him. He turned the handle so minutely it made not the faintest sound, and inched the door away from the frame until he could just distinguish a supine figure on the bed. When it didn't stir he pushed the door wider—was about to throw it fully open when he saw the light from the hall spread across the floor. Before he was able to draw another breath he stumbled backwards, almost dropping the hammer as he dragged the door after him.

He didn't see much, but he couldn't have borne to see more. Though the girl sprawled on the bed had changed her position since his last sight of her, she didn't stir as the light touched her. Something did, however. He might have tried to believe that he was seeing shadows of the clutter on the floor, except that he heard the rustle of movement—of a great many small things no longer bothering to hide. As he heaved the door shut he saw darkness pursuing it, a darkness so solid he had to tell himself he couldn't see it destroying the wallpaper and glistening like moisture on the brick it bared. The slam of the door put an end to these sights, but Oswald backed away until his heel struck the rest of his purchases, which emitted a clang like a bell summoning him to his duty. Now that the room was shut he could turn his mind away from whatever was within. Perhaps it might bring her to her senses. Or might she even welcome any infestation of her room? Was that why she had taken to living like some creature less than human in its lair? The thought made him scratch at the air in front of his face and then at his cheeks as they started to crawl.

The thud of the hammer on the carpet recalled him to himself, and he managed to control his hands before he bent to his tools. He dug the chisel into the doorframe at the level of his eyes and gripped the handle while it shuddered with blows of the hammer. By the time he'd gouged out a chunk of wood twice the breadth of his thumb, his hands were aching and shivering. He couldn't rest yet, although there was no sound from the pestilential room—no sign, when he forced himself to glance down, of spidery legs groping under the door. He tore the celluloid off its cardboard backing and took out the gleaming metal socket, which bruised his finger and thumb as he held it steady in the splintered niche in the doorframe while he secured it with its pair of screws. The head of each screw was incised with a cross, he saw, and surely that must help imprison the contents of the room. He slid the shaft of the bolt, which was thick as a young girl's finger but far less easy to break, into the socket so as to line it up. He drove the point of the screwdriver into the door through the holes in the metal plate and inserted the four screws, which he twisted as tight as his stinging fist could turn them. Only when an up-right of each cross was absolutely vertical did he relent, dropping the screwdriver at the foot of the door. As he clasped his hands together to let them soothe each other, he felt like falling to his knees to give thanks for the strength that had enabled him to complete his task.

He could pray while he worked. He still had to clear away the mess she'd made and had caused him to make in the hall. If cleanli-ness was next to Godliness, he thought, what must its opposite be next to? He stored the tools in the cupboard under the sink, then he set about filling the carrier bag with all the litter: the splintered chunk of wood, the bits of metal he had pulled out of her face, the fragments of the telephone equipment she'd forced him to smash. "Crazed devil," he muttered, which was all he seemed able to say for the moment—he would surely be able to pray once he had an op-portunity to catch his breath. Meanwhile the sight of the spillage from her bag enraged him, and he stalked along the hall.

The five-pound note and the coins he consigned to his pocket, where they had originated, after all. A card in an envelope and some bits of scrawled paper and a container of false medicine he threw into the carrier, and considered sending the Bible after them. Despite its having been defaced, he couldn't; God forgive him, it was the only Bible in the place. He tore up the loose pages on which she ap-peared to have drafted her fiction and stuffed them among the shards of plastic, and picked up the book. Its binding felt unpleasantly soft, and he bore the volume quickly into the main room and dropped it on the table to meet its dim blurred twin. Much of the table was oc-cupied by her schoolwork, which could wait while he finished clear-ing the hall. There was still one item on the floor to be put with the rest of the rubbish, and he meant to throw it away unexamined, since he had no desire to see her eyes. When he crouched for the bus pass, however, he found her face turned up to him.

His breath trembled out of him like the beginning of a sigh, and then he took a long harsh gulp of air. He'd almost allowed himself to be swayed by memories of her, but he wasn't to be tricked again. Try as she might, she couldn't conceal how she already had been at the time of the photograph. Her hair wasn't cropped, but now that made him wonder sickly whether it had been infested. Her eyes were doing their best to appear as innocent as her mother would have liked to see them, but the longer he peered at them the more false they became. All those months ago, just after he'd informed her that they had a place in Nazarill, her face had been invaded by metal emblems of wilfulness, their poison seeping into her blood. He felt as though her shrunken plastic gaze had trapped him in a crouch not far short of a genuflection, but he'd show her who held the power. He seized the slippery image of her and bent it until it snapped.

He flung the halves into the carrier as he took it to the kitchen, where he thrust it into the bin. The action drained enough of his anger to let him be calm as he restored Heather's books to their place. "There," he told each of them, and smoothed any crumpled pages before he closed the book and caressed its binding. "Rest now. She can't hurt you any more." By the time he'd positioned the last book on the shelf his words had acquired some of the qualities of a prayer. Now he could pray properly, he thought as he fetched the vacuum cleaner from his bedroom.

He found it difficult to think of words as he vacuumed the hall, but they came to him as he made himself advance the wide grim mouth of the cleaner to the crack beneath her door: "Please God let nothing be alive." He said more as he progressed slowly through all the open rooms, pressing the mouth against every accessible surface, but he kept returning to those words. Whenever he replaced the mouth with the pinched nozzle and thrust that into the secret places of the apartment, he felt he was crushing some unpleasantness which she had brought into the home. Each time he changed the attachments he switched off the cleaner and listened, but there was no sound from beyond the bolted door. "I know you're there," he muttered as the tube in his hand sucked at a pair of swollen eyes. "Do your worst. God will give me the strength."

23

A DIFFERENT STORY

"As Overseer, Mr. Highstool, surely—"

"Superior Overseer, madam, if you please."

"Forgive me for not using your full title, but as long as you're that—"

"My *full* title, madam"—here the grey-faced man inserted his thumbs behind the lapels of his frock-coat and rose up on his perch behind the desk that towered over her—"my full title, I say, is Superior Overseer of Permissions for Cemetery Placements."

The supplicant clasped together hands raw with so many years of work as washerwoman and mother, and lifted them to him. "I see that's what you are, indeed I do. And as you are, you'll permission me to have a little stone put up for my Amelia's Christmas, won't you?"

"Have you not read"—the functionary pointed both his sharp pinched nose and a long grey fingernail at the front of his desk—"have you not perused and digested the notice which I myself wrote in my finest copperplate?"

"I see how fine it is, sir, indeed, but I can't."

"Can't read!" announced Gustus Highstool to a drip-nosed clerk who that moment was scurrying past his cell. "True enough, there is no profit in teaching the poor their letters, but sans ability, what use may a stone be to you?" This was addressed to the grey-haired widow stooped by her years and her grief, whose attention he now drew once more to the notice. "No permissions will be granted after three o'clock of any Friday," he read very slowly aloud.

"I understand, sir, but if you'll forgive me—"

"Forgiveness is the business of a priest, not mine."

"I was going to say, sir, one thing I was taught to read was a clock." Here the woman ventured to indicate such a machine beneath the window thick with stalactites of ice. "And if you'd care to look, sir, you'll see it's not quite three."

"Not quite, you say? Not quite?" The official adjusted his pen in its well before devoting himself to the chore of unbuttoning his coat. This accomplished, he painstakingly drew from the fob of his waist-coat a repeater, and was about the task of raising the lid of the watch when the clock began to utter its tinny chimes. "I believe you are mistaken," he said, and snapped the lid shut in his fist as he repeated in triumph, "No permissions will be granted after three o'clock of any Friday."

How grey is life passed in a cell! Some seek the cells which are their lives, while others have such cells built about them. Some, of whom we have invented Highstool as our first representative, draw greyness about themselves like a cloak; while others, like the widow pleading at his desk, are greyed by the lives society requires of them. And what a factory of greyness is such a place as Nazarill! At the time of our initial visit it is sodden with a fog which creeps about the corridors, and resounding with sneezes and coughs; but even at the height of midsummer, sunlight never penetrates many of the cells where clerks stoop over their work as a spider crouches to its prey.

What sunlight fails to dispel, might fire destroy? Perhaps some thought of the kind—some echo of the past—was awakened in the slow but honourable brain of the widow's only son as, plodding without complaint over the cruel stones of the approach in his boots whose soles were worn thin as the last wail of a pauper's child, he beheld his mother weeping on the steps of the grim offices. "Mother," he cried, "you maun't take on so, straight you maun't," and to comfort her brought forth from the least ragged of the pockets of his father's jacket his dead little sister Amelia's once treasured.

Rob had had enough some pages back, but it was the dialect, even if it was remotely possible that someone somewhere had ever spoken like that, which proved too much for him. The item in the ragged pocket was a tinder-box her father would strike to amuse her, he saw in the instant of shutting the dull brown cover on the dull brown pages. They emitted a thud which succeeded in sounding muffled with dust, specks of which flew towards the chunky mantelpiece and its row of photographs. He gazed at the six ages and thicknesses of himself and wondered all over again why he'd bought the book.

After Amy had left him to be stared at by the clientele of Tea For You, several of whom had begun viciously stirring their tea as if brewing up a spell to drive him out, he'd lingered to prove their opinion couldn't touch him, until the manageress had asked him to leave. By then Pickles was nowhere to be seen, otherwise Rob would certainly have turned his rage on him. He'd been making for the way home, glowering at anyone who glanced at him, when the bookseller had waved him over to the van he was loading. "Tried to catch your girl's eye before. I found her book in a library sale."

Rob's instinct had been to retort that she wasn't his girl, but he hadn't wanted to discuss it. He'd said only "How much?"

"It's not worth marking up this late in the day. It's yours for what it cost me. Twenty pee."

Though there had been some satisfaction in exchanging the weight of all the coppers in his pocket for the musty book, Rob had hardly left the marketplace before he wanted to take *Nazarill* back. Why hadn't he left it for Amy to buy? He'd spent half the weekend convincing himself that the only way she would find out he had it was to ring him. Last night he'd given in and called her, and had learned she'd been sent away to recuperate.

This felt as if she had been wrenched out of his life and replaced with memories whose underlying nature it dismayed him to contemplate. How much was he responsible for her condition? Ought he to have demonstrated skepticism earlier, or not at all? At first he was tempted to take the novel as a promise of her returning unchanged—tempted to feel that because he was keeping it for her, she would have to come back as eager to read it as ever—and then he saw it might make her worse than however she was or, if her retreat cured her, might cause her to relapse. Home from school this Monday evening, he'd attempted to read it so as to judge how it could be expected to affect her, but became distracted by the antics of the prose. He was beginning to think of taking it to the recycling bin in the market car park when he heard a key in the front door, and then his mother's voice in the hall. "Who's in?"

"Just me."

"You'll do to be going on with." As soon as she'd divested herself of the padded jacket she always wore in the car during winter she tramped into the living-room, raising one shoulder and then the other as if they could be rendered straighter and shoving her square jaw forward, and Rob had the impression that she was making an entrance to perform a speech she'd rehearsed. "Sometimes I think we must be crazy," she declared, "the people we let loose on the road."

"Anyone special?"

"Not special enough. Too many of them. I've lost count of the folk I've met driving who seem to have forgotten everything I taught them except how the car works. Last week I had one come at me out of a fog with no lights on and flash them to say I should have had mine off."

"That was last week, though."

"That's right, last week." She seemed, not by any means unusually, less than certain whether he was making fun of her, and responded with her usual comical frown. "Today I had someone your father sold a car to coming at my learner round a bus at fifty, that's twice his age. I smiled sweetly at him and pointed at our name on the roof, but he was too busy getting where he couldn't wait to be to notice. I suppose you're thinking I'm a bit crazy myself."

"I wouldn't say that to anyone."

He felt unfair for having made that sound like a rebuke, and was thinking how to make amends when she glanced away from him. "School?" she said.

"Like usual."

Ordinarily she would have changed the subject once she had provoked this retort, but now she said "The book, I was meaning."

"No."

"That isn't like you, reading an old book for fun."

"Didn't say it was," Rob said, and found he wanted to continue— might even do so with a little more encouragement, although discussing his feelings with either of his parents was a habit easier to break than to regain. Brooding in his room to music seemed unlikely to do him much good, any more than smoking a whole joint by himself yesterday on a lonely stretch of moor had—doing so had made the wind on his face feel like the opposite of Amy's breath. He dragged his gaze away from the book to find his mother's attention waiting for him, but both of them were hoping the other would speak when a rattle of keys narrowed itself down to the insertion of one in the front door. "Now there's your father," she said with some impatience, and stumped out of the room.

In the shortest possible time his father's rotund pink face, bristling red on top and not much less along the upper lip, presented itself around the door. "Dinner as soon as I'm down," he announced on his wife's behalf, and was heard to jog upstairs with a muffled "bugger" at missing a tread, and soon after to roar an assortment of sentences to the tune of the first line of "La donna è mobile" through the rumble of the shower, "Best prices at Hayward's Cars" proving as always to be his favourite. He reappeared wearing his bathrobe, the same shade as his face now that was towelled pinker, and urged his son to the kitchen, tilting his head to glance at the title of the book Rob had dropped on the chair. "Who'd have thought it," he murmured, and seemed to forget about it. Having set the table, he stowed his lanky legs beneath it and shared descriptions of the day's customers as enthusiastically as he attacked his meal. "She wouldn't try out the Mini till I managed to fit all of me into the front," he eventually said, then squinted at Rob over the last slice of steak and kidney pie. "You and the chef share that. So what's the significance of the tome?"

"Positive, I'd say," said Rob's mother.

"Where do you get that?" his father said, laying his utensils to rest.

"Reading some old classic when he doesn't have to."

"It's not quite one of those, is it, old chap?"

"Oh, I see, I think," his mother said, and hid a knowing smile behind her hand. "Our baby's growing up. What is it, *Fanny Hill* or *Lady C*?"

"You're fiddling with the wrong switch, Marge. It's—"

"It's a story about Nazarill," Rob said.

"Oh."

The syllable might have expressed sympathy or disappointment, neither of which Rob welcomed. "I don't think I'll be seeing her any more."

"Oh dear," his mother said with, he was pretty sure, some relief. She led a few seconds' silence for the death of the relationship and broke it with "Don't tell us about it unless you want to."

"Now, Marge, he doesn't need our permission for that, and he knows it, am I right, old chap?"

Perhaps his father was genuinely unaware of doubling the pressure on him, but Rob saw he couldn't get away with just a nod of agreement. "We had a row," he said. "Maybe you heard."

"How could we?" his mother said as though she would have been entitled to sound a good deal more accusing. "You'd walked out with her when I was trying not to cross her father."

"Heard about it."

"I didn't, Tom, did you?" She barely waited for that answer before demanding of Rob "Why, whatever were you up to?"

"Shouting at each other where they drink nothing but tea."

"Not that embalmed bunch. Of all the folk to choose, the maiden aunts of Partington and women that manage to be grandmothers without having any children. If anybody needed shaking up . . ." She hid another grin until she'd tempered it with some reproof. "What was said?"

"They didn't have to say anything, they only had to look."

"I can see how they would," she said, and mimed their characteristic expression accurately enough to suggest she didn't think it entirely inappropriate. "But I meant what was the argument over?"

"Something I didn't believe."

"Tell me to shut them with a clothes-peg if you like, but I can't say I'm surprised." When he only shrugged she said "Was it about that old place up there?"

"Everything is for her these days."

"Never mind, love. You'll be at university before you know it."

Rob had begun to envision the solaces which she was implying lay ahead when his father spoke. "Maybe the clothes-peg's needed over here, and call me a slow old sod if you want, but if you won't be seeing her any more, why are you reading that book?"

"You're a slow old sod," Rob's mother obliged at once. "Weren't you ever his age? Can't you see he's still thinking about her?"

Rob was, but with so much less pain he was surprised and even rather pleased by himself. His nine months with Amy were receding to a manageable distance, and if he didn't indulge for a while in remembering how she'd felt to him and looked at him, they would stay there. If she had wanted him she would surely have phoned by now, since she must realise that her father wouldn't give him the number of wherever she was. This morning he'd awakened thinking that if she needed him she would phone while whoever was looking after her was out of the way, but now the absence of a message on the answering machine seemed no worse than inevitable. "I've started not to," he said.

His father made to speak until Rob's mother pinched the air in front of his lips to hush him. "I think you're taking after me," she told Rob. "It used to be if two people broke up they were supposed to return all their gifts to each other, but I've always believed you should keep something to remind you of the good times."

Rather than complicate the moment with an explanation, Rob tried to deal with his father's unconvinced look. "It's just a story about when Nazarill was offices. I don't really know why I'm reading it. I think I've given up."

That earned him twin smiles of affectionate skepticism which might have ended up irritating him if they hadn't been interrupted by the phone. When a female voice made itself heard through the speaker of the answering machine, his mother picked up the call and agreed a time with her latest pupil. By then Rob and his father were clearing the table, and the subject of Amy was cleared away too. While his parents settled down in front of the evening's first comedy programme to the sound of an audience laughing before the Haywards found occasion to, Rob retrieved the copy of *Nazarill* and carried it upstairs to put it out of the way of his school coursework.

As he drew his bedroom curtains he saw Nazarill looming above the town. The glow from the marketplace glimmered on the long pale building and drained the colour from those of the upper windows that were illuminated. For a moment he had the impression that the building, to which the lit windows seemed irrelevant—cartoonish rectangles pasted to the facade—had turned into a ghost of itself, as dead as the chimneys that crowned it. That was a last trace of Amy's thinking, he decided as he turned away with a shiver. The beacon of her apartment, to which he'd often looked before going to bed, was no longer lit for him. He switched off his light and went downstairs to the dining-table to start work, knowing that at least his parents wouldn't trouble him while he was studying. More than once during their conversation he'd sensed that his mother could have said more if she had chosen to, but he was grateful to her for restraining herself. Whatever she might have left unsaid, he preferred not to know.

24

MORE OF A CELL

"Your mother's dead, and you're mad, and you're staying here in Nazarill."

As she awoke with her father's voice in her ears, Amy had to remind herself that it had been just a nightmare. She must have been wakened by her own cry, and surely her parents would have heard it. She had only to lie still with her eyes shut until they came to reassure her. If she held onto her breaths and stopped them from panting and shivering, if she made herself take long slow deep draughts of air, the duration of the next breath would be enough to bring them—to be on the safe side, the next two breaths. She prolonged those for all she was worth, though they caused her jaw to twinge, no doubt because she had been lying awkwardly on it while asleep. She closed herself around the second inhalation despite its stale taste, and listened hard, but there was no sound except for the hissing of blood in her ears. She would have to call out for reassurance, and she was opening her mouth to do so when the kind of ache which she was expecting to declare itself in her forehead fastened on her jaw. The pain shocked her eyes open, and she yanked at the lightcord, and saw that she was where she was most afraid to be.

Perhaps it wasn't entirely the room she'd seen in her nightmare after her father had held her up to Nazarill, but too much of it was: the four hats hovering on the wall, the three necklaces adorning the flattened glass throat of the mirror. For as long as it took her to force her lungs to work she expected the door to be thrown open, reveal-

ing her father with a fire behind him, and then she remembered she
had already heard him say what he would have said—had been wakened by the echo of his words. He'd uttered them before he'd
punched her into her bedroom, bruising her jaw. Her headache
seemed in retrospect no more than a premonition of this, but why
did she feel that the new pain might be an omen of worse? What was
the worst that could happen now that he'd spoken the words from
her nightmare?

The worst, she thought, might be that she lay there on her arse waiting for it to happen. She worked her body up the bed until her shoulders rubbed against the plump headboard. Since her movements
hadn't aggravated the various aches above her neck, she grasped the
edge of the mattress and swung her feet slowly to the patch of floor
she always kept clear for her first step. When she pressed her clammy
hands against her knees and stood up, however, both she and the
room wavered, the latter so badly that she was afraid she was about
to see it change. To steady herself she threw out a hand to meet its
cold flat glassy twin, and the necklaces jangled against the mirror as
though they were trying to snare her reflection. She saw a threatening quiver pass through the dimmer of the two rooms she was in, and
thrust herself away from it. She squeezed her eyes shut once she had
her balance, and when she opened them she was sure enough of herself to make her way to the door.

She planted her feet wide in the space between it and the contents of her room, and having cupped her hands behind her ears,
rested a palm against the slippery wood and leaned her head towards
it. She could still hear no sound from outside. She shifted her hand
to the doorknob, and felt the metal grow slick with her sweat until
she wiped both with an unbuttoned cuff of her jacket. She gripped
the knob and twisted it slowly, even slower, manoeuvring it very
gradually past the squeak it often gave when it was halfway turned.
She felt it turn all the way, and closed both hands around it to control the movement of the door as she inched it open. Or rather, as
she tried; because the door shifted a fraction of an inch and then
came to an absolute halt.

At first she thought she'd failed to turn the handle completely
after all. She relaxed her grip before twisting the knob with both
hands and every vestige of strength. This time she heard metal scrape
out of the socket, and felt the door give its fractional lurch. She

swelled her lungs with air that made her cranium feel fragile as an egg, then she grasped the handle so hard her palms began to throb, and threw herself backwards as violently as she could—so violently that when the door refused to yield she almost lost her grip on the handle and sprawled on her back. She imagined her father clinging to the opposite knob, his feet wedged against the uprights of the frame, before she wondered whether objects no longer quite so much like hands might be clutching the knob at the far end of the shaft from the knob she'd again taken hold of. The thought would have made her shrink away if she hadn't managed to remind herself that surely none of the denizens of the secret places of Nazarill would have the strength. She sagged against the door and then, as though to take the hindrance by surprise, she heaved at it. This time she heard a faint unfamiliar sound through the crack between the door and its frame: a constricted rattle, a metallic snigger. As though his voice had been triggered by the metal, her father spoke.

He wasn't far from the door—perhaps not even as distant as the other side of the hall. He sounded groggy, roused from sleep, but ready to be more awake. "Throw all the weight about you like," he mumbled loudly. "Exhaust yourself. That bolt will hold you, I warrant."

For a second she felt as unable to move as the door had become, and then she was driving her shoulder against it, kicking it savagely, yanking at the handle, flinging her body about as if she was struggling to release herself from a shackle. When she saw that her actions no longer made much sense and that she would indeed exhaust herself if she persisted, she relinquished her grip and stumbled away to fall into a sitting position once the backs of her legs encountered the bed.

Soon her father greeted the silence. "I hope I hear you beginning to see sense. You must stay in there until I am persuaded that you can be released."

"Just watch me," Amy whispered, knowing that was one feat he couldn't perform. His voice sounded increasingly blurred, closer to sleep—surely too close for him to reflect whether he'd left her any means of escape, as she saw he had. If she unscrewed the hinges of the door, the room couldn't hold her. She held onto the edge of the bed while she looked for a tool.

There was none to be seen: nothing in the clutter on the floor or amid that on the dressing-table. She could fetch a hanger from the wardrobe, except that all the hangers were so thin that any she tried to use would simply bend and most probably snap before a screw moved. She was beginning to raise her fists in despair while she trapped a screech between her teeth when her gaze roved to the bag she had forgotten throwing into the room. She fell to her knees beside it and tipped its few contents onto the floor.

If only she had thought to retrieve the pills Beth had given her! Just now, however, it was more important that she had her metal comb. She leaned over to pick it up and laid it beside her in a wrinkle of the quilt, and waited, and then made herself wait longer. She had no idea how much—far too much—time passed before her patience was rewarded by an absurdly welcome sound: her father's snoring.

"You stay asleep," she whispered. "It's past your bedtime. You sleep and dream about . . ." She didn't know what she would like to think he was dreaming: certainly not about her—the notion threatened to trap her once more in the nightmare he had built around her. Perhaps he should be dreaming about her mother if that had the potential to revive his old self, except that Amy didn't care to imagine her mother's memory engulfed in the brain he had now. All that mattered was that he stay asleep while she removed the screws from the door, and if he needed anything like as much sleep as her eyes were crying for, he should. She pushed herself up from the bed, reassuring herself that the creak of the mattress wasn't audible outside the room. Two stealthy paces brought her to the door, where she inserted the point of the metal handle in the topmost screw. As soon as she twisted the comb the point slipped out of the groove.

She had expected as much. She slid the edge of the handle into the groove and steadying the improvised tool with one hand, bore down on it with the heel of the other. The screw held firm as the handle started to bend. She tried the screw below it, and the next, and had to kneel to reach the last, the angle of whose groove caused the comb almost to touch the floor. None of the screws gave so much as a millimetre, but each bent the handle further. By the time she wavered to her feet, rubbing sweat out of her embers of eyes with the back of her free hand, the metal was curved as a grin. It wasn't mocking her, she told herself, it was showing her how to proceed. She sat on the end of the bed again and trod hard on the tip of the handle while she grasped the comb with both hands and levered it towards her. At once, before she was expecting it to, it snapped.

Most of the handle was quivering beside her heel, but an inch or so was left on the comb. Surely that had to be strong enough. She padded to the door again, encouraged by her father's snores, and fitted the end of the remains of the handle into the highest screw, or thought she did. It required two attempts to turn it, during both of which the stub of metal only scraped across the disc, to convince her that the tip of the would-be screwdriver was thicker than the grooves.

At her second try the metal teeth scratched her hand. She wrapped the comb in her handkerchief and did her best to move the screw using the edge of the stub, but it wouldn't stay lodged in the groove. When she persevered it slid off the disc and dug a splinter out of the wood, and her father emitted a louder sound, bordering on the articulate, as though he'd sensed the damage and was trying to awaken. Once she was certain he'd subsided she attacked the screw with an effort that trembled her wrists, only to have the comb deal the wood another gash. "Bastard," she said through teeth she nearly clenched until her jaw hinted at the pain she would experience if she did, and let the comb drop at her feet. She didn't know if she'd meant her father by the word, or the improvised tool, or the whole of life and anything that might be responsible for it. The cloth fell open, displaying the comb, and she was about to retrieve the handkerchief alone when she saw that she might have been wielding the tool the wrong way round. "I didn't mean it," she murmured, less sure whom or what she was addressing—surely anything that could help her—and picking up the comb again, inserted the edge of the tooth farthest from the handle into the groove of the topmost screw.

It fitted perfectly. The angle, though, was awkward, since the groove was close to vertical. She muffled most of the comb once more in the handkerchief and pressed the tooth into the groove with all her weight, then she grasped the knuckles of the hand that was gripping the comb and exerted whatever strength she still had. She felt metal twist at once.

It was the end of the comb, she thought; she'd wrecked that now. Even when she lowered it towards her face and saw that it didn't appear to have bent, she had difficulty in believing it had held. She lined it up in the groove, which remained almost vertical, and threw more force than she had thought was left to her into her wrists. This time she felt and heard and, best of all, saw the screw turn at least an inch.

Her earlier struggles had been worthwhile after all; they must have eased the screws. She waited until an untroubled snore indicated that the faint squeak of metal within wood hadn't alerted her father, then she returned to her task. Three increasingly effortless twists, and she was able to wind the screw out with her fingers, nearly cutting their tips on the sharp edge before she protected them with the handkerchief. She felt the screw lose its hold on the wood, and at once it was gleaming on her palm. As it came she thought she heard movement beyond the door.

It might have been her father shifting his position while he continued to snore, except that she had the impression it had been closer to her than he was. It had sounded as though something had permitted itself to grow audible as it scuttled unevenly to her door and settled down to wait for her.

Amy closed her fist around the screw, digging the helix into her skin, and glared at the door with her overheated eyes. "You can't reach me," she muttered. "You have to stay out there. You don't scare me. Try scaring him."

Her words seemed to promise at least the possibility of reassurance. Unless she believed in them she couldn't go on, and she mustn't falter while her father's sleep was giving her a chance. When no response made itself heard outside the room she forced herself to relax her nervous grip on the screw, which she shied onto the bed, so as to apply the wrapped-up comb to the remaining screw of the upper hinge.

It wasn't as forthcoming as its companion had been. She redoubled the grip of her hand on her fist and fought to turn it with her whole body, using her straight arms as a single lever. She felt metal shift—the tooth slipping out of the groove—and rammed it back in as a trickle of sweat found her left eye. That had started to blink as though it had been seized by an uncontrollable nervous tic—she was desperate to clear it of the stinging, but even more determined not to slacken her hold—when the screw executed a half-turn with a protesting squeal.

Amy wiped her eye, then let her arms hang by her sides while they trembled towards stillness. Her forehead and jaw were working on joining their aches across her face. She might feel worse before she'd finished, she told herself fiercely, but she ought to try not to be tense: apart from the mechanical snoring, there seemed to be no activity beyond the door. So fatiguing were her efforts, so dulling to her brain, that if she allowed herself she might even forget that anything was out there. When the tremulousness of her arms reduced itself to a throbbing that might, given time, have become pleasurable, she drove the tooth into the groove and twisted her hands along with their painful spiky contents. The screw turned nearly half a circle at once.

She was able to grasp it between finger and thumb, though for an unpleasant second as she unscrewed it her nail was caught beneath the rim. Before her father had snored thrice the screw was nestling in her palm. About to swing round and aim it at the bed, she froze. Something had come into the room behind her.

She thought she smelled how damp and mouldering the intruder was. She was sure she felt its chill on her back. Since it was making no noise, she was unable to judge how close it was to her, and so she had to look—had to, no matter how much her body was shivering as if to shake her out of herself, to extend her that chance to escape. She staggered around on her wavering legs and raised the hand that held the comb. She'd forgotten it no longer had a point, even supposing that would have been any defence.

But the room appeared to be deserted. Whatever had joined her had hidden itself, and she could only wait until it poked any face it had left from under the bed or out of the wardrobe. "I've seen you," she whispered, but the words were barely out of her mouth when she ceased to understand how she'd hoped they would reassure her. Perhaps they brought her a response, however—a glimpse of movement which she tried desperately to locate. It was in the dressing-table mirror, she realised. It was in the room in the mirror, which was no longer her bedroom.

There wasn't a great deal within the glass: not even much of the light from the lamp overhead. Where she ought to have been seeing her Clouds Like Dreams poster in reverse, she saw a dim surface of bare brick, crawling with trickles of moisture whose movement she had originally glimpsed and flickering with the glow of some flame. Her bed wasn't in the mirror, nor was the crowded top of the dressing-table. To give herself a view of the rest of the cell she would have to venture away from the door.

She took one reluctant step, and saw the bare wall draw back to accommodate her, revealing more of its glistening bricks. Another step, and she saw how she was helping the unsteady dimness in the mirror to expand so as to draw her in, the image of the cell taking on more depth as her sense of her room shrank. One more step would take her to the bed, but she was suddenly afraid to find that since it was apparently incapable of producing a reflection, she wouldn't be able to feel it if she tried to touch it with the hand that so far was the only part of her trapped in the mirror. Then her room would be the cell in the mirror—her cell.

Except that was still just an image, she told herself, so long as she didn't let it take hold of her mind. If she turned her back on it, it couldn't do that—if she turned she would see her poster, not bare brick. The poster had been at the edge of her vision all the time she'd been trying to unscrew the hinges, she was almost sure it had. She closed her eyes to ward off the sight in the mirror, and swung towards the door, and forced them open.

The Clouds Like Dreams poster hung on the wall beside the door, the four androgynous faces framed by tents of curly hair. She rubbed her free hand over them to convince herself, though she wished she couldn't feel a hint of brick through the layers of poster and wallpaper and plaster. She made herself crouch to the lower hinge while with an effort she stopped herself from wondering what more of the cell she would see if she looked up at the mirror. Once she was out of the room, and not until then, she would look back. She dug her trusty comb into the third screw and concentrated all her mind on the promise she wanted her actions to be.

At first the screw absolutely refused to budge. She had to lean her weight leftward over it, a position that felt dangerously close to sprawling on the floor. If she was as helpless as that for even a movement, she knew she would be bound to glance at the mirror. She crouched forward, leaning her right shoulder against the slippery wood, and just as she concluded that it was supporting her too much for her weight to affect the buried helix, the screw yielded with a screech and dumped her on her knees.

The door had scraped her shoulder through her jacket and sweatshirt, and the carpet might hardly have been there, her knees felt so bruised. Nevertheless she remained on them with her eyes shut, willing her father not to have heard anything through the door. A mumble escaped him, and then there was silence except for her heart in her ears. She was attempting to arrange herself into a position in which she would be able to keep still if she should hear his chair creak and his footsteps approach the door when he snored once, then again less emphatically, and rediscovered his rhythm. At once she gave the screw a full turn which allowed her to fasten the tips of her finger and thumb on the edge.

She was so relieved to have the screw in her grasp that she almost turned to throw it on the bed. She let it drop beside its predecessor, which at some point had fallen from her hand, and redoubled her grip on the comb. The lowest screw would be the hardest to extract, but merely hardest, not impossible. She lined up the tooth of the comb in the nearly vertical groove of the screw, and lowered herself into an awkward crouch that started her legs shaking, and freed a hand to mop her wet fragile throbbing forehead. She thought the smell of stony damp had returned, but she wasn't going to let it deter her. She took a breath that felt like metal in her chest, and closed both hands around the comb, and the doorbell rang.

This was so unexpected that for an irrational moment she found herself wishing away whoever might be at the downstairs entrance so that she would have a chance to deal with the last screw. She heard her father give vent to several syllables that sounded unrelated to any recognisable words, and then he began to waken. "Wait till I come," he protested, and his voice lurched past her door. "My legs are prickled. Why must you rouse me? What is here that anyone would wish to see?"

He sounded even less like her father, and by no means fully awake—perhaps insufficiently so to realise that not only he would be audible through the intercom. Amy pressed her ear against the door and closed the eye that might have glimpsed the mirror. She heard his footsteps stumble to a halt, followed by a silence that seemed ominous, especially when he demanded "What device is this?"

He'd forgotten how to use the intercom, she thought in a panic. By the time he remembered, if he did, the caller might have decided it was too late or too early, whatever the time was, to call. She tried to clench the whole of herself around a silent wish. As her sight began to pulse with the pressure of her closed eyelids, her father said "Who's there?"

He was answered by a burst of static which, as Amy let her eyelids rise and dropped the comb that was biting into her palm, became
a voice. She couldn't tell whose voice it was or the name it announced, not through all the static and her door, but that didn't matter. Someone real and alive and surely unconnected with Nazarill
was within earshot, and the moment her father spoke again she
started to kick the door and pound on it with her fists. "Help," she
shouted. "I'm locked up in here. He's imprisoned me. Come and let
me out or he'll do worse."

25

NEARLY THERE

Before dawn on Tuesday morning Rob found he couldn't sleep. He kicked off the quilt and eased his curtains open on the view of Partington. A low mist had gathered at the edges of town, dousing the lights of Little Hope Way and Nazareth Row and almost blotting out Nazarill. Only the oversized chimneys were visible, deformed emblems of lifelessness that the crouched hulk was brandishing. At least, Amy might have seen them in such terms, but that was no reason why he should. He turned away and headed for the bathroom.

While he was dressing, his gaze kept drifting to the bedroom window. If he faced away from it he was confronted by the Clouds Like Dreams poster she'd bought him in Hedz Not Fedz, not that he had ever liked the band as much as she did. The mist was shrinking in anticipation of the dawn, though Amy might have thought Nazarill was drawing the concealment around itself. Rob dragged a black polo-neck over his head and brushed his hair in front of the mirror, feeling compelled while he did so to keep trying to decipher the word EKIL. He turned away at last, only to be confronted with the book he'd perched on top of his school rucksack in the hope of knowing what to do with it today. He couldn't make that decision until he'd at least glanced through the rest of it, and so he took it down to the living-room.

It was much as he'd expected. Mercy Steadfast, the indomitably hopeful widow, made her way through the administrative labyrinth Nazarill represented, each chapter introducing a functionary yet more grotesque than his predecessor, while the widow's slow but honourable, not to mention increasingly ragged and down-at-heel and weather-worn, son Humble allowed himself to be exploited without, as it kept transpiring, any pay at all from a series of horrible jobs he undertook in the belief that he would be able to add to washerwoman Mercy's pittance. Rob had had enough as soon as he learned their names, but he skimmed onward to confirm that the son did indeed attempt to set fire to Nazarill with his late sister's treasured tinder-box on Christmas Eve, only to be caught in the act by a kindly white-bearded stonemason on his way to give the Cemetery Placements overseer a generous helping of his mind. What could apparently be simpler, once he'd refused to quit Gustus Highstool's cell until he obtained permission for the widow's stone as well as those he'd planned to argue for, than that he should donate a stone to her and carve it and raise it on the grave just as the bells began to peal for midnight mass? "Right," growled Rob with all the incredulousness he had in him, and rubbed his cheek beside his eye, and shut the book so vigorously that he drove out a few specks of dust it had held in reserve. Slamming it didn't help him determine its fate, however, and he should.

He dropped the book on his chair and stared out at Nazarill. The mist was allowing such windows as were lit to hint at their colours, but he could see no trace of light in the Priestleys' apartment; perhaps her father was visiting her after all. Apart from the odd coincidence, the novel had absolutely nothing to do with Amy's stories, but why should that have any significance for her? Rob watched the corner of the top storey for signs of life as the chimneys caught the dawn and deadened their portion of its glow. The mist was sinking into the grounds as the glow was lured down the pallid facade when his mother found him.

She said nothing until she'd completed her journey to the kitchen to start coffee, and then she came to him and put her arm as much around him as he'd let her since he was about thirteen. Her white towelling robe smelled like all the bathtimes that went with the second earliest of the photographs of him. She glanced at the prone book and out of the window, and said "It just takes time, love. I remember how it was with somebody I knew before I met your father."

"You kept remembering how you'd felt together, you mean."

"I won't go into the gory details if you don't mind."

"I wasn't asking you to," Rob said, wondering instead why people of her generation referred to gore when they meant sex. "Only it isn't like I suppose you meant. I keep thinking it's my fault how she's gone."

"I'm sure it's not, so don't."

"You can't know."

"Aye, that's true," she said, and took her arm away from him. "I'm a parent, and we don't know anything."

"You don't know how she is now. You haven't spoken to her since you wouldn't let her in the house."

"That should have been enough," his mother said, and prolonging her accusatory tone after it might have seemed inappropriate: "So what are you feeling to blame for?"

"Maybe I shouldn't have started believing her and then turned against her like that."

"It can't have been much to believe in if it was only you that did. You mean her tales about up there."

"Stuff she thought she'd found out, that I thought she had."

"You know where the clothes-pegs are, but I'd have to say imagining all that about the place she lives it's no wonder she went, well, we can't say mad or crazy these days. But I believe with all my heart it wouldn't have mattered what you did, not when a girl like her gets an idea into her head."

A smell of coffee strayed into the room as though to represent good sense with one of the clichés Rob most loathed. "Come and have a mug and whatever you want for breakfast," his mother said, "so we can get you off to school."

Just then a window of Nazarill bared its light. Without the mist to soften it, the uncurtained spark seemed to pierce straight into his brain before he realised that it wasn't in Amy's apartment but in the one next door. He had to blink away the afterimage as he followed his mother. He sat on a chair which appeared to be an undernourished relative of the dining-suite and accepted a mug of coffee, into which he stared until his mother said "What are you having?"

"I'll get it. Just some cereal." He rather hoped his undertaking to eat would send her on her way so that he needn't do so, but before he could mime any intention of serving himself she was shaking Sticky Rotters into a bowl. She planted the bowl and a jug of milk in front of him, and watched as he drowned the sugary cylinders and fed himself a spoonful. If she intended to supervise him to the last mouthful, he thought, she could listen to him as well. "I wish I knew where she was, that's all," he said.

His mother ducked over her mug. When she'd blown on her coffee and sipped it she said "Was when?"

"Is now. She's not at home."

"What makes you say that?"

"I tried to call her at the weekend, but he said he'd sent her away and wouldn't tell me where."

"I expect he knows best," Rob's mother murmured, and scrutinised her coffee.

"That isn't what you're thinking."

"It most certainly is. He's the only parent she has."

Rob's mother lifted her gaze to him, and he was resigning himself to having fallen foul of parental solidarity when his father wandered into the kitchen. "I take it we're talking about Amy's dad."

"*We* are," Rob's mother said, "but I think we've finished, haven't we? What can I offer you while I'm being the chef and the waitress?"

"Sorry. I wasn't . . . Sorry, sorry."

Rob might have thought he was apologising for somehow having implied he meant to take advantage of her if it hadn't been for the fierceness of her glare which cut him off short. "What were you going to say?"

"It wouldn't have been anything worth the breath, old chap. I don't know what your mother was saying, do I? You sit down, Marge, I'll get my own—"

"She was talking about Amy's dad always being right like you and her."

"Well, I'm sure you must have had enough of him," Rob's mother said.

This was one attempt too many to do away with the subject. "Have you spoken to him since I did?" Rob demanded.

"I'd have said if I had," his mother assured him, and managed to appear as offended as her tone, but Rob saw his father turn away too quickly to the coffee-pot.

"You've . . . you've been in touch with someone," Rob pursued, and all at once knew. "It was Amy, wasn't it? You spoke to her."

"Why on earth would I have done that? Eat up now or you'll be late for school."

"I'm driving. No rush." If Rob hadn't been sure of himself by now, his father's reluctance to face the two of them would have convinced him. "When did you talk to her? Why didn't you tell me?"

His mother pursed her lips and breathed so hard her nostrils flared while she narrowed her eyes at her father, whose back was exhibiting signs of besiegement. When none of this rid her of Rob's questions she muttered "I shouldn't think you'd want me to after what she said."

"I won't know if I do or not unless you tell me what it was."

"You know." It was clear she intended this to be sufficiently reproving to forestall further enquiries if it hadn't conveyed her answer, but since Rob shook his head she went on. "The thing she told you to do that made you come home not wanting anything to do with us. You needn't think I'm repeating it."

In other circumstances he might have been touched or amused. "How do you know about that?" he said.

She went through the routine involving lips and breathing hard and glaring at his father. At last she said "I picked up the phone when your friend thought she was talking to the machine."

"And did you say anything to her?"

"What would you want your mother to say to a girl who'd just used that word?"

Before Rob could insist on a real answer, his father abandoned his defensive posture. "The point is, son, it sounds as though the poor girl's even worse than she was when she sent you packing, even more out of control."

"Thank you, Tom. Well done."

"Did she say where she was?" Rob said.

His parents didn't quite look at each other. At last his father said "Maybe she doesn't know, the way she is."

"I'm sure her father has to know what he's doing."

"But did she mention a place?"

Rob's mother gazed straight at him, and he had so little idea what she was thinking that he felt he no longer knew her. "No," she said.

"What did she say, then?"

"I couldn't make head or tail out of most of it. Look, Robin, we'll discuss this tonight if we must. You're going to be late for school."

"Then don't keep holding me up by not telling me things."

It seemed that a look of rebuke might be her sole response. At last she said "I think she wanted to say she was sorry for making a scene. Now will you please eat that up if you're eating and—"

"Will one of you phone her father and ask where she is?"

Rob's mother turned an incredulous stare on her husband, who apparently misinterpreted it. "To be honest with you, son—"

"*Tom.*"

"I can't see what harm it will do, Marge. You aren't going to charge off to see her, are you, old chap?"

"Shouldn't think so. I just want to know how she is."

"I expect her father can tell you that," he said, and shrugged a shoulder at Rob's mother. "From what Marge heard her saying, it looks as though she's at home."

"Then why did he say she wasn't?" Rob demanded.

"Maybe she's come back since you spoke to him."

"But the idea was to get her out of there. She wouldn't want to come back, not this soon anyway." When his parents failed to disagree with him, Rob dropped his spoon in the soggy cereal and stood up. "I'm going to phone."

"I hope you're satisfied," he heard his mother say, and his father protesting "We couldn't have gone on keeping him in the dark." As Rob lifted the receiver his mother came to the kitchen doorway and folded her arms, pointing her elbows at him. "Don't start one of your half-hour conversations. School's more important, especially this year."

"Not to me," Rob whispered into the mouthpiece, having turned it and himself away before dialling Amy's number. It occurred to him that if her father refused to speak to him he could ask for one of his parents to be told any news of her. Except that the voice that responded before the phone could ring wasn't her father's but a woman's, intoning "The number you have dialled has not been recognised. Please check and try again."

Had he misdialled while attempting to ignore his mother? He spun the creaky dial again, and was raising the phone to his face when the indifferent voice cut in. "The number you have dialled—"

Rob silenced it and dialled the operator. As he waited for the zero to become a person, his mother pushed past him to settle the weight of her gaze on his face. "Do you realise what time it is? You can't afford to be late for school. Come and take this away from him, Tom."

"I won't be late."

"I don't want you driving like a mad thing either," she said, so fiercely anxious that Rob almost desisted. Then a voice that might have been understudying for the announcement of unobtainable numbers produced itself. "Operator, how may I help you?"

"I'm trying to get this number," Rob said, and gave Amy's.

While he loitered the phone kept up a hiss of static which suggested a distillation of his mother's reproach. At last the sound retreated to let the operator tell him "That line is out of order. I'll inform the engineers."

"How soon will they be there?"

"I'm afraid I couldn't say, sir."

Rob planted the droning receiver before hurrying upstairs to brush his teeth and grab his rucksack. He considered adding *Nazarill* to its burden, but left the book on the chair to lie about his intentions. It was no more of a lie than his parents had allowed him to believe, after all. He tried to imitate someone bound directly for school, which wasn't enough for his mother, who said as she opened the front door for him "I hope you've left yourself plenty of time to get to your first class."

"I have, I promise."

He might as well not have spoken, for she looked no less worried, wrinkling her nostrils at the hint of mist in the air. He couldn't very well admit the rest of the truth—that his first period that morning was free, since one of the psychology teachers was off sick. She watched while he unlocked the Micra and switched on the engine and, to console her, the headlamps. Having returned half the wave he'd given her, she closed the front door as he manoeuvred around the first of the potholes in the slope to the main road. There was no traffic to prevent him from driving straight across and up the nearest street to Nazarill.

Children were hurrying along the street, some of the girls dressed in the uniform Amy had to wear. The memory made the seat beside him feel deserted, and he heard her saying "It's a nice little Microbe." Beyond the railings at the end of the street the mist was trailing away through the grounds to let the facade confront him with the pallor it appeared to have extended to the daylight all around it. The drive glistened like the tracks of a plague of snails, and he found himself beginning to detest the place as much as Amy had. If she was inside and didn't want to be, it was time someone listened to her.

The windows of her apartment caught the sunlight and twinkled mockingly at him, aggravating his dislike, as he drove between the drooling gateposts onto the gravel. He was halfway along the drive when a car swung around the left-hand corner of the building and came for him. It was a bronzed Jaguar driven by a red-faced woman wearing a white blouse and a severe grey suit. She stopped her car abreast of his and ran her window down. "Can I help you?"

"I'm here for Amy," Rob said, having leaned across to wind down the window that had once been hers. "Have you seen her?"

"Is she home? I understood from her father she was away undergoing treatment."

Rob experienced a shiver that felt as though Nazarill had cast its pale shadow over him. He could have understood if Amy's father had lied about her whereabouts to keep him away from her, but if he'd also told the other tenants that she wasn't there when she was . . . "When did he say that?"

"Within the last few days," the woman said, employing her demeanour to ensure he recognised her for the magistrate Amy had mentioned to him. "Are you implying you know otherwise?"

"I'm here to find out. I'll ask him to tell you where things are at, shall I?"

"I'm sure we would all appreciate that," the magistrate said, and having completed a stare at Rob which more than doubled the force of her words, sped off.

Rob drove up to the front of Nazarill and halted in its shadow. He would only waste time by parking round the corner, and so he climbed out of the car. As he switched off the headlamps the ground-floor corridor darkened beyond the glass, and he seemed to glimpse movement. If somebody was coming out, he would do his best to talk his way in—but when he peered through the glass nobody was in sight. He couldn't have seen any of the doors opening or closing; he must have seen shadows vanishing as his lights did. He strode to the wide doorstep and rang the Priestleys' bell.

There was silence, or at least no more than the usual sound of Partington mumbling to itself, until a girl screamed. He turned to see her dodging out of Little Hope Way as three of her schoolmates pelted her with scraps of litter. A metal shutter clattered up beyond the gates of the marketplace as though to hasten her on her way, and then Partington subsumed her protests into its vague murmur. Rob was about to give the bell a second try when the grille beside the twin columns of bellpushes spat words at him. "Who's there?"

It was a man's voice, and so it must belong to Amy's father. If the intercom was capable of rendering it so unrecognisable, the same ought to happen to Rob's, and in the moment of locating the button under the grille he changed whatever plan he'd half conceived. "Parcel for Miss Priestley," he said.

The response was slow in coming—slow enough that Rob had time to wish he hadn't left his car where it would be visible from the front windows. For the moment Amy's father couldn't see it, and eventually the wall said in something not much like his voice "Leave it without."

Rob ducked his head towards the grille, too late to be certain if he'd overheard another sound—surely only a high-pitched distortion. He poked the button as soon as he thought of an answer. "I can't leave it. It has to be signed for."

"She is unable to sign for the nonce."

The voice seemed increasingly focused on the microphone, filling it to the exclusion of any other sound. Rob imagined Amy's father pressing his lips against the underside of the metal to produce the close electronic whisper, and couldn't help shivering as though the mouth in the stone had breathed at him. "Then can you sign for it?" he said.

"What manner of package are you seeking to deliver?"

Rob hadn't anticipated such a question. "A. A book," he improvised, "or some books, it looks like."

"We have no need of any more books here."

"It'll have to be signed for before I can take it away," Rob said, growing desperate.

"Then let it be left where I bade it be left."

"I can't do that. The instructions are, they're if it can't be delivered it has to be sent on, forwarded, and I'll need an address."

"I leave you to light upon one you find appropriate."

"No, I mean I need it from you, the address where I can send this to her."

"Her whereabouts are nobody's affair but mine."

"They're hers as well, aren't they?"

Rob wasn't sure if he'd discarded his role; perhaps a postman might just conceivably have said that. The grille crackled with static like the driest laughter he'd ever heard, which was transformed into a whisper that sounded as though it was embedded in the stone of Nazarill. "I think not. No longer," it said, and then the grille was as dead as the wall.

Amy was upstairs: Rob was certain of that now. "Hello?" he said after the fashion of innumerable characters abandoned by phones in films, and leaned on the doorbell. When it provoked no response he struck the closer of the glass doors with the edge of his hand. An ominous low note resounded through the corridor, and he imagined he saw all six doors stir with the vibration. That wouldn't gain him entry to Nazarill, and so he pushed a fist's worth of doorbells and poised his thumb on the intercom button. "Special delivery," he would say, or was that pretence past standing up? "I need to speak to someone about Amy Priestley" would be better. He could be calling on behalf of her school—of a friend of his parents, a teacher, who'd asked him to find out how Amy was. Only there was nobody to persuade of this; the grille wasn't even bothering to raise his hopes with static. Then he saw that in his haste, not that haste impressed him as quite enough of an explanation, he'd rung all the ground-floor doorbells. He rubbed his hands together to rid them of the chill he seemed to feel seeping out of the wall, and was about to jab the lowest of the second-floor buttons when two whitish globes appeared at the far end of the corridor and glided towards him.

They weren't the lifeless eyes they appeared to be, of course. They were the headlamps of a car approaching up the drive behind him, a car moving so slowly that the muted crunch of gravel beneath its wheels resembled an increasing burst of static from the intercom. Rob turned to meet it, vowing that whoever the driver might be, they were going to admit him to the building. "Her school sent me," he heard himself say in his head. The Triumph, which was brown as an official envelope, pulled up behind his car, almost butting it, and the driver climbed out with a double slam of boots on gravel. "What are you hanging round here for, Hayward?" he said.

It was Shaun Pickles in his uniform. Beneath such hair as he permitted himself his bony face was as studded with dull angles as a fist, one reddened by anticipation of delivering a blow. Rob told himself he mustn't allow his dislike to get in the way of any help the guard might be persuaded to offer. "I'm trying to reach Amy," he said.

"Better do as she told you, and quick."

"She'd tell you to if she saw you," Rob said, and was momentarily so confused that he wondered if Pickles might be there at her invitation, but she couldn't have changed that much. "Anyway, what's it to you?"

"Plenty. We're friends of her father."

"So?" Rob retorted, and forced out a question that almost blocked his throat. "Do you care about her?"

"A damn sight more than you have, did you but know."

"Then help her now. Help me to. She's up there and she doesn't want to be."

"Doesn't know what she wants, more like, and no wonder with the likes of you trying to stuff mad ideas like that into her head along with God knows what else you need arresting for."

"It isn't my idea, it's hers. She called me."

"Isn't that nice after her telling you the other thing. And what did she whisper in your ear?"

"I wasn't there, my mother was."

"Then your mother wants to learn how to take messages. Your used to be girlfriend's gone away. Wanted shut of you, I shouldn't wonder."

"Her father told you she'd gone, didn't he? I don't know if she went or not, but now she's here."

"Watch who you're saying is a liar." As blotches flared on his cheeks, Pickles struck Rob as more and more like an overgrown schoolboy in the wrong uniform. "Who says she's here?"

"I do. I heard her before."

"What did you hear, you bloody pothead?"

"Amy, when I rang the bell." Rob knew he mustn't sound even slightly uncertain, and indeed with everything he said now he was convincing himself. "He answered it, but I'm sure I heard her trying to call to me until he blocked her off somehow. He's keeping her up there against her will."

"Sounds right to me."

"I'm serious. Somebody ought to see how she is."

"I'm bloody serious too, and don't you mistake it. Somebody's seeing to her all right, the way she needs to be seen."

Rob restrained himself from lashing out at the stiff smug face, which he was beginning to identify with the impregnability of Nazarill. "If that's what you think I haven't time to stop you. Just leave me to think different."

"Can't do that. Her dad asked me to keep an eye on his property."

A hot wave of rage passed through Rob before it was overwhelmed by the chill. "Amy's not property."

"She is at her age."

Rob clenched his fists and turned his back to hold them away from the guard. He was ignoring him in order to identify the next bell he should ring when he saw there was no need: several people were descending the stairs. In the dimness that was coated with the daylight on the glass, he thought at first the girl in the middle was Amy. When he pressed his forehead against a door he made out that she was younger, not least by the way she shrank back from the sight of him. He straightened up and smiled and displayed his palms, but her father came stalking at him while she followed timidly alongside her mother. The man yanked the door open, drooping one corner of his mouth as though to counteract the asymmetry of his face and ensure it didn't appear remotely comical, an ambition by no means achieved. "What do you want?" he demanded.

"Amy. Amy—"

"I know who you mean. She's not here."

"She told my mother she was. I'm just going up to check. It's fine, I've been up before."

The man blocked his way while continuing to hold the door ajar, and his tall stooping wife pushed their daughter forward. "Go out quickly, Pam. He won't hurt you." She squeezed through after the girl, who fled to stand beyond Pickles for protection, and added her stare to her husband's. "You've been told she isn't here. We live next door, so we should know."

"I've been told all sorts of stuff. I want to see for myself."

"Then ring their bell," the man advised, further lowering the corner of his mouth, and shut the door behind him with a glassy clang that sounded final.

"He already has. He isn't wanted," Pickles said.

Surely Amy still had friends who would be sufficiently concerned to let him in, Rob thought, and was pressing bells in the middle of the column when the woman said "Can't you do something about him?"

"That's what I'm here for," Pickles said, and took a gravelly step towards Rob. "I'm warning you—"

"Come away, Pam. No need to watch." The woman steered the girl in the direction of the car park while her husband lingered. "You'll handle him, will you?" he asked Pickles.

"You won't be seeing him round here again uninvited."

"That's what my family wants to hear," the man said, and hastened after them as Rob, having failed to break the stony silence of the grille, made to push another gathering of bells. Behind him Pickles said at the top of his voice "You've been told to go by the people who live here. Are you going to get in that pile of junk now and stop bothering people?"

"Not until I know if Amy's here I'm not," said Rob, and knuckled the bellpushes.

"Then I'm escorting you off this property." As he spoke Pickles closed a wiry hand around Rob's wrist. Rob leaned his weight on the buttons so as not to be shifted and said "Better let go of me. We're not at school any more."

"Are you coming quietly or do I have to use force?"

"Don't try it," Rob said, clenching his teeth as the bones of his wrist began to ache. "Fuck off, Picknose, or I'm—"

"You may say that to your girlfriends if you've got any, but you aren't saying it to me," Pickles snarled, and planting his free hand on Rob's left shoulder, twisted Rob's arm up towards it, hard.

Rob's forehead struck the glass door, producing a gong-note that reverberated in his brain. The dim corridor lurched into focus, and he saw the six doors tremble as though they were preparing to spring open. Then a blade of pain drove itself through his arm and deep into his shoulder, and he reached behind him with his other hand and grabbed the back of Pickles' neck.

Perhaps he was remembering some film; he didn't know where the instinct was coming from. He shoved himself away from the doors with his feet and immediately bent forward with all the strength he could summon to throw his adversary over his shoulder—or rather, he started to do so. As Rob made to fling his body forward Pickles let go of his wrist and stepped back to release himself. Before he could, Rob sprawled on his back, having had no time to let go of Pickles' neck.

The guard's weight came with him. His arm was still twisted behind him, and gravel bit into the length of it. When Pickles struggled off him and stood up, Rob attempted to roll over, but the pain that filled his arm was so intense that he crouched into a sitting position instead. A lump of gravel seemed to have lodged itself where the arm met the shoulder. He braced himself, gripping his thigh with his free hand, and tried very gingerly to move the twisted arm. The rush of pain brought the front of Nazarill toppling at him. The lump embedded in his flesh wasn't gravel, it was a knob of the bone of his arm.

Pickles was watching from a safe distance. "Serve you right," he said, then frowned as Rob's vision blurred. "Come on, get up. You're not hurt that bad."

Somewhere out beyond his pain Rob heard a car start and coast over the gravel. The sound of bits of stone grinding together beneath the wheels suggested that his injury was expanding into the world. The car halted with an unnecessarily violent crunch of gravel, and a window was lowered. "Everything in hand?" said the voice of the man who'd barred Rob.

"He did himself an injury trying to resist while I was bringing him away. Does anyone know first aid?"

Apparently nobody did; there was silence apart from the panting of the car. Rob tried once more to coax the arm from behind him, but the pain nearly overbalanced him onto it. "Hospital," he gasped as tears flooded down his cheeks.

"Can you take him? Maybe one of you could drive him in his car. I'm expected at the market in five minutes."

"I suppose I could," the woman said, not by any means immediately. "You can tell them at the library I'm on an errand of mercy, Leonard."

Rob heard the slam of a car door, and footsteps disturbing the broken stones. As a piece of gravel struck the hand with which he was supporting himself the woman said "I can't do anything unless he gets up."

"Here, for God's sake." Pickles grasped Rob's uninjured arm and hauled him to his feet with a vigour that shifted the dislocated bone in the flesh. "Behave yourself while you're with this lady," he murmured in Rob's ear, "or I'll do for your other arm."

Rob couldn't argue or otherwise react—hadn't even room within himself for resentment. All he wanted was that the pain should go away or, for the moment, simply not grow worse. He suffered him-self to be marched to his car, where the passenger door was opened for him from within. He heard and smelled the spicily perfumed woman assume the driver's seat while he propped himself on his left shoulder against the shampooed upholstery, and then there was a pause he didn't understand until she said "If I had the keys it would be useful."

"Trousers. Can you get them?"

She greeted this idea with a solitary tut, and he thought she was going to insist that he produce the keys. Then he felt her fingertips probing his pocket, fastidiously avoiding contact with his thigh. The keys left him, and the engine cleared its throat. As the car began to swing round she said "I'll go as gently as I can."

As the Micra completed its turn Rob saw the other cars start to follow as slowly, and had the impression that a funeral was leaving Nazarill. The façade withdrew into the mirror, mist draining cur-tained windows of their colour while adding to the pallor of the stone. Until his injury was fixed he could do nothing except hope—hope that Amy would be safe for all the time that might pass before he would be able to come back.

26

THE SILENCING

"Come and let me out or he'll do worse," Amy shouted, and had to snatch a breath. In a moment she heard the intercom responding to her father or to her, though she couldn't distinguish whose voice it had. Whoever was out there wouldn't be able to hear her except when her father was speaking, and so she made herself wait until he did. "Help, he's locked me up," she cried, but something was wrong: he sounded muffled. She'd heard him speak several times, separated by bursts of noise from the intercom, before she deduced that he'd cupped his hands around the microphone and was talking between them so as to exclude her cries.

"Help," she almost screamed. "You can hear me. You must hear me." Her bruised jaw ached from being forced so wide the skin at the corners of her mouth felt close to tearing. She no longer knew what room she would see if she looked behind her, she only knew she couldn't bear to be robbed of the solitary hope she had. She clutched at the doorknob and set about shaking the door, having remembered that it was secured by just the bolt and a single screw. Could she wrench it out of the frame while her father was distracted? Even when she flung all her weight backwards with both hands gripping the knob, the door hardly stirred. She let go of it and encircled her mouth with her hands, and tried to concentrate her pleas so that they must penetrate any barrier. It seemed to make less sense now to restrict her shouts to the times when her father was speaking; how many chances to be heard might she deny herself by stopping to listen? She paused only for breath, as little of it as practicable, and so she didn't know when he ceased to speak. The sudden appearance of his voice directly outside her room felt like the springing of a trap. "Let there be an end to your ravings. Your friend has departed."

Amy's cupped hands found her cheeks and dug their nails in. "Which friend?"

"The one you so vulgarly sent on his way, I believe."

"You're saying Rob was here?"

"Was without, rather. I understand the bird had some name of the kind, and I am certain he has hopped away for good."

She let go of her face rather than injure it. "What did you say to him?"

"Why, that you are in the place that will do you most good. You yourself have ensured he will assume that is anywhere but here." Her father's voice was moving away into a room. "Now cease your useless prating and spare my brain for a little."

She didn't need to be told not to attract his attention further. The thought that Rob had been so close—was perhaps still outside, not entirely relieved of whatever suspicion had brought him—had renewed her desperation to escape. She stooped for her comb and tried to fix her gaze on the screw she had to attack, but she couldn't avoid catching sight of the mirror from the corner of her eye. She gripped the comb through the handkerchief as though the dull bite of the metal teeth might help reinstate reality, and confronted the image in the mirror. Nearly the whole of her poster was there, together with a sample of wallpaper, and not so much as a hint of bare brick.

For a prolonged moment she wondered how she could be certain that the scene beneath the glass was more present or more genuine than the view of the cell had been, and then she managed to put the uncertainty out of her mind. "Stay there. Just be there," she whispered at the reflection, and crouched quickly to the screw. She wedged the metal tooth into the groove and leaned awkwardly over the comb, clenching her hands around it, then bore down on it as hard as she could.

Sweat prickled her forehead like a gust of hot ash as the teeth of the comb dug into her palm, and her wrists began to shiver. Just as she was about to let go until her palm stopped smarting, she felt movement. Metal had shifted, had twisted. She threw all her weight against the clumsy tool. With a snap that seemed to travel through

the bones of her arm on its way to her skull, the tooth at the end of
the comb broke off.

Amy's knees struck the floorboards through the carpet, and tears
sprang out of her eyes. She rubbed away the moisture with the back
of her hand before she could give way to despair. The comb had
plenty of teeth left, and the next in line must be almost as strong as
the one she'd lost. She poked the broken fragment out of the groove
of the screw and tried to manoeuvre its neighbour into place, tried
to stay calm as she fiddled with it, tried to believe it would work.
Once she saw that the length of shaft which had held the end tooth
would get in the way however she angled the comb, she tried to snap
it off, first by wedging it under her heel and then in each of the holes
for the screws she'd withdrawn. None of this had the least effect on
the idiotic half-inch of metal. When the teeth pierced the handkerchief and found her already tender palm she flung the comb across
the room.

It clashed against the mirror and fell among the mass of jars and
sprays and bottles on the dressing-table, where it struck an object
that sounded more metallic than glass. What had it found? Amy
made her way over, watching herself approach across the room that
was still her room, and discovered her manicure scissors. If only they
were the scissors she had used last summer to cut the legs off an old
pair of jeans! But perhaps those blades would have been too large
to deal with the screw, and in any case they were in a kitchen drawer.
Those on the dressing-table looked pitifully fragile, but she had to
try them. She'd barely started levering at the screw with the thicker
blade when it snapped off, and the other blade took no time at all.

"Think," she pleaded with herself. "It's only a screw. Think." She
dragged her gaze around the room in search of another improvised
tool, but the place might have been the bare cell she was afraid to
see, its contents offered her so little. She ran to the wardrobe and
rummaged in all the clothes that had pockets, but the only secret they
were keeping was a half-used book of matches with which she lit her
incense sticks. She imagined trying to twist the screw with a fingernail in the groove. While the notion made her cringe, she could think
of nothing with which to engineer her escape besides herself.

And perhaps her father had told her how, if she was getting on his
nerves even more than he acknowledged. She strode over to the door
and began to kick it, chanting "You can hear me. You can hear me."

Before long he responded from across the hall with a weariness that afforded her some hope. "Be quiet in there."

"I'll be quiet when you let me out, and till then I won't stop."

"Do as you choose, as is your wont. You will exhaust yourself before you wear me down," he said, and started to pray, more loudly as she redoubled her kicks and her chanting. He faltered at "deliver us," and had to recommence. When his words gave out at the phrase a second time he shouted "Hold your tongue, or I—"

"You'll what? You can't do anything to me unless you come in here."

This time she would be ready for whatever he might try. Let him throw another punch at her—it would bring him across the threshold so that she could dodge past him. Bolting the door on him would give her all the time she needed to escape. She was straining her ears to detect any sounds that would betray he was trying to take her unawares when he spoke, still across the hall. "Your subterfuge is a poor effort. Can you contrive me no better diversion?"

All she had left was the truth. "You'll have to let me out sooner or later."

"Indeed? Pray explain."

"I need to go next door."

"I think not. I fear you have made yourself unwelcome."

"Next door here. The bathroom."

"I cannot see how that will be necessary when you have supped so sparingly of late."

"What are you going to do," Amy said, her voice uneven with an element that only sounded like laughter, "starve me?"

"I shall pray that fasting will bring you to your senses and to God."

"It won't, so what's going to happen instead? Am I supposed to die in here or what?"

"Should that come to pass I shall pray you repent at the last so that your soul goes up to Heaven."

"You're mad," Amy whispered, and as the words became audible she knew they were no longer an insult or an exaggeration. She was overcome by a shiver that made her feel walled in by damp bare brick. Perhaps the cell in the mirror was where she would die, she thought—where she would be imprisoned once she died. She returned to kicking the door, an action which suggested what she could shout. "That's your head I'm kicking. Can you feel it? You will soon if you don't yet. I'll kick it till you open my door."

She was anticipating that when he'd had enough he would rush her door, but when he responded he was no nearer. "You will injure none except yourself, and any harm you do yourself will have only God to help it." He didn't sound entirely unaffected, and when he set about praying louder than before, she knew she had reached him. This time he was less than halfway through the prayer when he broke off, yelling "You fiend, you'll not best me." He was staying where he was, however, and her foot was beginning to ache. "You won't be able to pray till you let me out," she called, "you won't be able to think," searching her mind for a monologue she could use to rob him of his self-control as an alternative to bruising her toes against the door. There was plenty of material in the room—all the books her mother had bound for her. The biggest volume, a collection of fairy tales and nursery rhymes, lay on top of the others, but now she realised she needn't consult it; she could recite from memory. Before she was conscious of deciding which of her old bedtime verses to perform, she was projecting her voice through the door.

" *'Come dance with me, young and old, out from the tree.*
There are songs to be sung, there are marvels to see.
Come dance with me, young and old, under the moon.
You'll have wings on your shoulders and dew for your shoon.'
'Dance away to the moon, Mother Hepzibah, flee.
In the morning they'll come to play prickles with thee.'
'Let them come to my hovel, whoever they are.
I've games that I'll play with them,' says Hepzibah . . ."

It seemed to Amy she had read this only once, and perhaps not to the end. Her father was raising his voice in yet another bid to scale the prayer, and surely he must lose his temper very soon. She rested her fingertips on either side of her nose and the edges of her thumbs gingerly against her jaw.

" *'They've come, Mother Hepzibah, come with the dawn.*
Your cat she is drownded, your friends they are flown.'

'*Good day, Master Matthew, for that's who you are.*
Will you trip the old dance with me?' says Hepzibah.
'*Bring her with us, stout fellows, bring her to the oak.*
She'll dance us a jig 'til her neck it is broke.'
' '*Tis no dance with no partner, and it's Matthew I name.*
In a twelvemonth from now you shall see me the same.
I'll come for to find you, wherever you are.
And we'll dance in the air,' says old Mad Hepzibah.
They pricked her and spun her and swum her until
They left her to rot on a rope on the hill.
'*Why, what ails thee, Matthew, thy face is so white?'*
' '*Tis her dead eyes I see turn to me every night.'*
'*Come open the door to me, Matthew my swain.*
'*Tis a year since I promised you'd see me again . . .' "*

Had Amy ever read all this? She felt as though she was dredging up the last lines from within herself. If to any extent she was making them up, couldn't she take control of them? Her hands sank away from her face and clasped themselves in front of her. For the moment she was addressing only herself.

" '*You're a poor partner, Matthew, so die in your bed.*
I've daughters and friends I shall dance with instead.
We'll dance through the fire, we'll dance into the sky.
The power of the hill means none of us shall die . . .' "

She was trying to understand her own words, and grasp how responsible she was for them, when her father broke the silence which she hadn't even noticed overtaking him. "Perhaps this will put an end to your ungodly chanting," he yelled, and tramped into the hall so resolutely that she felt the floor quiver. Instead of unbolting her door, however, he headed for the exit to the corridor. Had she driven him out after all? Then what had he meant by his threat? Just as she realised, she heard a click from the end of the hall, and her room vanished.

He'd switched off the fuse that controlled her light. As her eyes jerked back and forth, desperate to free themselves from their blindness, he came to her door. "I imagined that would pacify you," he said.

Amy began to kick the door, around which she was starting to perceive the faintest thread of a glow. "Turn my light back on. Turn it on now."

"I think not."

"Turn. It. On. Or. I'll. Wreck. Your. Head," Amy cried, punctuating each word with a vicious kick.

"Your performances no longer trouble me. I rather think the dark will quieten you ere long," he said, turning his voice away from her and taking it into a room. A door slammed, extinguishing much of the rectangle from which light had seemed capable, given enough time, of leaking into her room. The darkness fitted more of itself to her eyes, and she felt it settling into her brain, robbing her of words. When she continued to kick out she had the dismaying notion that despite the ache that spread through her foot, she was kicking only the adamant blackness. But it wasn't quite as unrelievable as her father must want it to be. She had only to cross the room in the dark and find the book of matches in the wardrobe.

Some effort was required before she managed to look away from the door—from all the light she had. She couldn't distinguish so much as the hint of an outline in the depths around her, but she had a sense of something crouching low a few feet into the room, where her bed ought to be. Of course it was the bed, and she shuffled until her body was turned towards it, and moved forward.

If only she had thought to take the matches while she was searching in the wardrobe! Her shins bumped hard against the corner of the bed, and she flailed the air to keep her balance. For a moment of panic that made her eyes feel overcome by cataracts she was afraid to touch walls closer than they should be. She could feel her bed, she was in the room with which she'd had to grow familiar, not the cell in the mirror. She made herself sidle to the right along the footboard, in the direction of the wardrobe.

As soon as she relinquished her contact with the bed she felt lost in the dark. Her feet were beginning to encounter objects on the floor. Some were soft as flesh without much bone to keep it firm, some were hard as exposed bone. They were hers, she kept telling herself, even if more than one of them seemed to draw itself back as her foot touched it. She thrust a hand into the darkness where the wardrobe was supposed to be, though she couldn't help clenching her fist, and took another hesitant sidelong step. At once her knuckles collided, more loudly than she would have preferred, with the wardrobe door.

She ran her hand over the flat featureless surface to locate the chilly sliver of a handle, and found its twin with her other hand, and pulled them both. She felt the doors pass on either side of her like the halves of a breath as she ducked into a blackness which pressed its smells of cloth and wood into her face. She groped in front of her, and one hand brushed against a dangling boneless arm. It didn't belong to the coat she was trying to find, but she thought it was close. Her fingers ranged over a gathering of empty sleeves which stirred at her touch, and she had time to wonder what she might do if she met anything like an arm in one of them, just as an object harder than cloth and larger than any of her buttons presented itself to her fingertips. It was indeed the book of matches, which she pinched between her nails with all their strength—to ensure she didn't drop it, surely not for fear it would be snatched out of her grasp—and having extracted it from the pocket, closed her other hand around it. She elbowed the doors shut, and was pushing back the cover of the match-book on her palm when she hesitated. Was she certain that she wanted to see the room in which she was imprisoned—the room which seemed to have abruptly grown cold and damp?

Not seeing would be even worse. She prised up a match and tore it out of its rank and pressed it against the striking strip. When she felt it start to bend she realised that unless she struck it she was liable to render it useless, and so she dragged it along the strip. It sputtered but failed to ignite. "Don't," she whispered, "you're all I've got," and scraped the edge of its head on the strip. This time the match flared up.

The jaundiced flame was so unsteady it had to be suffering from the damp she could smell in the air. Its light didn't extend nearly far enough; most of the glow was concentrated in a blotch on the wardrobe door. She turned away as quickly as she thought the flame could stand, and held the match above her head.

The cluttered floor began to heave like a sea of shadows. Dark shapes leaned out from behind the furniture and dodged back and crept into view again to obscure the flickering walls. The gloom was so unstable that only the pattern of the wallpaper persuaded her the walls weren't bare and crawling with moisture, and the pattern might have been stains of damp, except that surely it was too regular. At least she could see to find her way back to the foot of the bed, guarded by the four dim faces which appeared to be floating in the cloudy air—but the light was also showing her that the match-book was considerably less than half full, with only seven matches left. She wouldn't feel safe lying on the bed; she was going to sit on the end of it with the presence of the faces on the wall to reassure her the room hadn't changed, and the matches in her hand if she absolutely needed to see in order to believe. She paced around the bed, stepping over huddled objects that snatched at her feet with their shadows. She had reached the corner of the mattress when the flame stung her thumb and forefinger. She shook it and it died, and in that instant she glimpsed a face raising itself to peer at her out of the dark of the room.

She almost dropped the matches. For a moment she didn't know which way she was facing or where the intruder might be in relation to her—sneaking up behind her or waiting directly in front of her for her to strike a match and illuminate its face? Then she discerned the meagre outline of the door to her left, and made herself turn towards the depths of the room as she fumbled for a match and nearly broke it off too short to be of use. Digging a nail into its root, she twisted it out of the book and dragged the head along the strip.

The shadows sprang out to greet it. Some crawled about the floor while larger shapes nodded from behind the furniture. The swarming of dimness on the walls seemed to be the only other movement. Amy was striving to persuade herself that she must have imagined the glimpse—that if she didn't control her imagination, she was lost—when her gaze was drawn where she least wanted it to go: to the mirror.

Her poster wasn't in it. Bare bricks were, even less well-lit than the walls around her but visibly coated with moisture. Was there also an object at the base of the mirror, the top of a rounded brownish lump crowned by a few strands of cobweb or vegetation or hair? She stared in panic at it, willing it to sink out of sight or at the very least not to move. The match burned down to her finger and thumb, and with a cry she dropped it. As its fall extinguished it she saw the discoloured lump rear up to gaze at her over the edge of the mirror, or rather to show her the lack of its eyes.

She became aware of crushing the matches to uselessness in her fist. She had to pry it open with her other hand before she could locate another match, and pinch it between her shaky finger and thumb, and jerk it free and scrape it on the progressively bald strip. The room and its shadows wavered up as the flame did, but all she could see was the head of the figure crouched beneath the level of the mirror.

More of the shrivelled peeling forehead was visible this time. It was waiting for the last instant of light before it raised itself further, Amy recognised, as though it was playing a mad version of some childhood game. What might it do when the matches were spent? She mustn't risk finding out—mustn't use her last match. The flame shivered at the thought as her hand did, and although it was no more than halfway down the stalk, gave up. Its failure was the signal for her companion to lift its head, displaying the holes which were the best it could do for eyes and a good deal beneath them, though not much that was worth calling a face.

Amy dropped the smouldering match and flung herself at the door. Her free hand clutched the knob, and she began to rattle the door in its frame. She didn't want to infuriate her father now but win him over. "Please put the light back on," she called. "I'm better now. Please let me out or put the light on."

Her skin was tingling unpleasantly, and a faint reek of singed carpet had added itself to the increasingly damp smell of the room. Her ears had started to ache along with her forehead and jaw as she strained to hear her father and willed nothing to be audible in her room. "Can't you answer?" she called, jerking the door harder and fighting to control her voice. "You've cured me. Can't you tell I'm cured? I'd just like the light on to see."

She was struggling to think of more to say when she heard a sound that had to be welcome—the opening of the door across the hall. The outline of her own door brightened somewhat, and as she tried to take that as a good sign, her father said in a voice which sounded resentful of being roused "If you are cured as you say you must know there is nought to fear."

"I didn't say I was afraid," Amy managed to inform him, though she had trouble with the last word. "I can't see to do anything, that's all."

"You have no need to do anything. Comfort yourself with the dark and find peace in it. You ought to recognise you are not alone in it."

Somehow Amy kept her voice even, reminding herself that the

only way to overcome the presence in her room was by persuading her father, but her body did its best to shake itself away from the threat of being touched in the dark. "What do you mean?"

"What should I mean? You betray yourself by asking. Is God not with you?"

"Oh, I see. I thought you meant—" There was no subject Amy would have less liked to pursue. "You're right. You don't need me to tell you, do you? I know it's true now," she said, gritting her teeth. That failed to relieve her tension, and she couldn't help thumping the wall beside the door with the side of the fist that held the matches. "Oh no," she whispered, and before she knew it she had let go of the doorknob and retreated a step into the dark.

She threw out a hand and found the knob again, and hung onto it while she attempted to convince herself that the wall had felt as it had seemed to feel solely because of her panic. She inched her fist towards it, gripping the matches tight but not too tight, trying to believe in them as a talisman of the light which would show her the room hadn't changed. None of her preparation was any use. Her knuckles touched the wall, then grated against it as though that would crush her sensations, but there was no mistaking them. Her skin was chafing against bare rough moist brick.

She pulled her hand away and rubbed it convulsively on her sleeve, and almost relinquished the doorknob in order to light a match. She had a sudden notion that so long as she maintained her grip on the knob she would be holding back the change from overtaking the room, and besides, the matches were a final hope that she didn't want to exhaust until she absolutely had to, not while there was the slightest chance of coaxing the reaction she needed from her father. "I said I'm better," she called, trying to concentrate in her voice everything she was desperate to achieve. "You have to come and see, or how will you ever know if I am?"

Her father didn't respond for some moments—long enough for her to wonder if more of the contents of the mirror than the bricks she'd seen reflected might be with her in the room. Then he said "You are clever as the devil, but I see through your ruse."

"What ruse?" Only her headache prevented her butting the door in her frustration. "I'm telling you the truth. Why won't you believe me?"

"Because you tell me you have found peace, yet I hear you are as diseased as you were when it was necessary to put you away."

He was beyond persuasion, she could hear that now. All she had left were the matches, and at once she knew that the best they could show her would be too similar to the nightmare she'd experienced after he had lifted her up to Nazarill—the three necklaces dangling over the mirror, the four hats on the wall, their shadow jerked by fire. He'd lifted her because he was afraid. He'd overcome his fears at her expense, and that had brought her where she was now.

Or had he quite overcome them? The contrary idea seemed to crystallise her thoughts into a hardened point aimed straight at him. She gripped the doorknob harder and leaned her forehead against the wood that still belonged to her bedroom. "I'm not as nervous as you," she said, her lips nearly kissing the door.

"What idiocy are you mumbling? I cannot hear a word."

"Now you can," said Amy, and sharpened her voice. "You were scared of this place before we came to live here, and you're still—"

"Be silent, fiend. I cannot hear you. Your ravings find no purchase in my ears."

"You can. You're trying not to. You're in the place you wanted to forget you're scared of. You're in the spider house."

"Our Father. Our—"

"You won't be able to blot me out, because you know I'm right. You're alone out there in the spider house, and you will be unless you let me out."

"Be still, you wretch, you poison, you betrayal of my flesh. Bow to the word of God. Our Father Which, Which—"

"Praying won't make it go away. It's all around you, can't you feel it? It's the spider house that won't let you pray, not me."

"Hold your tongue, droppings of your mother. I shall hear none of you. Rave until your voice deserts you. My ears are stopped."

"Then you won't be able to hear the spiders coming."

"You hellspawn," her father screamed, and slammed the door across the hall. Amy heard a thud which she guessed was the impact of his knees with the floor, because he began repeating desperately "Our Father, Our Father, Our Father—"

"You can still hear me. There's nowhere in here you won't be able to. I'm in your head. You can't get rid of me." She no longer knew where her words were coming from, but she sensed they were working. "Better not stay alone out there much longer," she said.

"Protect me against the wiles of the fiend. Our Father, dear God, Our Father—"

It was her feeling that a great deal of her panic had been transferred to him that allowed her to let go of the doorknob and, with far less urgency than before, strike a match. The glow spread over the door and illuminated the wall. No bricks were to be seen, only wallpaper. She ventured to touch it, and having confirmed that it felt as it looked, turned to the room. Clouds Like Dreams were in her mirror, and she could see no sign of a figure lurking at the bottom of the sheet of glass.

Then dim lumps wobbled out from behind her four hats while strings of shadow entangled themselves with the necklaces in the false room beyond the glass, and she remembered her dream of Nazarill on fire. The match flickered out, though she hadn't extinguished it, and she saw darkness leap into the mirror—for the moment, only darkness. "Better let me out before you see them," she called. "They're all around you, the spiders in the spider house."

At first she thought she was speaking too low, but then she heard her father. "Dear God, silence her. Take away her devilish voice."

"If you don't let me out they'll come out. They're watching to see if you—"

The door across the hall crashed open, and she sucked in a breath to help her brace herself. She was retreating an arm's length from her door—she wasn't prepared to relinquish the knob until he pulled the bolt—when his footsteps dashed into the kitchen and halted. She sensed he was at his wits' end, ready to open her door if he could think of no other course, and she mustn't give him a chance to think. "They're coming. They'll be everywhere you look. They want you to be all alone with nobody to help you. They won't let you out of here unless I'm with you. Open my door while you can get to it, before they come in the hall."

He'd ceased praying. There came a screech of wood on wood as though he'd shoved a bench away from him, having sat on it. She mustn't be afraid of provoking him further. "They're coming, millions of them, all the spiders in the spider house. I can feel them waiting. They're giving you one chance to let me out, and if you don't they'll—"

She didn't know what more she could have said—what nightmare she might have summoned up for him—but there seemed to be no need. While she was speaking she heard him tramp into the hall, and as she ran out of words, he wrenched the bolt back so violently she felt the force of it through the doorknob.

As the door tottered at her, holding itself almost upright on its single hinge, she released her hold and made to dodge around her father. At once she realised she should first have pulled the door off balance to ensure he couldn't shut it again, but it was too late for either plan. Her father lunged at her, jabbing a hand into her face.

She would have thrown herself aside if she hadn't been momentarily paralysed by the sight of the item in his hand—the large scissors from the drawer whose wooden screech she'd heard. "Forgive me," he said, but he wasn't speaking to her; his eyes were blank as death. Perhaps his last prayer had been an attempt to head himself off. Amy opened her mouth to cry for help, forgetting that nobody would hear, and backed away, but he was faster. The scissors plunged into her mouth.

She felt the blades close on her tongue and, with a considerable effort, meet. She saw them snatch a reddish object from her mouth and shy it into the hall. Her father turned away at once, as if he had no further interest in her, and heaved the door shut after him. He must have observed that all was not right with it, because once he had bolted it he shook it hard. Apparently satisfied, he moved away, and she heard the scissors clatter into the drawer.

He couldn't really have used them, she tried to tell herself. Her father couldn't have done that to her, not her father. But her mouth felt invaded by a wound too big for it, and at the same time robbed of part of itself. The metallic taste of the scissors was intensifying, filling her mouth until she was unable to pretend it wasn't the taste of blood. It was making her faint, and so was shock, through which the pain had only started to declare itself. When she tried to cry her outrage at her father, nothing came out of her except a choking inarticulate gargle and a mouthful of blood which she heard splash the door.

She had to see the worst. She shuffled unsteadily around, though her faintness threatened to collapse her legs, until she was facing the mirror. Her hands were clumsy unfamiliar tools she was using in her blindness to locate a match and tear it out of the book. Her sense of the rest of her body had been cut off by the violation of her mouth. She managed to focus in her hands the very little awareness she had

to spare, and found the strip on the match-book with a distant finger. The match scraped and caught fire, and she saw herself.

Her chin and her throat were bearded with liquid which, in the
uncertain light, looked black. More than that she couldn't see across
the room, even when she forced her mouth to recall how to open.
She held the match in front of her and followed it towards the mirror, her legs wobbling against the bed and only just supporting her.
By now the light on the wall at her back was too meagre to show her
whether the surface had reverted to naked brick, but she couldn't
see her poster. She seemed to be watching herself as she was led into
a cramped dark place by the spectacle of herself, mouth gaping in
anticipation of the horror she had yet to experience. She swayed to
a halt before the mirror and brought the match close to her face
while she tried to poke her tongue out of the hole framed by her
bloody teeth. Any muscles that were left in there flinched from the
agony that responding would involve, and all she could see in her
mouth was blood. The sight released another wave of faintness
through her, and the blood spilled from her mouth. It put out the
match, and she was overwhelmed by the dark.

She supposed that was partly her faintness, since she felt herself
falling. Most of her struck the bed. Her inability to see made more
room for her pain, and her body tried to shrink around it in an effort to squeeze it smaller. Then her limbs and fists and clenched feet
relaxed as another gush exploded out of her mouth, and she fainted
from loss of blood. In her last moments of consciousness she realised
she still had a voice, even if it wasn't audible to her ears. "Let me out,"
she said with it, and knew she no longer meant it for her father. "I
don't care what you do to set me free," she vowed as she was accepted by the dark.

27

THE SPIDER HOUSE

There was a problem with the door. As Oswald pulled it shut it began to lean into the room. He had to grab the handle two-handed while the scissors dangled from one thumb. As he heaved the door upright he couldn't avoid a glimpse of the denizen of the room. Then the door was in place, despite whatever she had sought to do to it, and he rammed the bolt home. When he tried the door it held firm. It was as secure as the rest of Nazarill, and the evil beyond it was silenced at last. He strode into the kitchen to return the scissors to the drawer.

Though he narrowed his eyes as he shut the implements away, he couldn't entirely fend off the sight of them. They weren't as bad as he might have feared—hardly even reddened. He'd done no more than had to be done, and now he should put the unpleasant but necessary incident out of his mind before it drove him as mad as she had made herself. Brooding about it would only corrupt him, weaken him as her wiles had failed to do. Surely his courage in taking up the blade had earned him peace. He clasped his hands together and closed his eyes. "Let my mind dwell on You now, O Lord. Let all my thoughts be good."

He was able to pray again. She was no longer able to destroy his ability to speak to his maker. He would pray until the memory of the incident was locked away as of no further use. After all, he thought, she had little reason to complain; she had taken pleasure in mutilating the body God had given her. He opened his mouth to raise his voice, and seemed to feel the faintest hint of tickling on his face.

As his eyes sprang open the sensation retreated, and he clasped his hands until he regained control of his thoughts. Of course, he hadn't finished cleaning the apartment, and the nerves of his face had been reminding him. Why, there was a disgusting example of slovenliness in the hall—a piece of reddish meat lying on the carpet opposite the bolted room. He tore a wad of paper towel off the roll above the sink and having picked the lump of meat up, not without a shudder, dropped the package in the kitchen bin. The plastic lid clunked shut, allowing him to forget the repulsive contents while he set about searching for anything else she might have scattered about the flat to trouble him.

He was responsible for some of it, he remembered. He'd left the table strewn with her schoolwork. It had been an emblem of his hope that she would come back to herself—perhaps he'd even hoped that it would somehow help her come back—but there was no point in further deluding himself. He gathered up the armful of books and papers and dumped them in the kitchen bin, which just had space for them. The Bible he let lie, because surely its holiness must be equal to any damage it had suffered. "You are my strength," he murmured to it as he surveyed the room.

He could see nothing untoward. Apart from the bolted room, he'd brought the vacuum cleaner to bear on every inch of the apartment which could conceivably have required it, after all. He shouldn't be tempted to repeat the operation so soon; it would suggest an enfeeblement of faith. Instead he went to the window, to gaze at a world which he had forgotten was out there.

The town was subdued by the afternoon. Beneath a slab of cloud the colour of the gravel drive and as extensive as the sky, the only movement he could see was of several women surmounted by hats, who kept shaking their heads as they made their loquacious way across the marketplace to the tearoom. The red segmented lines of roofs wormed up towards the moor, and he recalled that dozens of those roofs protected families that were also under his protection. He needed to return to work, and now that he'd dealt with his domestic problem he would, just as soon as he'd caught up on his sleep.

As he passed the bolted door he heard only blessed silence. She must know better than to start her kicking; she'd been taught not to play any more tricks. Nevertheless he left his door open an inch before lowering himself onto the bed, where he shut his eyes and crossed his hands on his chest. Surely he'd achieved enough to indulge in the luxury of praying himself to sleep.

"Now I lay me down to sleep, I pray the Lord my soul to keep...." He must have been very young when he had last said that, because the remaining words had deserted him—and then it came to him that he'd suppressed them on her behalf. She hadn't liked them as a young child, when she had been taught the prayer; perhaps this aversion had been the first sign of her ungodliness. If only he had seen that it betrayed her unwillingness to put her faith in God! But brooding over it would be to risk the sin of despair. "If I should die before I wake," he said, "I pray the Lord my soul to take," and found he was too weary to frame any more prayers. That felt entirely different from being unable to remember them, and he let his hands relax.

His eyelids were at least as heavy as his hands, and more difficult to lift. All the same, he forced them open when, on the edge of sleep, he had the impression of hearing a noise, hardly even a whisper, by no means articulate and perhaps not even audible. As his rolling gaze was slowed by what appeared to be a small crack at the bottom of the lower pane, he wondered if it was a draught he'd sensed. If so he couldn't feel it, and his body was growing more stubbornly ponderous by the second. His mind sank into itself and drew his eyelids down. Just as sleep engulfed him, floating his thoughts apart, he imagined that the softest of kisses touched his lips.

Whose would he have wanted it to be? Not the infested creature's—he couldn't have borne the contact of the unclean mouth that was safely locked in its lair of a room—and so he wished it to have been Heather's. That was his last thought as he gave himself up to sleep, and he experienced the stirring of a hope that the wish might be transformed into a dream. When one came, however, it wasn't Heather that it brought to him.

He was in the same position on the bed. To judge from the sky, not much time had passed. He was lying there, as incapable of conscious movement as anyone asleep would be, when he heard some small presence approaching over the carpet by the bed. His immediate notion was that it might be the magistrate's cat, which had somehow managed to survive his treatment of it, an encounter which it suddenly seemed crucial for him to take back if he could. Impracticable though the proposal was, it did allow his hand to move, to reach over the edge of the bed to stroke the cat's head. Then his dream made room for the thought that the animal was unlikely to be in good shape, and he succeeded in retrieving his hand before it could touch or be touched by the visitor. He had returned it to the clasp of his other hand when a series of soft uneven footfalls arrived at the far end of the bed, and a small head wobbled into view against the grey light from the window.

It wasn't a cat's head. It was unclear to Oswald what kind of creature it belonged to, since there was very little of a face to see. He had a confused fancy that the intruder was related in some way to the pictures in the hall; it appeared to be at least as pop-eyed. The globes bulging from its head lacked pupils, however, and were pale as the exterior of Nazarill. In the dream he wondered if it might be someone's idea of a pet, because it sat on its haunches and jerked its front legs up before its fleshless torso as though to beg. Then it pawed at its eyes that weren't eyes, and just as he identified them, the cocoons were dislodged from the sockets.

The many-legged contents of the torn globes spilled over the remnants of a face. He heard a rain of objects strike the carpet as the head ducked out of sight, whitish tatters dangling from its eyeless sockets. He was struggling to regain control of his immovable body—even to be capable of praying for the gift of movement—when the glistening mass swarmed on its countless legs over the end of the bed, as swift as fire on oil.

All the bulbous bodies wobbling between their spindly scuttling legs were green as mould. He could hear their soft rush towards him, a triumphant whisper; he thought he could smell the poisonous moisture of them. Any of this should be productive of a scream, and if he could only cry out he must waken. Now their weight was gathering on his shoes, and in a moment they were teeming over his ankles and onto his legs beneath his clothes. He forced his mouth open, the whole of him straining to yield a scream. He felt a substance stretching between his lips—the substance whose invisible presence had kept tickling his cheeks and whose accumulation he'd taken for a kiss. The realisation came too late to prevent him from gasping for breath.

His gasp sucked in more than air. At once his tongue and the interior of his mouth were coated with the substance, and things were crawling over them. Those sensations drove a sound out of him, and

not only a sound. With the gurgling cry in a voice he scarcely recognised went the contents of his mouth, or most of them. As his teeth
clamped shut to ward off any further invasion, he felt them close
on an object that writhed and immediately burst. A despairing
shriek prised his jaws apart and sprang his eyes wide, and he was
awake.

His tongue and the roof of his mouth felt thicker than they should,
and he seemed unable to rid himself of a poisonous taste. Surely
these were effects of his wakening without having slept enough. If
the light through the window was exactly that of the dream, that only
meant it was somewhat later than when he'd laid himself down on
the bed. He ought to pray again—pray as long and as hard as was
required to wash away the lingering nightmare. "Now I lay me—"
he began with a vigour which he hoped would clean his mouth, but
found he would rather not invoke the notion that anything might
happen to him while he was helplessly asleep. Some stronger and
more positive prayer was needed—one which would persuade him
that he was alone in the room, that the bare quilt would stay bare,
that there was no cause for him to glance over the edge of the bed.
He clasped his hands together so hard that they shuddered, and was
about to pray for the faith to close his eyes as an aid to recalling every
prayer he knew when something ran across the ceiling to dangle from
its legs above his face.

Oswald flung himself blindly forward and sprawled off the end
of the bed. His momentum brought him to the window, and his palms
slammed against the glass. If there hadn't been a crack in it before,
there was now—but perhaps he had previously seen the silhouette
of a thread of cobweb. As his face almost collided with the pane he
saw that the entire length of the bottom of the double glazing was
stuffed with white cocoons. The impact of his hands must have jarred
them, because the thousands of bodies they concealed boiled out, a
frantic mass that reared level with his face.

They were trapped within the cracked glass, but for how long? He
reeled backwards a couple of steps before he managed to turn away
so as to bolt for the hall. As he turned he glimpsed darkness retreating under the bed, and heard the whisper of its rush across the
carpet. He dodged wildly away from the bed, and became aware that
he was being followed, a body quivering above him like a gob of
black poison about to drop. He groaned and fled to the door, but his

pursuer easily kept pace with him. It would fall on him as he struggled out of the room, he thought in despair. But the door was still
ajar, and in a moment he was past it, and it was slammed, imprison-
ing all the horrors in his room. Once he'd shaken it to convince himself it wouldn't open as soon as he let go he dashed along the hall,
stretching out a hand to grasp the latch of the door into the corridor. His sense of imminent release was so vivid that he saw what he
wanted to see, and was nearly at the end of the hall before he realised
that the latch was no longer to be seen.

It was there, but it was hidden by a thick grey veil at least two feet
across. Where the grey surface clung to the doorframe, a brownish
shape reminiscent of a baby's hand appeared to be caught in it. For
a moment Oswald was able to imagine the shape was a hand which
a child had pulled off her doll, and then it produced the rest of its
limbs as it sidled heavily down the web and poised itself over the
latch.

Oswald clapped his hands over his mouth, bruising his lips as he
backed away. A terror of stumbling over some unsuspected intruder
whirled him round, and he elbowed a picture-frame. The picture
began to sway as though its pop-eyed subject was performing an insane dance, and the inhabitants of the nest it had concealed scattered
from behind it, scurrying over the panels in every direction. All the
bulging eyes resembled cocoons pressed to bursting. As he flinched
between the pictures, hugging himself for fear of dislodging them,
he hardly knew where he was going or why, even as he lurched into
the main room. Then he saw where his instincts were leading him,
and sprinting to the window, made his fingers venture to the catch.
Nothing appeared to be lurking in it, and he managed to steady his
shivering arm while his finger and thumb levered the segment of
metal out of its niche. The sash was released, and he heaved it up and
hoisted himself over the stone sill.

The lawn gleamed up at him. Frost that lingered in the shadow of
the building had rendered the grass as pale as Nazarill, and he knew
that the ground would be unyielding as stone. Though it was less than
forty feet below him, he saw at once that he couldn't jump; at his age
he would only smash himself. "Help," he screamed instead. "Someone please help."

There was no response. Few people were visible, and they were
all enclosed by the windows of shops around the distant marketplace.

A second plea, louder and more shrill, had no effect other than to crack his voice. In a fury of hopelessness he dragged the sash down and stared through it at the silenced indifferent streets, and became aware of movement on either side of him.

The curtains had stirred in a draught as he'd slammed the window, and now they were still. He jerked his open hands at them in an attempt to keep them so. For some seconds they hung inert; then, as he was about to let his hands sink, the heavy velvet shifted— rippled with the life teeming in the material. Both curtains swayed towards him as if they or their denizens were about to overwhelm him. He'd thrust out his hands to beat them off before he realised he would touch not only the velvet but also its contents, giving them the opportunity to swarm onto him. He retreated, flapping his hands, and floundered in the direction of the hall without the least notion of where his panic might be driving him.

The sight of the Bible lying on its vague reflection halted him. It was the one item in the entire apartment which seemed capable of helping him, yet he'd come close to overlooking it in his terror. He swept it off the table and held it tight, ignoring how softened the covers felt. "God be with me. Help me overcome all creeping things," he prayed, and advanced into the hall.

He saw the Bible work at once. The paper eyes were eyes again, and they looked cowed by the book. Whatever might lurk behind the pictures was staying well out of view, and so he marched past them, holding the cross on the front cover towards the bloated object that had crouched over the latch. He thought he'd seen the Bible work— but as its shadow fell on the grey expanse, the creator of the web only twitched the tangled strands and raised its front legs slowly and deliberately as though to acknowledge him.

Oswald brandished the Bible above his head and struggled to send himself forward. Surely the weight of the book was sufficient to crush the swollen body against the door, or failing that, at least to knock it to the carpet, where it would be stunned enough for him to tread it underfoot—except that he couldn't bear the possibility of failing to cripple it or of proving unable to finish it off. As his hand waved the Bible, miming his inability to strike, he saw the spider's moist jaws work; he felt its inhuman attention focus on him, a gaze concentrated by its minuteness. Was the creature preparing to leap off its web at him? He flinched back several feet, and a thought managed to articulate itself. He should indeed be heading for the kitchen. Any spider was afraid of fire, and should be doubly so of the one he would be bearing. "A holy flame," he declared, both an apology for the action he was proposing and a prayer that it would save him. He ran to the cooker and twisted the nearest control.

It achieved nothing—not the feeblest hiss of gas. He poked his face at the gas-ring which ought to have responded, and then his head jerked away, so violently he felt his throat stretch. The outlet on the ring was choked by a whitish blob; every ring was plugged with a co-coon. "God rot you all," he screamed, and twisted every control as far as it would go, and heard a solitary muffled hiss. One of the out-lets wasn't quite blocked, but he couldn't see which. Before he had time to think, he'd jabbed the ignition button. The left-hand front ring flared up, setting fire to the cocoon. Within the reddish flame small bodies writhed and instantly were lumps of ash.

The spectacle filled Oswald with a joy indistinguishable from rage. He plunged the topmost corner of the Bible into the ring of fire. The covers only smouldered, but in a few seconds the pages caught fire, slowly enough to reassure him that he wouldn't need to dash along the hall. He held up the flaming Bible and saw himself re-flected in the window, a hero with a sacred weapon, as he reached with his free hand to turn off the lit ring.

Perhaps it was the heat which brought five legs groping out from behind that control, and as many from behind its neighbour. Oswald managed not to cry out or recoil. He thrust the blazing pages at them, and was heartened to see them flinch. He was loitering to prolong his enjoyment of the sight when it occurred to him that the fire in his hand could ignite the pent-up gas. Shielding the flame to slow its progress into the book, he marched down the hall, past the intimi-dated pictures. "Here comes fire," he announced. "Here comes death."

The guardian of the latch renewed its grasp on the web, and its poisonous balloon of a body twitched up towards Oswald. It looked as though it was offering itself to the flame, and he didn't hesitate. He shoved the blazing pages into the midst of the cluster of legs, and was almost certain that he saw fire gleam like realisation in the pin-point eyes. There came a bubbling hiss, dreadfully loud, and the legs splayed themselves in a convulsion. The web shrank in tatters away from the latch, and a lump of fire dropped from it, writhing and shrivelling. By the time the lump struck the floor it was a charred remnant which lay smouldering but still.

Oswald flicked the rags of web away from the latch with the Bible and glanced about for somewhere to dump the book, which was more than half consumed by now, and threatening to scorch his fingertips. He couldn't bear the thought of retracing his steps only to relinquish his protection. He tossed the Bible against the skirting-board as his fingers began to sting, and clamped them on the latch. With his other hand he slipped the key into the mortice-lock and twisted it, and used both hands to haul the door open, and stepped into the corridor.

The panels were no longer visible, and little of the lighting was. As far as his vision would stretch in the clogged dimness, the walls and the floor and the ceiling were an energetic mass of blackness. His step over the threshold sent the host on the floor scuttling away from him, only to gather itself and rush at him, its countless legs waving, its multitude of bodies quivering. He heard a concerted soft patter filling the corridor as he fell back into the hall and grabbed the Bible. As his fingers closed on the binding, the kitchen exploded.

The impact hurled him against the door, slamming it. He saw a gust of fire from the cooker cross the kitchen doorway to engulf the table and the benches, all of which burst into flame. He'd kept hold of the Bible, which had left a sample of its flames on the skirting-board. Immediately after the explosion he heard glass shatter, and then the sliding fall of a sash—of the window he'd neglected to secure. A wind surged into the hall, turning the fire of the Bible almost white. Before he could drop the book, the flames leaned towards him and streamed up the whole length of his arm.

His jacket sleeve and the shirt inside it were a single wad of fuel. When he tried to fling the book away, the cover adhered to his fingers, and he felt as if he was doing his utmost to tear off strips of their smoking flesh. His other hand clutched at the little of the book that wasn't yet ablaze, but a draught so purposeful it might have been a breath sent flames up that arm too. He had to wipe the Bible down a panel of the wall to part it from the hand it was destroying. The block of fire fell against the skirting-board, but he hadn't time to extinguish it. Fumbling at the buttons of his jacket with his less injured hand, he staggered around to the door. He couldn't even bear to look at the fingers which had held the Bible, never mind trying to use them to grasp the latch. Abandoning his struggle with the buttons, he forced those charred fingers to close around the metal knob.

He felt the skin over his knuckles tighten and split open, but the knob turned, and his weight dragged the door towards him. The fire was swifter. As the gap between door and frame showed him that the corridor was deserted, he felt flames meet across his shoulders. The nape of his neck caught fire, bowing him into a convulsion as though he could duck out of reach of the blinding pain. A last instinctive thought remained to him: he was beyond escaping from the fire, and so must phone for help.

He spun giddily in the midst of the smoke of himself, stretching his arms wide in a crazed notion that doing so would keep some of the fire away from the core of him, and saw there was no longer a phone in the hall. He'd smashed it to prevent Amy from calling for help. He'd done far worse, and the sudden flood of memories convulsed him more savagely than his physical agony had. As though the flames were leaving his mind nowhere to hide, he remembered everything at once. He remembered saving her from falling into Nazarill, her small hands gripping his for protection, and he remembered the effort he'd had to exert on the scissors as they bit inside her mouth.

The flames had reached his scalp, but it was the memory that almost sank him to his knees. Instead he thumped his back and his skull against the wall to put out as much of the fire of himself as he could. It didn't work; indeed, he felt flames spreading down his legs. Nevertheless he limped towards her room, beyond which fire swarmed fluttering out of the kitchen to snatch at the hall. "I'm coming, Amy," he did his best to call while trying to keep his voice gentle. "Don't be afraid. I won't touch you, I won't come anywhere near you. I only want to let you out and then I'm staying here."

There was no response from beyond the bolted door. Of course, he thought, he would never again hear her voice. The upsurge of appalled shame he experienced was almost enough to render him incapable of venturing even as close as her door, but he compelled the lumps of fire that were his feet to advance one more step, and another. It was a draught that stopped him.

It came from behind him, where he would least have expected it. It whipped the flames around him to embrace every part of him that wasn't already on fire. His legs wobbled one more step and were no longer capable of supporting him. He fell yards short of Amy's door. He heard his body strike the carpet, but he didn't feel the impact; perhaps he had nothing left with which to feel. That wasn't true, because he felt helpless grief at the sight of flames blustering out of the kitchen towards Amy's door. Then fire raced crackling over the panels of the wall above him, and he knew the fuel of that fire was himself.

28

BEYOND THE HILL

As Amy rose towards consciousness she seemed unable to see or to breathe. A substance heavier and more solid than darkness was filling her up on the way to her brain. If it shut down her awareness once more, that was fine with her. Being aware would only bring her pain and a knowledge of imprisonment and loss. There was no point in trying to remain alert in case someone came to save her, because nobody would. Now she understood why she had made so few friends: people you relied on went away when you most needed them, as her mother had and, in another sense, her father. Having understood that, she could forget it, and everything else too. Neither seeing nor breathing was much of a reason for her to fight off the dark, and once she gave in to it she wouldn't miss them. Thinking was the feeblest reason of all, especially when a multitude of dreams was waiting to be dreamed, requiring nothing more of her than relaxation. It was time she returned to the dark.

Except that some presence at an indeterminable distance from her consciousness wouldn't let go of it. A profound lack of sensation had occupied her body, annulling even the pain which she would have expected to be suffering, and so she doubted that the troublesome element was part of herself, unless it was the very lack. Perhaps it was the darkness that was more than darkness—which, now that her reluctant awareness grasped it, was much more like smoke. How could she have failed to smell the acridity of it? She couldn't stand her unawareness now, and so she lifted herself off the bed.

At first she was unable to locate the floor. Perhaps, she couldn't help thinking, there was less of it to find. The notion that she might be stepping off into a void as empty as her vision almost sent her into retreat, but imagining the worst might be less bearable than knowing. Besides, now she was managing to make her way in the direction where her instincts told her the door stood, although she could still feel nothing underfoot. Her eyes might as well have been replaced by the dark; it was impossible to judge whether she was seeing the faintest outline of the door or whether this was an impression her mind felt obliged to provide. But the door was where she had taken it to be, except that as she reached out to it, the block of ash it had apparently become fell away, revealing the hall—revealing that the hall was hardly there.

A single picture lay at the foot of the opposite wall, the face under the cracked glass charred beyond recognition. Presumably all that was left of the panels was the soot which clung to the brick. She could see into the blackened cave that had been her father's bedroom; it no longer had a door, nor any glass in its window. Most of its floor, like that of the hall, had been consumed, leaving a few joists and random lengths of floorboard chewed by fire and, by the look of them, consisting mostly of ash. Through the gaps between them she saw the yawning depths of Nazarill. For a moment she thought the roof at least had survived, and then a star gleamed in the ribbed blackness overhead.

So her nightmare of a fire had come to pass without her even being aware of it. Not only the fire but also any fire-fighters had apparently come and gone, abandoning her unnoticed in the ruin. The disaster seemed to have driven her father away, at any rate; she didn't care that he hadn't saved her, only that he was gone. There was silence throughout Nazarill except for the whisper of ash in a wind that fluttered the black fur of the wall, and then she heard a chunk of the roof slither off the bricks on which it was resting and plunge in a series of shattering crashes all the way down to the foundations.

If she'd been tempted to wait to be found—her room had protected her, after all; she assumed its lack of ventilation had kept the fire at bay—she felt too vulnerable now. What could she do? Calling for help had proved useless before, and now she had no voice. In any case, when she considered the lights of Partington beyond the charred hole where the window had been, they seemed no less dis-

tant and indifferent than the star overhead. Nobody would help her
except herself, but when she gazed along the very little that remained
of the hall floor, she wasn't sure that she would be enough. The
prospect of the black gaps between the remains of floorboard balanced on the shrivelled joists made even her perch on the threshold
of her room feel increasingly precarious, but if she left it she was by
no means convinced she would be able to distinguish any footholds
in the shifting smoky darkness. Her plight was threatening to shrink
her into a point which would have room only for panic, but she
mustn't let that happen. "Help," her mind said.

She meant the appeal for herself alone, and yet she wasn't entirely
surprised when a response came from outside her. There was a creak
of wood at the far end of the hall, where the doorway gaped emp-
tily, as a small dim shape entered the apartment. Deft as an acrobat,
it ran across the scraps of floor to Amy and sat up on its haunches.
Before she could glimpse its face in the dark it shuffled round and
began to pick its way more slowly towards the corridor. A yard or
so from her it halted and turned the shadowy blotch of its head to
her. It wanted her to follow, and was showing her the route.

It might have been a cat; it was about the right size. The darkness
allowed her to take it for someone's clever pet that had strayed into
the building and was guiding her, as clever pets did in stories she'd
once read. Even if it was what she suspected it might be, it was all
she had, and it had come when she'd called. As the dim head wobbled, beckoning, she abandoned her refuge and lurched onto the first
of the stepping-stones which were all that survived of the floor.

She wavered on the exposed charred joist, and the three-storey
void surged at her to pull her down. Then she had her equilibrium,
and immediately advanced to the next perch. She recalled from stories that the trick was never to look down, and so she kept her attention on the next footing she had to reach. It was like learning how
to walk again, but more exhilarating. Her guide must be sure of her,
because it had turned away and was demonstrating the next few steps
of their route. She couldn't be less sure of herself than it appeared
to be of her, and in almost no time that she was aware of she gained
the end of the hall.

The corridor had been reduced to its essentials, a dark three-
storey tunnel crossed by skeletal portions of blackness. As a wind
moaned along it beneath a sky that was uncovering its stars, the

black-furred walls appeared to shudder. The naked drop beneath her might have troubled Amy if she hadn't concentrated her attention on her guide, which was staying only a pace ahead of her now. She rather hoped it wouldn't turn to her; she was beginning to distinguish the outline of its body, which was less complete and regular than she would ideally have preferred. As though sensing her wish, it kept its head hunched low between its shoulders while it led her past the doorless gutted apartments to the stairs, or rather where the stairs had been. All that remained of them were stubs of joists protruding from seared brick.

Her guide sprang onto the highest joist at once. Surely it wouldn't have done so unless the carbonised stump was capable of support-ing Amy too, and once it leapt to the next she launched herself after it. She caught the rhythm of the descent at once, and soon she and her companion were skipping down the excuse for a ladder, even managing to swing themselves around the bends in the staircase without breaking their headlong progress. Since the joists were so close together, Amy was able to observe more about her guide, not least the dark lines between its ribs—lines much deeper than shadow. This failed to disconcert her, and she found herself reflecting instead that she was so certain of her balance she might have leapt from floor to ruined floor rather than bothering to use the remains of the stairs. Perhaps she'd needed them as some kind of reassurance, she thought as the lowest joists carried her down to the level which had been oc-cupied by the ground floor.

It was hardly more than a pit now. Just enough of the floor had endured to make Amy feel capable of picking her way to the exit. She would have to pass all the rooms she'd feared, but she could tell they were deserted. She glanced into each hall as she came abreast of it. The blackened bricks were dripping, presumably with water from the hoses the fire-fighters would have employed, but if the vis-tas beyond the charred doorways resembled cells, those cells had been liberated. And so was Amy about to be, just as soon as she fol-lowed her guide, which had pranced lopsidedly out through the blis-tered opening where the glass doors used to stand. Amy sprang from the last stump of wood ribbed with black ash onto the step and from it onto the gravel.

It was odd: she couldn't feel the chunks of stone beneath her feet, any more than she remembered having felt the footholds she'd used to make her way out of the ruin. She found she was unwilling to look down at her feet. Her reluctance might have troubled her more if she hadn't sensed that her perceptions were being overwhelmed by the shadow of Nazarill, a dark stony presence which, however impalpable, seemed to be exerting itself to hold her within it. Having managed to escape from the building, she could surely elude its shadow as her guide, which had dodged around a corner, apparently had. She darted forward and felt the shadow clinging to her like a fog that was more than fog, trying to stretch after her as she reached its edge alongside the buried roots of the oak. Then she was beyond it, and sensed it drawing its darkness into itself. She was free at last—free of Nazarill and all it represented—but where had she to go?

Beyond the gateway she saw the dull glow of the marketplace and the static lights of the rest of the unhelpful town. Past them all was Rob's house, invisibly dark. He'd tried to help her at the end, but she didn't think she could go to him now, not only because the lightlessness of his window showed he was asleep. It must be the middle of the night, yet she wasn't even slightly tired. What else ought to strike her as unusual? Something else uncommon for the time of night—some quality of Nazarill. She hadn't looked towards the building when it occurred to her to wonder how, when the night was so dark, the ruin was able to cast the shadow she had seen. She swung round like a weight on a rope, and saw. Behind the hulk the crown of the hill was glowing.

For an instant she imagined it was catching moonlight, but there was no moon in the pierced ebony sky. Besides, no moon could have made the ground shine so brightly. The grass, and the scattering of wild flowers which had crept back in the absence of the gardener, seemed transformed into luminous pearl, and from several hundred yards away she could distinguish every separate blade of grass, each leaf and petal. The spectacle mesmerised her, and before she was conscious of deciding to approach it she was drifting uphill over the frozen lawn.

She kept well away from the ruin, which was surrounded by a patch of blackened earth like a frustrated attempt to extinguish the glow of the hill. Now she was past, and the light swelled up within her, ousting her sense of herself. She wasn't even convinced she was seeing her shadow, it was so feeble and thin, and yet she was afraid of damaging the flowers over which she was passing; the minutest details of them were intricate as crystal. "You don't need to be," she thought, or was it she who'd thought it? She was almost at the summit now, and she wanted to make out her shadow in case the light did away with it. She looked down and saw not only her shadow. She saw twelve more, six on either side of her, all of them as shrivelled and malformed as hers. In the moment of their growing visible, each of the nearest extended a hand to her.

It seemed impolite not to take them, especially when they were no more incomplete than hers. The fire had reached her after all, she saw. At once her hands vanished from her sight, and she was holding onto her invisible companions with the essence of herself in the midst of the pearly glow. "We shall see everything save ourselves," said another voice within her.

"We rescued one another."

"We shall be whole at last."

All the soft intimate voices, even those which had yet to speak, already seemed as familiar to Amy as her own. They belonged to her truest friends, whom she would always have. "Let us go up," another suggested, and in a moment they had glided to the crown of the hill.

The moor stretching to the horizon shone with a moonless moonlight—a luminousness that was as much a part of her as of the landscape. Beyond the moor were further mysteries, and beyond them the sky and the stars, and other revelations whose vastness she feared for the moment to contemplate. The wind in the mile after mile of shining heather was the secret voice of the moor, and she thought it was promising her that she and her companions would be equal to whatever they encountered; she felt herself being given a promise. It might take eternity to keep it, she thought as they began to sail effortlessly over the moor—as she became aware that the consciousness she was acquiring might be capable of holding within itself every living thing around her, and every individual detail, and the awesome whole of which they were a part, beginning with the world. Beyond that she dared not venture yet, and so she fixed her awareness on the moor that was sharing her light. As she revelled in the start of her voyage she felt herself being raised up with an immense gentleness by the stars.

SET US ALL FREE

The day before he was to leave for university Rob finished packing late in the afternoon, and then he wondered if he had. He surveyed the pile of suitcases and the huddle of cartons in his room, but they weren't the answer. The view that had been nagging at him throughout his preparations drew him to the window. A slow procession of builders' lorries was emerging from the gates of Nazarill. The spectacle made him feel hollow, abandoned by the year he'd known Amy. Just about now he might have been meeting her to arrange when they would see each other once he was settled in his new accommodation. When he swallowed with an effort and turned back to his room it was only to be confronted by the poster she had bought him.

It could stay on the wall, he decided in that moment. Packing it would be to try and fail to bring Amy with him. Even without it he was bound to be wakened in the night by memories of her. Thoughts of actions he should have taken were the worst, harsh as a beam shone into his eyes in the dark. His parents kept telling him he would form new friendships, maybe more than friendships, and he supposed that would have to be so. Perhaps he would feel better about it once he told Amy he was going; perhaps visiting her would reach him in a way that the clump of smugly mysterious faces surrounded by clouds was unable to achieve. He liked the band and the fake magic of their lyrics even less now, and if it weren't for Amy their faces would no longer be in his room, but they were the nearest thing he had to a picture of her. Working his arm to rid his mended shoulder of the twinge it still sometimes experienced, he hurried down-stairs and out of the house.

The September sky was veiled by cloud. A vague disc of pale light was lowering itself towards the horizon of the moor beyond Nazarill. The air smelled of early autumn smoke. Usually this first sign of the dying of the year appealed to Rob—when he was younger it had promised fireworks to come, and Christmas—but now it reminded him of the stench of the ruin of Nazarill on the day after the fire, the day he'd wakened from his medicated sleep to learn of the disaster. He hunched his shoulders at the thought, digging out the twinge again, and found his way along the lumpy road in the direction of the church.

At the end of the row of houses above the iron-tied wall a path wandered through a thorny sprawl of brambles along the ridge. Generations of churchgoers from the row had tramped it clear, and eventually it led alongside the railings of the churchyard to the gate. Now grass and wild flowers were reclaiming the path, and Rob had to disentangle himself from more than one spiky twig. Elaborate extinguished candelabra of gorse surrounded the path, concealing his approach. Perhaps he would see who kept leaving flowers at the Priestley grave.

The grave was near the top of the slope that rose to the church. When Rob stepped out of the brambles by the railings, the building obstructed his view. Rather than learn the identity of the mourner, he thought, he would prefer to have this farewell visit to himself. He was halfway along the boundary when the grave came into sight. Shaun Pickles was straightening up from laying a wreath against the headstone.

Rob was filled with a rage so fierce its glare seemed to reflect off everything he was seeing, and then it subsided. The last place he wanted to fight with his old enemy was at Amy's grave. He was edging into hiding when a thorny creeper snagged his ankle, and the creak of the mass of vegetation as he tried to free himself drew the guard's attention to him.

Pickles' face stiffened and grew more mottled than ever, its red blotches flaring as the pallor of the rest of it intensified. Then he appeared to control himself, presumably having grasped that Rob wasn't there to spy on him. "I'll be gone shortly," he mumbled.

No doubt he was embarrassed, but it sounded rather too much

like a brusque dismissal. "So will I," said Rob, and walked to the gate.

Pickles murmured a few quick words over the grave and crossed himself, then descended the grassy slope. "Off on your travels, are you?" he said with a ponderous humour that was new to Rob.

"My mind is."

Pickles twitched his eyebrows but didn't comment further. "I don't reckon she'd have hung round here much longer either," he muttered instead.

"Maybe I'll do some of the things she would have done."

"I'd not be surprised," Pickles said in a tone designed to convey that he was keeping most of his disapproval to himself. "She didn't think much of us."

Rob concluded that he meant the town, since he had turned his gaze on it. He continued to look past Rob while he licked his lips and put his tongue away before declaring "I thought I was doing right, you know."

Rob's shoulder was reminding him of its injury, but he did his best to keep it still, because to draw attention to it would distract them from the memory of Amy's fate. "That's all right, then," he said.

"Of course it's not all bastard right," snarled Pickles, slamming the heel of one hand down on top of the gate between himself and Rob. "I wasn't to know about him though, was I? You don't expect them to be like that when they're mad. You don't think they could be so plausible and sly that nobody notices what's up with them."

"Some of us had an idea."

"Aye, well, that must be why you're off to university and I'm stuck here, because you're so clever." Either he regretted having allowed his bitterness to show or was determined to persuade Rob to his view. "My parents never noticed, let me tell you. You couldn't know what goes on in a mind that's gone like that. I mean, locking her up, that's going too far."

"Just locking her up?"

"He couldn't have meant to set the place on fire, could he? Not when he knew she wasn't able to get out. Nobody's that mad, not Mr. Priestley at any rate."

Rob had the impression that however sure of himself Pickles was trying to sound, he was close to pleading. Rob didn't feel he could say much to help, but he tried. "I think the fire was waiting to happen."

"I don't know what you mean by that. You sound like her."

"I wish I'd been more like."

Pickles blinked at him and returned his attention to the town. After a pause he said "My mother thinks Mr. Priestley never got over losing his wife."

"That'd do it, would it?" Rob said, and was ashamed of his sarcasm. "There was more to it. Aim was right, they shouldn't have moved into that place. Maybe nobody should."

"Don't start that up again, nobody wants to hear. We need all the new people we can get. People are business." Pickles unlatched the gate as though, Rob thought, he was its keeper, then held onto it while he glanced up the slope at the grave. Rob wasn't sure if he was meant to hear what the guard said then. "I couldn't ever be like him."

"Pray you won't be."

Pickles gazed at him to indicate that there were any number of responses he could give. No doubt questioning Rob's right to advise him to pray was among them. All he said as he opened the gate, however, was "I see your arm's fixed."

"More or less."

"Well, there you are," Pickles said as though conceding a point, and it wasn't until he swung his upturned palm towards it that Rob saw he was referring to the grave. "Your turn. All yours."

Rob stifled his resentment. "You're the one who's looking after it," he said, and dodged clumsily around Pickles to head up the slope.

He heard the latch click shut. When he reached the foot of the grave he looked over his twinging shoulder. The guard was already out of sight along the main road. Despite his absence, Rob felt no less awkward as he gazed at the wreath leaning against the granite headstone at the end of a rectangle of gravel like a sample of the drive that led to Nazarill. He had no idea how to act or what to say—not because he felt watched, but because he had no sense at all of any presence.

Amy's gilded name and dates were concealed by the wreath, but that wasn't the only reason. How could she be expected to rest with her father? If he hadn't left so much money to the church Rob wondered whether he would have been allowed into his chosen spot. Perhaps Rob should take his leave of Amy on the moor—and then he asked himself reluctantly if he should visit where she'd died. She'd thought the place was capable of holding onto the dead, and if she'd believed that in her last moments . . . He wanted to believe it meant nothing, but he hadn't ventured anywhere near Nazarill since the day after the fire. Now he wanted to be certain it was keeping no secrets about her. He turned away from the stony grave and hurried out of the gate.

Townsfolk were climbing the streets towards Nazarill. It looked like a ritual, and indeed it was—of going home. None of the people he observed letting themselves into their houses glanced uphill, perhaps preferring to ignore the sight of the windows of Nazarill, every one of which was draped with a pale substance that billowed in the wind.

Rob tramped past the locked marketplace and stepped onto Nazareth Row. The sign clamped to the left-hand gatepost of Nazarill waved a stiff greeting at him. MAJOR NEW REFURBISHMENT, the sign proclaimed. LUXURY APARTMENTS—ONLY 13 LEFT. The removable numerals shivered as the polythene that filled the windows bulged as though the place had drawn a breath. "You're dead," Rob declared, and strode between the stone posts.

The long facade was pale as ever, having been cleaned by the builders. As Rob stalked up the drive, kicking gravel towards Nazarill, the moors crouched lower behind the roof, leaving the whitish sky, and he felt as though the paleness was trying to insinuate itself into his skull. The blankness of the windows lurched at him again as he reached the threshold and tried the handles of the massive oak doors. Of course the doors were locked, and he paced backwards to stare up at the windows that had been Amy's.

None of them had actually belonged to her. Unlike him, she'd had no landscape of her own. He couldn't bear the notion that the least trace of her might still be imprisoned in the windowless room. Those were her father's windows Rob was gazing at, and when the polythene in them flapped as the rest did he knew that was only the wind. "You aren't here, I know you aren't. I hope you're wherever you'd like to be," he said. The wind bore his voice towards the moors, and he was about to move away from the building, whose shadow had begun to lay an insidious chill on him, when he heard something flutter like a wing, although all the blind windows had grown motionless.

It was on the ground, at the corner of the building which the Priestleys' apartment had included. As he glanced in that direction ìe glimpsed movement dodging out of sight—not a cat, he thought, ɔut some less common animal. When he ran around the corner, how-ɛver, he could see no sign of life—just the wind streaming through ;he grass and over the top of the hill, and carrying with it a charred ;crap of paper.

As the scrap danced to the crest of the hill he managed to pin it Iown with his fingertips. It was a fragment of a page from a book of verse, he saw when he turned its blank side over—from the foot of ì page, he deduced. It contained just two lines:

The monks and the rest would have crushed it, you see.
But the power of the hill shall set us all free.

That was the extent of the words, but not quite the whole of the nessage. Beside the last word, and as faded as the print, was an nked cross. It looked very like the one Amy had drawn on the soli-:ary Christmas card she'd sent him.

Rob gazed at the moors as he folded the scrap carefully and slipped it into his safest pocket. He felt as though he was sharing the andscape with her—the ranks of heather turning into mist as they :eceded towards the horizon, the hollows secret with shadow, the Iusk rediscovering the subtle twilight colours of the moor. He stood :here until nightfall, when he imagined her exploring the mysteries ɔf the dark. "Goodbye," he said into a silence as wide as the moor, 'and thanks." Pressing his hand on his pocket to guard the message, ìe turned downhill to the world.